THE COAST OF

Akron

THE COAST OF

Akron

ADRIENNE MILLER

FARRAR, STRAUS AND GIROUX / NEW YORK

Farrar, Straus and Giroux
19 Union Square West, New York 10003

Copyright © 2005 by Adrienne Miller
All rights reserved
Distributed in Canada by Douglas & McIntyre Ltd.
Printed in the United States of America
First edition, 2005

Library of Congress Cataloging-in-Publication Data
Miller, Adrienne.
    The coast of Akron / Adrienne Miller.— 1st ed.
        p.   cm.
    ISBN-13: 978-0-374-12512-7
    ISBN-10: 0-374-12512-0 (alk. paper)
    1. Artists—Family relationships—Fiction. 2. Problem families—Fiction.
3. Artists—Fiction. 4. Secrecy—Fiction.   I. Title.

    PS3613.I5323C63 2005
    813'.54—dc22

                                                            2004024348

Designed by Jonathan D. Lippincott

www.fsgbooks.com

1   3   5   7   9   10   8   6   4   2

This is a work of fiction. All characters are products of the author's imagination and bear no resemblance to any real people. Public figures are used for the purpose of satire and the portrayal of them is not intended as a representation of fact.

The author is deeply grateful to Eric Chinski, Christy Fletcher, Zoë Rosenfeld, Tom Bissell, Jim Rutman, Neal Bascomb, Diane Bartoli, Heather Caldwell, Karim Abay, David Granger, Johnny Dougherty, Emily Robichaud, Matt Klam, Gene Miller, Patricia Buckingham Miller, and F. and the I.

FOR JOE

THE COAST OF

Akron

1

Wyatt's glasses were crooked again. Merit rinsed her hands in the kitchen sink, shook them, and took three long, resolute steps toward him. She removed his glasses. Wyatt had just come in from mowing the lawn. He smiled. She smiled. Merit and Wyatt had been married for five years.

Merit held the glasses up to the ceiling light. Somehow, every pair went immediately lopsided on Wyatt. These years of repositioning (on three different pairs of glasses) had led Merit to think—and she'd voiced this suspicion more than once, alas—that maybe his ears were crooked, just a little bit.

Wyatt wore long pants (mosquitoes), although it was August and, at 7:00 p.m., ninety degrees. This past week, he'd rigged up an ultraviolet-light mosquito killer. A fan drew the mosquitoes into "the unit" (Wyatt's term) and into a tray of water. He'd cleverly added a few drops of liquid soap to the water, which, he'd explained, lowered the surface tension. The unit didn't work tremendously well, in Merit's opinion, so now Wyatt was, for reasons unclear to Merit, trying to create carbon dioxide. Merit wasn't sure how one created carbon dioxide exactly, or what it had to do with the mosquitoes; she didn't like the idea of killing animals, even insects, and didn't ask.

Wyatt leaned over the sink and washed his hands with dishwashing liquid. Merit got a good look at his backside. Was his ass actually clenched, or did it just appear to be? She had never known. Wyatt could whistle, which Merit could not, but he was, pound for pound, as dreadful a singer as Merit was. Unlike Merit, however, he was oblivious to his talentlessness. His two current around-the-house favorites were "Band on the Run" and "Lady." If Merit were ever to tell Wyatt how bad his singing voice was, he would certainly disappear into his study, probably for hours, and would possibly stop talking to her for the rest of the day. She knew she was capable of hurting Wyatt. She knew she could hurt him more than he could hurt her.

For Mother's Day this year, Wyatt had bought Merit a miniature Persian rug mouse pad (priced at a remarkable forty-five dollars on Merit's fact-finding journey to Alfredo & Me Gifts at the mall) and two packs of paper cocktail napkins decorated with a field full of rusty greenish triangles that were meant to be either sailboats or pine trees. Merit had been curious about why he'd bought her a Mother's Day gift at all. But she hadn't commented on it.

Wyatt fixed things. Wyatt built things. His motto (Merit's husband was a man with an actual motto) was "In God We Trust. All Others Must Use Data." One of Wyatt's "personal goals" (Wyatt was, unlike Merit, someone with personal goals) was to have, within two years, a house whose lights were entirely controlled by sensors. He called his dream the Smart House. Merit had no idea whether the term came from some magazine or what, but she did know the term irritated her the way the words *condiment, slough, slacks,* and *doily* did, too.

The overhead upstairs hallway light had been the first step Smart House–ward, although the motion sensors there weren't exactly what you'd call foolproof. Sometimes, at night, when Merit lay in bed, she'd hear Wyatt curse, "God*damn* it, *Wyatt*" (after he'd stubbed his toe) outside in the black hallway, and she couldn't help thinking sometimes that her husband's in-progress Smart House could maybe be just a little bit smarter.

Merit's home with Wyatt was very different from the house in which she herself had grown up. She liked that.

When Caroline, Wyatt's daughter, was small, Wyatt built her bedroom furniture (furniture that, much to Caroline's recent adolescent humiliation, was still in her room). He had also built her a dollhouse, a sandbox, and a jungle gym. Last year, Wyatt had made a wooden enclosure—Merit refused to call it a "pen"—for their pig, Arabella. (Their animals, Merit knew, made Wyatt nervous.) The enclosure was constructed of three-foot-high cedar planks, the same planks that were being used for the deck. *Uniformity* was one of Wyatt's watchwords. On one of the enclosure's walls, he had mounted a fan, a very large fan, four feet in diameter, which, even on calm days, even under optimal sanitary conditions, was unable to entirely overcome the . . . well, odor. To give him credit, though, Wyatt hadn't complained when, five years ago, just weeks after she'd moved in, Merit brought Arabella home unannounced. Arabella had been advertised in the paper as a Vietnamese potbellied pig.

Only recently had Merit been able to admit to herself she'd been had. Arabella's present weight: approximately five hundred pounds. Wyatt had never once suggested he and Merit give Arabella away to a farm, where she'd surely be more comfortable and among her own kind, and had never made any "If we get nuked, at least we'll have Arabella to eat" jokes. Arabella was furry and piebald and wagged her tail like a dog. She had tusks.

There was a rabbit, too. Name: Tonya. Tonya wasn't allowed out of the bedroom. This was another of Wyatt's rules. In an effort to protect the bedroom walls from rabbit urine, Wyatt had taped up sheets of polyethylene film. Every quarter year he removed the previous quarter's rabbited plastic, measured each wall again, and cut four more pieces of premeasured polyethylene. Any occurrence of rabbit urine through plastic on any area of the bedroom walls (not to mention any occurrence of rabbit fecal matter anywhere other than in the bedroom's approved rabbit-fecal-matter receptacle) meant FAILURE in all caps and would require a redoubling on Wyatt's part of rabbit-containment efforts. The only mean thing Wyatt had ever said about Tonya was this: "It's like living with a goddamned squirrel." He'd said this through gritted teeth one night in bed. He'd awakened because Tonya was urinating on his face. Merit worried Tonya hadn't really ever liked Wyatt. Now she knew.

Merit's animal thing was entirely antithetical to Wyatt's nature. If it were up to Merit, the animals would just be allowed to run amok, but for Wyatt, who wished to organize that which was by definition unorganizable, the animals meant too much potential for unpredictable spontaneous interaction.

Wyatt owned a sweatshirt that said PERFECTION IS OUR GOAL and an older, pre-Merit one that said REËNGINEERING! Caroline, Wyatt's daughter, had drawn in two dots over *reëngineering*'s second *e* with a blue Magic Marker. Merit guessed Caroline had seen the umlaut usage in a magazine to which Merit subscribed but which she never read. Caroline was thirteen. Merit still didn't know if the kids in her class made fun of her.

"Maybe this side is a little bit bent or something," Merit said, even though she knew it wasn't. She held the glasses up for Wyatt to observe.

"Could be the nose pads," Wyatt said. "Jiggle the nose pads around."

"It's not the nose pads. Look."

"Here. Give it here."

"Just keep your pants on, mister," Merit said.

Merit slid the glasses back on his face, careful not to stab his ears. Oh, hopeless! They were even more crooked than before.

"Much better," Merit said.

"Hey, Caroline. Question for you," Wyatt said. "What do you think of when you hear the word *extruder*?"

Caroline was stuffing steaming potatoes into the opening of an appliance Merit referred to as the "that thingy—you know, the one that squishes potatoes." Wyatt called it, correctly, "the potato ricer." Caroline already was five eight. She would probably soon be as tall as Merit, although Caroline's real mother wasn't very tall.

"*Extruder* makes me think of . . . *extrusion?*"

"That's your answer?" Wyatt asked. " '*Extrusion*'?"

"Why would I know anything about extruders?"

"An extruder, Caroline, an industrial extruder, extrudes some kind of rubber or plastic that's forced under pressure."

"Wyatt," Merit said. "Shhhhhh."

"This potato ricer is a kind of extruder. I mean, it's not technically an extruder, but it's extruder*like*. Do you see this, sweetie? The opening is called a 'die.' And it forms whatever cross-sectional shape you want. It could be weather stripping or tire tread. It could be hose. The reason I'm telling you this, Caroline, is that the potato skins are blocking up the extruder die."

"Wyatt," Merit said. "*Shhhhhh.*"

"Honey, I'm just trying to help you guys be more efficient. Now the thing that gets me, and tell me whether I'm wrong, you guys, but my sense is that cooks don't want to do something that makes them feel as if they're following a process. That's why recipes are always so confusing. Think how much more efficient it would be if recipes were written as diagrams. But cooks would hate that, because then they'd feel like engineers, wouldn't they?"

Merit faced the window. Outside were the fence, the sky, a garden hose, Arabella's enclosure (Merit imagined Arabella's happy white tail whipping through the murky air), and a birch tree with hacked branches.

"And no one wants to be mistaken for an engineer. As we *all* know," Wyatt said.

The birch tree had previously been green and tree-looking, but post-Wyatt–pruning attempt, the tree was a nontree, a moon tree, a tree from a damaged planet, where children had overthrown their parents, the parents crawling on all fours, wheelbarrows chained to their backs.

Merit, without turning, said, "But a diagram would take up too much room in a cookbook, don't you think, Wyatt?"

Merit turned.

Wyatt removed his glasses, took his special crazy zebra-patterned special ophthalmologist-bought eyeglass-wiping hankie from his front pocket. Kleenex was the stealth enemy, according to Wyatt—green Kryptonite to plastic nonglare coated lenses.

He wiped. He put the glasses back on.

Maybe it was the *nose* that was crooked.

"It'd be neat, actually, to interview you." Wyatt tidily folded his glasses hankie and tucked it back in his shirt pocket. "Then I could really get a sense of your process."

Caroline ran her finger along the end of the extruder, stuck her finger in her mouth, and sucked. Then the finger went right back in the bowl. Merit saw this little maneuver but said nothing.

"It'd be so interesting to do a flow chart of the whole process of meal preparation. Picture two columns: One is like things—stuff—formally it's called Data; the other side is called Actions."

Merit depressed the button on the top of her electric pepper grinder (birthday present last year from Wyatt) over a bowl of broccoli. How weakly it whirred, how pathetic, sort of like a dying version of Wyatt's Weed Whacker. A straight-to-the-madhouse sound.

"Actions are verbs. As an engineer, you have to sort of remind people of the difference between nouns and verbs."

Pepper was not forthcoming. Merit pressed harder, the whir more impotent. Wyatt talked passionately about how difficult it was to get people to think in "process terms." Merit had heard this lecture before. She banged the pepper mill on the side of the bowl. The batteries fell out of the grinder and onto the kitchen floor.

Merit's father had often told her that perhaps she needed to handle objects with "rather more finesse." Everything, he once said, must be thought of as a fabulous prop. Her father was a professional in matters of style.

Before the batteries rolled to a stop, the dog appeared, sucked them into her mouth, and then trotted off elsewhere. It was no mystery where Rosalita went, because the overhead Smart Light in the dining room clicked on.

Wyatt was still talking. Merit told Caroline to trade a treat for the batteries.

"Those things in the plastic tube that look like ham?" Caroline asked. Merit answered that those would be them.

"You do know that ham is pig and pig is Arabella, don't you?" Caroline asked.

"Caroline honey," Wyatt said, "there are some things it's better *not* to think about too hard."

Caroline galloped down to the basement. The basement was where Rosalita's food was, and also the big freezer for stuff from the garden, canned goods, washing machine and dryer, and Caroline's childhood toys. A chalkboard was down there, too, a child's blue Fisher-Price chalkboard, on which Caroline had, at the age of about eight, roughly when Merit came into the picture, written the beautiful word *whippersnapper*. It was still there, beautiful *whippersnapper,* and Merit knew she would never erase it.

Merit thought she heard the dog chewing the batteries. She held her hands up for Wyatt to shush.

"But Merit, this is fun for me! All I'm saying is that you've got to understand how things work in terms of systems."

Caroline slammed the basement door.

The dog bounded into the kitchen and another light came on. Dog nails scrambling on linoleum: Merit loved that sound.

"Can I ask you a question, Wyatt?" Merit asked. "Don't the lights sort of bug you sometimes?"

"Oh, they don't bother me. They make me feel like royalty. I stand there, open my arms, and the lights go on. It must be how Jesus felt."

"Did Rosalita just burp?" That was Caroline. In her hand were two slimy-looking batteries.

"Caroline, Rosalita can hear you," Merit said. "You'll hurt her feelings."

Wyatt held the potato ricer aloft and dug into the device with a fork, scooped out the potato skins, and flung them into the sink. The potato skins clung brownly to the sink's side. He fed potatoes into the mouth of the ricer, pressed down on the handle. Both Merit and Caroline were there to watch the potatoes ooze into the big white ceramic bowl.

"See?" Wyatt said.

The light in the dining room clicked off, followed by the light in the living room.

"It's sad when the lights go off," Merit said.

"It's not sad," Wyatt replied.

"I think it's sad, too," Caroline said.

"No, it's not sad," Wyatt said. "All you have to do is wave your arms."

After all that, Wyatt didn't even take any potatoes, and Caroline only picked at hers. Merit was quite aware that Caroline was discreetly spitting her food into her napkin and feeding it to the dog when nobody was looking.

Caroline tilted back in her chair until the front two feet were off the floor. Merit used to do that, too, when she was little.

"Sweetie, how many times have I told you not to lean back in the chair?" Wyatt asked.

Caroline tilted back a little more, and then a little more still, holding on to the edge of the table, removing her grip for a second, then two, then grabbing hold of the table again.

"Hey," Caroline said. "Is Jarlsberg the same thing as Swiss cheese?"

"It's made in a similar *process* to Swiss," Wyatt said.

"It has all these little holes or whatever like Swiss," Caroline said.

Caroline lost her balance, grasped for the place mat. She was quick and got off the chair before it hit the floor. The dog barked, and the Smart Light in the eating area clicked on. That Caroline didn't go down with it seemed for a moment triumphant, as if she'd escaped from a car the second before it nose-dived off a cliff. She surveyed the situation—the upended chair, the potatoes, the broccoli, the tofu steak, the spilled soy milk, the glass—as if she'd accidentally killed something.

Wyatt chucked his paper napkin onto his plate and leapt from his chair. "Are you hurt?" he asked. "Tell me where it hurts. Are you hurt?"

"I'm not hurt, but the chair is, I think. Am I in big huge trouble?"

He crouched down, jiggled the chair leg.

Merit bent down next to him. Their eyes met. Little bits of grass clung to his lenses.

"Oh, Wyatt," Merit said, "it's only a chair."

When Merit was a kid, when she, her mother, and her father all lived together in "Uncle" Fergus's house, she'd fallen off a dining room chair one evening. Although that chair had been substantially sturdier and more expensive than the one now in question, it had broken, too. Fergus hadn't seemed to mind that she'd broken his chair, though. Weird, really, because he'd cared enough about his chairs to fold towels over the seat of

Merit's chair, and his own, before every dinner. Although she hadn't hurt herself, Fergus had carried her up to bed, brought her an ice pack and a heating pad, and sat with her until morning. She had no memory of her mother or father that night.

Merit started collecting the mess into a napkin. If nobody else had been around, she probably would have just picked up the food from the floor and eaten it.

Caroline had already split the scene. She was on the floor in the family room now, watching TV at a low volume.

The dog licked the floor by the table.

"You're sure you're not hurt?" Wyatt asked.

"Caroline," Merit said, "dinner's not over yet."

Merit went back into the kitchen. Wyatt started unpeeling an orange.

"I'm just watching the news," Caroline said. "I mean, I'm not watching cartoons or QVC."

"She's right, Merit: There are many worse things to watch than the news," Wyatt said.

Caroline lay on the floor, bare feet kicked up in back of her. She was wearing an ankle bracelet made of red yarn. When you accepted the contract of adulthood, lying on the floor just never really presented itself as an option. Merit herself didn't really sit on the floor all that much anymore. Except for tonight, when she'd gotten home. Earlier tonight Merit had lain on the floor for one whole hour.

"Want a piece of orange?" Wyatt asked. Merit wasn't sure to whom he was speaking. "It's a strange color. Is it supposed to be this way?"

"Blood oranges," Merit said.

"I thought they tasted darker. Can something taste darker?"

"Caroline?" Merit said.

"It's a shame we can't grow them here," Wyatt said. "We can't really grow anything here in Akron."

Although Caroline wasn't technically Merit's daughter, Merit had very clear ideas about how she wanted to raise her. She wanted Caroline to be a freethinker. Merit had, for instance, been a militant recycler, until she got a flyer from the garbage company indicating a policy change. She'd then tried a compost heap, then tried (briefly) freezing their garbage. Aspirin was the only real drug allowed in their house. If they ever got mice, Merit would, naturally, never use mousetraps, being of the belief that the mice would just leave when they were ready to leave. As a parent—or "parent," as she thought of herself—Merit's philosophy was something along the lines of: Let Caroline do what she needs to do. Merit's parents had never really been very "parental," either, and Merit had turned out okay. You couldn't control people, not even your children. Especially not your children, even when they weren't really yours. You couldn't control your parents, either, Merit understood. Not that she'd really ever tried.

Just last year, Caroline was still playing with dolls. Caroline was twelve then, and Merit had been in their house for four years. Merit had made a sane life for herself, one without lies. So had she needed to manufacture something to worry about? She was good at creating problems for herself, she knew. Merit lost sleep over the question of Caroline and her dolls. Wasn't twelve sort of too old to be playing with Barbies? Caroline kept them in a boot box in the Wyatt-built cupboard in her room, and it required a strong woman indeed to be able to confront them, naked and wound around one another like bodies in an open grave.

But just as soon as Merit's doll worry was becoming something of an obsession, she found the lidless doll box in Caroline's trash can. Merit didn't look again at the contents of the box as she carried it out to the garage.

Dolls freaked Merit out. Always had. One of the only times her father ever scolded her happened when he found a doll whose face she had erased with nail polish remover. Her father told her a story about a bad little girl who erased her dolls' faces and how the bad little girl grew up without a face herself. Caroline had never erased anybody's face, but Merit knew Caroline was already more (oh, how to say?) emotionally stable than Merit was, or would ever be.

After Merit got home from work tonight, she'd lain on the living room's carpeted floor, which smelled of chemicals she didn't know the names of but that Wyatt surely did. She'd stared up at the ceiling, listening to, and understanding in some vague way, Mozart's Requiem, then Fauré's Requiem, then Mozart's Requiem again, concentrating on the Lachrymosa, track number seven, programmed on repeat. She'd cried, and conducted, and wiped her nose with her shirt sleeve, and felt it all. Was it like this for everyone? The longing, or whatever it was? Unfulfillable, unresolvable. Whenever she cried, she cried for the same thing, although she had never really been sure what that thing was. She liked to imagine music touched something deep in her. She loved to listen to Mozart or Fauré and to think about art, which she knew she didn't understand, and imagine herself as rare and alone, which she suspected might not be true, which she was so afraid was untrue that she couldn't tell anyone about it. Not her mother, father, nor Fergus knew she loved, for instance, *Don Giovanni,* a love that she knew seemed undergraduate and obvious in the extreme. Some evening maybe she would listen to it while she was in the kitchen, stirring the risotto or whatever, on her second bottle of wine, and wonder who there was to tell about all she knew. Wyatt didn't know the longing part of her and never would. And then there was Caroline in her bare feet, and her *whippersnapper,* and her childhood habit of hiding inside the cabinets Wyatt made for her. Merit had been a hider, too, when she was a kid. Her favorite place to hide had been a big tire stuck upright in the playground across the street from their house, the house she and her mother had moved to after they'd left Fergus's. Whatever Merit was feeling now, she relished, basking in the exquisiteness of its vague presence. But maybe she *was* rare and alone and total. Maybe she could love only things that were unreal, like her father.

It had been two summers since Merit had seen him or the house. He had wanted to give Caroline a drawing lesson. Merit had tried to dodge the invitation for months, having elected not even to mention it to Caroline. She got busted, though, when he called Caroline herself (something he'd never done before) and told her (according to Caroline) to "ask that gorgeous daughter of mine why she's keeping you away from On Ne Peut Pas Vivre Seul."

Caroline had even heartbreakingly attempted the name of the house, calling it "On Nee Puke Paw Veeve Soul."

Caroline didn't know the truth about who the real artist in the family was. Wyatt did.

So two years ago, the four of them—Merit, her father, Caroline, and Wyatt—had sat by the reflecting pond at On Ne Peut Pas Vivre Seul. A statue of a peeing boy was in the middle of the pond. Merit knew that pond; she used to wade in it and drink from the statue when she was a girl. Only Fergus knew this about her. Fergus orbited them that day, serving half-lemonade/half–iced tea drinks on a silver fish-shaped platter. Merit and Wyatt didn't do much of anything but sweat, tormented by the sunlight. Merit's father talked to Caroline about how to draw a peony bush; he did not show her how to draw. Caroline's peony bush ended up being pretty good.

Merit had always really respected how good her father was with words.

Merit got a letter from him once, after her mother took her away from him, that ended like this: "Dance well. Look both ways, but jump. Feel it all, beautiful Spider." He had enclosed a sketch of himself with the letter. He'd enclosed a goddamned picture of *himself* with the letter about *her*. He had not drawn it himself, although he didn't know Merit knew that.

The worlds he inhabited were ghostly, backlit, undefined. The places he moved through contained, in her imagination, no hard surfaces. When she was eight, he told her he'd written a song for her. Had Merit understood more about music, had she understood more about him (and herself), she would have known Lowell wasn't really the composer of "The Ash Grove," nor was he a composer at all.

When she cried, did she cry for the same thing? And was she always crying for her father, the painter Lowell Haven?

2

We were late, as always. My fault again, of course. Didn't we have enough boxes of Kleenex back in the house? Did I *really* need to insist that we stop and get my antihistamines *now* of all times? Lowell was driving fast because we had a little less than three hours until the party started. My legs stuck to the upholstery and I liked it. Lowell hates it when I wear shorts.

At one point, I felt a sneeze coming on. I took a tissue from the glove compartment. I sneezed and glanced at Lowell. Were the driving gloves really necessary? We were just going around the corner. His eyes widened psychotically. He screamed again about how much *pain* my Kleenexes, my allergies, my pathological lateness, my miserable outlook on "life," and me in general caused him. Me, who had been holding back on any phlegm expectoration because I really did *not* want to set him off. Aren't I considerate? Aren't I a nice person? I screamed to Lowell that he could be *such* a fascist, and it really was so unfair.

"At least it is not my life's goal," he said in his low Lowell voice, "to do my business in every public toilet I pass, *Ferrrrgus.*"

Lowell parked the car in my driveway with a horrifying screech, stepped out, and threw his gloves onto the seat. He slammed the door and plucked the grocery bags from the back, one, two, the car bouncing back when he shut the trunk. As he marched up the hill, the cobbles under his boots went *crunchcrunch*. Ninety-five degrees and the man was wearing riding boots. Did he look back at me? He did not.

I sat in the car and reflected for several minutes about how dead I felt. Death comes first to the gut. I watched Lowell disappear underneath the entry arch.

Lowell thinks he's better than I am. Actually, to be perfectly accurate, Lowell thinks he's better than everyone, but we're talking about me for once, not everyone else. Because he does not admire me, he has never revealed himself to me. He has never given of himself. Look into his eyes if you don't believe me. His eyes, which say, I am completely alone, and want to be. His singularity, and its deadly glamour. None of us is immune to it. The funny thing is that everybody else who loves Lowell hates me because I got him. They think I *have* him. Which is, of course, not quite true.

"I want to look at you all the time," I remember saying to him once decades ago, when Jenny and Merit lived here with us. I remember when he made me feel simultaneously ecstatic and suicidal. To this day, I look at the breathless planes of his face and wonder . . . Oh, never mind.

The smell of hot leather was doing nothing for me. I unbuckled my seat belt, and it flew from me as if it couldn't wait to get away. Am I the only one who constantly feels as if the physical world is conspiring to defeat me? The car made that time-bomb *tick tick* and sounded as if it wanted to collapse, too. It strikes me as unspeakably sad to think about the lives of objects. I had to get out.

I'll tell you what Lowell's anti-Kleenex crusade is about: a complete disgust of my physical being. He's always, for instance, complaining that he finds ancient balled-up tissues of mine all over the house. Whenever he finds one in bed, it's armageddon. That's what happened this morning—the wadded tissue held at arm's length like a dead thing, and then the speech that followed—always the *speech*—about how he's always theorized that a Kleenex box on any couple's nightstand equals a miserable sex life.

It wasn't always like this.

As I walked up to the house (why didn't the stones crunching under me sound as fascinating as they did beneath Lowell's feet?), I imagined a scenario in which I went away somewhere, then came back svelt and tan and unsniffling, and Lowell took me into his arms and said to me . . . Oh, never mind. Just as I was enjoying this melancholy little fantasy, I fell down, slipping out of my sandals completely. They were Roman emperor–style, with crisscrossed laces. Who did I think I was? Caligula? Cla-Cla-Claudius is closer to the truth. The cobbles, those cruel little blades, dug into my knees and hands. Nothing seems sadder than a fall, nothing in the world, when there's no one to help you get up.

There was the sky. A dandelion puff twisted in it, then vanished. There was the ragged brown August Akron grass. I shook the stones from my shoes, extracted a Kleenex from my pocket, and wiped the scuff marks away.

I tossed the Kleenex on the ground and limped up to the house, the sixty-five room brick Tudor Revival–style house that once gave me such pleasure. The vista, spread out in front of me like this—the insane sky-line of the manor house, its crenellation-like teeth, its fenestration-like eyes, the corbeled turrets, the false battlements, the valley, the soft hills, the sky, the light—used to make me nauseous with love. I used to love this house with a purity with which I've never loved anything, except Merit.

I kicked open the gate. Atop the fake coat of arms above the keystone in the archway is a banner that says this: *On ne peut pas vivre seul.*

The lion's head knocker was cold in my hand. I pushed into the door. *Locked.* Thanks awfully, Lowell, *much* appreciated. I rang the doorbell to my own house. The ring inside was low and serious, and if this weren't, you know, my *house*, I would have thought the lives led by the people within were incomprehensibly great. The latch clanked and the door creaked open slowly, slowly, ghostlike, like a house of evil into which I was being beckoned. Who was behind the door, opening it? I stepped in-side, into the bleak and awful Tudor-homage foyer of my bleak and awful Tudor-homage house. Lowell's enormous self-portrait as King Arthur (how rippling his muscles! how flowing his hair!) between the two elec-tric torches efficiently establishes the tone.

I took the photographs on which the portrait was based.

To either side of the torches are tasseled lances. (Sad to say, we've had parties here in the past during which the lances got a swinging.) There were boxes, large unopened boxes from various catalog companies, stacked up Fergus height in the foyer's corners. On top of the boxes was a mail stack.

"Hello, Fergus." A voice that wasn't Lowell's. "Lowell arrived five minutes ago." I peeked behind the door. Andrei. Andrei is Lowell's special little friend, an artist aspirant (but of course), who was at this precise moment wearing a jauntily tilted fur hat. Tartan piping was involved. He shut the big portcullis door and greeted me, kiss kiss. Lots of cologne. He'd had some work done to his face.

"Did you two drive separately?" Andrei's English is so blandly perfect, it sounds like a language-lab record. Had he had cheekbones before? He looked fantastic.

"No," I said. "I was just doing some troubleshooting out there in the car." I was sweating. My mouth was dry. The following body parts hurt: knees, hands, and stomach. I needed a drink. The deeply dreadful thing was, I needed Lowell. When I let myself be sad, really sad, I still get terrified that he's left. Ridiculous, I know. It would take Lowell years to pack up all his stuff.

"I see," Andrei said. "This is interesting." Andrei said something was wrong with the lock and that Lowell had instructed him to stand there and let the guests in.

So Lowell hadn't locked me out.

"It would appear that you are the first guest," Andrei said.

Ah, let's not forget, I reminded him. *I* own this house.

I told him to go make me a drink. As I passed the boxes (which I really did have to figure out something to do with), I quickly sifted through the mail. There was another letter to Lowell from that magazine reporter, that Bradley W. Dormer person, who's written Lowell a letter every month since the retirement. A snippet recalled from last month's letter: "As I've been reminding you for five years, I attended your Whitney retrospective every day of the show. I hope this doesn't sound too fatuous, but your work has changed—some might say 'challenged'—the way the world sees. But why, Lowell Haven, do you remain in darkness? Why are you so enigmatic? And why did you stop painting?" Lowell has, in his more lucid moments, told me he won't talk to any journalist because he no longer has anything to say, not since the "long, joyless struggle" (as he now calls his artistic career) came to an end. Would that all magazine profile subjects had such a solid grasp of their limitations, I said.

I never found art to be a long, joyless struggle.

I stuffed the letter into my pocket and followed Andrei through my manor house in silence. Don't you love it? My manor house. Andrei, with his hat and his small hard ass, led me through the great hall (ceiling: three and a half stories high) with its Lowell as literary syphilitics portraits and vast Gabsa Gul rug, which took one hundred assiduous Ashgabats six round-the-clock weeks to weave; through the music room with its Lowell as Mozart portrait and its wide-paneled oak floor, which is buffed to a sheen so glowing that it looks licked; down the hall past the dining room with its worm-brown carpet runners, which I wasn't paying much attention to because I'm always powerless in front of the collection of *Canterbury Tales* Lowell portraits hanging upon the dark wall. Lowell painted himself as each character. The paintings were a gift to me. Sometimes I take down the painting of Lowell as the Wife of Bath (I don't enjoy looking at Lowell as a woman), but within a day, it always appears right back on the wall. The haggard, robed, white-bearded Lowell as the Franklin is a glimpse into the rather near future, I'm afraid, Lowell's and mine.

Lowell and Fergus. Question: Who is the more free?

Andrei took me into the kitchen. The kitchen and Lowell's now-unused studio are the only bright rooms in the house. I put my sunglasses back on. One would have thought Andrei would have had my drink order down by now. I told him, for the zillionth time, I wanted a Kahlua and skim milk, no ice. Wordlessly, he prepared my cocktail. He moved with the brisk efficiency of one who knows where everything is, one who feels a bit too much at home: liquor cabinet, glasses, stirrer, linen cocktail napkin, milk. (Andrei, you might suspect, has been here for quite some time.) One of my things with him is that I always try to catch him blinking.

He handed me the drink, which was viscous and warm, and not unlike . . . Oh, never mind. I downed it in one chug, feeling weirdly, I don't know, thankful and small, watching Andrei unblinkingly watch me as I drank.

That *hat*.

I felt like an orphan who'd been given half a cup of oatmeal.

Lowell's grocery bags were on the island in the middle of the room. Not unpacked, of course. That was old Fergus's job (or, more accurately, Mrs. Valdez's, but you see my point nevertheless). I obediently rinsed my glass in the sink.

Ah, *there* Lowell was, down below by the reflecting pond. Somebody else stood with him: a *woman*. How . . . novel.

"Andrei, tell me something. Who is that person down there?"

Somewhere in the dark corners of Eastern Europe there existed a prostitute who wondered who'd stolen her miniskirt. You know how all cheap hookers look the same from fifty feet—curly hair, shtetly body? Lowell appeared very crisp indeed, crisp and ironed and egg-still in his boots and ivory jodhpurs. His hair shone a cartoon blue-black in the sun. He wasn't even as big as one of the filthy plate-glass squares of the window. The woman to whom he spoke made big, annoying, affected arm gestures. Any show of feminine leg would be absolutely lost on this crowd tonight, be*lieve* me. Lawless blond hair. White sneakers. Did she have claims on him, too? Oh, yes, apparently so, because she touched Lowell's face with one of her soft little lotioned female hands.

"Who, Fergus?" Andrei asked. He was giving his bicep, which he flexed and ran his hand over, his full attention. Unappetizing stubbly arm hair. The woman threw her head back and laughed, her mouth open wide enough to toss coins into.

"Who is that . . . *person?*" I asked. I pointed. Lowell looked far too amused about something.

"You are a very low talker. You—what is the word? *Mumble.* You mumble, Fergus."

Is Andrei actually human? We've never been clear about this.

The mullioned widows were so dirty, I could have written Lowell's name on them. "Lord" Lowell Haven. How many glass squares would that have taken up? Ockwells gave me permission to copy their windows, I should add, back when I believed in things like windows.

"I just think we must allow Lowell to enjoy himself today." Andrei scooched in front of me to wash his hands in the sink, completely blocking my view. "That is Drisana-Nari. She is gorgeous, don't you agree? She arrived while you were doing your little errands."

He shook his hands, tepid water splashing my face. He didn't blink at me, just smiled with those chalky, hypocalcified teeth. My face was hot and my breathing constricted, both signs I was about to lose it. I thought of Jenny. I couldn't help it. Lowell was paying the woman the same kind of slavish attention he used to show Jenny, when she still existed to us.

"Sweetie," I said, "why don't you go back to your friend in Cleveland Heights and get your arms waxed? You're starting to look ethnic again."

"Now all of you, all of our dear, dear friends, know that our beloved, if tiny, Fergus is the undisputed champion when it comes to whipping up the neat little lunch basket. I remember when—this was quite a long while ago—I was painting one of my early-stage self-portraits, *Boy Scout, or: Murderer?* Fergus and I were first getting acquainted then. He invited me and my family here, into this very house, an invitation we had no choice but to accept. How *could* one resist? We sat over there, at that side of the table, directly underneath where the *Wife of Bath* now hangs, so this room certainly does have a, as the phrase goes, 'place in my heart.' Fergus served me and my wife a glass of champagne. In it was an ice cube—just one—into which a violet was frozen. Let it just be said that champagne, from that evening onward, became, perforce, more of a mystery than it—"

Ah, yes. Here we were at dinnertime, toast time. Lowell is never anything less than spectacular at toasts. How nice he always is to look at up there. How nice he is to look at, and to hear, even if you aren't exactly listening. His hair is still robust, still shines as black as an animal eye. There are some university courses that devote at least a third of one class to his artwork. (Although I still don't know what there is to "learn" about Lowell's work. Maybe that he's infatuated with his own myth? Maybe that you out there, you small, colorless individual, have neither self nor myth?) Back in the day, the celebrity wranglers at your glossier periodicals fought one another for access to him. ("An *artist* written about in a *glossy magazine?*" you ask. To which I say: Never forget how spectacularly good-looking Lowell is.) He'll make you think he knows Ovid in the original. Holderlin, too. He can use the word *rodomontade* in a sentence and make it sound as if it should be there. He moves well. He speaks well. You'd buy anything he'd care to sell you. Lowell never lets me sit next to him at his dinners, of course, because then, he says, I'd never talk to anyone else. He's probably right. That woman, Drisana-Nari, was next to him tonight. She hadn't left his side all evening. Lowell introduced us during cocktail hour. As I held my hand out, she switched her drink from one hand to the other and wiped a hand on her dress. As we shook, she said, a little too tensely (it seemed to me) into her shoulder, "Never trust a person with cold hands." Then Lowell slid in between us and solemnly told me to go stand by the front door and greet people. Instead, I slunk into the kitchen and made a man-sized Kahlua and skim amid all the hired-help hubbub (their leader: Mrs. Valdez) and then hid upstairs in my bathroom until dinner.

Lowell was at the head of the table, naturally, and she was to his right. I think her expressions came from ads in her favorite women's magazines. As he speechified, she gazed up at him, her heliotrope, the refined gentleman whose age is so impossible to pinpoint, up there with his black lustrous hair and his crimson velvet jacket (white French cuffs peeping out from underneath) and his movements, which are so economical and pristine that they remind us how miserable are our own flailings, the famous painter Lowell Haven. She looked around the table every so often to see if anyone was watching her. Nope, darlin'. No one.

"Then we came to the emu, which Fergus served in a sarcophagus. Over the sarcophagus he'd folded one of my early portraits—a photocopy, a photocopy!—*Lowell, Number Eight*. He removed the lid. The smell of the steaming emu came abruptly over me like a summer storm. I dug my fork in, and as it bloomed on my tongue, something within *me* blossomed. I remember, as well, what I said to Fergus after the first bite: 'Bloody hell,' I said, 'this is the closest I've gotten to an orgasm in *years*. No offense to my *wife*.'"

He had already mentioned Jenny twice. I would try not to think about this. Whenever I make the mistake of bringing her up as a topic of conversation, Lowell raves and sputters and threatens to leave me once and for all. The last time this happened was two Christmases ago, when I wondered aloud if we should send Jenny a Christmas card. He's never recovered from her—and Merit's—abandonment of us. The odious part of me has often been grateful he finally knows what it's like to be alone.

We're richer than everyone who comes here. We are always the richest people in whatever room we're in. We're rich because I'm rich, but when you've been "married" for as long as we've been (about five million years), one of the rules is that you have to say "we," even if you do still have separate bank accounts. All these people come to our dinners because they like the way they feel when they're with us. Let's be perfectly clear about this: Identify the issues at the beginning, and you'll hate me less later.

I got the money by turning my father's land into shopping malls. Don't you admire my passion? The month after he died, I sent myself out on a package tour of English country estates. Package tours are a humiliation, but I'd been to England only one other time and didn't know how else to travel alone. I had stayed with Jenny when she was living in London. That was almost thirty years ago, and it was otherwise a *weekus horribilis*, although I did take some nice pictures. I met Lowell then, too. We had a brief encounter with Jenny in a doleful little English restaurant.

Little did I know then, when Lowell oozed into my life, that I hadn't only met my match; I had met myself.

So, four thousand blueprints later, and this Tudor aesthetic makes me want to throw up all over my six-hundred-dollar Roman emperor–style shoes. What's awful here is that I did exactly what my parents did, although on a preposterously bigger scale—the week after Mother and Dad got married, they bought a whole houseful of furniture from Ethan Allen. They were kids then (what it *does* to me to think of my parents as kids) and they didn't put an enormous amount of thought into their purchase at the time. But then, hel*lo,* it's twenty or thirty years later and you're stuck with the decisions you made when you were so young. You're stuck with the same goddamned furniture. Every decision is always a commitment, isn't it? So this is all to say that I'd love to have this house trashed and start afresh, but Lowell won't let me, you see. Lowell loves this house with a purity with which he's never loved . . . Oh, I'm sorry; I forgot: That was *me.*

"In these vast stretches of forlorn land that Fergus and I later encountered on our travels, there was a certain mystery. A lonely desertscape shimmering like a mirage, one will never again be—"

Lowell says he's English. I personally am Akron-born, -bred, and, -educated, although I don't generally admit that right off the bat. Would you? I used to lie, used to say I was from Rhodesia, although I still don't even know what Rhodesia is. Lowell and I are both champion liars, so we've got that in common at least. However, Lowell's memory, unlike mine, isn't flawless. So when I tell you I've forgotten something, please recall I'm lying. I remember everything, lies included.

Lowell, when he painted, painted self-portraits. When he sold his best work several years ago and finally got rich and abandoned his painting, he became a famous host. Until that point, his interest level in meeting amusing people would have been, on a scale of one to ten, a five. Now, Lowell loves meeting every amusing person ("amusing" because their heads are all amusingly mucky with artistic delusions) from miles around—from Cleveland, Toledo, Columbus, Gambier, Dayton, Sandusky (but never Cincinnati; NB: Cincinnati *never*)—befriending that person, inviting him over to our house, making him feel loved, accepted, unjudged, pretending to be fascinated by him, by his "art," encouraging him to call at any hour of the day or night (which that person does). What the guests don't know is that Lowell's role as the host is only temporary. Oh, Lowell does, at the beginning, stock the guest's medicine cabinet with Mason Pearson hairbrushes, and, yes, he would order three dozen cases of sparkling rosé wine from Luxembourg if the guest happened to casually mention he enjoyed a Luxembourgish sparkling rosé from time to time.

Next, however, the guest will be discarded, as Jenny and Merit discarded us.

Lowell says he doesn't have to try too hard to make friends, since amusing people with amusing stories to tell are just drawn to us. Just drawn to us. He means drawn to *him*.

Some of the people, after Lowell has finished with them, after they've ceased to be amusing, can't understand why they've been icily dismissed. Every once in awhile, we'll get some tiny gray person—they all have that swollen face of the dispossessed—hovering like a ghost at the front door, meekly requesting an audience with Lowell. I turn them all away. Some drop to their knees and weep.

I've trained myself not to pay too much attention to his fantastic and amusing of-the-moment friends. Most recently, there was the Antioch girl with the tortoiseshell headband, whose artwork we referred to, when we were feeling munificent, as Neo-Expressionism, and who, I recall, at the dinner table once expressed her amazement that Lowell hadn't bought one thing for himself during that day's late-afternoon shopping excursion; before her, there was the sockless Oberlin boy, a conservatory student, who, in my recollection, talked about only two subjects: Bjork and Lowell. If I were to allow myself to think of the boy as a real human being, I would remember the scabs on his ankles, which I recall having thought had something to do with a bicycle, although I never had any evidence to support that theory. He walked with a faint limp, and his stomach rumbled all through one late-night viewing of my DVD of *The Music Man*. We'd already had dinner that evening, and he didn't ask for anything else to eat (nor did I offer). Last year, we had the Californian tree photographer Ray-Ray. Did my best to avoid *that* one.

He loved Lowell very much.

So, we have these tremendous dinner parties a few times a year. The scene at these dinners: *fabuloso*. Attractive and amusing people—men dressed as women, fabrics flowing, bracelets clanking, people working with vigor on songs, dances, poetry, sketches, easels spread-eagled on the lawn like demented giraffes, Lowell checking in on everyone's progress, governing them like an uncompromising king—moving purposefully and gracefully through my ill-conceived Tudor mansion on the coast of Akron, Ohio.

That's a lie, of course: Akron, Ohio, has no coast.

What the people don't understand is that the pain of knowing Lowell will outlast the pleasure.

". . . didn't know Fergus would *crash* the truck and we'd be left stranded in the Sahara without a sandwich to our names. We should have known better than to let our dear little Fergus drive, given that his mummy and his dad had been his chauffeurs his whole life, which, despite—"

He was making all this up, by the way. (And we never eat our emus. The emus are my friends.)

I used to hate these dinners, used to care about whom I was going to be seated next to, but now I don't. The horrible first moments of introducing yourself to the person to your right, the person to your left, deciding immediately which side you'll talk to, which side you'll exclude, the snarly first moments of not being able to figure out which wineglass is yours, the desperation of trying to find a common thread of conversation ("Your parents are dead? Mine are too!")—none of that matters to me anymore.

". . . Certainly we wished we'd brought a little more with us to eat. Our only hope was that someone, some nice fellow in a lorry, would stop by and rescue us. Here was the miracle, though: Fergus had serendipitously brought with him about two dozen silver packets of freeze-dried ice cream, which we'd bought months before at that wondrous museum in Washington, D.C., the American Air and—"

This night was just like any other. Me: Kleenex in my hand; the toast: convoluted but excessively eloquent; the guests: my enemies. I watched Lowell. His eyes, which are a changeable black-gold, moved as meaninglessly over me as they would a urinating stranger.

I didn't remember the name of the guy next to me. He didn't seem to be paying attention to Lowell, and wasn't even bothering with any perfunctory civility by pretending to listen. While Lowell went on about my shortcomings, this guy—attractive in a big-nosed way—traced the bottom of his wineglass. A seductive little move.

". . . Neopolitan. Pink, white, brown. All three flavors had peculiarly different—"

The big-nostriled man was now lighting a cigarette, bent into the candle flame. I looked down at my plate and felt a frisson of terror when I saw a used Kleenex on top of it. How had that gotten there? The smoke made my eyes water. I sneezed. The nose gentleman glanced my way and mouthed, *Bless you.* His nostrils were not small—was that his brain glistening up there? The smoke dragoned out of them, the nostrils, and what a menacing little picture that was. I wanted a cigarette, one of his.

". . . We'd bought the ice creams to send to my daughter, Merit, who was at this point a young child. But thank God Fergus hadn't gotten around to making a trip to the post office. We sometimes joke that we wouldn't be alive, the two of us, were it not for Fergus's forgetfulness. Or was it his rapaciousness that kept us alive? Jenny doubtless would have waggled for the latter. But that's neither here nor—"

The only true piece of this anecdote was the bit about the freeze-dried ice cream. Lowell and I did once find a pack of it, one pack, hidden behind the marshmallow peanuts at Rausch Drug and Gift Emporium. That was just a couple of months after Jenny and Merit left us. I tried to keep them here. I even wrote Jenny a *check*. I would have done anything to get them to stay. We were buying sleeping pills for Lowell and candy for me. I felt the foil-packed space-age ice cream behind the ersatz peanuts and made a comment about how nice it was to feel something hard after having felt so many soft things. Lowell was intrigued. He tugged the tight little ice-cream pack from the rack.

"I promised I'd find this for her someday," he said, shaking the pack at me. "I *promised* Merit."

I had to steady myself on the counter. I was shattered. Why? Because it was another promise of Lowell's I'd known nothing about. And because he and Merit had nothing to do with me.

I tapped Nostrils on the shoulder, pointed to the pack. He moved closer, nostrils dilating. Shook a cigarette from the pack. We held each other's eyes for two beats longer than is generally considered appropriate. His nostrils really were something. What nationality is that, big nostrils? Nostrils held the candle up to my cigarette very politely. I was too shy to meet his eye. Sucked powerfully, coughed a little, sneezed, sat back, enjoyed. Lowell as the Wife of Bath sits (*not* sidesaddle) on an exhausted white horse. He as the Wife wears spurs and red hose. A hat so queer that Andrei would wear it. The Lowell in the picture looked out at me furiously, something hideous blazing in his black eyes.

I took the pictures of Lowell in these costumes; Lowell painted the pictures.

"At any rate, Fergus kept us alive and nourished and well. Perhaps there wasn't a great deal of art to these humble meals, but let it just be said that I owe my very existence to them."

Do you see what he does? Do you see how Lowell butters you up, so that the dagger goes in smoothly, smoothly?

Mr. Nostril reached into his jacket, took out a toothpick from the side pocket, and studied it. Wonderfully expressive nostrils. They had something very important to say. He brought the toothpick over the candle flame, held it there, and let it burn. The scarlet stone in his ring caught the light of the flaming toothpick. The ring looked medieval and secret and cruel. (Genuine ruby? Your certified gemologist and appraiser Fergus dearly hoped the answer was a stentorian *yes*.) His fingernails were slightly, just slightly, too long. I had an image of the burning toothpick exploding, a fireball leaping up to my face. Skin grafts, people in white, pig skin, unspeakable pain, darling, don't stare, it's just a man with no face.

"Three days without food. How many of you have gone three days sans—"

The guy sitting next to the nostrils man had thinning yellow hair, longish, a look that I sincerely, sincerely hate. Fakirlike, he gazed up at Lowell. His eyeglasses were wire-rimmed, and, in side view, you could see one of the lenses was much thicker than the other.

"Other miracle is that Fergus found a bottle of Benedictine in the glove compartment, next to his ubiquitous box of *Kleenex,* come to think of it, a bottle that he has throughout the years claimed appeared quite literally from the desert air. We opened the bottle with great gusto, gulped it down, the liquor smoldering on the tongue like shellac. As Rabelais said, 'That which is meant to cleanse the—' "

The burning toothpick smelled like a fireplace in winter. Yellow Hair glanced sideways at the nostril man, hit him on the upper arm, and mouthed, *Oooh, stinkypoo, put it out.* Nostril's nostrils were going crazy, and he rolled his eyes and shook out the toothpick, but not so quickly as to seem entirely submissive. Lowell made a sniffy-sniffy face and looked coolly around to see what was burning. It was the first time during the toast he'd looked into my eyes. He should have known I don't set fires.

"Which, in a circuitous way, brought dear, dear Drisana-Nari into our lives. It was back to our little Akronian villa, where truffles may not quite grow on trees, but good friends—"

The woman, Drisana-Nari, was turning as red as rubber. She didn't know where to look, her eyes darting helplessly around the table, with no clue about where to rest them. Just relax, honey, I wanted to say. It ain't about you. Lowell put his hand on the back of her chair cosmopolitanly.

" . . . had seen Drisana perform several times, and I was dumbfounded by the resourcefulness of her—"

I think I need to mention at this point that Lowell had never once brought up her name, ever. Nostrils stabbed out his cigarette into the ashtray. He drew bored little circles in the ashtray with the bent stub. There were remnants of dirt underneath his long nails. A sexy whiff of rot about him.

"We—Drisana-Nari, Andrei, Fergus, myself—want you to feel well cared for, gastronomically and otherwise. This, my friends, is our fondest—"

Nostrils was now etching lines into the table with the burnt remains of his toothpick, which clumped blackly here and there on the white tablecloth. The black lines became a word, then two words. The two words were *SHUT UP.*

"And may you never be strangers—"

In the eyes behind Yellow Hair's oily glasses was a wild gleam when he saw his buddy's etched *SHUT UP* upon the tablecloth. He started rubbing the graffito, hysterically going at it, revved up and on speed, on the wrong speed, like a silent movie.

"And we shall see you all very soon, I'm sure—in a few weeks, in fact—at what will certainly be a cartwheeling, *epic* party in honor of our gorgeous and gifted new friend Drisana-Nari."

Excuse me?

"Our little Fergus over there will be handling the arrangements. The dream, my friends, continues shortly."

Everybody's real dream had finally come true and the goddamned speech was over. The idea of planning another party, and one for that *person* over there, made me want to take the biggest syringe on the market and jam it into my ear canal. Had I had the proper equipment at that moment, I would have stapled my tongue to something.

Lowell sat down. Drisana-Nari stroked his hand. I had a drink. I had the whole glass. Nostrils had placed his wineglass over his black *SHUT*

UP, and he held it there, at the base. I smiled at him. He smiled back. I found him charming.

"If you want to know the truth, Fergus," he whispered, his hand still spread out rigidly over the bottom of the glass, "Trevor and I come to your dinner parties only to see you. Lowell can be such a . . ." Here he was searching, searching—for what perfect word was he searching? " . . . *turd* sometimes."

Ahhh!

"You look so . . . amazing, by the way, Fergus."

Or at least I think he said "amazing."

Double ahhh!

Lovely guy. Yes, indeed, wonderful, wonderful man. What *was* his name?

Our legs were now brushing against each other, and, despite the impossible admission of Drisana-Nari into our lives, despite the prospect of another party and its attendant horrors, a surge of—what?—bounteousness went through me. A feeling of uncharacteristic generosity. I felt good. I *felt.* Expanded. Bigger. An increasing openness in the chest. I pushed my plate away and leaned back like a glutted emperor. Maybe it was the tuna, the noodles, or the distinguished vino, or the fact that I'd done about an hour of demanding back stretches earlier in the day and could finally sit in those impossible goddamn "Glastonbury" chairs, which had cost me about ten thousand dollars apiece, even though they were made in North Carolina circa 1982, without being incapacitated by a Rockette line kick of back spasms, or maybe it was the fact that I'd just had a little moment with someone, but I was feeling flush with goodwill.

Lowell was enjoying a little drinkie himself, his signature Manhattan. He looked fantastic. How he laughed. Confident and elegant and very much alive in his red smoking jacket. He fed Drisana-Nari a cherry from his cocktail. She ate the stem, too. Now she and her hair were leaning into him, engaged in some kind of private whispered conversation. Elsewhere at the table, men were passing around massive rhinestone earrings and laughing. Each successive man who clipped the earrings on would shake his head so they flopped excitingly around. It was actually very nice, this repeated desire to make them go sparkly sparkly for the benefit of the watchers, the wearer unaware what he actually looked like. It is a tragedy, is it not—never being able to see oneself? I suspect Lowell would have chosen another subject for his artwork if he didn't believe this, too.

I noted nobody had eaten anything. I drank a few more glasses of wine.

So what happened next was that I woke up on the floor of the music room. How I got there, I don't know, but there I was, too drunk, too vomitous, to move. I always try to avoid the music room because of the suits of armor. They'd never scared me until they scared Merit. I just know that when I die, they're going to put me here, stuffed and powdered. The ceiling was very far away, the pattern, a molded plaster crest of some family that wasn't mine. I have no crest because I have no family. I lay there on the floor, listening to the ocean sounds of my own head, feeling my body beating. I was drunk. I was vulnerable. It was important I not vomit all over the floor.

I remember a blurred male figure swooping around with an elaborately immense hookah. I remember thinking it looked expensive. I remember watching Lowell bend at the waist and take a puff off of it, the embers glowing a hotter orange when he inhaled. The elegantly dissipating smoke rings were a schoolbook drawing of white blood cells, fat and round and white. Lowell was upside down in my view of him then, and he looked very evil indeed in his bloodred smoking jacket, the tube in his mouth snaking down to the hookah like a cave-dwelling life-form, an underground thing. The terror of tree roots, tubers. Don't you think the devil probably wears a crimson velvet jacket with tasseled belt?

Then noises, a commotion, human voices.

"Fergus, wakey, wakey, if you don't mind."

I wanted to go home and lie down. Remembered, though, I was home, and I already was lying down.

"Fergus, it's time, please, for you to get up."

Most of them don't even bring *wine* to these things. Isn't that just so unspeakably rude?

I fanned my face with my hand and breathed.

"Fergus: *NOW.*"

These words were directed at me, and they were coming from Lowell.

Something hit me on the forehead. It took me some time to figure out I wasn't mortally wounded. There the culprit was, over there by my foot. A piece of bread, a roll. I squeezed it and crawled over into the corner, right underneath the suit of armor, which I'd never considered a friend. I shoved the roll into my mouth and ate it up. No one ever eats the rolls at our parties. I keep telling Lowell it's a big waste of money and that we should stop serving them.

Then: music. A sitar? Since when did we have a sitar? There it went, and a high, piercing voice fluttered around the room. Did the voice belong to a male or a female? Who knew? Who cared? A young man—slender, soft-faced, seemingly without genitals—danced gaily on the stage. The music room has a stage, on which all our legendary performances happened. The man/woman was wearing a sari. So many candles up there, so easy to knock over.

I've always known I'll die in a fire.

Then, act number two. Was that Drisana-Nari? I'm going blind, too, I think. I squinted. Yes, it definitely was Drisana-Nari. She'd taken her sneakers off and was now barefoot. She performed two dances, the first one involving, from what I got out of it in my low-functioning state, a scrambled egg. I really do think that's what she was playing, the whole kitchen-egg life cycle: the egg broken, the egg scrambled, the egg cooked. The second dance had to do with a hammer. She played not only the hammerhead but the hammer *claw,* and that, you see, was what made her into a spectacle. Her face: the hammerhead; the back of her head: the claw. Pound, pound, pound with her face; then she flipped herself around and went pull, pull, pull with the back of her head. She had no dignity. None. *Perfect* for Lowell.

She had been the kind of child who always had chocolate smeared over her face. I just knew it.

Lowell stood off on the other side of the room, smiling and clapping urbanely. The suit of armor remained immovable, immobile, immutable, saluting.

A sneeze coming on.

Boinged up, yanked Kleenex from my pocket. Ahhh, got it. I opened the Kleenex and sneaked a peek. Hello, *that's* odd, I thought. What *was* that smell? My lip curled up in disgust. So easily identifiable, so familiar, but . . . what? I couldn't quite get at it. An odor high and thin, not thick enough to be a taste like most smells are, but higher than that. It was an aroma that stung like horseradish or chlorine, pool chlorine, which had always seemed so unclean and brought to mind pale dead skin on the underside of waterlogged feet on the mildewy cement of bathhouse floors.

It was a smell that made me think of . . . sex.

And then I was thinking of Lowell, and then Drisana-Nari, who in my fantasy was faceless, only a body with a head of lawless blond hair. His ass and her hair. Lowell would not appreciate being thought of in this way. Probably neither would she. And then: another, subtler whiff of it. A smell clean and filthy both.

How completely disgusting. Did I extrapolate immediately where the tissue had come from and for what it had been used? Yes, indeed, I did. A tissue I'd that morning picked up from the bed and put in my pocket. A tissue into which someone had ejaculated.

That someone being, let us hope to God, Lowell.

I gagged. I made an attractive "I'm going to be ill all over the place" sound and lay back down on the floor. I curled up fetally.

"Fucking hell, are you all right, Fergie?" I felt someone moving, the footfalls on the floor. Lowell was standing over me now, but the chandelier was so bright and the suit of armor loomed over me like Claudius's ghost. Someone had put the armor's right arm out, as if it were heiling Hitler. I held my hand up to block it. I understood for the first time what had scared Merit about the suit of armor. She was a little girl then. Merit was once a little girl, as inexplicable as that now seemed. I'd once put that armor on to show her there was nothing to be afraid of. But when I'd clomped around the room, Merit ran to the harpsichord and hid underneath it. On the floor, she'd curled caterpillarishly into herself, clutching her white patent-leather shoes. When Merit was young, she seemed not to possess hamstrings. Lowell was coming toward me now, his entire body the size of my thumb. How tiny he was, and how easy it would be to crush him, to flick him away like a ladybug. One never knows the size of anything unless one is right up next to it, staring it in the eye.

"Fergie, my God. What the devil's wrong with you?" he asked. He was Lowell-size now. He crouched down and spread his hand over my forehead, as if taking my temperature. I could feel his soft breath on my face, and I breathed it in but felt nothing. My heart.

"I'll start getting the invitations to the next party out tomorrow, Lowell," I gurgled.

The suit of armor arm was giving me a sign of some kind. It cast a long shadow. I closed my eyes against it, that hateful arm, and saw a pattern, houndstooth, and then it occurred to me that every pattern we've ever seen with our eyes exists already in the brain, and Lowell's hand came down over my nose, and I smelled it, but there was nothing to smell, and I could feel him moving in closer to me, and his hand was over my mouth and I bit the skin of his hand, softly, softly, but tasted nothing, and I thought of Merit, and all the people who'd been here before, in this house, and all the ghosts here, and how nothing is ever left untouched, and I breathed the room's air and smelled nothing, and our smells—mine, Lowell's, the house's—were indistinguishable to me, inexorable to the flesh, and I sucked on Lowell's hand, and his eyelashes swiped my forehead, butterfly kisses dealt by long Lowell lashes. As I get older, as time passes, all I want to do is hold on to everything forever, and that's a need that might strike you as sad. If you hold on to something, then it can't disappear, can it? I sucked the flesh of his hand and listened to his eyelashes. Oh Lowell. My poor little ladybug Lowell, oh Lowell, my butterfly. Yes, Lowell, you can't very well cry with closed eyes. I've told you that forever, and it might very well strike you as sad.

3

Merit's problem at work—well, one of them—was that she hired the guy in the Kafka T-shirt. She initially liked his, as they say, "attitude." (Who comes into a first interview wearing a weird T-shirt with Franz Kafka's head silk-screened on it, and *shorts*?) She had also enjoyed how he sat in her office's leatherette waiting area before their second interview, writing something that almost certainly had nothing to do with the interview at hand into a dirty spiral-bound notebook with the softing gray-edged paper of the criminally insane. The tip of his pencil was blunt and probably unsanitary. On the second interview, he wore the same fringed stoner moccasin boots a boy she'd had a crush on in school used to wear, a boy who, the last day Merit ever saw him, famously stood up in study hall and announced, "The President has been shot," then hightailed it out of the lunch room (it was 1993, and the President had not, in fact, been shot [confirmed later]), his boots' fringe and his leather jacket and his long hair flying. The boy, whose name was Micah, was never heard from again. But no one in Merit's crowd cared much about Micah; he was merely a peripheral element in school, a burnout, a person who had been deemed in kindergarten already nonessential. And it was with Micah, his specter, that Merit became aware of time passing, that she understood her days were marked with his vanishing: It's been a week since I've seen him; it's been a month since I've seen him; it's been a year; it's been two; it's been ten. When she was younger, she sometimes counted the days like this with Lowell, too, marking the time since she and Jenny left the house. It's not like anyone knew this about her. She divided her childhood into two parts: before she was eight, when she and her mother lived at Fergus's, and after she was eight, when she and Jenny lived alone together.

And so during the second interview with the guy with the Micah boots and the Syd Barrett hair and the definitely unwashed Kafka T-shirt, Merit knew she had found herself a new assistant.

A straight-backed chair was across from her desk; whenever anyone sat in it, she felt, behind her desk, like the world's least-liked principal. The lighting situation in her office wasn't the best, either, and the swivel lamp on her desk shone like an interrogation lamp upon the face of whoever sat across from her. Merit noticed when people were uncomfortable.

She asked the Kafka T-shirt guy (whose name was Randy) three times during interview number two if the light bothered him. He said, "No worries" each time, although he did repeatedly squint and shield his eyes.

Randy had dropped out of college the year before, a semester before graduating, and Merit found herself stating something in the first interview that she didn't know she believed until she said it, which was that most truly smart people didn't graduate from college anyway. Neither of her parents had gone to college, and they were both, in their own weird ways, really smart, she said.

For some reason, during the second interview, Merit mentioned to Randy that Lowell Haven was her father. Merit hated to hear herself say that, for a number of reasons. In this instance, it felt as if she were pulling rank on her young interviewee. After the information was presented, Randy smiled radiantly, his braces shining in the interrogation lamp. (He had braces.) He smiled that way, she imagined, because he was impressed she was the offspring of a semi-semifamous artist, although she suspected she might just be flattering herself (and Randy) by thinking this. Upon leaving her office on the second visit, Randy gave her a copy of his self-published physics/literary journal, so Merit was therefore left with no choice but to believe Randy was something of a boy genius, and perhaps even an artist himself. Such a boy genius artist would definitely know who Lowell Haven was.

But it soon became clear—in, oh, his first hour in the office, after the plastic *South Park* figures went up all around his cubicle, followed by the sheet of paper that read "Phone Etiquette" ("Rule #1: Answer the phone distinctly but pleasantly, stating your name and, if applicable, your department. Example: 'Bob Smith, Systems.'"), which he'd taped to the outerfacing wall of his cubicle—that her initial impression of Randy had perhaps been too generous. That he would actually think to bring in—on his *first day*—*South Park* figurines and a page of sarcastic phone-answering rules left her scratching her head. (Also, on the first day he kicked—literally *kicked*—the fax machine.) From day one onward, Randy's hunched, heated phone conversations (too intense to be office-appropriate, Merit thought) became commonplace. These were two of the overhead Randy phone sputterings on day one: "My old lady" and "I need to find out what she said to *Cooper,* man."

Randy's spelling problem didn't reveal itself until a few days later. Merit's big joke (which wasn't really funny enough to be called a joke, she knew) was that Randy believed *bean,* as in legume, was spelled *been.* It wasn't very nice, she knew, to mock his spelling problems, and *bean* versus *been* wasn't the best example of a misspelling anyway; beans didn't come up all that much at work. Merit sold ad space at a regional magazine.

Neither of her parents had ever expressed the slightest interest in her job.

Randy did wear the stoner fringe boots almost every day, although the Kafka shirt was, sadly, never seen again after the two interviews.

And another thing about Randy: How hard was it to collate photocopied documents? After he'd copy something, she'd have to do the collating herself, spreading the Randy-photocopied papers out on her office floor. She'd close the door so Randy wouldn't know what a big pussy she was. Why didn't she just say, "Dude, collate the copies next time. Thanks."? Problem solved. Done and done.

Merit now thought, Randy hadn't, in fact, ever heard of Lowell. If he had, he'd certainly do a better job at collating copies, spelling names in phone messages, etc.

Randy smelled exactly like you'd expect him to smell: patchouli. And still she felt an attraction/repulsion thing for Randy. She could admit this only to herself.

She had a nickname for Randy. His personalized E-mail screen was a computer programmer's idea of a court jester: a crude line drawing of a mental defective (eyes pointing in different directions = mental defective) in a dunce cap, a scroll in one hand and something that was probably supposed to be some kind of horn in the other. E-mail was Randy's preferred mode of communication. Her nickname for him, inspired by the novelty E-mail screen, was "the Tooting Subordinate."

Merit sat in a bathroom stall at work. Rebecca, her boss, was planted silently in the stall next to hers. Merit ID'd Rebecca by her feet, which were stuffed into the lace-up shoes Merit had seen so often—huge, immobile—underneath her huge glass-topped desk. The thick gray socks on the feet looked itchy and hot. The feet were pointed straight ahead, dead-looking, the feet of a (very large) ventriloquist dummy. Merit had made a little pact with herself that she was going to remain in the john until Rebecca moved her feet. This ran very much counter to one of the unspoken rules of all ladies' rooms everywhere, which was that you did your business and *got out.* One didn't linger.

Nose blowing.

Rebecca's left foot slid back a little, and Merit was free. Merit soaped her hands, rinsed, dried with one paper towel. Rebecca blew her nose again, flushed, banged open the stall door. Merit tucked her overloaded makeup bag under her arm and mouthed, *Bye* to Rebecca. The bathroom door sort of slammed, which Merit hadn't meant to happen.

She went briskly down the hall, past the window and the sink with all its dirty dishes, and into the little kitchen area. She crouched down at the dorm room–size fridge, her bones or whatever cracking distressingly, a sound so private and thus shameful that Merit always felt, whenever it happened, she should apologize for it. She took out her blueberry yogurt. A Post-it note that said NOT YOURS MINE in the Tooting Subordinate's *America's Most Wanted* scrawl had come detached from one of the refrigerator's many Rubbermaid containers and was stuck to the icy side rail.

Big purposeful steps clomping down the hallway now. That sound was Rebecca.

"The people here are little babies who need their mommies to clean up after them."

Rebecca, unlike lots of other ladies, didn't have a perfumy afterwind.

Merit stood over the sink with her yogurt. The four years she'd worked at *Ohio Is,* Merit's lunch break went, on non-client-lunch days, exactly this way: standing at the sink, eating a yogurt or a protein bar, looking out the window, checking for any sign of life in the yard next door. Today, the dog yapped away and the empty backyard swing swung as if being ridden by a spook or neighborhood demon, or the disgruntled ghost of a former regional magazine ad salesman.

Merit ate blueberry stuff out of the bottom of the yogurt container with the spoon she kept in her desk drawer. She just thought of the word *runcible.* She washed her nonruncible spoon and slid it into her back pocket. She popped the lid back on the half-full yogurt container, because otherwise there'd be a big mess in the kitchen area's garbage can. Merit wanted to make things easier for Claudia.

Claudia was the cleaning woman. She and her husband ran the cleaning service (which they owned) together. Merit had gone to high school with Claudia, although it wasn't like they'd been friends then. Merit usually got to work too late to see her, but the times she had been in early, they would usually talk—gossip about people from high school mostly. She still couldn't tell what Claudia thought of her. In the past, Merit had heard Randy bitching to another assistant about how "even the fucking maid" earned more money than they did.

Randy stood over the fax machine. He was yelling.

"Geniuses! Could somebody tell these geniuses that they don't need to send the same fucking ten-page fax to every single person on this floor? They do this all the time. It's wasting toner, and tell them I can't fax anything for hours when they do this." Randy shook his frizzy head at the folly of it all and sneered uglily at the fax machine.

"Sorry about that," said Merit, who was always apologizing for something, even to her Tooting Subordinate.

"Yeah, well. That's *life,* isn't it?"

Randy really had a way of laying things out, explaining how it all worked. His braces made him sound as if he were eating even when he wasn't.

Merit shut her office door. This was in violation of an unwritten, unspoken office code, but let everyone think she was complaining about them or talking to a headhunter or masturbating. Just let them think whatever.

The phone's message light was on. She told it to leave her alone. She gave it the old middle finger. Her black chair was coated with hair—hers and the animals', maybe some of Caroline's, but let's hope to God none of

Wyatt's. (Wyatt's hairline's alarming recession of late was a topic ver-boten.) She picked up the phone and let it dangle down, the cord un-twisting itself. She punched in her PIN. She had the same PIN for everything in her life that required one: Fergus and Lowell's address. One new voice-mail message: a male client who wanted to give her a "heads-up" that he had to "reschedule" and "could do the twenty-fourth or the twenty-sixth" and who signed off by saying, "Talk soon." Merit deleted the message without writing down the guy's number. Maybe she had the number in her aged Luddite Rolodex; maybe she didn't. She was feeling reckless today. Hey!

Three E-mails from the Tooting Subordinate.

One: subject line: "THIS IS STUPID"; message: "We need to get somebody else to order fax toner for the fax machene."

Two: subject line: "THIS IS STUPID, NUMERO DOS"; message: "And printer tooner."

Three: subject line: "CALL 4 U"; message: "Call from I think it was your Mommy."

Merit opened her office door. The door banged against the wall. Randy was settled back at his desk. At his cubicle area, she crossed her arms over the breast-high plywood partition and pointed to her ears (a little hint to him to take off the headphones).

She thanked him for taking the message, then asked if he had any de-tails about it.

He leaned back in his Aeron chair (bought back when they were flush, back before the ad recession) and whipped the headphones off. He sighed histrionically.

"She went into this *rant* about how no one has any style any-more, about how people look like 'peasants squatting along the side of the road, giving birth'; then she asked me totally belligerently why I was at my desk at lunchtime. I was like, okay, chiquita. I was like, Whatever."

Yes, he had indeed spoken with Jenny. Merit asked if there were any specifics about her reason for calling.

" 'Specificity' is not her strong suit, methinks," he said. The head-phones went back on. He turned back to his screen. Merit denied her-self the pleasure of smacking Randy. Was she mean for imagining the headphones going flying right across the cube? Yes, she thought, she certainly was.

Merit closed her office door gently, practiced the breathing thing from her yoga tapes, and dialed her mother's number. She guessed from the tenor of her message, as Randy'd explained it, that Jenny was drunk.

Jenny answered on the first ring. She asked Merit if she had a "weensy, itsy-bitsy sec." She was definitely drunk.

Merit lied and said she was busy. *Swamped* was the word she used, one of the words she most hated in the lexicon.

"I got an invitation to a party. Guess whose? Come on, guess."

Merit was afraid she knew the answer to this question. She said nothing.

"Fergus and Lowell's. Such dolls, aren't they?"

Merit coughed into the receiver.

"Really. They're *dolls*. Mr. and Mr. Lowell Haven have a *new* artist, apparently."

Merit's E-mail chime went off.

"Oooooh!" Jenny said. "What have we won?"

"It's just my E-mail; ignore it, Mom."

"We won a million bucks!"

"I need to figure out how to make it stop dinging; just ignore it."

"Noooo, don't do *that*. It sounds happyhappyhappy. We'll throw our own party with our million bucks and we'll be happy. We'll throw a million-dollar party and not invite Lowell."

"I thought I threw all the Goldschlager out. Please say you don't have some secret Goldschlager stash under your bed."

Was this a situation? Was Jenny drunk enough for this to be officially deemed a situation that would call for Merit's swift and decisive attention?

Silence. Jenny was probably crying.

Yes, this was indeed a situation.

The car was a Jaguar. It was a twenty-first birthday present from Merit's father, and it was presently stalled at the side of the road, by Pfiffin Elementary School. Whenever anyone at work seemed impressed Merit owned a Jaguar, she'd say, "What good is your Jag-u-wire if it's broken down along the side of the boo-lay-var?" It was not a good joke; Jaguars were English and boulevards were French. Merit knew this.

Merit never really listened to Wyatt during her little prepardedness drills. She'd never once bothered to open the trunk during a breakdown, but she knew the contents of the trunk (Wyatt had put a checklist in the glove compartment): two umbrellas, three flashlights, eight nine-volt batteries, a bucket, a sign that said CALL POLICE, a Black Watch–patterned blanket, a roll of duct tape, a pair of heavy gloves, an ice scraper, a roll of twine, a shovel, an itchy wool shirt, a couple of disgusting (according to Merit) cranberry-flavored energy bars, a three-pack of paper towels, a three-gallon bottle of mineral water, a pair of Merit-size steel-toed boots, a pair of rag-wool leg warmers, a pair of cheapie pink sunglasses from Cedar Point, a plastic funnel, a battery-powered hot plate, a battery-powered radio from the National Weather Service, a tin of steel-cut oats, and the rattan produce bag for her Saturday shopping trips. There was no room in the trunk to carry groceries or haul lumber or do anything like that.

A bumper sticker in back of the car said IF ANIMALS COULD SPEAK WE WOULD ALL BE VEGETARIANS. Merit had stuck it there, not Wyatt.

Merit weighed the pros and cons of calling Wyatt now on her cell phone. She decided not to, not yet. It would worry him. He would be worried. Wyatt worked fifteen miles away, but once he heard she was in trouble—Was this even officially trouble? She'd vote no, but he'd probably say, "Oh, my *Lord,* sweetie, what were you thinking and why did you wait so long?"—he'd get himself there, somehow (although Wyatt was otherwise a very cautious driver), in five minutes. Also, if she called him now, she knew she'd have to watch politely as he drew another statistical control chart that explained why they needed to get rid of this terrible car.

Merit had always suspected the very fact she even drove a car in the first place made Wyatt nervous. During the course of their seven-year relationship, she had been the driver and he the passenger only three times. The first time she'd driven, Wyatt had said through his fever: "This concerns me more than you can imagine"; the second, returning home from a funeral: "I fear for you, Merit, for us"; the third, drunk, and seizing the Oh Shit handle: "I'm scared."

Merit cranked the key. She cranked it again. Her hapless Jag had been jinxed from the beginning, she supposed, because of, well, the little accident she'd had before she even managed to get out of the driveway on the morning of her twenty-first birthday.

At 8:00 a.m. that birthday morning, Lowell and Fergus had shown up unannounced at Jenny and Merit's back door. Lowell's special knock (*of course* Lowell had a special knock) awakened Merit, who was, at this point in her life, rarely up before 11:00 a.m. She put on her splotchy glasses, stumbled downstairs in her sleepy-time shorts and T-shirt, and encountered at the kitchen's screen door (which no one except Jenny and Merit ever used) Lowell and Fergus.

"Hallo, darling!" Lowell exclaimed. "Look at you looking *so* gorgeous on your big birthday!"

Lowell was dressed in a red robe that might or might not have technically been called a kimono. He brandished a bouquet of pink peonies; Fergus carried a white baked-goods box. She invited them inside and hugged each individually. Lowell's hug was full-hearted and frank; Fergus's one-armed hug (the box) was somewhat squirrelly, but almost embarrassingly sincere. Usually, when Fergus saw Merit, he'd open his mouth really wide—he just couldn't *believe* it was *her!*—in what Merit always thought of as an unsettling silent-scream/silent-laugh hybrid. Whenever he did this, Merit always wondered if he were imitating some trademark gesture of *hers*. Fergus did the mouth thing both before and after the hug.

The ceiling creaked; Jenny was, as Jenny always was, up. Merit put the peonies in water and opened the box: cupcakes, beautiful pastels, spring colors. She thanked them. She asked Fergus how he was, because she knew he very much wanted to be asked that.

"I'm exceptionally well," Fergus said. "You can always tell when they grow up, can't you?" he asked Lowell. "They look so *tired* in the morning." He was talking about Merit.

She didn't know why, but this particular foot-in-the-mouth exclamation was a real kick in the chest. Although she loved him, in a way, a lot of things about Fergus were kicks in the chest. When Merit was six years old, he told her she was the best friend he'd ever had.

Lowell did a sly eye roll at Merit. "Well put, Fergus," he said.

Fergus didn't know about Lowell. Merit knew who the real artist was, but Fergus, because he was in his own little world, did not. Was "allergic to reality" a good way to phrase Fergus's condition?

"Your mother's been up since dawn, I'm quite sure, no?" asked Lowell. "Should you perhaps run upstairs and tell her we're here?"

Merit hollered for Jenny. No *way* was she going to go upstairs.

Fergus glanced wildly around the untidy pink kitchen like an ensnared bunny. The ceiling creaked again. The kitchen, unlike most of the other rooms of the house, didn't have any paintings of Lowell hanging on the walls.

When Merit was younger, she'd been in awe of Lowell. It was too weird to think about now. To be in awe of the actor, but to scorn the artist? Actors were not artists, Merit knew now. In the paintings from that era, Lowell was in various yoga poses, Kabuki makeup, his stare rigid, black. Merit didn't understand the point. Over Christmas vacation, Lowell had invited her over and shown her two new paintings. Once every couple of months, until he "retired," Lowell would invite Merit over to look at his new projects. She pretended with Lowell because she always pretended with Lowell. She had become really good at putting on shows for him, although hers certainly weren't as good as his shows for her.

One of *his* best shows at the house happened when she was eight, when he gave her a piece of sheet music. It was a song he'd written for her, he said. Merit hadn't sat down at the grand piano in the music room since she and Jenny had moved away from Lowell a few months before. Sitting at the grand piano, she played, less haltingly now than a year before (it was in C major, and in three-quarter time, and was easy to play), the most beautiful song she'd ever heard in her entire life. Lowell stood over her like a god and sang the words as she played. The words he said he'd written were exquisite and sad, and when he sang the line "I only remember the past and its brightness," he began to cry. Merit stopped playing and watched her father's face. "I wrote this for you, Merit," he said through his tears. "Isn't it beautiful? I want to give you everything that's beautiful." The song was called "The Ash Grove."

In the kitchen on Merit's twenty-first birthday, Fergus wore black leggings and orange socks with smiley face jack-o'-lanterns on them. It was March. It wasn't October, or even early November, when pumpkin socks would have still been somewhat socially acceptable. Merit's birthday always fell on her spring break, and, since Merit wasn't a Myrtle Beach type, and since she certainly didn't want to take a road trip with people her own age, she was always home for her birthday. The jack-o'-lantern's eyes were upside-down empty black triangles. Fergus's grin as he stood there with Lowell by the kitchen door, looking so cornered and shaky, was pained, mirthless. And it was a grin, not a tooth-baring smile. Merit knew Fergus was ashamed of his teeth.

Lowell suggested they, he and Fergus, sing "Happy Birthday." They sang. Lowell did his little thing of fake conducting. Merit felt uncomfortable, deeply uncomfortable, and maybe even a little ashamed, by the attention, and wondered if maybe she should make Lowell and Fergus a drink. That was the mannerly thing to do, was it not? Or maybe *coffee?* But she didn't know how to use the coffeemaker. Merit knew Fergus's singing voice well, but whenever she heard it, she was always surprised by its depth and quality. Because there was no ignoring this essential fact about Fergus's speaking voice: He was a man with dire sinus issues. Lowell's singing was strong, firm, clear. They finished the song, then clapped delightedly. They clapped, Lowell and Fergus, for themselves.

Lowell gestured to the bakery box and asked Merit if she'd like to partake. *Partake* was the word he actually used.

Merit said something about how it was so early in the day for cupcakes. She still wasn't really all that awake yet.

Lowell pouted. *"Ohhhh,"* he said.

In Fergus's eyes was a desperate, feral look, as if this, finally, were the end.

Lowell said, *"Please?"*

Merit didn't want to hurt Lowell's feelings. She was annoyed with Fergus already, so his feelings were not considered. Lowell offered her a cupcake. Merit accepted and took a careful nibble. Lowell and Fergus were watching her, and smiling hugely—Lowell smiling with his excellent teeth, Fergus smiling, too. A few more little delicate bites. Merit really did have a sugar problem. Once when she was a little girl, she ate twelve Lowell-prepared weekend pancakes because she couldn't stop. This was the first and last time she could remember Lowell ever cooking. He told her that morning that Escoffier once told him he had the genius and passion to be a Michelin three-star chef. He was lying, of course.

Merit bit down on something: hard, metal. Now, Merit was no metallurgist, but she knew metal when she tasted it. Fergus's mouth hung open. His tongue was visible. The ardor of Lowell's gaze as she chewed made her think she was the only thing in the world capable of bringing his heart happiness.

She felt it with her tongue then, the metal object, and knew what it was: a *key.*

She spat the key into her hand. Lowell, smiling beautifully, offered a silk handkerchief in a cloisonné pattern. He'd had it *ready.* Jenny had still not appeared.

"It's the car you want when you're twenty-one but can't afford!" Fergus said. He was very excited. "It's a useful piece of art! Finally!"

All eyes rotated to Fergus. Lowell gave him a little fake shove, then said, his excellent teeth theatrically clenched, "Fer-*gus*."

"Ooopsie. My fault," said Fergus. "As always."

Jenny had been hiding in her bedroom, with the door closed.

After Lowell and Fergus left, Merit knocked on the door, just as her mother had raised her to do. She was told to enter.

Merit was adrenalined right then, and her fantasies were exclusively concerned with imagining what her friends would say about her new car. It was the dashboard she kept thinking about, the elegant dashboard, with its femininely circular dials. Merit didn't know much about cars, but she knew two things: It was a Jaguar, and it was a lovely high-class pine color. She did not know yet it would turn out to be as reliable as a Volga.

Merit opened Jenny's bedroom door. Jenny sat on a big white chair by the window, a paperback biography of Edmund Burke, singed a little bit around the edges and thoroughly water-warped, open on her lap. Jenny had accidentally set fire to it the night before, when she was cooking Merit's birthday-eve dinner. Merit had been in the kitchen at the time, cracking open a pop can (wanting to remain a child, still, on the eve of her twenty-first birthday, making the point to herself by drinking a pop), when the book Jenny was reading—a little too close to the gas stove's flame, it turned out—caught on fire. For as long as Merit could remember, Jenny'd always read while cooking ("mitigates the *stu*pefying boredom," Jenny once said during one of her less maternally spirited meal preparations). Merit seized the flaming book with a pair of barbecue tongs and hurled it into the sink.

Jenny's black hair shone iridescent blue in the sunlight. The pale skin, the dark hair: *chiaroscuro* was the art-school word for it. Merit believed then, as she did now, that her mother was one of the handsomest people she'd ever seen. And then you had Lowell. Given her genetic pool, Merit always thought she should have turned out to be Catherine Deneuve. Alas.

"Oooooh! Happy birthday, pumpkin!"

Merit shuddered. "Pumpkin" had been an adorable childhood sobriquet, but it was only brought out now, in early adulthood, as heavy artillery. She didn't see any presents anywhere in the bedroom.

"Why didn't you come downstairs?"

"This might be hard for you to swallow, Merit, but he's a dangerous man for the psyche."

Jenny went back to reading the book. She actually went back to reading the fucking book. There was a time in Merit's life when she couldn't even stand being in the same room with her mother. This birthday was getting toward the tail end of that time frame, but it was within that period nevertheless.

"I can't believe that's the first thing you would say to me on my twenty-first birthday. Why is it always about him?"

"It's not about *him*. It's about *art*. Read Edmund Burke, and you'll understand."

Merit was too irritated even to bring herself to look at Jenny right now. They were surrounded on all sides by huge canvases of Lowell. Some were propped up against the pink walls. Some were hung on painting stretchers. These canvases were life-size, and the only finished parts were the eyes. Merit was having a hard time moving in front of those disembodied eyes. Unfinished paintings had always made Merit uncomfortable in the way, she imagined, watching someone you love out cold on an operating table would make you uncomfortable. Well, sort of like that. How do you describe somebody's eyes, especially when that somebody is your father? Jenny always painted the eyes first, repeatedly telling Merit you couldn't have art until you had the eyes.

Merit asked, because she knew Jenny wanted her to, what, exactly, Edmund Burke said about art.

" 'Art is power.' Or words to that effect. What time are we leaving?"

As Jenny rose from her white chair, the sodden book plunged soundlessly to the white rug. Even the year before, Merit had felt it sounded pompous to tell people her parents were artists. She was embarrassed by the word—and, looking back on it, embarrassed by them—and therefore didn't really tell anyone the truth. The truth was too complicated to get into anyway.

In her dorm room one unpleasant afternoon the second semester of her sophomore year, while arguing with a guy she'd been dating for two months, she'd realized that perhaps she needed to be more forthcoming about what kind of painting it was her parents did. At the end of the dorm-room fight (doesn't matter what it was about), the guy yelled, "Well, what do you expect from someone whose parents paint *billboards* for a living?" Merit thought, *What?* She'd said they were *painters*. She threw his backpack out into the hallway and the boy scurried outside after it. She slammed her door, and the boy was history. (Merit's retort, by the way, yelled down to him from her dorm room window: "Oh, and Jason? I hate your madras shorts, you stupid asshole.")

The truth was too complicated.

Their art didn't have a life out in the world anyway, not like, say, M. C. Escher's or Gustav Klimt's or Maxfield Parrish's did. . . . Those were bad examples; nobody except for college freshmen and the interior decorators of shrinks' offices really cared about them all that much, either. The Uncle Sam I WANT YOU poster and the classic design of a canister of Bon Ami cleaning powder—those were art forms that lived, that survived, that existed with everything else for everyone. Where did Lowell, with his kimono, and Jenny, with her Edmund Burke, get off? The world would get along just fine without them. Maybe they knew this already. Maybe that's why they were so crazy.

Jenny came toward Merit. The scene, through Merit's dirty glasses, was like watching a cougar move through formalin.

"Can we go later in the afternoon?" Merit asked. "I'm going back to bed."

The plan had been for Merit and Jenny to go shopping at Beachwood Place. Merit hadn't been able to figure out anything else to do for her birthday; but they *did* have to do something car-related now, Merit supposed, so the forty-five minute drive to what was arguably the best mall in the whole state of Ohio actually ended up making sense.

"You're going back to bed? That's how you want to remember your twenty-first birthday? 'What did you do for your twenty-first birthday, Merit?' 'Ooooh, I went back to bed!' No, no, *no!* Get your clothes on and let's go *now.*" Jenny sometimes sounded like a boss who'd taught herself to speak in a professionally condescending tone because that, she thought, was what it took. (What it took to get *where* was the question.)

"So maybe we can drive my new car?"

Merit tried very hard to contain the buzz in her voice. She wanted to seem affectless, bewildered; also, she thought Jenny would approve of the cunning with which she revealed this information. Merit held the key (chocolate cupcake remnants attractively wedged in its groove) out so Jenny could see. She knew the car would hurt Jenny, because, for one, Jenny was broke.

"*That's* what he got me for my birthday."

She waited for Jenny to correct her and say, "Fergus bought you the car; Lowell, as we all know, has no money."

"Hmm," Jenny said. She sat down in her white chair and opened her burned book. "I only have to believe what I want to believe."

Lowell's judging eyes. Canvases of them.

"Mother," Merit said, "have you ever asked yourself why you still paint pictures for him if you hate him so much?"

The painting *Lowell's Murder* hung on the wall by the window. In it, an abstract figure, a bullet-pierced, crimson-streaked sky. Jenny was staring at the picture.

"Mother, why are you still painting things for Lowell if you despise him? Why don't you just *stop*?"

Jenny's room hadn't been painted since . . . well, ever, not that Merit could remember. The pink paint was chipped all over the place, revealing ragged little maplike splotches of the wall's previous color (an insane asylum cornflower blue).

"*Merit*," Jenny said, "do you have any idea how much those pictures will be *worth*?"

This room always reminded Merit of something she'd read once about the Hermitage and how the Matisses and Picassos hung incongruously upon its cracked and rotted walls.

"I think you would have made some very different decisions in your life if you'd ever thought about *money*," Merit said.

Jenny was still staring at the painting. In it, Lowell's abstract head was obliterated to smithereens.

Merit decided she'd rather take a drive around the neighborhood that day than go back to bed. Jenny said no thanks; she didn't want to go for this initial spin because she had too much to do. Jenny went outside to wave good-bye, but she wouldn't leave the porch of their purple house. She waved aggressively at Merit, her bracelets definitely jangling, although Merit couldn't hear them over the motor. In her late high school to mid-college years, Merit had just found it so sad that Jenny felt the need to wear all that big jewelry. As if she were asserting her place in the universe.

Merit was in reverse, starting to take her foot off the brake, when she thought of something Jenny had said to her years before, when she was a girl: "You father is a classically tragic figure, Merit. Here is a human being who's never in his life—not even when he was a *boy*—made *one* meaningful connection with *anyone*." Not even me? little Merit wondered, although she did not ask.

But here was little Merit's larger question: Lowell had been a little boy?

Jenny was waving and smiling—like a child—as Merit began to back out. Merit's parents were so young—a decade younger than other kids' parents—it had always been hard for her to consider them fully adult. Jenny's smile from up on the porch was weird and huge, and it seemed to be getting bigger, expanding in such a way it looked as if it were going to overtake her entire face. The words *vagina dentata* invaded Merit's mind. She removed her foot entirely from the brake pedal, utterly devoid of nuance (she could hear Lowell now), and sort of forgot to look where she was going. She tried to find the brake pedal, but too late. It didn't take too long for her to figure out she'd creamed the mailbox. Jenny leapt down from the porch and ran out onto the driveway with nothing on her beautiful bare feet, but, weirdly, she was still smiling, and kept right on smiling, as if something extremely lovely had just occurred.

Merit had finally gotten her car started outside Pfiffin Elementary School. Now as she rolled her car into Jenny's driveway, Jenny didn't wave or in any other way greet her. Jenny was headed down to the road, carrying a familiar-looking Hammermill box from the closet in the guest room.

Merit twisted the key from the ignition. She watched Jenny. Even in full-blown mental meltdown, Jenny was charged with horrible authority. Now, as always, this authority wasn't directed toward Merit.

Merit parked, but not competently (the tires on the driver's side were on the grass). The seat belt got stuck in the door when she closed it, but Merit barely noticed. Her head was spinning in panic. The air was dense, vibratory. Merit knew better than to ask what Jenny was doing. Jenny's face was eraser red. She was, or had been, crying. Whenever Merit saw somebody crying, especially if that person was her mother, she'd want to cry, too, and usually did.

Jenny set the box down by the mailbox and pulled out a notebook—blue fabric, with a faded gold 1976 stamped onto the front and spine. What a nothing year: Merit hadn't even gotten herself born yet. Jenny, with a bracing Teutonic "auf," flung the book at the tire across the street. Although she was cocksure, her aim wasn't any good, and it landed in the middle of the road. Merit knew all about Jenny's intended target: the tire. That tire stuck into the playground was *Merit's* tire, the one she used to hide in when she was a child.

The cover of the detested notebook flapped open in the road as if seized by an imaginary hand. Things were written all over the pages. A Polaroid from within came loose, thrashed into the air, fell, trembled on the empty street.

Years ago, when Lowell would occasionally come over, he and Merit would often throw things at the tire. Once, Merit remembered, they threw some dirty, old, hardened paintbrushes.

"I don't *like* today," Jenny said. "I don't like today at *all.*"

Merit asked Jenny what exactly about today it was she didn't like, although she knew the answer. The handwriting in the notebook was Jenny's.

"*Mr.* and *Mr.* Lowell Haven," Jenny sneered.

Now was the time to ask the question.

"You're doing what, exactly, here?" Merit asked.

Jenny leveled an enigmatic Vivien Leigh nutjob eye flicker at Merit, the same look Merit got whenever she used to try to encourage Jenny to start painting again. She said, "You were smart, at least you were when you were a little girl. So why didn't you tell me what you knew about them?"

When Merit was a kid, Jenny wrote in her diary every night in bed. As a child, the very sight of the diary bothered Merit in a way she had been unable to define. Jenny always kept it on her bedroom dresser, by her jewelry box. Merit was never allowed to look at the journal, although it always seemed to her it was kept very much out in the open, as if wanting to be seen. A couple times throughout the years, Merit had gotten caught peeking. When she was about ten, she read this: "There is no hope for my life, other than Merit. Merit is my hope." Merit read this while sitting on Jenny's bed, and she felt both exhilarated and terrified. Jenny's response as she thundered into the room seemed to young Merit puzzlingly extreme.

Merit left Jenny outside. The invitation was on top of the upright piano in the living room, right where Merit knew it would be. Merit hadn't played that piano in years. She took the invitation upstairs to her old bedroom because she wanted to be somewhere Lowell's eyes couldn't see her.

Merit's bedroom walls were bare, except for the *Amadeus* poster, a freebie in a public radio station giveaway a long, long time ago. The poster was so old that she'd been a child when she got it, and did not yet understand the poster's references to both the Queen of the Night and the Statue. (Her current favorite line from *Don Giovanni*: "Where do those flames of horror come from?") The room was chillingly untouched from her late adolescence there—her notebooks from college, her collection of Joseph Campbell paperbacks, and her swim team and track trophies and a plaque from the year she played volleyball, all in the same places she'd left them.

She sat on the floor by the window. What had she ever done in here, in her bedroom? What *was* there to do, other than look out the window, up into the Akron sky of thermometer-mercury hue? As a child, she was never lonely. No one ever told her until later that she'd been lonely.

It looked like a wedding invitation. (Who was Fergus marrying? Himself?) The envelope, addressed by Fergus, was creamy, cheesily expensive-looking, foil-lined. There was a red wax seal, and layers of ingratiating tissue paper. Merit had always thought Fergus had the handwriting of an antisocial fourteen-year-old boy. Jenny had managed to tear the invitation almost, but not quite, in two, right down the middle. It was only marginally held together, a peeled scab hanging by a strip of skin. There was already a stain of mysterious blue on the back. The invitation said:

> *Out With the Old, In with the New!*
> *Celebrate the New Artist.*
> *Mr and Mr Lowell Haven*
> *request the honour of your presence*
> *at a costume ball*
> *on*
> *Saturday, the seventeenth of August,*
> *at half past seven o'clock in the evening.*
> *His Majesties have decreed*
> *all Guestes will be in masque*
> *to amuse and mystify His Majesties.*
> *At On Ne Peut Pas Vivre Seul.*
>
> *R.S.V.P.*
> *(But you knew that already, you bad little Guestes, you.)*

The door downstairs cracked shut. Jenny was tremendously late for work now. Merit would suggest—although Jenny wouldn't ask for her opinion—she take the day off. Jenny was, essentially, a baby-sitter on the kids' floor of the museum. Her job was to make sure no kids choked on the puzzle pieces (painted in some kind of ghoulish homage to Frank Stella) or vomited into the Teeny Weeny Land Magical Puppet Theatre Company hand puppets. The job was so farcically beneath her.

Even so, Jenny still never bothered to ask Merit about *her* job. Merit folded the invitation into her front pocket and went outside.

Merit kept looking to see if the neighbors were watching her gather her mother's plunder from the street, but since it was a weekday, and August, Merit was alone. She chased the tumbleweeding Polaroid down the road; disappointingly, there were no people in the picture, only the faded facade of a mansion that wasn't Fergus's but that looked like it. She had sort of hoped it would be a picture of Lowell.

With the Polaroid and the diary from 1976, Merit crawled into her tire. Yes, she knew all about this tire. A memory of her time spent inside it: When she came home from school one afternoon, she found the front door unlocked, the back door spookily open. Jenny was at work. Merit thought fast, put their dog on a leash, and ran across the street to the playground. She hid in the tire, with the dog in her lap, until Jenny came home. It turned out Jenny had, that morning before she left for work, forgotten to lock both the front and back doors. As far as Merit knew, Jenny never forgot to lock or close an outside door again. Jenny did, however, often forget to turn the coffeemaker off before she left in the morning. When she was a child, Merit wouldn't have been surprised to come home from school and find the house in flames, or, depending on when the fire started, completely incinerated. This character flaw—preparing herself for the worst—established itself at an early age.

Merit opened the diary to the first page. It was written in script, which Jenny rarely used anymore, although she had when Merit was a little girl.

Merit read:

30 May 1976

I must not waste another second! Today, today, today, my life begins today! I've never kept a diary before, but what good would one have done, when, up to this day, I was nothing? I didn't go to graduation today, naturally. I made no sense as a high school student, so thank God *that's* over. Childhood didn't really suit me particularly well. I found this whole adolescent thing very, very much for the birds. When people ask me what I'm going to do with my life, I say this: "I don't think *you'd* understand." It takes courage to do what you must do, of course. If one is to become great, one must endure by being untiring, exact, and alone. What will I make myself into? A great painter, of course. There's only one way to live: with applause. I shall stun my audience, just as Laurette Taylor stunned hers! I will, finally, have a life worth writing about.

Merit looked up at the house now. She thought maybe she saw Jenny moving around in her bedroom upstairs. The lavenderish paint job outside, applied right after Jenny bought the house, had washed out to more of a graying beige over the years. The worst area was the porch. Merit was thinking now about the porch, about the time before the paint had started to peel on it. Every Fourth of July, she and Jenny would stand on that porch and, in an annual bout of forced patriotic merriment, wave their sparklers around. And every Fourth of July, Jenny would remind Merit that summer was already half over. It had been years since Merit had held a sparkler, but she could still remember how it felt to have one zap her hand. Laurette Taylor? Merit had never heard of her. It was August now, somehow. Merit hugged her knees tighter to her chest, looked at the diary again, and thought about how late it had become.

4

31 May

"All your friends will miss you, Jenny," Mom said. "What friends?" I asked. She had to think about that one for a second. And then she said, "Fergus?"

1 June

All they ever wanted was to be nestled in their own complacency. The people in my class, doing whatever it is they do—mowing lawns, doing something unspeakable with a Q-tip, sitting around preparing to go bald. Boring people, lives vacillating between boredom and struggle, boredom the best they can hope for. Boredom is their art! My skin is vibrating with anticipation. It's only a few days until I leave for London. The ticket was the only graduation gift I wanted. Today, Mom asked me to write down what I predicted for myself in thirty years, said she intended to put it in a "time capsule," which I'm guessing is really just a shoe box underneath their bed. "How fun it will be when we open it thirty years from now," she said. I'm picturing how yellowed the tape around the box will have become, brittle, no fun to look at or to touch. I found a gold crayon in my bedroom desk and did a sketch of my imagined future self with it. In the sketch, my eyes are older, far from blameless (not to mention gold!). My third-grade teacher, Mrs. O'Connell, could already tell I was especially good at capturing a certain little glint in the eye. I studied them (my eyes) and I wondered if greatness were possible there. I *think* greatness may be possible, but I'm not 100 percent sure. I drew about a thousand little stars around my head. I also gave Mom a mimeograph of Goya's *The Straw Manikin* for the box. I need to start doing some BIG projects, not just these dumb little self-portraits. I'm eighteen already.

2 June

   Oh and to be away from Fergus's towering letters, his endless accusal, his pinkly swollen eyes! Did I mention he tailgated me yesterday? Here's Dad on Fergus: "I think that kid has a screw loose." The absolute, absolute worst was when he'd call me and get a busy signal. I'd hear about nothing else the next day. There he'd be the next morning, lurking creepily by my locker, always saying something like "So . . . I couldn't help noticing your phone was busy all night. . . . New boyfriend?" Then I'd be forced to say, "You're NOT my boyfriend, Fergus. Get a GRIP." He's consistently looking for a crrrrumb of hope, and I never give him one. (But here's to the gals who keep trying!) I could always count on him to shakily hand over a letter on unlined paper (only *I* know he has to use a ruler to write in a straight line), folded in thirds, and color-coded. Shouldn't there be a limit on the number of times one should have to read the sentence "We have to TALK!!!!!!"? He used to be my best friend; now he's merely an annoyance, something you extract from your belly button, then dispose of. So here's to my new FERGUSLESS life. And here's to more CAPITAL LETTERS, yes, a life lived in caps.

3 June

It will be a time of empire! Yippee! Whipped up by ecstasy. I think I know this painting that I found in Mom's book, *The Straw Manikin,* fairly well, but I don't know it completely. This is why I must go to London, of course, to study it and to paint it. And I'll paint it as many times as it takes to get it *right.* On the surface *The Straw Manikin* doesn't seem much more than a cartoon. It's a simple pastoral scene, really: The four women holding the blanket are tossing a man—or a mannequin—up in the air. But if you look closely, you'll find something hideous in this painting. And it's this hideous thing I must know. Call it the truth.

4 June

Crying on airplanes is one of my trademarks. On planes, I feel vulnerable, chosen, my lungs gurgly, overwhelmed. I was sure this one was going to go down, and then I got really sad: Me, barely getting started in life, then *gone.* At the thought of the world being robbed of me, I decided yesterday would be my first time to get drunk. I pressed the call button. When the stewardess arrived, I requested three Bloody Marys, but she told me that I could order only one "alcohol cocktail" at a time. "Ah, details!" I exclaimed. I drank six Bloody Marys anyway—one at a time. I was as drunk as an otter (whatever that means) by the end, but the sketches I did of myself were still pretty good. I rigged up a hand mirror to the back of the seat with two safety pins. I didn't notice who was sitting next to me. Being drunk wasn't all that great. It just made me sleepy.

And no, I'm not proud I've hurt Mom so much by leaving. Mom and Dad keep making me promise that I'll just think of it as a "temporary head-clearing year." They seem not to understand what an enormous snob I am and that enormous snobs are much more interesting than college allows one to be. On the plane I was thinking about how I considered my childhood just something to endure. I wonder if someday I'll think this is sad. Fergus said it was sad. Should a much-loved child allow herself to be unhappy?

Last week, Fergus said my trip was just another way of disappearing. "Adults don't disappear," he said. (And then I left.) But I must do good work, so I must make myself scarce. I must not care that my heart is stingy.

5 June

Thank God I brought only one bag. I'm writing this in a youth hostel, so that explains the smell. I didn't venture too far from the hostel today. I wish I could be one of these supertough and cool German travelers who go to terrible places like Marrakech, brag about how little money they spent (overheard tonight: "Ten marks I used in one month there!"), and live out of a backpack for a year. I think I brought too much stuff. I must ask myself, Did I really need to bring all *three* of my pairs of pointy-toed boots? Only assholes have a lot of stuff. I think it's funny when girls are called "assholes." Tonight, in the blackest part of the night, I walked around the neighborhood here, the darkness changing, swelling up and around me. Even the red mailboxes on the sidewalk are *so* ridiculously cute. I'm starting to panic about money already. I ate the four Cup o' Noodles I brought with me.

6 June

It took me THREE HOURS to get to Sex! First, I thought I'd try to get there without bringing my awful travel guide, but I got lost before I even made it to the bus stop near the hostel. I was looking for the bus stop, wandering around hungry. Eating alone in any of the restaurants around here seemed too scary, so I bought three packs of these things called "wine gummies" at a little store. That was my breakfast. I couldn't understand what the cashier said when she told me how much the wine gummies cost, so I decided to play it safe and give her £10, which was basically the same thing as paying for a pack of gum with a hundred-dollar bill! Sheer embarrassment! Then I went back to the hostel and got my guidebook. I ripped the cover off before I ventured back out. I found King's Road about two hours after that, but I was on the wrong end of the street, and it's a LONG street! Luckily, I saw some punks and followed them to 430. (I threw away my travel guide before I went inside the store.) The SEX sign is in huge pink plastic letters. It was so cool. (Fergus would have looked quite fetching in the rubber bondage gear.) I felt it was rude of me not to buy anything after hanging out in there for so long, but when they asked me if I wanted any help with anything, I just smiled and shook my head like the dull, docile girl I am. I didn't say anything because I didn't want them to know I was merely a boring American. The sky is a different tone here than in Ohio, the gray more delicate, softer: coyote fur under glass. For dinner, I ate the cereal I packed from home.

7 June

I was getting a little more used to things today and took the Tube to the National Gallery. It was an unexpectedly strange sensation to see the painting in person. No one stood by *The Straw Manikin,* everyone having gathered around the grisly *Saturn* (infanticide: instant crowd pleaser). I guess I got too close to my painting, because the guards yelled at me and told me to stand back. The colors are incredible! The four women who hold the blanket have very nasty smiles. The dummy's mask is white, his lips, cheeks, and chin rouged, like a mime, a marionette. He's floating, his body limp and fluid. I don't know if he's supposed to be a real man or a fake one. What do you think it means that I'm more interested in the dummy than the actual people in the painting? Or the actual people in real life?

I ate in the National Gallery's cafeteria twice today. Kippers shall be my new thing. I brought *Daniel Deronda* with me, although it was difficult to concentrate on it in the cafeteria. Let's be honest: I brought it mainly to hide my new map in.

8 June

Back to the National Gallery again today. Squeezed out my paints in the order of the prism, good old ROY G. BIV. *The Straw Manikin* is like being in love with something: All you want to do is look at it. A man is inside the dummy; I'm becoming sure of it—the color of his hands is more lifelike than the women's real flesh. As I was sketching the eyes (I'm doing this very unsystematically), someone, a male voice, said something to me. I haven't really talked to anyone for almost a week, and I was afraid I'd forgotten how. The voice sounded blue-blooded, middle-aged, self-satisfied. It stopped; then it made sounds again. It asked me if I was an "art lover." I didn't say anything because I don't like how men feel like they can just start talking to you. I wonder if men know they do this. It must be phenomenal to think everyone's interested in what you have to say. I suppose that's one of the tricks to life.

"So you're an *art* lover, are you?" he asked again, and lunged a soft, pallid face into my personal space. His eyes were brown, but toneless. He smiled a smile that was more gumline than teeth. The teeth were the same color as the gums. I said I was a painter and then went back to the sketch, but the man wormed in closer. He was fortyish, wore a battered corduroy jacket, and smelled like an attic. He was one of these people who have a constant cloud of dust hanging around them, receipts, whatever, falling out of their sleeves. He seemed to have about four arms. He popped his round head right in front of my canvas (his smile announcing,

These are my gums!) and said, "I'm Reginald Van Pelt. Hallo!" Reginald Van Pelt paced a circle around me, his head inclined at a thoughtful angle. He seemed to be engrossed by the real Goya, then by my semiblank canvas. He said some friend of his had made him come to the show, and he asked if I were American. How horrified I was to hear myself saying, "No, I'm from *Rhodesia*," in an *English accent*! Some British men like Van Pelt have this kind of bowl cut, medieval-looking, just this side of animal-fat greasy. His hair was beaver brown. He asked me if I wanted to get a drink, but I said I didn't drink anymore. He left without argument, as most people do. I was glad to get to work a little bit today. It's good to work, I think. That way, you don't think about how alone you are.

9 June

I forgot to write yesterday that Mr. Van Pelt gave me his number. Well, he did, and I called him today. I was homesick and I was lonely. "Oh, *lovey!*" he said when I explained who I was. He asked me if I wanted to get a cocktail, and I said okay this time. We met at a bar called Griffin, Toad and Tiggy and I ordered a tepid Schweppes. I peeled the label from the tiny bottle as Van Pelt asked me questions about where I lived, what I did for money, etc. I quoted one of Fergus's favorite lines (although I didn't give Fergus any credit for it), the one about how rich people never amount to anything, because they're not thirsty. *"C'est vrai,"* Van Pelt said, and tittered into his snifter of port. "Parents," he said into his glass, the glass going foggy. "That's really the only way to get any money. And mine left me a bloody *fortune.*" He put his baggy hand on my knee. I removed it. He told me I was a very rude little girl. I wish I'd been fierce enough to tell him he was precisely as threatening as Dudley Moore. His gums were gray from the port. Then he asked me if I wanted a job as his au pair. I'd only be working for him during the day. He said his wife was going to take a cheese grater to his scrotum if he didn't find someone soon.

Here's a truism for you: Whenever you think someone wants *you*, here's what you eventually find out: what they really want is your *work*. I did my poor bunny act, and asked him if he'd buy me dinner, too. He did. God, it's so awful being me sometimes. Tonight, I was thinking about how I didn't cry once when I was nine. I was tougher when I was a little kid. The problem with crying in a youth hostel in old Londontown: other people can hear you.

10 June

I was sad today because I know I've made Mom and Dad sad, my leaving them, Akron, everything, without any real goal other than to paint this ridiculous picture over and over. "A picture is not a plan!" Dad yelled when we were driving to the airport. Then I got even sadder tonight because I couldn't call them, since I still couldn't figure out how to work the pay phone in the basement of the hostel. No one was around to help me.

One nice thing did happen today, though. I met a girl, one of these impossibly self-sufficient Germans. We were both in the dingy sitting area, smoking, and she asked if she could give me her card. She dug into her Moroccan bag and took out a card that said she was Gerta Jurgen from Tubingen, Germany. She was wearing these very sturdy-looking sandals, which made my pointy boots—and me—feel as if we were trying far too hard. Eyeliner? Fresh-faced Gerta scoffs at the very idea! She said she'd give me a free consultation, and I asked, "A consultation in *what?*" Whatever I wanted, she said, but after the first one, she'd start charging me. The couch we sat on was squash-colored and scratchy. We talked. We smoked. She asked me if she could braid my hair, and she told me she was eighteen "alzo." I told her I was prepared to make any sacrifice, ready to suffer, willing to do whatever it takes. She said she was, too, and then she put her head in my lap. I ate three muffins at midnight.

11 June

Van Pelt lives in a castle in South Kensington. A molely man in an impeccable blue suit (the BUTLER!) opened the dungeony front door and examined me as if I were a coarse black hair sprouting from a feminine breast. I was invited to come inside. There were actual flaming torches on the hallway wall. The house smelled as if it were on fire. He walked and I followed him. I didn't know what to say, so I asked the age of the house. The butler told me it was from the same period as Compton Wynyates, which wasn't a very helpful answer. I listened to the unladyish bang of my pointy boots on the stone floor, and the butler pointed with a doughy finger to a harpsichord and said it had belonged to Gluck. The name Gluck echoed richly through the room, ricocheted off the dark paneled walls, hung there. On the walls were some terrible portraits, all done in that treacly pre-Bastille eighteenth-century style. They were a lie, each one of them. Mrs. Van Pelt's drawing room had butter-colored floor-to-ceiling curtains that looked like fabulous ball gowns. Van Pelt had told me earlier that my interview was just a formality, "so the old battle-ax will feel she's being included in some decision." She had platinum hair and was wearing a leopard-print jacket. Her face was full of depth and appraisal, and she wasn't my idea of a battle-ax at all. I think the interview went okay, although she kept looking at my hair, one particular spot on my scalp, as if something—a scorpion, a spider?—were crawling there. Every time I touched that place on my head, she looked away from me. She said she designed hats and was trying to get them sold at stores on Sloane Street. I asked her if I could see one of her designs, and she said, "Honestly? You'd honestly like to see one? Oh, that would be smashing!" She said no one had ever asked her to see her hats before. But then she said they probably weren't my style anyway, so I never got to see them.

12 June

I called Van Pelt from the pay phone at the appointed time, and he told me I got the job!

I was wondering something tonight: What if Goya painted *The Straw Manikin* just for money?

13 June

I wonder if Geoff (their butler, my boss) would think it was funny if I asked whether there are butlering lessons in England. I really must find out. Geoff is one of these pasty British guys from some depressing northern town who wants you to think he's an old-school aristocrat. Geoff took me on the house tour. One of the suits of armor once belonged to King Arthur, he said. He introduced me to the baby, which, now that I think about it, seems like something they should have done a couple of days ago. I've never really been around babies before, and it felt kind of weird. You know, like how it is when you don't know what to do with your hands. And what, really, is there to say to a butler about a baby other than, "Oooo, she's beautiful"? The baby's name is Nicky. Or Nikki. Last week was her first birthday, and she really is beautiful. There actually *wasn't* anything else to say, because beauty does overwhelm all else. Like other people, I keep my hands in my pockets when I don't know what to do with them. It's important, for this reason, always to wear pants with pockets. I've asked Van Pelt to pay me daily—in cash. The color of his face makes me think of the word *squeal*.

14 June

I was snooping in Van Pelt's room today (he and Mrs. Van Pelt have separate rooms) and took a pair of underwear out of his drawer. I don't really know why. What was I planning to do with them? I put them back and looked at myself and his red bikinis in his mirror and thought about what a bloody awful mess I was today. I'm less of a grown-up now than when I was *nine*! Need to remember to be strong, unsentimental.

After work I went to the Clarke-Bourke-Buffiningham Flat-Finding Agency on Oxford Street. I had to sit on a folding chair in the dingy waiting room for about an hour. All the action in the waiting room was centered on a hot plate with two rusted World War II–era steel kettles on top of it. Every five minutes or so, a different wan, shaky person from the back would come out and refill the kettle with water (the bathroom was somewhere behind me; the sink dripped constantly when it wasn't turned on). They'd all stand (with their chattering teacups and saucers) in front of the hot plate, pale arms crossed, waiting for the kettle to scream. Finally, a girl in red-and-white-striped tights called me to the back. (She'd not been out to the hot plate.) Her hair was short and dyed black and worn in a pomaded "Elvis." When I told her how much I could pay per week, she said "More of a bed-sit, are you, then?" Then she said she had a special one she was saving and pulled out an index card from the stack on her desk. She dialed the number, had a little conversation with someone on the other end, and told me to be at the flat in Kentish Town at 7:00 a.m. tomorrow. Must remember to find out what a bed-sit is.

15 June

New apartment in Kentish Town is fine, I suppose, and I have my own bedroom, but it's in a grim row of grimy houses. "Interview" with a girl called "Grunt" and a boy called "Scrumpy." The girl said I was okay because I was punk. I was called punk by an actual punk! Moving in tomorrow!

16 June

Gerta wasn't around when I left, so I put a note on top of her duffel bag. Thoughts about how you'll never see such and such person ever again are killers. It's true there's a death in each parting. A futon mattress was already on the floor in my new room. I taped *The Straw Manikin* to the wall over the mattress. It's pretty much as punk as you can get, actually, that painting.

Only interesting thing at work: I overheard someone, a man, say this tonight from the great hall: "I think I'm going blind from seeing so many beautiful things."

17 June

I met someone tonight. He's a friend of Van Pelt. Before we introduced ourselves, I watched him from the landing above the great hall. I couldn't hear what he said, but I knew already he wasn't my type. He wore a lavender suit. He didn't exactly sit in his chair, I noticed, but *perched,* and in so doing made perching seem quite the in thing to do. His mannerisms were actorly and sumptuous. Very much the contrast to Van Pelt—such a grim victim of gravity, leaning to one side, disastrously close to pitching leftward off his red settee. (Van Pelt also looked as if he were swaying.) But Mr. Purple was oblivious to Van Pelt's troubles. He leapt up, seized a torch from the wall, and spun around the room. He brandished the torch like a sword. He was a machine, humming along on the engine of his self-regard. Again: NOT my type. It was probably a grave social faux pas, but I went downstairs and plopped upon the tufted leather couch. He didn't notice I was there until I coughed. (So much for my awesome presence!) He looked as if he'd been caught at something and asked where *I'd* come from and said he thought he was *alone.* I guess everyone knows poor Reggie isn't a hell of a lot of company.

The man didn't look at me as he fumblingly attempted to return the torch to its hook on the wall. "I was just telling Reggie about . . . a demand *Picasso* . . . once put on me."

I actually would almost have believed, for a second, he was as suave as he was trying to be . . . had he not accidentally dropped the flaming torch onto the white bearskin rug. He jumped back from the rug, the bear, the fire and threw his hands in the air. "Help me!" he cried desperately. "Oh please help me!" He sounded suddenly much younger, and much less English. Van Pelt was teetering off the edge of his low stool. I leapt up— the bear's head was already in flames. The man was trying to rip off his purple coat, but the buttons made any Superman-moves difficult. I, however, was ready (thank God for pointy boots), and thrillingly willing. I stomped on the bear head and put that fire out. Van Pelt was swaying like crazy, one hand positioned on the rug, and kept muttering, "Rumpelstiltskin." Purple's hand was shaking when I gave the torch back to him. His hair is as black as mine (but probably not, like mine, fake), and his eyes are the black I've always wanted mine to be: velvety black with flecks of gold, the gold on the wall of a cave. In crudely commercial terms, he has the cleft chin of an unemployed thespian, cheekbones that could cut through cheese, and a snubbed nose, the upturn of which reminded me of—is this a stupid thing to say?—a slipper. For some reason, the nose made me think of Pinocchio's when he was still a real boy (although I can't remember what the human Pinocchio looked like). I asked him about Picasso and he slid the torch back into its hook, left his hand there for a theatrical moment, as if readying his answer.

"Picasso," he said, revolving toward me, "said this from his hospital bed in Mougins, 'I challenge you, Lowell Haven, to make me see anew.' " The man extended his hand for me to take. I took. "So many beautiful things," he said. He gazed straight into my face, taking it in in its entirety. "I think I'm going blind from so much looking." So *he* was the voice from last night. Obviously, this wasn't an original sentiment; he was just too dumb and scared to say anything real. He said, again, his name was Lowell. He smiled a lot, but I wasn't really quite sure what he was smiling at. The smile was creepy in its force, and I don't know if I believed it. Something bothered me last night, but I didn't know what it was. Maybe it was the same thing that made scratching sounds at my bedroom door all night long.

18 June

Today I watched Lowell from the window as he screeched up the long stone driveway. He disembarked from his red motorcycle, wiped his sunglasses with the tail of his shirt. He bent over the motorcycle's mirror, talking to himself and grinning, as if enjoying a conversation with a witty phantom. His hair is flowing and Byronic. And these purple Little Lord Fauntleroy suits really must go. A teacher said to me once that color is a lie. It makes sense she said this, because she had no imagination, and if you have no imagination, how can you possibly understand color? Purple would be a far better color on anyone else. Byron was a really miserable poet, actually. I read a couple of his poems last year and thought they were outrageously bad.

19 June

Day off. Went to the museum again, this time with a flashlight and the magnifying glass, both of which I applied to *The Straw Manikin.* Got yelled at by some stern-faced guard before I could determine, absolutely once and for all, whether Goya gave the dummy fingernails. Avoid received wisdom! Find the truth for yourself! Fergus says I have a tendency to talk like Chairman Mao sometimes. Speaking of whom (Fergus, I mean): He's already sent me a letter here, can you *believe*? Maybe Mom gave him my address, although Dad makes him so incontinent with terror that I doubt he'd call them. The envelope was waiting for me on the table when I came home. The letter is, as his letters have recently been, color-coded in ink. It began this way, in red: "J.M.: It is dangerous to proclaim war against such an armed opponent." I stopped reading after that. I think I deciphered the color code today: *Red* for what he believes, *blue* for what he thinks I believe, *black* for what I think I believe, *green* for what I think he believes. I wasn't bold enough to throw the letter away today, but who knows what tomorrow will bring. How can I tell Fergus that people are good for certain chapters of your life, and that the Fergus chapter of mine is now closed? Plus, who wouldn't be terrified by the way he's started copying all my trademarks, every fascinating Jenny detail—the very things I hope someday will make me very wealthy? First, he dyed his hair black. Then he started wearing eyeliner. Then it was stealing my music, then wearing scarves, then co-opting my other friends. Dad said he's started talking like me recently, and in English class last semester, the teacher asked me repeatedly if I were writing Fergus's papers for him. In this letter, I noticed his *K*'s were like mine, no uplift of pen. (It took me a long time to arrive at that *K*, and I don't appreciate its being snatched so cavalierly.) And then there was when he started buying my clothes. When he showed up at school one day with my boots, laced up in my special crisscrossed way, I knew he was in big trouble, psychologically speaking.

Why would someone do that, toss a dummy into the air? It seems like a strange thing to do. This is the question I asked myself all night. After the Goya study is done, I want to do some paintings of myself. Women artists never do full-size self-portraits, but I will.

20 June

Tonight, Geoff sent me into the taxidermy room to fetch him a (taxidermied) chipmunk. (Some questions are better left unasked.) Lowell was sitting on the floor in there, cradling a painting on his lap. His eyes were closed and his fingertips moved over the painting as if it were Braille, as if he were divining a message from it. I said something about how I used to think I could paint by osmosis, too. That was last year, back when I had *really* unsophisticated taste in art and used to lie on my bed with that Max Ernst book I found at a garage sale. Tracing my finger over *The Word or Woman-Bird,* often, but not always, made for a more satisfying Friday night than driving around the teachers' houses (and honking at them, and sticking our tongues out) with Fergus. Lowell, very defensively, said I was always sneaking up on him. I noticed that the red paint on the walls wasn't quite the paint's original color—the place where the painting had hung indicated the exposed wall had dirtied and darkened to its present cadmium red medium. Lowell said the painting was a Velásquez, but only a minor one. It was a painting of a queenly woman on a white horse. I went toward the painting, and him. The floor was cold, my feet were bare, and I stepped on something that hurt.

ME: "Mother*fucker.*" (I had stepped on a naked, detached little plastic doll arm.)

HIM: "We're too young to know this, but I'd suspect that when you're a parent of young children, it's very much part of the game."

ME: (I was flirting, despite myself.) "I adorrrre games." (I hadn't noticed Nikki was there, too, on the floor, on her back, kicking up at the ceiling.)

HIM: "Forever stepping on a hard detached plastic arm, a decapitated head, what have you."

ME: (I grabbed the painting, still flirting. Sad how conversations with men are easier when you're flirting. Sometimes it's easier to make yourself stupid—must do project about this someday.) "A court painter. Don't you think that's tragic?"

HIM: (He stood and lifted the baby into his arms.) "Tragic? Not at all! Geniuses *should* be hired."

ME: (I hung the Velásquez back on the wall. I could feel Lowell's eyes on me. Both mad and happy, chiefly mad.)

HIM: "I tell you what I'm going to do, Nikki. I'm going to give you a present. Yes indeed! Your daddy told me to give it to you. Your daddy and I have become fantastically close friends."

ME: "*How* close?"

HIM: (He bent down beside a stuffed lion, its motionless face fixed in a silent roar, ignoring the query about Van Pelt. Next to the lion was a box. Inside the box was a mass-produced plastic doll. He tore open the box, yanked out the purple cardboard backing. Doll attached to the cardboard via twist ties.) "Ridiculous! The people who design these packages are surely sadists. Each limb is bound with three ties. Do you see this?"

ME: "Or Boy Scouts."

HIM: "Do you see these knots? There are knots within knots. A mastermind is responsible for this, clearly, an evil genius."

ME: "Or a murderer."

HIM: "A Boy Scout or a murderer," he said. "Maybe I'll use that someday. When I get good enough."

ME: "Oh, so you're not good now?"

HIM: "No. I'm not. Remind me someday to tell you all about my tutelage under Pablo."

Why is he flirting with me if he's gay? More to the point, why am I flirting with him? Is this just the way it is in Swinging London? Remember: no ménage-a-trois with Lowell and Van Pelt if they try. He must be lying about Picasso. Should I be flattered if he's lying? If he's lying, does that mean that he's really trying to impress me? And if he's trying to impress me, does that mean he's in love with me?

21 June

I personally think he just comes over to have an audience. That's my new theory. I wonder if he exists when he's alone in a room. He seems to think he holds the key to the universe. I really hope he doesn't. When Lowell talks, he makes the seducer's point of including everyone. Whenever someone says something interesting or noteworthy (which is, for Van Pelt, approximately never), he rubs his excellent smooth chin, and says, "I shall have to use that someday." He's like Fergus, I think: a vampire. I asked him a perfectly innocuous question today ("How are you, Lowell?"), and he launched into a fancy, fiery little speech about how he'd just "learnt" the most marvelous thing in Matisse's letters about his (Matisse's) search for the perfect blue, how a dear friend of his from childhood owns these letters, which he had just read. Then he asked me how much time I'd spent in France. I held up the zero sign. He said he'd get me there soon. Do you think he really meant he wanted to take me to France? What should I do if he asks me? I wouldn't go, of course. Then he talked about how the blue of southern France is superior to the blue anywhere in Greece, talked about a 2,400-year-old Greek fishing boat that went down in the Black Sea, talked about the ancient Greeks' plundering of the ocean for gold. "Alas," he said, "gold's bloody history." I told him that gold was a lie, because all color was a lie. I supposed I wanted to sound sophisticated. I also wanted to see what he'd say.

"Eliminate color?" He sounded very hurt. "As the Fauvist would ask: Then why be alive? And furthermore, why would I want to become any sort of *seventies* artist? A dismal period artistically, wouldn't you say? I mean, *Hockney* is the best we've got?"

Van Pelt and Lowell met, I've learned, at an Eton reunion. Well, isn't that just plummy? Isn't that just so marvelously nifty? (Fergus says I have a chip on my shoulder about rich people, to which I respond, "And you *don't?*") Also, he said something about being the son of Josephine Baker. I don't believe that, either, although the color of his skin does make me think of beef bouillon. Even if *I* sketched Lowell (if I could get him to sit still long enough), I can't see how I could get at his inner qualities. Even the genius can't create what's not there. I think maybe I'd stop thinking about him if we could kiss, just once. Sessela from biology class told me everybody falls in love with the first person they kiss, so I must remember to be careful about that.

22 June

I'm SO mad today. I feel like MURDERING something. V.P. and Lowell were monkeying around earlier in the great hall with a racket-making Polaroid camera. Lowell stage-whispered for Reggie to "take a picture of her ass." That was me, my ass, he was talking about. I was bending over to pick up something, and V.P., who, as far as I can tell, spends his whole life fellating Lowell, hysterically obliged (gums shining in the torch flames), snapping a shot of my rear. I tried to grab the developing picture, but L. yanked it from Señor Van Pelt's hands. From where L. was standing, the stag horns above the fireplace appeared to be on top of his head. And so, with an appropriately monstrous image for Lowell, that's all I'm writing about today.

P.S. Whenever Mrs. Van Pelt sees Lowell, she excuses herself and goes into her bedroom. Tonight, she asked me if I understood what Lowell and Reggie *were*. She always locks her bedroom door when she retires for the evening. She's my only friend there, I think.

23 June

I found several interesting things when I was cleaning Lowell's room today. On the desk, a framed black-and-white picture of Lowell as a little boy. A fully formed miniature Lowell. It looks just like him, but shrunken—the ethereal face already lit with a burgeoning fiendish charisma. He's about three in the picture, and squatting on a cold black beach in a hooded sweatshirt that says I LOVE MOMMY and squeezing two fistfuls of wet sand. A woman's bodiless bare arm reaches for Lowell. The photographer had cut the woman off at her shoulder.

Also on the desk was a postcard of Josephine Baker, Paul Colin's drawing of her in a banana skirt. I picked it up. The back of the postcard had written on it, in purple ink in a foppish Jeffersonian hand:

Birthplace: St. Louis

Pig: Albert

Zouzou!

When I got home, I drank a tumblerful of my roommate's bizarre Goldschlager. I dug into Fergus's delightful letter again. "Your view of me is jaded. [Written in red.] He's only a worthless little prick, I know you think. [Written in blue.] Well, I've got some news for you, Jenny-pants, you're mental cotton candy. [Written in green.] Plus, I prefer people who don't go for the jugular 24/7. [Written in red.]" I stopped reading. I yawned. I held the letter over a candle flame, watched it burn. Scorched pieces of it fluttered black in the air, like injured bits of pillow down.

Oh, and when I was making Lowell's bed, I found a pair of men's red bikinis twisted within the sheets.

24 June

Tonight, I was in the torch-lit nursery with the baby. I was on the floor, sketching her, because, well, what else is there to do with a baby? A knock on the door. Door groaned open, although I hadn't yet given it permission to do so.

Lowell.

"Ah! *There* you are," he said. In his hand was a ceramic doll, blond hair, blue eyes, red bonnet. This was not the doll from a few days ago, but another doll, older, rarer. Lowell looked at my sketch, and as he looked, he pursed his lips, as if they were sewn by a thread. He bent down from his imperious height, kissed Nikki on her forehead, and cupped his giant's hand for a moment over her eyes then removed it. "It's the most ex-traordinary gift as an artist, when one can stare at one's subject all one wants and not feel as if one's violating the object's privacy. A nonreactive thing is the perfect object, don't you think?"

Nikki watched Lowell talk, her eyes following his lips. "She *is* old enough to stare back, actually," I said.

"Ah . . . *you*! You, I think, are like Orestes," he said, "pursued by fu-ries. What, you bright young confection of a girl, are you running away from? If I may indeed ask."

I held Nikki close to me. I was afraid I was going to cry. He said I *must* be in London for a reason, but I couldn't talk, because I knew my voice would quaver. I couldn't remember *why* I'd come to London, actu-ally, not at that moment. (Why was I here, again?) I placed Nikki on her burled-wood baby-changing station. He rubbed his long fingers together. The fingers cast a trembling shadow upon the wall. Nikki watched the shadow.

"Money? Why, for example, do you think I'm here, with Reggie? Money makes one behave very strangely," he said. I was close to tears. He was very kind in not mentioning it. Then he said fame was another pos-sibility for my trip to London.

"Well . . ."

"You're right: You're not interested in any notion so gauche as fame. Another guess: It's about the process of finding oneself. You seem to have a febrile brain; I've been watching you closely, and my sense is that we're going to have a problem, you and I. Here's an inspired try: You're a painter?" He was looking at my sketchbook, which was lying on the floor. He licked his demon red lips. He touched my hair, smoothed it. I told him what painting I'd come to London to study, and he said, "Ah! A Goya fan, are you, you clever little social realist, you. That's the Rossi knockoff, yeah? I find social commentary boring, but I suppose I'm glacially alone in this regard. I've seen the show ten times, you know. We'll go there together very soon." Then he asked me if I was from Ohio, northeast quadrant. He said something about my accent. I said I didn't have one. He spread out his hand and examined his manicure, which ad-vertised his breeding and privilege. "You may think that just because I'm a lord, I don't *know* anything. Fair enough. I have known some rather beastly lords. They show up at the House of Lords every day and collect their twenty pounds and contribute precisely zero to their kingdom or their world. They all wear decades-old suits, which have a terrible too-worn shine. You can spot a lord from a mile away. I knew a lord once who, when he had a hole in a trouser leg—and he often did—would color his leg—his actual flesh—with a black pen. He was a relation of Cornwallis's, or so he claimed. Everyone's related to someone in England, or had better be. He later murdered his daughter with a hammer. The issue involved an heirloom of some sort. You've got a smidge of baby powder on your nose, my dear. May I?"

He rubbed my nose. His hand was cold. On the surface, he appeared very festive and engaged, but something about him seemed utterly remote.

"It's always the scattered bags found after a plane goes down, all those tragic unclaimed pieces of luggage, that cleave me in two. People—let's be frank about this—are only remembered by the stuff they leave behind."

"Hm," I said. I was resisting his seduction, but yielding to it, too. I felt myself yielding. "Children? Art?"

Lowell said something I didn't quite follow about the eighteenth century, the "cult of the child," patricide, how things must be beautiful for their own sake, how things owe us that. He was rambling. I think he knew he wasn't making any sense, because he stopped talking in midsentence and let the baby take his thumb.

I readjusted my headband.

He was right next to me, yet he felt very distant. I would have needed my magnifying glass to really get a good look at him. I thought about what it would be like to kiss him, but then I mentally reprimanded myself for falling for his performance.

"It is only by the things a person owns," he said, "that a precise—what's the term?—*character study*—may be made. Consider the . . . fecund imaginative possibilities of this doll, for example."

He moved away from Nikki, who made a pained little face, reached for him again. Lowell shook the porcelain doll to further his point. One blue glass eye shut; the other stayed open. I asked him if he was pronouncing *fecund* correctly. I wasn't trying to be mean; I really just wanted to know. He said, timidly, almost childishly, "I'm sorry. I'm not a very good talker." We stood there, silent and uncomfortable. I told him I wasn't any good when I talked, either, and that that's why painting was important; the only time I didn't feel unmoored and away from myself was when I was painting.

We both looked at the doll, wordlessly. The doll's eyes were spaced far apart, like a prey animal, like Jackie B.K.O. I was thinking of Marie Antoinette awaiting the guillotine, dressing a doll.

Lowell said, suddenly, "Isn't it just a marvel that porcelain can generate its own cold? Isn't it a mystery?"

He touched the doll's head to my cheek. The doll's hair felt like human hair.

"You know what, Jenny, my adorable little bean?" How quickly he'd shaken off our uneasy moment together. With one hand, he mussed my hair. In his other hand was the doll. The blond doll hair peeped through his human fingers.

"No, what, Lowell?" I asked.

"When you cease believing in the mystery, then you're dead. If you ever see me taking a mystery like this for granted, please remind me to take a gun to my head." He handed the doll to Nikki, who drew it to her chest. She inserted the doll's head into her mouth, sucked. "No, I'd be too demoralized even to kill myself. *You'd* have to do it."

Why was he talking about a future with me? I don't want to have to imagine anyone else in my future, not for decades at least. I have to remember to carve my own path for myself. Must carve my own path. He looked at me. His eyes were deep and rich and black.

"Here," he said. His hand held mine. "Touch."

"Yes," I said. "Cold."

"Do you know what, Jenny?"

"What, Lowell?"

"There exist an enormous number of weak people in the world. I *loathe* them. I loathe them all. Do you know what, Jenny?" He eyed my sketch pad.

"What, Lowell?"

"We are not weak."

I'm beginning to think this whole London caper was one big mistake.

Hey, out there: Grab your toothbrush, your antiperspirant, and your contact lens solution and come along with me in my journey downward. Oh, come now, it's not *so* bad, here at the bottom. I can say with solemn certainty that these few days have been completely atrocious. But you know what? I'm alive. I'm getting through. I still set my alarm clock for 10:30 a.m.; I'm still shaving daily, still eating the food they put out for me, still wearing clean underpants. I even plucked my nose hairs this morning, which must mean that I'm doing at least some future thinking. Plucking nose hairs, as you doubtless are aware (don't lie to your Uncle Fergus now—he knows what you've been up to), makes you sneeze like a motherfucker.

It's actually not as miserable as you'd think, having your nightmare realized. This had happened to me before—a worst-case scenario coming true—and each time, I think, I'm *stunned* that wasn't worse. I remember, for example, how terrified I was by the idea of getting fired from a job . . . until, that is, I finally got fired from a job. It was my first job, actually. Actually, it was my only job. It was three years before my father died. This is pertinent information, because I had no money then. I was working in the kitchen at a nursing home and got the ax for refusing to remove a pair of dentures from a bowl of ice cream. "There is such a thing as dignity," I remember saying to my boss, a woman who wore a gold-tone eagle brooch and who smelled like a macaroon. "There is such a thing as going too far." I mentally referred to my termination afterward as a "mercy killing," and I spent the rest of the summer watching TV and sitting on the bathroom sink, squeezing my face in front of the mirror. I'd never been happier. Not a day goes by, though, when I don't think about the death-heaviness of that place.

I broke my ankle a few years ago, too (fell off my carousel), and I found I rather liked being an invalid. I got fairly good at it. I wonder if dying is easier than we suspect, too.

So, yes indeed, this Drisana-Nari person is here to stay. I should add that this isn't a tremendously shocking development, given that we always have roughly three to six scroungers staying with us at any time. I just open my eyes anywhere in my house and, hello, I'll see a stranger doing something I disapprove of *in my house.* Gee, I wonder who *that* is dirtying up my steam room? Who's that in the billiards room, by Lowell's *Self-Portrait Emphasizing My Feminine Features,* the one whose cue just dug spastically into my table, green felt flying? Who just rode past my window on a bicycle, naked, grinning and waving? If you're me, you have, at this stage in the game, learned not to ask these sorts of questions.

So how could I have protested the advent of Drisana-Nari?

This time, though, something feels much worse. Could it be this? Your significant other has a girlfriend, that girlfriend moves in, a coming-out party is to be thrown for her, and your significant other has designated *you* the official party planner? Isn't that enough to drive anyone gibbering straight to the loony bin? I had only two hopes for the night; Merit would be there, and I would tell her everything I hadn't yet told her.

I should add, however, that Lowell has used the New Lover excuse to throw a party before. This is not a first. So why the seasick feeling? A year and a half ago, for example, I organized a macrobiotic buffet in the great hall for Lowell's temporary Marin County friend Ray-Ray. Three days after the party, the mammothly eyebrowed (and surprisingly high-strung) Ray-Ray packed his bags and left the premises for good. He still calls sometimes. Annina, a self-deprecating, and, it seemed to me, entirely broke (she once asked me for some money), representational painter, got herself a Fergus-planned Red Party two autumns ago. As the party theme perhaps advertised, all the guests wore red. The next morning, Annina was nowhere to be found (and I actually did look for her). When I (transporting an armful of wrecked red Parisian crepe-paper streamers to the Dumpster out back) asked Lowell, "Where *is* Annina?" he said, "I'm afraid I don't know *whoooom* you're talking about."

Here's my fear: What if this time the lover *doesn't* leave?

"Drisana-Nari was, like absinthe, the toast of Pittsburgh," I overheard Lowell say to someone from behind the library (the room that contains his Turner Award and the secret passageway to his five-years-unused studio) wall this morning. Reasons for relaying this remark: The house is less sturdy than it looks, and Lowell actually talks like this. I haven't actually seen Drisana-Nari in the, as they say, "flesh," since the dinner party. That was a few days ago. Since then, I've gotten the invitations out (keeping myself busy by addressing each one by hand), and am steadfastly ignoring the ringing phone with its early-bird RSVPs.

This afternoon, I saw the woman's shabby bags and her trunks and her cello case and her ridiculous harp spread out all over the music room. That really got to me. Was it monsoon season? Were we Calcutta Central? Of course, I was left then with no choice but to sneak the sticky bottle of Kahlua from the kitchen and slink outside with it to the emu colony's pen.

I sat on the ground and looked at the emus. The emus stood and looked at me, orange eyes full of ruth and meaning. You've got to love the good old *Dromaius novae-hollandiae*. I always find it necessary to remind guests they're dealing with a two-hundred-pound, six-foot-tall creature with an exceptionally tiny brain. If it's the size of a doughnut hole, we've got to consider ourselves lucky. Their feathers look like hair, and when they get mad, watch it, because when they kick, they can really disembowel a fellow (and they have). We've got two boys (Harry Bailey One and Harry Bailey Two) and three girls (Hermengild, Jane Seymour, and Simone de Booboir—one of Lowell's "associates" named that one). Simone is "with child." What does one call a bird who's incubating her eggs? Is she "pregnant"? Do you see how little I know about the circumstances of conception, the conditions of *life*? At any rate, the entire scene—the bird goo, the five birds standing around like a big, stupid, happy, clucking family, their orange nobody-home eyes and bizarre feather fur, the woman bird and her egg-warming rump—really did calm me down. I thought about how nice it would be to be in a big green egg myself and have a large warm thing pinning me to the ground.

I drank the whole bottle of Kahlua. Glugity, glug, glug. Just for the record, whenever I don't say "I sneezed," just assume I did. The emus looked startled every time I let loose a big honker. They weren't as troubled by my crying. I cried and stuffed the empty bottle full of rocks. This became my little project. It seemed like a good idea. I thought of that children's fable, the one with the half-full water bottle and the birdie who plops rocks down inside so she can get a drink. I sang campfire songs and remembered every single thing that had ever happened to me. I remembered the faces of people whose names I never knew and never asked. I wondered if I've been living a lie: What if it's true I've never really had any love in my life?

I stumbled back to the house at sunset, leaving the bottle where I'd find it later. I applauded my birdlike ingenuity, pleased, at least, I would be prepared come next rainfall.

I staggered in through the kitchen, thinking it highly unlikely I'd run into Lowell or his new aficionada this way. The downside of the route, though, was that I'd certainly come across Mrs. Valdez, our remarkable yet uncomely cook. It is she who mans the kitchen. (*Man* really is the appropriate word here.) Just so you think I'm not thoroughly impenitent, I do know when I'm being unkind.

Ah, yes, of course: There she was, hovering over a sputtering botulism-ridden pot. (She makes V. Sackville-West look like Bardot.)

"Hello, *papita,*" she said. "Is good, no?" She lifted the top and a puff of steam escaped, *Macbeth*-like. She gazed into the pot and made a *nummy-nummy* sound, pinching her fingers to her mouth.

"Is what good, my dear?" I asked. I sighed. Lowell, as you might suspect, is better with her than I am. It takes so much *effort* talking to her. I wasn't in the mood. I was, as you'll recall, drunk.

"Here. Try. For you." She dipped a spoon into the pot, then brought the bubbling spoonful of hell up to my mouth.

"No, thanks, sweetie, although it certainly does look delectable." What I needed right then was a good long finger down my throat (and a toilet).

"*Eat.*" She put her hands on my shoulders and looked me square in the eye. So frank. So blunt. When was the last time Lowell had looked at me with that level of interest? When had anybody? Merit used to, but she was a little girl then. Jenny loved me, too, but that love turned straight to the other thing. I sent Jenny a letter once when she was in New York that said, "You'd better never hate me." She wrote me back and promised she never would. How childish I was to believe her. She never approved of my love for Lowell, or Merit. Valdez sucked her stomach in and turned to her side. She rubbed her belly. "Skinny," she said. "You skinny. Too much. Too many."

"Me? Skinny? Ha. Don't *think* so. Skinny, *me?* What a *laugh,*" I said. That sounds phonily incredulous, I know, but I really did mean it. I lifted up my shirt and shook a spare tire of flesh for our jumbo-size señora. A mouthwatering picture, no?

"*Skinny!* Skinny, *papita,*" Señora Valdez said. Was she serious? Was she just fucking with me? Was this everyone's week to fuck with loathsome, lipid-plagued, self-tanner-accident-prone, stinging BO, rotting, contemptible Fergus? She smiled. She grabbed my tummy and shook.

"Have you ever seen *Return of the Jedi?* I'm . . . Jabba the Hut. He's incredib— He's this monst—" With that, I exploded into tears and sunk to the floor. She kept her hand on my stomach until I was halfway to the ground. There could have been no more unerotic touch in the world.

"*¡Aiie, papita! ¿Cómo?*"

I find that I've been spending quite a lot of time on the floor these days.

I was on my back now. She came to me. I tried to shoo her away. She loomed in closer. I tried to shoo her away again. This time, she went bye-bye. As she shuffled toward the stove, I watched the ample lines of her underwear through her dress.

The señora bustled toward me, bowl in midbrandish. Up like ghosts the steam came. She extended her other hand for me to take. I took.

She led me into the dining room. I followed, a little wobbly, but I followed. She set the bowl of stew on the table and pulled out a chair for me. I sat. She tucked a napkin under my collar, just as she's been doing for years. The white of her left eye contained a mysterious speck of brown, as if a bit of her iris had come detached. I wondered if it hurt her. I wondered why I'd never noticed it before.

Into tears once again I exploded.

My cheek was smooched against the reproduction gateleg table as if I were a second grader enjoying a postrecess desk nap. My tears slid down my face and pooled onto the table. I didn't even think about how the oak would warp. I licked my tears. The table was smooth on my tongue. The tears tasted like tears taste. I heard her trundle out of the room.

I considered the wallful of *Canterbury Tales* Lowell portraits. There are twenty-nine portraits, each pilgrim on horseback. The whole story makes me so sad—Chaucer had intended to give each pilgrim four tales, but he never even made it to *one* for each character. He lived; he died. At least he tried.

Lowell as the Friar is wearing a black cloak and an Olivia Newton-John–type headband. By the way, the real headband he wore when I took the pictures that became his studies was *mine* (this *was* the early eighties, recall). I had to have the beaver hat for Lowell's high-style Merchant shipped in from Russia. I still don't know what's in the Summoner's envelope, although its brushwork is particularly lush. The Knight is too Boeotian for me. Lowell as the Wife of Bath has the best outfit. The Lowell Wife smiled cruelly at me as if he/she had something to say. Maybe it's the puckish gap in his/her teeth (the real Lowell's teeth don't possess such a gap, of course) in this particular portrait that makes him/her look as if he/she is holding on to a secret that, if revealed, would destroy my life.

Lowell has never been very good at painting horses.

To myself, I said, "Whan that April with his showres soote." Years ago, I memorized the whole of *The Canterbury Tales*. It took me two years. Lowell quizzed me every day. Sad, really, when you think about what your life used to be like.

"The droughte of March hath perced to the roote."

"Experience, though noon auctoritee, were in this world, is right ynough for me."

Lowell as the Wife wears this quite outrageous hat. If you stare at something for long enough, don't you expect it to come alive? You know how you have your most cherished possessions, the ones you'd run back into your burning house for? Here are mine: the *Canterbury* portrait cycle, my photographs of Merit, and Lowell's letters. Let the rest go up in flames. Let the rest go.

"To speke of wo that is in marriage."

Lowell painted these portraits for me.

Lowell painted these portraits for *me.*

There exist in the wall stair two full-scale oil portraits, one of Lowell as Richard III and one of me as Hamlet. Lowell painted them. The year after he, Jenny, and Merit came to live with me, we hosted a Shakespeare-themed party. Come dressed as your favorite Shakespeare character, that sort of thing. It was our first party. What a different time it was then! Lowell was painting so feverishly, so prolifically, and so well, and he wouldn't emerge for *days* at a time from his mystery studio, which none of us (except for Jenny), not the person who owns this house (that would be me), were ever, ever allowed to enter. Oh, I was so happy when Jenny, Lowell, and Merit were here! I'd never met Merit before they moved in, you know. And my previous encounter with Lowell, years before, hadn't gone well (largely my fault). This was in London, and I wasn't—and am not—a good traveler. He had insulted me dreadfully then (years later, he told me he was "troubled" by me at that first encounter, that he was certain we, the two of us, "shared genetic material"). But Jenny had been so kind to me after my father died, and we talked on the phone every day and I told her everything about my house and she told me everything about Lowell and Merit. Pre-Merit, I don't think I'd ever actually talked to a child, not since I myself had been one. I remember how natural it felt with Merit, how immediate it was, and how right. I opened my door for them, and there she squirmingly stood, a dark-haired four-year-old in overalls and eyeglasses. She waved at me, then opened her arms. No one had to tell me to squat down to her height when I embraced her. I just *did.*

The first party was my idea. I was Hamlet. I was in my twenties then, and full of shit, so I thought it fitting. Jenny was in full eye makeup as

Lady Macbeth (Lowell took her into his studio and painted a white dagger on the breast of her black cape). Merit was Ophelia, which I thought was quite the inappropriate message to send a young girl. Jenny agreed with me, but insisted it was Lowell's idea. Before the party, I sent Valdez off to buy rosemary and fennel for Merit's costume; Jenny and I dashed around the great lawn, gathering pansies, daisies, and violets. (Columbine and rue: not found.) Later, Merit and I sat on the floor in the music room, singing Cole Porter songs and stringing the flowers and herbs onto a garland. I had turned each of the suits of armor toward the wall for her. I didn't want her to be afraid.

Lowell was Richard III that night. He threw the costume together in about a minute, but it *worked*. It takes a true beauty to want to uglify himself; at Halloween, it's the average girl who gets dolled up as a French maid or a sexy witch or a princess so she can, for one night, play at being a belle. A real beauty would have no problem going as a fork.

Lowell painted me in the Poor Yorick scene. I didn't sit for Lowell, because no one sits for Lowell. He used photographs when he painted other people, which turned out to be only once. Am I flattered? Less than you'd think. (*I* took the photographs; although this time, he shot me.) The star of this picture? You guessed it. The huge shadowless skull. Disturbingly, the skull is about twice the size of *my* head. Not that this is such a bad thing, really, because my hair is closer to pink than I feel comfortable admitting, and I look stiff and scared. But Lowell and I do look young. We do at least look young.

He worked with a brilliant palette during these early years, the paint thickly worked. As you might expect, Lowell's Richard portrait is the more eye-catching of the two. I talked about myself first just now because people always talk about themselves first. But Lowell's is the one you can't look away from. Lowell's great subject: himself; his landscape: his body.

Lowell, because he's an actor and an artist, disappeared entirely into the role as Richard III. He is utterly hidden away. He is unrecognizable in a prosthetic nose, prosthetic hunchback, cape and crown. It's a face devoid of mercy. His black eyes gaze at you, neither catching nor reflecting light. They are the eyes of someone who will look away from you first, whether in bed, on the street, or on the stage. He is the one who rejects you . . . but one whom you can't help but respect for rejecting you, because you know he's made the correct decision. Lowell, you see, understood Richard's poison all too well. I remember that right after the pictures went up, we were standing on the creaking stairs, admiring them (admiring *him*, I should say), and Lowell said his performance in the Richard portrait was based on the most wretched man he'd ever met. I have never asked him who that man was.

Which is all to say that I tend to use the back stairs more frequently than the main ones. Who wants to be confronted by the specter of his own invisibility?

And I did have a legitimate reason for being upstairs, too. Cause: Kahlua; effect: bathroom. Certainly I could have used any of the umpteen downstairs powder rooms, but those were for public use, and I certainly wasn't in the mood to confront any dark surprise in one of them.

En route to my WC, I crept through the lightless back hallway, off of which are all the guest rooms. I guided myself by feeling the linenfold wall. Door after door was closed. A lovely torture chamber of the mind, this hallway. Behind each door you'll find another nightmare. A thin band of light shone underneath the doors of some of the rooms. Did I hear some squeak of laughter coming from beyond that door? The grunt of coitus from beyond that one? Most of the guest rooms have a special "theme": Behind one door is the Arthur Room, behind another the Lancelot Room, and then there's the Gawain Room. The best guest room in the house is the Guinevere Room, at the end of the hall. (I never read any Malory, so don't ask me about it, although I can fake my way through any conversation.) The door to the Guinevere Room was open. This was Drisana-Nari's room. I knew this because Lowell puts all his favorites there. (Merit's childhood room has no theme. I'd never reduce her to gimmickry.)

The Guinevere Room's light was on. Clothes were scattered over the four-poster bed, lying atop its entrail red hunt-scene bedspread, a hand-me-down from my own bed. Her clothes were so wrinkled, they looked as if they'd been balled up for a decade in a garbage bag. How nice. Toiletries spread out on the bureau, cello disrespected on the floor, cello case propped against the wainscoting. I imagined how horrifyingly alive the cello case would look in the dark. I popped in the room for a closer look. Crept over to the chest of drawers, which I'd had made for me by an outfit in Lisbon specializing in Crusades-era furniture. (I used to get my periods all mixed up.) Items on the drawer belonging to our unaesthetically minded visitor: a pack of *Simpsons* playing cards, deodorant, Blistex, keys, a pink Oral B toothbrush with a dried dollop of toothpaste on the handle, a box of tampons, tweezers, a hand mirror, a paperback biography of Marc Bolan, and a tube of Cover Girl lipstick. The detritus of an actual human life.

It was the lipstick that fascinated.

This Drisana-Nari had lipstick because she had lips, which meant that she was a human.

I need to have things spelled out for me sometimes.

I picked up the lipstick. I put it to my cheek. I unrolled, or whatever you call it when you make the lipstick go peekaboo. The lipstick wax had grooves in it from somebody's—from *her*—lips.

She was a real, live, actual human adult female and she had a mouth and this had touched—

"Hello, *Fergus.*"

I spun around.

Andrei just has this way of *materializing.* He stood in the doorway, hip jutted cavalierly out.

"I always said you would make a very beautiful woman."

Andrei has about two brain cells up there, which, if you rubbed them together, wouldn't even make a pinwheel go. The arms were once again hairless.

"Have you seen Lowell?" I asked. "I was just . . . looking around for him."

Andrei shook his head as if trying to shame me, and he plucked the lipstick from my hands.

"Does anyone ever know where Lowell is? No. Nobody knows. 'Where is Lowell?' 'Where is Lowell?' That is all everyone ever wants to know. What is the word, Fergus, for when you tell the teacher that a student has been cheating?"

Why do we keep Andrei around? I felt as if I were going to sneeze. I was going to let loose a really monumental one very soon.

"Tattletale? Is that it? I think that I will do you a favor by not playing the tattletale at this instance," Andrei said. With a flourish, he held out the lipstick. I reached my hand out to take it, but—

Achoooooo.

The Death of Arthur etching (not a Lowell painting, just a little thing I picked up at a flea market in Brimfield) on the wall rattled. The items on the chest of drawers vibrated as if a giant were making his evening rounds. The hands on the grandfather clock stopped.

The lipstick fell onto the floor and rolled under the chest of drawers. (The sneeze went *everywhere.*)

"God bless you, Fergus," Andrei said. He crouched down to the floor. He could be charitable sometimes, just like anyone else. I wiped my nose with my hand. I wiped my hand on my shorts. I, too, bent down.

And—although this shouldn't come as a surprise to anyone, although you'll say, No shit, Fergus, you poor naïve creature, what did you expect? Lowell hasn't been sleeping in your bed for four nights and counting, after all—there was, on the floor, underneath the chest, back by the wall, next to the cheap lipstick case that had just rolled to a halt, between Andrei's brown outstretched hand and my pink outstretched one, one of Lowell's sock braces.

6

It was surprising, but nice, that Randy had somehow made himself the designated purchaser and presenter of Ronnie's good-bye card and surprise good-bye gift. Merit didn't know how this had occurred, because the person in this role was always the one with the closest working relationship with the departing employee. Randy, as far as Merit was aware, had never exchanged word one with Ronnie. Ronnie was the associate promotions manager, and he coughed pretty much constantly and regularly used the drinking fountain in the little corridor that led into the women's rest room. He was the only man in the office who used it, although it was true the fellas didn't have their own drinking fountain, and it was also true the ladies' drinking fountain wasn't really technically *inside* the ladies' room. Still, though, Merit disapproved.

Merit certainly thought Randy's role of card/gift purchaser was a step in the right direction. She had worried Randy wasn't really a part of the office's social life, and so was pleased he was finally making an effort. And who knew? Maybe he and Ronnie were closer than she'd previously imagined.

Eleven of them from the ad/sales department were at the Chinese restaurant where they always went for special office occasions. The restaurant was in a strip mall, but what wasn't? The wrapped mystery gift was on Randy's plate, the card on top. Although Merit thought it was great

Randy had gone out and bought Ronnie a gift, she couldn't help but be concerned, a little bit (and she didn't really even *like* Ronnie), about the contents of the wrapped box. It looked like a shoe box; usually they gave the person leaving a Cross pen. Randy had wrapped the big shoe-looking box with the Sunday comic page from the paper. "The Family Circus" was on top, perfectly in the middle. Merit suspected its placement was deliberate, but she wasn't completely sure.

A female staffer made a comment about how the table seemed wobbly. Merit remembered how Fergus once tried to adjust a wobbly table when the two of them were eating at a restaurant in a Cleveland hotel. Fergus made the restaurant staff fetch one matchbook, then two, then a white Lucite cutting board (it was wet, Merit remembered, with little chopped-up parsley pieces on it), then a big wooden chopping block. That did the trick. Merit thought then that Fergus futzed at the table just so he wouldn't have to talk to her. But she had been about eighteen then, so anything she had believed at that stage of the game was suspect, she now understood.

Rebecca, who sat at the head of the table, tapped on her glass with her fork, demanding order. Randy had an important "parting gift" for Ronnie, Rebecca announced. Merit had never before noticed how many people in her office had names that started with *R*.

Randy scratched his head and squinted the way he always did when he was preparing to say something he considered significant. His eyes were exasperatingly blue. He had great hair, all who knew him had to admit—curly, lush, and so well tended—although Merit did imagine he was unclean in other personal areas.

"Ronnie," Randy said, picking up the card between two fingers, "I just want you to know something."

Ronnie coughed once into his fist.

"What I'm going to say might come as a kind of a shock, so get ready," Randy said. He sounded really worked up, as if a big testimonial were coming. There was a catch in his voice, just a little one. Ronnie coughed into his fist again, continued coughing. His hands were baby hands, and men with baby hands made her shudder, and she did.

"I just called to say how much I love you, Ronnie. And I mean it from the bottom of my heart."

Alanna, the magazine's accountant, whom Merit liked a lot, and who really did resemble George Stephanopoulos (although Merit knew she was mean for thinking this), brayed so loudly it was as if she thought Randy were Madeleine freaking Kahn.

"Ronnie," Randy said. He shoved the card down the table. "I have something to say to you: You complete me."

Ronnie coughed a rich, fulgent cough. For the first time, it occurred to Merit that maybe Ronnie wasn't actually coughing just to annoy everyone.

"No, I mean that, Ronnie," Randy said. "What can I say? You make me a better man."

Ronnie tore into the envelope, coughed twice.

Merit had no clue where or what Ronnie's new job was. She felt bad about this. She also felt bad about her send-off on his farewell card, and she hoped some of her coworkers' good-byes were as lame as hers. Merit was quite ungifted at signing work cards, she knew; it had taken her ten minutes of deliberations to come up with, "Ronnie, congratulations on your new job! We'll miss you! Take care, Merit." Later in the morning, the card (craftily hidden inside a manila folder) had mistakenly ended up back on her desk again. A green arrow had been drawn, pointing to Merit's pathetic little *auf Wiedersehen.* Next to the arrow was written, in Randy's frightening hand, "Ronnie, congratulations on your new job! We'll miss you! Take care, Randy. (VERY ORIGINAL.)" This had made Merit smile when she saw it. She couldn't help it. (And, no, none of her coworkers' send-offs ended up being either very witty or heartfelt.)

"Ronnie," Randy said, "this is all I have left to say to you: You had me at hello. *You had me at hello.*"

"Hey, Randy," Ronnie said. "Fuck you."

"I know you say that out of love. Open the box." Randy scooted the big box down the table. The tablecloth bunched up, causing adorable accountant Alanna's water glass to knock over into her lap. Merit, who was sitting across from Alanna, gave her her napkin. She rooted around in her bag for some tissues.

No tissues, but she did have lots of tampons. Tampons are built to be absorbent, and they would have, with some disassembling, done the job, but that would have freaked everyone out.

Ronnie shook the big shoe-type box and held it up to his ear. He ripped away at Randy's wrapping job without even making a comment about it. Ronnie allowed little bits of shredded *Akron Beacon Journal* to flutter to the floor.

It was a Rockport box, containing, voilà, a pair of black rubber-soled Rockport lace-up shoes.

"Holy schmoly," Ronnie said.

"A pair of shoes!" Alanna said.

"Are they your size?" asked Rebecca.

"Yeah, they are," Ronnie said, taking the shoes out of the box and dangling each up by the lace so everybody could have a look. "These are amazing! Thanks, man. I take back when I said, 'Fuck you.' "

Randy squinted. He scratched his head. He said, "I know how you're always saying you need new shoes, comfortable ones. So I got you some. *New shoes*, man!" He was smiling and his braces were on full display, like something for sale.

"Shoes! How nice of you," Alanna said.

Everyone around the table, including Merit, uttered similar words of approval. Merit seemed to be alone in thinking a pair of sensible black Rockport work shoes was a weird choice of a going-away gift . . . but thoughtful, so *thoughtful*! Randy and Ronnie had discussed footwear in the past? The things you found out about people! Randy could have done worse, much worse, for a gift, Merit felt.

Ronnie passed the shoes around the table, which seemed to Merit suspiciously like something out of a bridal or baby shower. The shoes were passed to Merit. She turned them over. Size eight, just as she had guessed. They smelled weird, chemically.

Merit's paper place mat again reminded her she had been born in the Year of the Snake. She didn't care for that, and mentioned it to Randy, who told her the Year of the Snake was the cool year to be. He asked her what her astrological sign was, and she told him, and he nodded, squinted, and looked away. Alanna said she was the Year of the Dog, then started talking about how her dog had fallen into her swimming pool last night, and how she'd had to construct, lickety-split (Alanna was from Georgia), what she called a "lariat" out of a piece of rope she found on the floor of the garage, and how she'd gotten that loop around the dog's neck on the third toss. Alanna said she'd had very vivid fantasies in her youth about being a cowgirl. Merit wondered why Alanna hadn't just jumped into the pool herself; it would have been much more efficient. Merit thought, What if something like that happened to *Rosalita*? It was un-likely, though, because she and Wyatt didn't have a pool. Lowell and Fergus had a pool, though, and, come to think of it, Rosalita *had* sniffed around its perimeter once when they took her over there two years ago for Caroline's infamous drawing lesson. Merit made a mental note not to take the dog to Lowell's again, should the opportunity ever arise (if, say, they were invited to a costume party there or something).

Conversation at the table was broken into two main topics now: one about the decline in the durability of footwear, the other about the arrogance of a certain advertiser who was now not even taking their calls.

"Hey," Randy said to Merit and Alanna, "so I heard that Michael Jackson song today, 'Smooth Criminal.' It was on in the drugstore. 'Annie, are you okay?' You know that song?"

Merit nodded enthusiastically.

"Yeah, I know that song," Alanna said. "Here's something I always wondered about in that song: Who's Annie?"

"Totally! That's my point exactly!" said Randy. "I mean, what's *Annie* got to do with it?"

It was true, Merit had to admit. Who was Annie? No one knew! Oh, Merit was in a good mood today, such a good mood—it was Friday, and it would be three o'clock before she got back to her desk, so she could just blow the rest of the day off, and she had the feeling, although she hadn't wanted to admit it before, that Randy was looking at her—like *looking*—in a maybe romantic-type way. But she couldn't be sure. She was bad at telling things like that. Randy's arm was completely hairless. She imagined licking it.

Servers had arrived and were beginning to set down steaming plates of Chinese food. Merit scooted her chair in to make way. Hers was the first meal delivered, and several people seemed to consider it with distaste. Randy got Peking duck and Alanna got some kind of chicken. Rebecca said she was flabbergasted that her Grand Marnier shrimp turned out to be deep-fried; Merit wondered what she'd expected. Rebecca sent it back and told them to bring out "some kind of steamed fish, whatever you have," which Merit found a brave choice. Merit had broken the "no seafood in a cheap Chinese restaurant" rule once, back when she ate animals, and had learned her lesson. Everyone at the table just sat there, watching the newly plateless Rebecca for some sign about what to do next—everyone, that is, except Randy, who dug right on into his Peking duck with his hands.

"What are you waiting for? *Eat,*" Rebecca said.

One by one, people started picking up their forks.

Merit's hands were in her lap. She told Rebecca it was okay, that they'd be glad to wait for her. Jenny had taught Merit the meal was never to start until everyone at the table had been served. It had taken a great deal of time for Jenny's edict to be of use; when Merit was growing up, she and her mother had never really attended any group meals together (they weren't big on the party circuit), unless you counted early child-hood dinners with Lowell and Fergus, which Merit didn't.

"Merit," Rebecca said. "Don't be strange. Eat. Please."

Merit knew she'd sounded like a suck-up just then, and she was em-barrassed. She studied her plate, cautiously picked up her fork, and aimed it at her thrilling steamed vegetables and brown rice. In the early years, after she'd left her mother's house for college, Merit would sometimes eat steamed vegetables and brown rice three times a day. Jenny's refrigerator was then, as it was now, stocked with things like double-cream Brie and foie gras, boxes of éclairs and packages of deli ham. Merit would have thought Jenny would have written more about food in her late-adolescent diaries. Like all children, Merit was still unable to see her parents as full, valid human beings with lives separate from hers. In 1976, she hadn't been born, so there was a way in which Jenny and Lowell's lives hadn't re-ally even begun. As Merit was reading the diaries, she'd realized she was looking for some mention about how Jenny could already *sense* her, how she *longed* for her already, although she didn't even exist yet. Merit knew this was crazy.

Merit noted all conversation at the table had stopped. People were chewing and making sounds. She tried not to be judgmental about the meat eaters of the group, who were the noisiest masticators. Merit watched Randy rip apart his entire duck with his hands, and she couldn't help but wonder how his employment reflected on her, in the eyes of the others in the office, what they thought about her for hiring such a non-corporate-type person, someone who just seemed so, well, *unsuited* to an office environment, someone who really should have been working in a . . . Well, who knew where Randy should have been working, actually. It was hard to picture him anywhere, really, especially here. If she could just put her mouth on his arm, just for a second, then . . . Well, she didn't know what. There wouldn't be anything wrong with that, nothing she couldn't share with Wyatt, even. She'd done that before, put her mouth on arms that weren't Wyatt's, and it was okay, sort of. Randy licked his fingers.

"Randy," Rebecca said, "it was Annie Oakley."

"Huh?" Randy said. There was grease on his face, and Merit wanted to lick it off. She was a messy eater, too, so she understood.

"You heard me," said Rebecca, who then drank her entire glass of water without coughing.

7

25 June

No work today. The Van Pelts went to the Isle of Man for a couple of days. (I adore the names the British choose for things.) Don't know if Lowell went with them. Went to the library at the British Museum and did some research on Josephine Baker. What I found: twelve children, all adopted, ten boys, two girls. No names given. She died last year, in New York, at the age of sixty-eight.

When I came home, Grunt was sitting at the head of the kitchen "table." I say "table" because it's really just a plywood door propped up on cinder blocks. It seems kind of fetishistic, the way she likes to sit at the end of the door and do things to the knob. Maybe she just likes fondling something round? Grunt asked me again how old I was, and I again said twenty-seven. She called me a liar and dug her grubby fingers into her paper sugar-cube cup. She popped two into her mouth and crunched loudly. I told her if those were ice cubes, I'd say she was sexually frustrated. She called me a slag and stuck her tongue out at me. I haven't written much about her yet, but Grunt has an unbelievably tiny, delicate doll's face. Her face is so translucent, it's as if she's missing a few layers of skin. When I moved in, I told her that she looked like Mia Farrow, but it didn't take long to learn she considered this a radically uncool comparison. She looks like a doll, but she's a jaguar.

She asked me if I'd heard Scrumpy and her going at it last night, and I lied and said I hadn't. Then she asked me if she could borrow my mascara. Must have been fun watching me trying to wriggle out of that one. She stomped up from her chair, dumping the whole cup of sugar cubes into her kilt pocket (I have now learned that kilts have pockets), and said how she'd forgotten to give me a letter. She riffled though a heap of junk and pulled out an envelope. Did I recognize immediately the psychotic block handwriting, the color coding? Oh boy. Sure did. The envelope was heavy. There were about twenty stamps.

I held the envelope up for Grunt to take a look at. She has a little side business as a handwriting interpreter, so her expert analysis was key. She said she'd seen it already, then clomped into the kitchen and picked up a butcher's knife. "I could tell something was off with the geezer by the handwriting," she said, and thawked the grapefruit into two. She squeezed one grapefruit half into a green glass bowl. She drank the grapefruit juice, licked the bowl, and said he was one of those "batty boys that's clingy and needy when he's around you, but then when he's not around you, he's like, 'Go away, go away.' " She said I'd better watch my arse, then asked if I'd care to join her in the other grapefruit half.

Grunt's Fergusian diagnosis: "The johnny's mental, nothing more to be said."

Grunt's real name is Emily Thistlewaithe. I told her Fergus was my best friend.

26 June

Fergus went through a big Latin phase junior year, but, from the looks of things, I'm afraid it's not over yet. I still haven't been able to open the letter, but I did go into the bathroom, stand on the toilet, and hold the envelope up to the ceiling light. Far too many pages for me to make out anything other than this, on the last page: "SUGREF—SINIF." The last time I saw Fergus sign off with "Finis" was last year, on a book report in Mr. Fitzwilliams's class. It was an unappreciated little flourish at the paper's end. Fitzwilliams gave Fergus a *D* (the paper was about Thomas Mann, that abominable snoozefest) and made a big point in class of telling us that we were seventeen and should now officially be able to spell second-grade reading-level words. I remember Mr. Fitzwilliams's knotted yellow chalk-dusty fingers pointing to each of us, accusing us one by one. Fergus held it together for a few minutes, but when Fitzwilliams called him up to the board and asked him to show the class how the word *finish* was spelled, Fergus started bawling and ran outside into the hall. Even from inside the classroom, we could hear him crying and muttering to himself. I went after him maybe a minute later. When Fergus really cries, and he was really crying, his face turns a strangulated red. When Fergus cries, he scares everyone. He was banging his head against the lockers and saying to himself over and over, "It's Latin. It's

Latin. It's Latin. It's *Latin*." I told him *I* knew *finis* was Latin, and wasn't *my* approval more important than old chalky Fitzwilliams's? Fergus hugged me and said he was sorry. His mom called our school the next day and got him moved to the third-period English class. I moved to that class, too.

So this is all to say that "FINIS—FERGUS" is as far as I got in his letter today.

27 June

Back at the Van Pelts' today. No Lowell. Mr. V.P. asked me to prepare a tray of tea and biscuits for him to eat while he watched the BBC news. But oh, how I want to be alone and work! To be hidden and apart! But all these PEOPLE keep getting in my way. Must remember not to need people. Or money.

28 June

I'm confused. Today was going to be my big day to beat Lowell, but I'm not sure who won. I guess it's obvious, just by watching Lowell, that he's related to *somebody*. And his skin *is* sort of beef bouillon–colored. But he's lying about Josephine Baker.

Tonight, I went to the library to collect the tray after the BBC news. Van Pelt was asleep, and Lowell was telling a story. He talked about riding a carousel in Paris, and said he remembered reaching up for the gold rings hanging above him. He said he thought they were real gold, but he was only a child, so what did he know then?

"And Mother—*Josephine Baker* to *you* [here he gave the unconscious Van Pelt a little wink]—clapped for me every time I bobbled past her."

It was my chance. I had my opening. I picked the tray up like a good servant and said I was sorry to hear the sad news about her death last year. Our eyes met, Lowell's and mine. He was silent for a moment, in the way people are when you've gone too far with them, when you've probed too much. Then he said I was a little one-man press conference with all my questions. (But I hadn't *asked* any questions.) It seemed as if I'd hurt him. Although I still didn't believe him.

He said, "A tragic end to a miraculous life. But relationships don't end, ever. Relationships always adjust and transform, Jenny, even when they're one-sided."

Van Pelt was snoring lavishly on his red couch. I took the tray out of the room, washed the dishes, and went home.

29 June

This morning. Slapped awake by a pounding at my door. I had fallen asleep with my clothes on, and my makeup, too. I shot straight up, did a quick damage check in the mirror. Not good. Eyeliner on my nose, for starters. Right earlobe, too. The pounding on the door turned into feral scratching. I put two and two together and figured out what was making the insane clawing noise: Grunt's rings. I pulled open the door. Grunt stumbled into my room, already wearing platform boots. I didn't know what time it was. A male voice from out in the living room shouted, "There's a girl here to see you!" That was Scrumpy.

"It's not a *girl,*" Grunt said.

I wasn't really awake yet. I wasn't exactly following. She said he called all "geezers" "girls" because that was his sense of humor. I'll never understand British comedy. Scrumpy (who was eating something) shouted that the guy outside was a "pouncer." I thought, Pouncer: Lowell. Oh God, I didn't want Lowell to be here. I mean, I *did* want Lowell to be here. I wanted him here, and I didn't. I stepped into the living room, and Scrumpy (sitting on the sofa, plate of muffins in his lap, tighty whiteys and a black Sex Pistols T-shirt that had a few random chunks of Band-Aid-colored couch foam stuck to it) said the pouncer outside had told him he'd had to ring the doorbell with his forehead because he had so many bags. "What did the pouncer look like?" I asked. Scrumpy said, "You think I'm going to let in someone I don't know from Adam who's wearing a cape and has the face of a *Scotsman?*"

I knew what pouncer in my life matched that description. And it definitely wasn't Lowell.

From the top of the stairs, through the little window high on the front door, I could see the top of the fuzzy little head that belonged to only one person. I stood by the front door and listened to the soft singing outside. Fergus's big solo number in the talent show last year. Blew everyone else out of the water with it, even Topher Sheets's repellently eager-to-please Travolta impression.

"... Then I long for my Indiana ..."

I opened the door.

". . . HOOOOOOMMMMME!" Fergus was doing a little soft-shoe dance, twirling on a black cane, ignoring everything but Fergus. Behind him, on the stoop, lay about ten black suitcases in various states of toppledness. We didn't hug or anything, because neither of us dared to.

"I'd been out here so long," Fergus said, "I was starting to think you'd forgotten all about me."

30 June

Fergus is snoring now, so I finally have time to write today. I'm not painting—what a disgrace—so I'll just *write through* today and I'll feel better. The first thing I did yesterday, after we'd hauled all Fergus's suitcases into the apartment, was to run into my bedroom and hide his unopened letter. I tucked it inside this journal, which I then locked in my suitcase. Fergus hasn't quoted directly from the letter, but it's clear that in it were two important announcements: He'd decided we'd made up, and he'd decided he was coming to London to visit me in a week. What else can I do, other than play along and pretend I've read it? This is turning out to be pretty easy to do. You can make someone believe anything, so long as you let him do the talking. It's probably not worth bringing up with him tomorrow morning, but I'd like to remind him that decisions, like, oh, crashing at someone's flat in London, should involve more than one person. We've discussed this before, how he needs to consult with other people. Maybe I'll brush off this old chestnut later in the week. It's all part of the same problem with Fergus: He seems to think we're having a conversation we're not actually having. So does that mean our friendship is just one endless monologue?

Here's us this morning as I was getting ready for work. Fergus was sitting cross-legged on my bed; I was straddling his suitcases, putting my eyeliner on.

"You probably think I can't take care of myself while you're at work."

"I know, Fergus, I *know*. Who's going to change your diapers for you?"

"You think that's funny now, Jenny, but in about seventy years, you actually *will* be changing my diapers for me."

I wasn't planning to change anyone's diapers in seventy years, especially not Fergus's. "No, but seriously," I said, "maybe you can ask Grunt, or possibly Scrumpy, to suck your thumb for you while I'm gone."

"Noooo! I don't think those two are going to be sucking any part of my anatomy today," he said. "Sorry, Grunt and Scrumpy. I know life's tough."

Please. Fergus is an even bigger virgin than *I* am. For the last several nights, I've gone to sleep thinking about Lowell. What does that mean? I'll probably die a virgin, just as Fergus no doubt will.

"That sounds like a cartoon. *Grunt and Scrumpy.*"

"Those two smell. Your whole apartment smells."

"Don't look at me," I said.

"What's *that?*" He meant the reproduction of *The Straw Manikin* taped over my mattress.

"That's my Goya. You like field trips, don't you, Fergus? We should go and see it in person." I was taunting Fergus again. How quickly we'd fallen back into our old roles.

"It's in a museum?"

Fergus's reflection in the mirror didn't look like the real Fergus at all. He was trying to smooth down his hair. It wasn't working, Fergus. And *stop* with your snoring! It's very difficult to write this.

"Where *else* would a painting be?"

"In some rich person's house? I don't know how these things work. Is there a furniture section in the museum?"

It's very strange to see someone else's reflection. Fergus doesn't know what he really looks like, and never will.

"Because you know how in the Met, in New York, there are all these fake rooms from Versailles and other places? Because I'd go if they have those. I like to stand in those fake rooms and pretend. Jenny?"

"Yes, Fergus."

"Are you mad at me?"

"No," I said. In Fergus's reflection, one eye was substantially higher than the other one.

"That's good."

"*Should* I be mad at you?"

"Jenny?"

"Yes, Fergus." I swung around. I was looking at the real Fergus now. His eyes seemed aligned, more or less.

"Do you think I could possibly go to work with you today?"

"Fergus!"

"I promise I won't get in the way."

I turned back to the mirror. His eyes were uneven again. "There's not a desk you can crouch under, you know. It's somebody's *house*."

"Is it really big, this house?"

"What did you do yesterday anyway, while I was at work? You were being very mysterious about this last night."

"I brought *The Canterbury Tales* with me. Is it big? How rich are they?"

"Did you even go out at all?"

"I don't understand how to tip here, in restaurants. Are you supposed to tip?"

"You didn't even leave my flat, did you?"

"How many rooms did you say?" he asked.

"Fifty, give or take a dozen," I said.

"Fifty!"

"You think this is an accomplishment? To have a big house?"

"Are you fucking *joking*? *Fifty?*"

"The guy, Van Pelt, doesn't even work. He doesn't do anything."

"Oh, I want to see it! I want to take pictures of it!"

"Fergus, it's just some family inheritance. The guy didn't even build it."

"I just want to experience your new life here, all of it," Fergus said. "Would you begrudge me that?"

I found one seat on the Tube train this morning and gave it to Fergus. I stood over him vigilantly. I feel like his mom sometimes. He held his bag tightly on his lap, like somebody's granny. (If I were the kind of person who gave one hot blistered damn about other people's opinions, I would have been embarrassed by him.) There was a scene at our stop in South Kensington when Fergus and I got separated. As I slid through the crowd out onto the platform, Fergus got sort of, well, trapped back in the train. I watched his hair in the train window, watched it bob wildly, moving like a live thing, a glowing red aura, amid all the strangers. I squeezed my way over to him and he screamed that I'd left him. His bag was hanging by one strap. We got out at the next station, waited for the train going in the opposite direction, and rode back to the original stop.

"How can you carry a bag when you're wearing a cape anyway?" I asked. I was hurrying him along the sidewalk, leading him by his elbow.

"We need to stop somewhere and buy safety pins. *Look* at this."

"*Fergus!* I'm late. We're late. What time is it?"

"Are you going to force me to carry it like this all the way there?" We were trotting briskly.

"Is your *Canterbury Tales* in there? Is that why it looks so heavy? Did you bring your camera?"

"I know you think that it's my fondest wish to make you late for your job, late for everything, but it simply isn't true," he said. He was lagging behind me a little. I could hear a rattle in his lungs. When we were growing up, his mom would drive him all the way up to Cleveland every Saturday to have his lung capacity tested. The big rumor in school was that Fergus had only one lung.

"Here. Let me carry it," I said.

"No, I wouldn't hear of it. I know how late I've made you. Wouldn't *dream* of it."

I tried to grab the bag, but he kept pulling it away from me. The strap hit a passerby, a woman in a trench coat. She massaged her arm and gave us a little look.

"Do you see that gate up there?"

Fergus said yes, he saw the gate.

"That's it," I said. "That's the house. Think we can make it in twenty seconds?" I was forty minutes late by this point.

"Oooh! It's like *The Sound of Music*. When Julie has a look at the house for the first time. There's a great history of governess film and literature. Jane Austen, the Brontës. It's a standard convention in women's art. What's the name again?"

"We need to run, Fergus." I had not seen Lowell at the house yesterday, nor had anyone mentioned him. I think there was indeed a possibility, a rather strong one, that he was avoiding me—for catching him in his mother fib.

"The people, what's the name?"

"Van Pelt. You're not moving fast enough."

In a way, though, I was relieved Lowell *hadn't* surfaced. Mom always says you should ask yourself the following question before making any big decision: Can any good come of this? So: Lowell. Can any good come of him? Danger follows a liar. There's nothing truer than that.

"Perfect. Van Pelt, von Trapp. You couldn't have written it. Is that German? Not a very English name."

"Bye. I'll see you at the front door. Just open the gate and come up," I said.

"No, no, no! Don't leave me, Jenny. Don't leave me!" he pleaded.

Fergus's uncoolness is one of the things I think is so great about him. In order to be cool, one must be an unexcitable flatliner. Fergus, on the other hand, exists in a permanent state of shaky excitability. And never has his uncoolness shone through more than it did when we walked through the Van Pelt door, through the torch-lit foyer, and into the great hall.

"Fergus," I said, "close your mouth."

In junior high, I called him "Mouthbreather." I thought it was a good nickname, until one night, during one of Fergus's and my marathon phone calls, Dad got on the downstairs phone and demanded that "Mouthbreather" stop immediately.

"Fergus, close your mouth. That's how the world works."

He turned and grabbed me. He spoke in a churchly hush. "This is the single most profound artistic experience of my entire life."

I hadn't been painting much in the last couple of days, so maybe I was feeling proprietary about profound artistic experiences.

Van Pelt took Fergus on a tour of the house.

"Your friend here seemed quite taken with the little home we've rigged up for ourselves," he said when he brought Fergus back to me in the nursery. "He took more pictures of our house than the chappie from *Harpers and Queen* did."

"It's stupendous," Fergus said. "I've been here before. I really feel as if I need to tell someone that: *I've been here before.*"

"Oh, and Jenny," Van Pelt said, "did I mention this to you yesterday? I think I may have forgotten: Lowell told me to tell you good-bye. He left the night before last."

Fergus is calling for me to get him a glass of water. He always does that when he wakes up in the middle of the night. My handwriting is getting really horrid, and Lowell's gone.

1 July

"I hate to bring this up, Fergus," I said, "but I think reincarnation goes along class lines."

We were at the pub around the corner from the apartment. Fergus was freaking out the entire table—Grunt, Scrumpy, and me—with a drunken speech involving how he'd starting reading about Hinduism recently, and that his long-standing, mutely held suspicion was now officially confirmed: He had been a medieval king in a past life. Fergus was scaring me. He was scaring everybody. I tried to steer the conversation in a less insane direction. And I was trying not to think about Lowell. I told him that reincarnation goes along class lines, so if you're a peasant in this life, you'll always be a peasant. Grunt and Scrumpy, being anarchists, seemed to enjoy my comment, and both raised their pints in my honor.

"But I'm *not* a peasant," Fergus said.

I don't know what Scrumpy puts in his hair to make it stick up in those three spikes. Could be egg. Could be glue. Not really sure.

"I am NOT a peasant!" Fergus said. "We're very . . . upper-middle-class."

I told him that land doesn't equal class, and that just because his family may own all of northeast Ohio, it doesn't mean he's an aristocrat. I nastily told him no one is more interested in maintaining the social hierarchy than God. I was in a bad mood tonight.

"Ah, now she's bringing the big boy into it," said Scrumpy. "Cheers."

"My family is richer than your family, and you *know* it, Jenny," Fergus said. He looked into his empty glass. He tilted it, then, coming to terms with the concept that there wasn't one drop of Kahlua left, set it upright. He'd had three cocktails, so maybe that explained something. I'd never seen him drunk before.

"You're evil to me," Fergus said. "Why are you being evil to me?" He flipped his collar up and wrapped his cape around himself.

"Don't worry Fergus," I said. "I'm sure you were a very respectable peasant in the sixteenth century. I mean, look where it got you today."

He hugged himself and dipped his head into his cape. Fergus has a lot of hair, but from the top view, through the orange cloud, a sad patch of scalp shone through. Fergus's head started to bob, and it was clear he was crying. Then he started weeping audibly. Grunt and Scrumpy shifted uncomfortably on the bench.

Fergus raised his head from his cape and said, "I was just trying to tell you something about myself."

Fergus wouldn't talk to me the rest of the night. I think he's fallen asleep now. I'm writing this on the door table in the kitchen. I was playing with the knob for a long time tonight, thinking, He's just like a doorknob; you can turn him to the right, or to the left, and he'll always go back to the center. I'm not really sure if that's true about Fergus, but I like how it sounds.

2 July

Today, Fergus left. Also, I ran into Lowell!

It started—or *I* started, I should say—chipperly enough. But how quickly the storm clouds of calamity do descend. My alarm clock went off, and I willed myself on my feet, just like the overachieving straight-*A* student I was when I wanted to be. And Fergus seemed to have forgotten, at least for the first twenty seconds he was awake, that he was mad at me.

"There shall be no dillydallying around in bed," I said, trying to tug the blanket away from him. He held it tightly. On top of the blanket were the Polaroids he'd taken of Van Pelt's house. Last night, he'd fallen asleep with them, like a mogul with his money. "Let's go get breakfast before I leave for work. I want bangers and mash. Yes siree, bangers and mash!"

Fergus turned away. "Don't get too close to me. I don't smell all that great." I yanked the blanket down and the pictures went flying. He was wearing my green velour underpants. I wondered aloud where he'd gotten them. He told me. I asked him why in the hell he was going through my suitcase. Then he said, "Jenny, you didn't even *open* my letter. You said you read it, but you didn't read it, Jenny."

I didn't say anything. I didn't tell him I'd lied, because it seemed like the kinder choice. This was my opportunity to apologize to him, but I didn't take it.

"You lied to me. You're a liar, Jenny," he screamed. *Incensed* approaches the tone, but there's not enough howl to it. I sat down next to him on the bed. He got up and said he wanted to go to breakfast. He shimmied into his boots and tossed his cape commandingly over his bare shoulders. I suggested maybe he should put on some real clothes or something underneath his cape.

"A *cape*, Jenny," he said, "*is* an article of clothing. Did you not know that? Let's go."

"Yes, Your Majesty," I said. "As your vassal, I—"

"I was just drunk last night, by the way," he said. "You should know not to pay attention to me."

Hard to believe, I know, but Fergus has been in London for only three days.

At the restaurant, Fergus opened the menu immediately. Mom has always told me it's quite rude, looking at the menu as soon as you sit down, but how was Fergus to know? He's not much of a gourmand. (Sour-cream–dunked Doritos was his idea of a luxe after-school snack.) I asked him what he was going to order.

Bangers and mash.

I told him he was copying me again. The harder Fergus works for my approval, the farther from him I want to run. Poor Fergus. Poor gormless little peacock.

He didn't look up.

"You really *do* look up to me," I said cruelly. "Bangers and mash, that's just the beginning. It's great to see what a role model I've become. Although your hair dye's faded and you haven't been wearing eyeliner this week. . . ."

"Think what you want to think. You will anyway," Fergus said. His eyes were still on the menu, and they were following his finger. Whenever Fergus reads with his finger, it kills me. Just temporarily, only for a second, but the finger really does slay me. I told him how sweet it was that I'm his hero; then he said my idea of our relationship and his idea of it are really quite different. He slapped the menu closed and pushed it off to the side. His eyes were red. He said, "Here's what I think: I think the person I am is *here,* and the person you think I am is over *here.*"

He sure didn't look eighteen suddenly. He looked about four hundred.

"The Fergus *you* think I am is here, sitting right here with you in this restaurant, but the real Fergus is over there, out on the pier, up on the Ferris wheel, up in the blimp, waving to you. Waving so you can see me."

The big theme (the only theme?) of our relationship has always been how I don't understand him. He may be right about that, but he doesn't understand *me,* either. He's never even thought to try. I asked him about the person he assumed *I* was.

"Oh, I know it might seem crazy, but we're talking about me for once, Jen. . . ."

"Hallo there, Jens, my dear!"

Blindfold me, put me in a room for a million years, and I daresay I'd still recognize the voice. In the mirror above Fergus's head was a reflection of Lowell. Lowell, in the reflection, looked exactly like Lowell. He was wearing black leather pants, rather tight in the crotchal area. I was so glad to see him.

"Mwa! Give us a kiss. I was walking by and saw the lovely back of your lovely head in the window. Decided to pop on in. How are you, gorgeous? And hallo there. I'm Lowell; *who* are you?" Lowell extended his hand to Fergus, who shook tentatively. With his free hand, Fergus pulled at his cape, trying to prevent any extravaganza of skin.

Fergus gave his name, first and last, and sort of folded himself down into the cape.

"You must think quite highly of yourself, Fergus Goodwyn," Lowell said. I didn't stand up because Fergus didn't stand up.

"Uh?" Fergus said (although it sounded more like *ugh*). He didn't seem four hundred anymore. He seemed more like four.

"Dining with the top girl in the whole of London!" Lowell said. "What do you think of *that*, Fergus?"

"I think it's fine," said Fergus.

"I enjoy saying that name. Rolls trippingly off the tongue: Fergus, Fergus, *Fergus*. I had a horse named Fergus, actually, when I was a boy."

"How neat!" I said.

" 'How neat'? Spectacular girl! Isn't she a spectacular girl, Ferrrrgus?"

"No! No, she's not!" Fergus said. "You're lying!" Fergus either loves you or he hates you. With Fergus, there are no shadows, no shades.

"Actually, I didn't really have a horse named Fergus, so I suppose I am lying. Ring me and we'll go out, yeah, Jens? We're all liars, Fergus: you, me, and Jens. One, two, three: all of us liars," said Lowell. "My horse's name, actually, was Reggie."

"Oh!" I said. "Mr. Van Pelt said you'd moved out."

"Had to, didn't I? Reggie questioned my integrity. Don't forget," Lowell said, making a sign-language phone with his gloved thumb and pinkie. "Ring me up, Jens. We'll talk about durable pigments, art's refuge. Say, how's the painting going?"

I told him Fergus over there had been a big distraction to me these last few days.

"Now, that's not what we want to hear, is it? Get back to work, you! Toodle loo, then! Lovely to meet you, *Ferrrrgus the Distracting*."

I watched Lowell's reflection swagger out of the restaurant. Fergus got to watch the actual Lowell. I didn't, of course, have Lowell's number.

Fergus was crying in his heavy chair. "Is everyone you know here as big a faker and a fraud as you are?" he asked. "I'm going back to Akron. Today."

I reached for his hand, but he pulled it away.

"You've made me feel even more alone than when I got here," he whispered.

I must be the worst friend anyone can have. And I really must be a very bad person.

I'm going to tell you a little bit now about what it's like to be depressed and on your own in your ancient-looking but seventies-built house in Akron, Ohio. Are you ready? I spend a lot of time on skin care. I spend hours looking at myself in the mirror, searching for some secret. I contemplate all the ways I've ever let Merit, Jenny, and Lowell down. One of my youthful fantasies was to be on equal terms with Jenny. But when that finally happened, after I wooed her and wooed her and she finally moved to my house, I threw all my attention onto Merit and Lowell. And I never supported Jenny's art. How did I disappoint Lowell? I was never enough of a person to satisfy him. And Merit? I never took her away with me. We could have started over, but we didn't. Now it's too late, for all of it.

I also enjoy flipping through terrible magazines (why is it the terribler the magazine, the more vaguely excremental its smell?), the ink leaving a ghostly backward impression on my overmoisturized leg, and I think, and even say aloud sometimes (to myself), God, Michael Douglas really *does* look like an old woman these days. I lie on my bed, staring darkly at the stark linenfold wall, but I don't really see it. I think about all the parties to which I've RSVP'd but to which I've never bothered showing up. Weddings, even, I've ignored, weddings of friends (so-called) of mine. Shouldn't I be taken into the parking lot and beaten with several baseball bats? But here's how I justify my pathologically no-show nature: Why, it's just little old *me;* they wouldn't even detect my absence anyway. I've had these thoughts as the functions were happening, while sitting on my bed, filing my toenails over a fifty-pound walnut wastebasket. Was it love that yielded the invite? Was it even fondness? No and no, I think not (although thanks for asking). Were the inviters perhaps social climbers? Ah, Sherlock, with your Sherlock hat and your Sherlock pipe and your extremely misguided pince-nez, how right you are, how very right.

You'd be both impressed and aghast were I to tell you the precise number of Fergus-hours I've consumed thinking about how I clearly possess this quality (What's the opposite of a quality? A defect?) that repels people. I wish someone would identify once and for all what exactly this quality/defect is, so I can take it with me to a psychiatrist, deal with it, and move on.

Here's an example of what I'm like: Whenever I have a good time talking to someone at a party, it will be months until that person hears from me again, if ever. (I haven't called Nostrils, by the way, and won't.)

I think about how I wish someone would acknowledge, finally, I am not someone who inspires great feeling in people.

I think about how tedious I am, even to myself.

A rather paltry life, that, you're saying to yourself. Sitting around moisturizing and fretting doesn't exactly constitute a rich, vivid existence. Well, just so you know, I do try and wedge into my busy day other electrifying activities. Here's one: I look at catalogs. No, correction: I *study* catalogs. I circle items I'm intrigued by, or mark with Post-it Notes the pages on which they're found, or else fold down the edges of these pages, order the items (could be a monkey-skull umbrella stand; could be anything, really, so long as it's unnecessary) either by phone or Internet, feel the afterbuzz (lasts for about ninety seconds), crash, go through a few low-blood-sugar hours, fall asleep (catalog in my lap), wake up (catalog stuck to my leg if I'm naked), walk around, eat something, make small talk with someone, make a Kahlua and skim, wonder where Lowell is, wait for the UPS man to show, hear the door knocker's bang, peek out of the peephole, wonder if it's a hired assassin posing as a UPS man—has he come to eliminate me or Lowell?—gather all the Fergus-resources at my disposal, make the sound that is commonly called "gulp" in certain kinds of books I used to read, open the door so awfully bravely (eyes shut tight, expecting the bullet, awaiting the bullet), sign the form, thank the man, holler to Andrei or whoever's around to go and fetch a dolly. Then, once the box is in my room, comes the whole loathsome process of finding a knife or pair of scissors, plunging the knife or scissors down into the tape like some miserable overdone Poe character feverishly plunging a dagger into a distasteful heart, peeling the tape away, then the trip to the bathroom to wash my hands of the ghastly stick, then dealing with the Styrofoam peanuts, then the bubble wrap and tape around the item itself, and then the big question: *What* do you do with the box?

It's all so exhausting.

So what's happened lately is that the boxes have become too much for me to deal with. They just accumulate there, unopened, in the foyer. Sometimes, when I'm in an expansive mood, I think about donating the boxes to an institution or halfway house or philanthropic-type organization, but then I forget.

Whenever I buy something new, I wonder, How will I get rid of it? Will I throw it away, or it will outlast me? Who will die first? Me or my Sportsblaster Pinball Gumball Machine?

From the time I was a little tiny boy, I wanted to live in a museum. I remember when my mother and I visited William McKinley's house and she whispered into my ear, her coffee/cigarette breath as good a sign as any that she'd already given up, "You can have a house like this someday, too." Achieve something great, buy a nice house: That sounded fair enough to me. That seemed very American. One of my big fantasies involved imagining bowing in front of a door in a grand house, saying (to no one), "What brings you to my palace?" My inspiration was a house in London, owned by (although I didn't know this at the time) one of Lowell's lovers. A lugubrious little noodle of a brain I've got, I'm afraid. Initially, I'd intended to do a faithful reproduction of the house, but my Polaroids of it didn't do me a lot of good. I'd taken eighteen pictures of Reginald Van Pelt's foyer, but not *one* of his knight's room. So I decided to make it up as I went along, as an artist would.

When I was a young person, I did get picked on, just so you know, by pimply-shouldered males, for whom high school was the zenith of everything ever. You want to know how I dealt with my life? By creating my own little fantasy. That's what you've got to do if you live in Akron, Ohio, and you really do consider yourself the dauphin.

Here's the problem, though, when you've achieved a sixty-five-room house: You need other people to share in the dream. That's where Lowell and Jenny and Merit came into the picture. If you have a big house, you need a family, don't you? I tried and tried, during the years Jenny lived in New York, to get her to move back to Akron and live with me. Finally, after she had a family of her own, she did come back to me.

One of my big concerns about Lowell and this house and ordering items from catalogs is this: What if all my effort is just misdirected energy? What if I never knew what to do with my life, and thus obsessed about skin care and catalog ordering and the house and Lowell *instead*? What if the house and Lowell and taking care of all the abject objects are my *job*? What kind of *woman* will I have become?

As for me, I always thought . . . I always thought I should be able to create something. Not a house, but something to look back on when I'm eighty, and say, This is me, this was me, and I made this. I used to think my house was my work of art, my photographic retrospective, my marathon, my opera, my magazine profile. But how wrong I was.

You might find it surprising that I live in Akron, Ohio.

Here's an interesting item. You'll discover there are only a few people on earth who could actually get away with wearing the sock brace. Most of these people are gay, English, and elderly. Does Lowell fit this description? Half check, no, and double check. The sock brace. Now, there's an invention for you, one that's meant to prevent the tragic exposed band of flesh between sock and pant which bespeaks middle management and heart attack and death at age forty-eight. To Lowell, such an aesthetic no-no is an unforgivable offense.

Obsessing about something is not the same thing as thinking about something. Oh my God, I'm so, so bored.

This morning, while sitting on my high canopied bed, picking at my toes, trying to think of something, although no thoughts other than the obvious ones would come, I came up with a new amusement.

I pretended I was a magazine journalist.

That was a new one for me.

I lay stomach-down on my bed and wrote a "piece" in the notebook I'm also reserving as my RSVP log. The whole setup (especially the journal propped up on my pillow) made me feel like an eighteen-year-old female diarist.

Keep in mind what follows is a rough draft, and I'm not even all that proud of it. But at least I had something to do this morning. Something to do and something to be—isn't that enough?

THE MAGAZINE PROFILE PRELUDE
By "Bradley W. Dormer"

This is a story about Fergus. Fergus: the most brilliant, fascinating, erudite, mysterious, talented, successful, generous, amusing, coordinated, thin, organized, beautiful, and perfectly proportioned human being who ever existed. Fergus: about whom it has been said, "The man's artistic genius surpasses even that of Goya." Fergus: Renaissance man. Fergus: medieval scholar. Fergus: Once you've heard one of his jokes, nothing else will ever be funny again. Fergus: Why can't he be naked all the time? Fergus: beloved by all. *Fergus.*

He is smarter than I am, smarter than you are, smarter than anyone you've ever met, and handsomer, and fitter, and richer. He's a quadruple threat, and, as such, would seem impossible to like. (How I hope to be proven wrong about that, though!) He is both unknown and unknowable, the dictionary definition of "a man of mystery," the last fascinator of our age. He has, unlike us, mastered the art of remaining hidden. Like every other American, I have my own suspicions about Fergus the man. Who is he really?

My editor never wanted to assign me the piece about Fergus. "*You* again?" she asked whenever I burst into her office.

I never even had to state the reason for my intrusion.

"Again," she said on my last attempt, "there's no *story* there." Her feet were propped unhygienically up on her desk, which I found distracting.

"No story?" I asked. "Oh, I'll get the story." A dead leaf was stuck to the sole of her shoe. I tried not to look. It was winter then.

My editor pushed backward in her auburn-toned leather chair, removed her feet from her desk. She stood. This, I had learned, was my signal to leave her office. It is good to understand the signals.

A profile of Fergus would be, I passionately believe, my masterpiece. For five years I've been trying to get this story. I've sent him flowers, balloons, liquor, a basket of stuffed animals, even a gorillagram. I've faxed his publicist regular biweekly letters stating my credentials (listing all my various prestigious magazine journalism awards and nominations), explaining my hook for the profile. The hook changed in each letter. Once, it was "Black-Tie Fashions with Fergus." When we were at war (when *aren't* we at war?), it was "Fergus on the Front Line." Do you know how many hooks that was in five years? Roughly five hundred. Do you know how hard it is to come up with five hundred hooks? I'd like to see you do it.

I've never received one response. It was coming down to this: My "career" was on the line. I had to, as we say in my business, "make this happen."

The best way to make someone like you is to pretend his obsessions are your obsessions. What, I asked myself, does Fergus love (other than us, of course)? Was the answer twofold? Indeed. Was the answer heart-stoppingly simple? Oh, it was.

He loved:

Art.

Himself.

Ah ha! I would fax Fergus a drawing of *himself*! Which *I* had drawn!

So what did I do? I enrolled in a six-week continuing-education course in elementary drawing! I really enjoyed learning about the basics of composition! And while I wasn't entirely lacking in the talent department, my teacher said (after the third class, when I confronted him out on the dark sidewalk) I was, if I didn't mind his saying so, "really bad at capturing life."

That gave me an idea.

Fergus is known to be the foremost medieval scholar in the world, is he not? Then why not draw a picture of something fabulously medieval, and unalive?

So, at my urging, my wife and I rented a car and drove to Lambertville, New Jersey, which is known to be the antiquing capital of the East Coast. A little store there (atmospherically called the King Charles Spaniel) sells what is perhaps the finest selection of medieval armor this side of Luxembourg, Italy, and Spain, and, of course, England.

Knowing my editor would not have been pleased had I sprung for one of the genuine suits of armor on the company's dime, I was forced to settle for a reproduction of a sixteenth-century English knight. I also purchased, with my corporate card, a stand and a sword.

At the store, they'd wanted to disassemble the armor and put it in a box, but I wouldn't let them. Fortunately for me, my wife, who played varsity lacrosse and hockey at Stanford and weighs a persuasive 165, had no trouble hoisting the two-hundred-pound suit of armor over her head and hauling it back to our charming bed-and-breakfast. I carried the stand and the sword.

The suit of armor turned out to be too tall to fit in the backseat of the rental car, so we were forced to perform an emergency decapitation. I held the helmet, and the screws, in my lap the whole way home. (Although there was no actual head inside, it was actually very heavy.) The red ostrich feather fluttered in the vent's heat. I tried not to look at the rearview mirror's reflection of the headless seated thing, but I couldn't help it.

At home, we moved the TV from the living room into the bedroom, then stationed the suit of armor right where the boob tube used to be. And for six weeks, I sat in what was formerly known as my "TV chair" and looked at the figure. I felt I got to know it pretty well. But you know what? The more I worked on my drawing, the worse it got. At the end of the sixth week, I asked my wife if she would be willing to help me out with some finishing touches. She uncapped a pen and said she saluted my ability to make even an inanimate object look even less lifelike than it already was.

Her revised drawing of the suit of armor looked so much better! I decided it was time to give it a life in the world.

I nestled the drawing into the side pocket of my calfskin briefcase and sauntered back to the office for the first time in six weeks. This was it, I told my assistant. I was ready.

"Do it," I said. "Fax it to Fergus's publicist."

For three weeks, no response. During that time, I slunk about in my magazine's editorial offices, thinking, Well, maybe I really *should* kiss the Fergus article good-bye; maybe I *should* root around on the Internet for some other story ideas. But wait. Ideas? I thought. What were ideas?

But we never know what jolly fate has in store for us, do we?

Because just yesterday afternoon, my assistant called me at home (I'm taking Thursdays off now), informing me I'd gotten a fax!

"Hold on a minute," I instructed my assistant, a recent Vassar grad.

I banged the handset down on the nightstand, leapt out of bed, slid into my fuzzy slippers, and knocked on the old noggin to make sure I wasn't still dreaming. I wasn't. I blew my nose. I did some other things. I manhandled the handset and told my assistant to deliver it to me straight-up. A Listerine breath strip was adhered to my tongue now.

"Who's doing what now?" I asked.

She again said I'd gotten a fax.

"Yesssss," I said. "Go on." I don't receive much in the way of faxes these days (or mail). My interest was piqued.

She said I'd gotten a faxed sketch of a suit of armor.

I swallowed what was left of my breath strip. "Is it *my* drawing?" I asked, mouthwash-fresh, yes, yet fearing the worst. "Did Fergus fax my drawing back to me? Is there an insult, like maybe 'You *wish*,' scribbled over it?"

My ever-capable and efficient assistant reassured me it was another suit of armor, drawn by someone else, and contained no me-directed insults as far as she could see. At the bottom of the sketch was a line of text, she said, handwritten. It read, "Nothing inside, is there, Brad?"

"Oh my!" I cried. "It's from Fergus! It's a communiqué!"

I didn't ask for any more details about the fax, deciding instead to put in a personal appearance in the office that very afternoon and see the blasted thing with my own two eyeballs. "I'm coming in!" I hollered, then told my assistant to call me a car. I couldn't change out of my dressing gown fast enough. Did I feel good? You bet I did.

In my Town Car, en route to the office, I thought about Fergus. I thought about Fergus, and nothing else.

Now here's a question for you: For any other person, wouldn't being ranked number one in the American Art Institute's list of the most important artists of the twentieth century be enough? Well, not for Fergus. No, nothing has ever seemed to satisfy this unsatisfiable Renaissance man. He lives in a midwestern town by the name of Akron, Ohio. "Akron, Ohio-born, -bred, and -educated," he once declared proudly, back when he still did interviews. His mysterious house is called On Ne Peut Pas Vivre Seul. It's on the coast of Akron, and has been rumored to have over a hundred rooms.

The Internet yields no photographs of the house.

The man's personal life? While it's famously off-limits, we do know the names of the main dramatis personae. Merit Haven Ash, Jenny Meatyard Haven, and someone called, I think, Lowell Haven. But have we ever seen them, Merit, Jenny, and Lowell? We have not. So the question remains: Are they real? Do they exist? Or did Fergus make them up?

It is true Fergus's parents are dead.

I sashayed into the elevator bank of my office building. My calfskin briefcase was with me, ready to collect its Fergus-faxed fax. I made some small talk with the lobby attendant, but I wasn't really paying attention. What was I thinking about? You guessed it.

As I was attempting, with my excitable hand, to unlock my office door, my assistant materialized from her dank cubbyhole. She indicated she had put the fax in my in-box (I'd given her, probably unwisely, a key to my office) and said something about how the whole fax situation was a little too "Dungeons and Dragons–dweeby" for her taste.

"Plus, how do you know it's from Fergus?" she asked. "It wasn't like it was signed or anything." What I recognized to be a red wine stain was crusted on my assistant's chapped bottom lip.

"Hey," I said, "do you have any alcohol at your desk I can have?"

A mug of mediocre merlot in my small trembling hand, I sat back in my chair and examined the fax. The artful, flowing script at the bottom of the page did indeed say, "Nothing inside, is there, Brad?"

Oh my! Fergus had written my name!

But what, exactly, was he trying to communicate?

And how deftly done the suit of armor was! And the virtuosically drawn Richard the Lionheart breastplate, well, *well*! The sad fact, though, was that Fergus's creation made my drawing look like the work of the class's laughingstock. Fergus's man's pole arm was, unlike mine, positioned at the charge. *Movement,* I thought; I wished I'd thought of that. My man, with the sword situated, as it was, between his legs à la Chaplin's walking stick, and the fringed miniskirt around the private region (my wife added the skirt at the last minute, assuring me it was both period-correct and necessary), wasn't really coming across as so fearsome a warrior as I'd recently believed.

In Fergus's drawing, the helmet had no visor (we medievalists call this an "open helm"). Despite the brilliance of the sketch, it was impossible to tell what was within the helmet. (I blamed our fax machine.) The area inside the helmet was black, yes, but what was the blackness? Was it nothing? Was it a bowling ball? I didn't know. The more I looked at it, the more confused I got. After a few more mugs of merlot, the head looked as if it belonged on the Grim Reaper.

That was it. I got up and whacked my skull against the wall, which is what I do when I know I need to knock the old brain back into its slot.

I found a piece of eight-by-eleven paper, and composed my response:

Dear Fergus,

   Thanks SO MUCH for the fax. So does this mean I get the story?

   Talk soon!

All best, as ever,
Bradley W. Dormer
Contributing Writer

The office had pretty much cleared out by the time I finally opened my door. I decided I'd be a sneaky little one and fax my letter to the 330 area code listed on the header of the fax, rather than to his publicist. The 330 area code was, I knew, Fergus's; 212 was his publicist's. That the man might have faxed his drawing to me himself, from his home, without any publicist's assistance, was almost too much to take.

I entered that number, which heretofore had been such a mystery to me, and hit send, and there was a connection; our machines communicated, Fergus's and mine.

I knew I'd make myself bonkers, squatting there by the fax machine, awaiting Fergus's response, so I called my assistant at her apartment (her roommate answered, and I didn't care for that) and told her to call me a car to take me home.

At home, I needed something to distract me. I'd brought back the fax's receipt-report, and I studied that for some time. It confirmed the document had indeed been sent. I ate some cashews. I studied the receipt-report again. Then I went into the living room and played with my suit of armor. I raised the visor and disassembled the whole thing. I put each body part on, piece by piece. It was only half a man, really, because his back was open, but this was okay with me, because his leather straps held you in.

The armor was uncomfortable (chain mail would have helped), but in it I felt powerful. I pulled the visor down and clomped around the living room. Had I remembered any of my medieval sayings, I would have said them. I imagined how I looked. With a shield, I thought, the picture would have been complete.

"Oh my God, Brad," a voice behind me said.

I swung around. It was my wife! She was holding something, something not small. I raised the visor. The thing she was holding was a five-gallon jug of Poland Spring water.

I bowed. "Hello, fair maiden," I said.

"God, Brad. What are you doing?"

"Hey! I almost got the story today," I said.

She lifted the water bottle over her head and marched in her Pretorian way out of the living room.

"Hey! I am going to get this story!" I shouted. "That's a fact!"

Despite its obvious demographic restrictions, it was the "piece" that should have been written about me long ago. And *piece* really is the perfect word choice; writing it felt like an amputation. (How can these magazine people *look* at themselves in the mirror each morning?) Composing it took less time than you'd think. It was only 11:00 a.m., but already I needed a drink. Mostly, however, I needed a bath. The contagion had to be washed away. I changed into my bathing suit and went for a vigorous soak in the whirlpool.

Earplugs, nose plugs, goggles, cap, Swim Ear are kept in a special locked drawer by my bed. (This drawer also contains: credit-card slips, packs of gum, a star-shaped gift tag, a Christmas card from 1995, which says, "Happy X-Mas, love you much, love Ole Lowell," some barrettes that aren't mine, in which strands of hair that aren't mine are ensnared, Seamus Heaney's extremely outstanding translation of *Beowulf,* a *Roget's Thesaurus,* several used Kleenex balls, some pictures of my childhood dog, a picture of my parents in front of a Christmas tree, circa 1956. When I had a diary, this is where I kept it. I wasn't the best at diary writing, being the kind of diarist who wrote exclusively about what he ate that day, who said what to him, and what he said back. No, I was never an obsessive diarist, not like Jenny. While (like Jenny) it's true I don't have anyone else to talk to, I don't (unlike Jenny) take an active interest in my life. One must be interested in oneself if one is to be a diarist.

This particular drawer does not contain sex toys, or K-Y Jelly, pornographic materials, or anything else along those lines.

("Ole Lowell" makes me think to myself, Olé, Lowell! Although it is difficult for me to picture Lowell in any kind of scenario in which a sombrero, blindfold, and piñata are involved.)

I tore off my clothes, stepped into my bathing suit, slipped into my sandals, gathered up all my pool supplies, and toodled on off to the pool, hoping no one would see me.

No one did.

Please note that when I travel, I always take along my inhaler, a box of raisins, and a little travel pack of Kleenex, and possibly several moist disposable towelettes.

Someday, maybe I'll draw a map of the manor house for you. Just know that the rec rooms are downstairs. They're the fun rooms, and the less popular of the fun rooms are where we hide Lowell's more recent work, his self-portraits having become increasingly . . . *pessimistic* as the years went on. We—or the "I" of we—thought it best to get the newer stuff out of the way. Gone are the monumental canvases from Lowell's earlier periods. In the air-hockey room hangs a triptych of Lowell's oils of himself falling down on three different suburban sidewalks. He didn't, for my photographs of this series, use a stunt double. These are the first of the paintings whose subject isn't *conspicuously* Lowell; the tumbling figure's face isn't visible, and the brush strokes are getting broader, more anxious, the color a maudlin, drippy yellowish gray. In the bowling alley no one uses (it only has two lanes; also, the balls notoriously smell) is a painting of a brown-skinned Lowell alone in a stark room, sitting on a Windsor chair in front of an open window, backlit by a gaudy red sky. The pinball room contains a series of monochromatically schemed paintings of an indistinct figure wearing a blunt-cut black wig. Even bewigged, Lowell is overwhelmed by the background's ugly flat brown.

In the whirlpool room is the frightful painting of someone who may or may not be Lowell (although—trust me—it is) being tortured by labial flowers. The pitiless work is well protected behind glass and sits directly across from my favorite whirlpool jet.

Before entering the whirlpool, I cranked the heat up to 105. I held on to the stair railing and descended, edging into the water and planting myself in my place. This is one of the paintings I cannot, *cannot,* tolerate. There are no radiant Lowell visions in this, one of Lowell's last paintings. It's all menace and malice, and I detest its lurid comic-book style: a close-up of Lowell's scribbly and indistinct head, the neckless head, open-mouthed in pain, being beaten with twelve creamy lilylike flowers. Each flower is held by a detached female hand. In each of the corners of the painting is a tiny photograph (which *I* took) of Jenny. I remember Lowell saying, after he finished this cycle, that he couldn't do it anymore. He said he'd ceased to understand his life. He said that the design he'd once had for himself had disappeared. "Jenny has taken my dignity from me," he cried, then buried his face in his hands and vanished into his studio for, as I recall, days.

Jenny always thought she was his inspiration, but she was wrong. At the party, we'll finally find out the truth.

Here is where I was, in terms of thoughts, when the door to the whirlpool room opened, bringing in a cold wind and the smell of chili-dog mixture. I've never understood why Lowell chose to juxtapose these pictures of Jenny's hideously grinning face to his own image.

After Lowell retired, there was nothing left for me to take pictures of.

"Oh, wow. Hot!" said a female voice.

Panic pang! There was, as far as I knew, only one female staying with us at present.

I decided to be a man about it. I turned around.

Our honored guest dropped one of my excellent bath towels down on the tile floor. As you might guess, I examined her closely. (Now is probably the time for me to state that I often tend to side with the womenfolk, in a way, always hating myself when I find I'm evaluating a woman's prettiness quotient. But at least I know I do it when I realize I'm in a really bad mental state.)

So let me just say this: She didn't really look like an Eastern European hooker, not all that much.

She was in the water now. "Feels nice," she said.

"We aim to please," I replied.

She smiled, a smile so sincere-seeming that I could not but be at least a bit interested. She removed a chunky silver ring from her right ring finger and laid it on the whirlpool's side. *Hot tub* sounds to me like chlamydia, like something from Aspen.

She splashed into the whirlpool, rolled her blond hair up in a sloppy bun construction, and leaned back, water gurgling onto her neck. I've never understood how they do that, women and their hair tricks.

"Ahhhhh," she said. She closed her eyes for a couple seconds, feeling what she felt. "I heard someone say something about you that I thought was very interesting."

"Oh?" I said. *I* got it; she was trying to "connect." You find that it's hard to hate anyone completely if they at least *try* with you, and talk about *you* with you, no matter how insincere the effort.

"I heard someone say when I was lying out in the sun, 'He's never met a mirror he doesn't like.' "

"Mmmm," I said.

"I thought you'd be interested in that. 'He's never met a mirror he doesn't like.' "

"Mmmm."

I inquired of this person what exactly her point was for telling me this.

"There was no point, really. I just take it upon myself to tell people all the things other people say about them."

"How extremely fantastic of you," I said.

"Have you noticed that it's hard to talk to someone you don't know unless you have something negative to say?"

"You seem smashed," I said. "Are you?"

"Oh, totally. I've been drinking since I got up. Didn't you hear the blender?"

The sound of the blender whirring indicated, I said, nothing more in this house than the making of fruit smoothies, or perhaps a protein shake.

"Not me. Piña coladas at nine a.m.: *parteee!* Woo hoo!" She did a little "I love fun" arm-waving maneuver, which I have also seen from the sunroofs of rented stretch limos on West Market Street on prom night.

She wore a robin's egg blue bikini, with brown piping. A vaguely French color combination. Not too bad, that.

"You didn't even tell me who said that about me and the mirrors," I said. I couldn't tell if she was trying to bury me or praise me.

"Don't know. Some guy with no chest hair who had a body like he had a personal trainer with him at all times."

"That narrows it down."

"You've got little clots of Kleenex all over your lip area, Fergus."

"In that case," I said, "pardon me for a moment." I grabbed my nose plugs from the side, inserted, took a big old Mouthbreather breath, and dunked myself under the water.

Back when I went to a therapist, she said something about how I didn't really deal all that well with hardship, how I tended to just sort of shut down all systems, to roll up into a ball like one of those pill bugs, a turtle in its shell, an ostrich burying its head in the sand—select an animal-behavior metaphor at random, pull down the lever, and enjoy. Underwater, I held my breath, counted to ten. I got some good thinking done that way.

I popped back up, removing my nose plugs in one elegant motion. "Why, hel*lo* there," I said.

"Hel*lo*," she said.

"How are *you*?" I asked.

"Oh, I'm having a marvelous time. And the party you're planning for me? How can I thank you?"

"You can't."

"You and Lowell are being so amazing about inviting me into your house, and letting me stay here while I get things sorted out. Life, *Karl. You* know."

"And did Lowell perhaps tell you who owns this house, that it's not his, but, rather, mine, and that the piña colada you inhaled this morning and the whirlpool in which you're presently marinating are, in actual fact, not his, but, rather, mine?"

"No, didn't know that. . . . But I'm not really into possessions."

"Mmmmm," I said.

"Maybe it's the industrial midwesterner in me—I guess Pittsburgh is the Midwest, maybe not technically, but definitely spiritually—but I'm more into accomplishment for its own sake."

"How 'up by one's bootstraps' of you."

"I mean, I don't know if you know this, but Lowell dragged me back from Pittsburgh when I met him a few weeks ago. I was doing one of my projects at a gallery. Maybe you heard about it? It was quite the thing."

"Lowell and I communicate less than you seem to think, but thank you," I said.

"I sat naked for four days in a tub filled with champagne and raw meat."

"That must have stung."

"Only on the first day."

"Must have been quite the pungent stew, at any rate."

"Only on the last day. Lowell came when it started, and he kept coming back every day. I didn't know who he was, and I couldn't talk to anyone when I was in the tub. When the thing ended, he came up to me and introduced himself. I'd never met a real English lord before! He said complimentary things about 'the extremity of the vision,' although he disagreed with the 'automatism'—I think that's the word he used—part of the project."

I assumed she was using the incorrect term, although I knew what she meant. "I'll bet," I said. Spontaneity is a big Lowell no-no. "Did the concoction look as menstrual as I'm imagining?"

"Probably more so. That was the whole point, one of them."

I wasn't really listening: Always keep in mind that the more charming the man, the more likely he is a metal rod up your Frida Kahlo.

"Can I ask you a question? He's pretty conservative, isn't he, as an artist?"

"Lowell? He used to be, yes, absurdly entrenched in what we like to call the 'figurative tradition.' "

"I don't really know much about his stuff," she said. "What I do know is that we don't really seem to have that much in common. As artists. You know what I'm saying? Plus: *paintings*? Who needs them?"

"As long as there are canvases and paint," I said, "there will always, I'm afraid, be painters. Anyway, Lowell is no longer an 'artist.' So you don't have to worry about *that*." I decided against telling her about a certain pesky journalist (name: Bradley W. Dormer) who's been obsessed, these five long years since Lowell's retirement, with getting the scoop about Lowell's vanished career.

"I keep asking him about his paintings, and all he'll say is, 'I will not explain my work to you or anyone else.' "

"Lowell isn't very nice. Have you not understood that yet?"

"Hmmm," she said. "So did Lowell like always swing both ways, or what?"

My little hand shook upon the bubbly water.

"Am I being rude? I can never tell when I'm being rude," she said.

"Listen. You'll like Lowell better when I tell you what I'm about to tell you."

And here I explained to my new friend Drisana-Nari that everybody thought Lowell was a truly terrible artist until around the time he got out of high school. "Lowell's late-bloomer status lends him a bit of the human touch, don't you think?" I asked her. "Every art teacher who'd ever taught him had tried—and, finally, failed—to discourage him from pursuing his vague dream to be a painter. Other people's conviction about his early talentlessness cannot, *cannot*, be overstated."

"No *way*," Drisana-Nari said.

"The technical dynamism you see is purely self-taught. His mother once told him, 'You can do everything, except for the one thing you really want to do.' Lowell said that statement made him so sad, and then so annoyed, and then so incensed, he decided he'd make himself not merely better, not merely good, but really, sincerely *great*. While he may not have started out with much talent, or many advantages, Lowell did possess a lot of will. And *will*, if you're Lowell, is the only thing that matters."

"Interesting."

"*In*teresting *and* true," I said, and it was true so far, although I was planning to plant a red herring or two for her to sort out later. "Throughout Lowell's childhood and adolescence, his mother had this . . . *thermos*— a miserable battleship gray—with a handle. Lowell's mother took the thermos with her everywhere she went."

"They have thermoses in England? Hey, my mom has a special cup, too."

"In my own mother's case, it wasn't a thermos, but a maize-colored plastic tumbler the dishwasher had somewhere along the line half-melted into a right triangle; Mother liked to drink out of the right angle."

"Hah!"

"We have a pretty good idea what was inside the thermos, although Lowell has claimed he cannot begin to guess. He looked inside the thermos once and only once. Lowell's mother kept it in a desk drawer at work and snuck outside with it."

"What was her job?"

"Don't interrupt," I said. "She was a teacher of high school Spanish. In the parking lot, she'd stand shivering in her short skirt, sipping liquid from the thermos lid, then bolt back inside and begin each of her classes with the greeting: '¡Hola, víctimas!' At the beginning, she was a good teacher, Lowell said, but she got into the very regrettable habit of threatening to paddle her students. Lowell even said something about her having some kind of paddle with holes. It hung nastily on the wall of her classroom. I imagine its being an unctuous Pepto-Bismol pink, although I may just be making that up."

"Do they paddle kids in England?"

"No. They don't. She never, never spanked Lowell, nor ever once threatened to. When Lowell was about the height of the kitchen countertop, she taught him how to prepare her Manhattans the way she liked them—in a martini glass: two parts vermouth and two parts bourbon, with two cherries. Lowell made this for her every day when she came home. They would share the Manhattan-marinated cherries, each eating one of them; then she would disappear with the Manhattan and the thermos into the teeny half bathroom downstairs and weep, for what seemed like hours, behind the thin plywood door. Lowell could hear every snuffle and gasp. Still to this day, I should add, you know Lowell *likes you* when he asks you to 'share his cherry.' His mother would emerge from the bathroom, carrying her empty red thermos cap—it looked like an organ-grinder's monkey's hat, he said—in one hand and the thermos by the handle in the other. She would throw away each Manhattan glass in the bathroom wastebasket. Every Saturday, she would buy a new set of martini glasses at May Company. Nightly, Lowell would ask her what was wrong. 'Is there anything I can do?' he'd say. She'd set thermos and the cap on the table and pat his black-haired head and sniffle and rub her nose and say how funny it was, how very funny, actually, to think that he was hers and that she'd made him. He remembers her calling him that: 'hers.' He was too gorgeous and perfect to be human, but she knew for a fact that human was what he was. 'I was there at the time,' she'd say. Then she'd run tap water into the thermos or maybe pour some orange juice into it. Lowell never once saw her *wash* the thermos."

"Hey, I've shared Lowell's cherry before."

"I *know*. As a child, Lowell would suggest to his friends that they play at their houses instead of his."

"I feel very uncomfortable about knowing all this. I feel like it's a betrayal of sorts."

"I should add by the way, Drisana-Nari, that Lowell's house was, and is, a fine middle-class house. I still ask to be driven by it whenever I decide it's a night built for punishment. His mother bought it herself, on her own; there was no *man* involved. It was her own goddamned house, which she paid for with her *own* goddamned money."

"Wait. Where is he from again?"

"But the house was a humiliation to Lowell, and so was she. Then add the thermos. He kept trying to throw the thermos away, but she'd always mutely dig it out of the kitchen trash can. And still she wouldn't wash it. When asked, Lowell would tell everybody in town, including parents and teachers, that he lived in the imposing gray colonial two streets down from his actual house. The colonial was, in fact, owned by a retired urologist, a widower by the name of Kunkle, who spent the entire ten-month northeast Ohio winter in Hilton Head."

"But Lowell told me he was from London, with, quote, 'childhood stopovers in Paris.' "

"From where do your people hail, Drisana-Nari?"

"Pittsburgh."

"Oh, great."

"I told you that before, Fergus. You're not listening to me, are you?"

"Have a little more faith in me, girl. Anyway: When the mother or father who was driving Lowell 'home' would ask why all the lights were off, why his big house looked so lonely, he'd say that his mother was performing in Paris. He was fine with being alone, he'd say; in fact, he rather liked it. He began telling everyone his mother was a 'musical comedy girl.' She bought him stuffed animals and novelty stickers instead of normal 'boy' toys."

"When I was a kid, I liked boy toys, too. I had trucks and cars and a little airplane and an airport and a Hot Wheels racetrack."

"I could tell this about you from the first. When Lowell was about eight, he once, experimentally, asked a kid for his toy truck. The kid gave it to him. Then Lowell started asking other kids, then others, for their toys, too. He would always get them, he quickly learned. His mother never asked him where his new trucks and soldiers came from."

"Why are you telling me all this, Fergus?"

"When he was ten, he told everyone he was filming a TV commercial in California. He stayed at home for a week, browning under his mother's sun lamp, and trying to teach himself how to be an artist by studying a book called *Now You Can Draw, Too!* He returned to school tanner than anyone in northeast Ohio knew possible, proud of himself for having that week filled a whole pad of paper with terrible—although *he* didn't say 'terrible'—sketches of his own beautiful face. When Lowell was about fourteen, his mother would sit on the toilet—lid closed—when he took a shower. The *thermos* would be there, on her lap. At fifteen, he moved into the attic. He'd come home sometimes and find her up there, lying on the red beanbag chair, a half-drained red thermos cap in her hand, sighing, saying that she thought he'd *never* come home. Sometimes he'd wake up, to find her next to him in his twin bed."

"This is totally breaking my heart. I bet he told a lot of people he was adopted."

"Wouldn't *you*?" I asked.

"I did," she said. "I do, still."

"Well, who doesn't? As a child, Lowell never understood why his birth certificate stated his birthplace as Erie, Pennsylvania. Later, he figured out that a nineteen-year-old girl who'd been knocked up in late-fifties-era northeast Ohio had to . . . well, best just to leave the area for a while."

"Oh my God. He told me that he was from London. He told me that he learned to drive race cars in Monte Carlo and that Peter O'Toole taught him how to drink at the Groucho Club when he was fifteen and that he lost his virginity to Maria Call—"

"Lowell entered a self-portrait in a high school art contest. His art teacher that year didn't really encourage it, but neither did she beg him not to. He received an honorable mention ribbon. He told me he was disappointed, but only for about two seconds, then moved on, determined to improve his standing next time. He got an honorable mention bow the next art contest on another self-portrait, and another honorable mention after that, the last contest, the one during which he finally opened the thermos."

"He's such a fucking piece of shit," she said.

"But, you see, none of what he told you matters. The one truth about Lowell is that he's a great painter. To continue: She took the thermos with her to this senior-year art show. In his high school gym, Lowell's mother drank from the red monkey cap and examined his first oil painting ever, a self-portrait. She shook her head at Lowell and said, 'That looks *nothing* like you. *Ooooh,* what I could do with that *face.*' She gently squeezed his testicles in the way mothers occasionally do. Mine was guilty of this, too, Drisana-Nari. She stumbled a bit, and some of her beverage from her thermos cup sloshed onto Lowell's first-ever oil self-portrait, and Lowell, although he knew enough to realize even a mystery cocktail couldn't harm a dry oil painting, snatched the red cup away from her, and the thermos, too, and strode with them into the boy's locker room, twisted open the pressurized thermos lid, and dumped the liquid into the sink. The plastic liner inside the thermos, which Lowell examined for the first time, was threaded with an intricate and very ancient system of hairline cracks. The drink, which was, of course, a Manhattan, spiraled down the sink. Little gray flakes of some kind of material clung to the white basin. Lowell shook the thermos. About a million gray flakes swirled around inside."

"I'm picturing a very toxic snow globe."

"Lowell said she never recovered emotionally after he threw the thermos away. It had been slowly poisoning her for years, he learned from their doctor at the Cleveland Clinic, but the old girl didn't seem to understand this information, or have much of an opinion about it, at that point. Before Lowell went off to London, he drove his mother to her sister's house in Kentucky."

"*Shit,* man."

"And he left her there."

"Have you ever met her?

"Not once," I said, lying again.

My eyes stung and water seeped from my ear holes. Drisana-Nari appeared to be sweating.

"Weird," she said. Our feet were inadvertently touching, Drisana-Nari's and mine. I was too paralyzed by this thought to move.

"Sad, isn't it?" I asked.

"I don't know what else to say," she said. Her arm reached around and undid her bikini top. The bikini's top half bobbed around in the bubbly maelstrom. Her foot moved away from me. Her breasts were not able to be seen. "Hey: *Lowell, Fergus*. Have you ever noticed that all last names are masculine? That all last names can be a boy's first name, when you think about it? You could be James Fergus or David Lowell. Or Fergus James or Lowell David."

"Touché," I said.

"I'm very interested in gender issues."

"Fantastic," I said. The blue bikini top bubbled toward me. I subtly shooed it away.

"That painting's . . . *interesting*," Drisana-Nari said, her monstrously blue eyes searching *Lowellbeat IV*. "Much more interesting than the ones upstairs, don't you think? I'm not so into the ones up there, where he's dressed up in costumes. I think they're kind of lame, but now I feel bad about saying that, because I know his biography."

I found it impossible to hate this person anymore. I regretted lying to her, to the extent to which I'd lied. I maneuvered away from the breast-holder bikini thing. "Just consider all of Lowell's work one big glutton-ous personal statement, and you'll be fine. *I* took all the photographs, you know. He based all his art on *my* work."

She sat up, and there were her breasts. Why, hello there. And no, I'm not going to evaluate them for you.

"Who's that, the woman in the little pictures in the painting?"

"That's Jenny," I said. "And I can't wait to see the look on Lowell's face when she comes here, to your party. Lowell loves surprises, especially those having to do with Jenny."

"Oh my God," Drisana-Nari said. "Why are you moving your feet like that?"

9

3 *July*

Living alone in London at the age of eighteen requires a certain level of adultlike self-scrutiny, which I'm not sure I'm ready for yet. So I won't write about myself, not tonight. Rain and swerving motorcycles and swans floating through the rain in a pond at Hampstead Heath. The rain seems older here than it does at home; the swans swimming through the rain seem older. Have I ever seen a swan before? I don't remember. I asked to leave work a little early today. I changed into a dress and took myself out for high tea at an old hotel and luxuriated and eavesdropped on fabulous old ladies chitchatting and watched other fabulous old ladies reading their elegantly tattered Jean Rhys paperbacks. Nothing seems understimulating, not even old ladies taking tea, so long as you're paying attention. The very thought of clotted cream now makes me go goose pimply! Perhaps I shall die a Londoner. I'm sure I've never seen a swan before; where would I have seen one?

4 July

Here are some of the choicer things that were said to me today at the museum:

"What are you doing hogging up the view, luv?"

"Miss, will you please be on your way, then?"

"Are you *blind?*"

"There are other people waiting to take a look."

"You're making my supervisor terribly suspicious."

"Don't you have a home? Don't you have something else to do?"

"Will you please get out of the way, so that my wife can have a look?"

"Oh, *you* again?"

"You're a very selfish little girl."

"It *is* an impressive piece. I wholeheartedly agree."

"Pardon me. So sorry. There's not much room here, is there?"

"Young lady, you *must* stand back! You're *far* too close!"

"My supervisor asked me to come over and have another word with you."

"When I was young, I used to love something that way, too."

Why can't they see that all I'm doing is trying to memorize every inch of *The Straw Manikin* so *then* I can transcribe it? And you know what else is sad? Everybody here seems much more interested in Gilbert and George than in Goya. They're very sinister fellows, I think. They've absolutely got to be.

Is it possible to capture life and put it in a painting?

5 July

I was taking my daily 2:00 p.m. "constitutional" in Kensington Square Park, with Nikki in her perambulator (the English have a lovely word for everything!), and guess who was sitting on a wooden bench there? Lowell (in a lavender suit) spied me before I spied him. He was already waving. With a hug for me and a forehead kiss for Nikki, he said, "I have a confession for you, Jens, and only you." And so, sitting on the park bench for an hour, while Nikki slept, he talked.

Lowell had misrepresented himself to me in certain ways and had been despairing since then. He'd been so unhappy in the last year that he'd come to need the oblivion of losing himself in something else. Ten months ago, he ran away from a person, and a place. Since then, he'd been bouncing from one "horrid situation" to the next. Last year, he was living in Paris in a shared-bathroom flat over a falafel shop in the Marais. He'd come to Paris to study printmaking with David Hockney. ("But my taste in art has matured, don't you agree?" he asked. Odd. A question that implied I already knew him.) Lowell would never be a painter, he understood, but he thought he could be draftsman, and Hockney was an inarguably brilliant one. So Lowell followed Hockney. He knew where Hockney's studio was; he knew what time he arrived, and what time he left. He knew which café he frequented for breakfast. And when Hockney was sitting outside his café one morning last autumn, Lowell approached, an elegant periwinkle scarf flung "round" his neck and portfolio in hand. He introduced himself. He called himself a "tremendous fan." Hockney smiled and invited Lowell to sit with him. Lowell ordered an almond croissant—in English. Rarely in Lowell's life had he been at a loss for words, but he was wordless then. They sat in silence under the colorless Parisian sky, watching the French women, who seem to allow themselves so many more moods than American women, and who were alluring even to them, click past. As Lowell was cutting a slice from his croissant, the knife slipped from his hand and clattered onto the pavement. Hockney pretended not to notice, pushed back his glasses, and took a sip of his superb espresso. Lowell asked him if he could possibly presume to bother him and would he mind looking at his portfolio. "Yes, yes," Hockney said. "I knew this time would come." He flipped each page in the bored and automatic way of someone who'd seen Lowell's self-portraits a million times already, closed the portfolio after about ten seconds, pushed it back to Lowell, and said it "wasn't his cup of tea."

Lowell said he doesn't think he'll ever be able to look into the face of a blond man with brazen eyeglasses ever again.

Depressed, discouraged, Lowell went out drinking alone that night. He was loaded on Pernod by the time he met a British man called Lytton. At a dive bar in Montmartre, Lytton, who was in his sixties, and who was dressed completely in white, propositioned him. Lytton and Lowell spent the next two weeks in Lytton's villa in Portugal.

Lytton was a rich but "essentially artless" man, although he did teach Lowell that white is the only elegant color for a room. (This is why children and animals cannot be permitted in the civilized home, Lytton told him.) Lowell went with him to London, but that lasted only a few days. Lytton told Lowell he was the most beautiful thing he'd ever seen, but he said that there was something about Lowell that made him want to treat Lowell vilely.

Lowell lived with five other men during the next six months. One of the men, some almost royal something or other, told Lowell he'd do anything Lowell told him to. He said he'd find a cliff and use it, *cheerfully*, if that's what Lowell wanted. He said he'd buy him an island. He also said, "I hate you for what I love you for." Lowell and Van Pelt met five weeks ago at a Tate fund-raiser. Van Pelt was obtuse, and an alcoholic, and told Lowell he loved him after he'd known him for only seven hours, then chuckled to Lowell, saying that he wasn't a boy to be taken seriously. But Van Pelt supplied two things Lowell needed: adoration and money. Van Pelt gave him a thousand pounds when Lowell told him he was leaving. Lowell is staying with someone called Scotto now, a duke. Obese, apparently.

"But worship leaves one with nothing," Lowell said. "What I want is to be *recognized*."

A light breeze was blowing, at last. Nikki had begun to stir, and I knew we didn't have much time left. Then Lowell did something so completely out of the blue, I'm not quite sure it even happened: He grabbed my hand and raised it to his mouth.

Sweltering day. The breeze did nothing to diminish the heat.

6 July

The more I learn about Van Pelt from Lowell, the more I hate him. Lowell says I should quit. I think I will, although I'd miss Nikki and Mrs. Van Pelt. Scotto's house has more style than Van Pelt's anyway. I haven't met Scotto yet, but Lowell says I'm not missing much. I must write about the bed this mysterious (and apparently quite vast) Scotto bought Lowell yesterday. It's a walnut sleigh bed, set upon four golden feet. They're men's feet, each foot pointing away from the bed. The feet are wearing Grecian-style sandals, laces zigzagging up the calf. The bed, I think, is meant to be a palanquin, and the feet are meant to belong to the porters. The detailing is very fine, and the toenails and toe segments are painstakingly done, but it took me a few minutes to figure out what was wrong with the picture.

They were all RIGHT feet.

When I told him, Lowell raced around the bed, from foot to foot, and said how he didn't understand how he could possibly have missed that there were no left feet. An artist must notice every significant thing, he said, then see *through* it. He sat down on his bed. The bed was so high that his legs dangled down like dwarf fingers. He got very quiet and morose and kicked his bare feet against the bed like a little boy and said this was probably a sign that he wasn't really an artist.

Then I did something I've never done before. I went over to Lowell and kissed him. I've never had another person's tongue in my mouth before. It seemed like just about the most intimate thing you could do. But that was until Lowell sucked the breath from my chest.

Then I sucked the breath from his chest, and he sucked his breath from mine. I don't know how long we did this.

Finally, Lowell spoke. He made me promise that breath would be a thing we'd always make together.

He didn't want me to leave, but I called a taxi to take me to my flat. On my mattress on the floor, I listened to my own breathing. I fell asleep eventually, and had dreams that I can't remember this morning.

7 July

I never really wrote all that much about when Fergus left, because I couldn't, but maybe I should now, so I don't forget what his departure was like. As soon as we got back from breakfast that morning, Fergus started packing. He had too many bags, so the five flinty trips up and down the stairs diminished the drama a lot, I thought. Before his last trip down, he tore around the flat and opened the refrigerator door and all the kitchen cabinets and drawers, put the toilet seat up, threw open the shower curtain, and peeled a carrot into the bathroom sink. (I, for one, didn't even know Grunt *had* a carrot peeler—or carrots.) He also took Grunt's butcher's knife and sliced the famous unread letter in long strips, right in front of me. Only someone who's on cozy terms with cruelty would think to do such a thing. The letter slices looked like a child's construction-paper chain for a Christmas tree. Fergus definitely got what he wanted out of his performance, because I feel sick whenever I think of it, or him.

Anyway, Fergus would be so mad he missed today. If I ever talk to him again, I'll tell him that he left London too early.

Somehow, Grunt and the foremost punk singer in the world are apparently *likethis.* That's how he introduced himself to Lowell and me. He was sitting on top of the door table in my flat, his feet on the table. He was belching into a bottled beer and watching Grunt's TV.

" 'Allo. I'm the foremost punk singer in the world," said Aloysius Canker. "Whot are you?"

(I'm just trying to transcribe him as I heard him, although I may not be getting him—or any of our British friends—quite right.)

Lowell ran right up to him, as if he weren't surprised to see him at all, as if Aloysius Canker belching in one's flat happened every old day. Lowell extended his hand to be touched, and introduced himself, stating his first and last name. His voice had become very low. Aloysius Canker looked about sixteen in the television's flickering smolder. His eyes were very blue, although that may just have been from the TV. Aloysius ignored Lowell's hand. He coiled up to Lowell's face. He sneered, hissed, and twisted back to the TV.

"You're really irritating me already, you," he said. He meant Lowell, although he was looking at the TV. "Although pleased to meet *you*, luv." Aloysius said. He meant me this time. I could sense Lowell's body tensing. (Does that mean you love somebody if you can feel what his body feels?) "But Bryan Ferry over there—or should I say Fairy—is really annoying me. I'm just trying to watch me *program.*" Aloysius was dressed in a T-shirt, on which someone had painted MADE IN HEAVEN with what looked like pink nail polish. The show on TV was a nature program about bees. Lowell said he was a "tremendous fan" of Aloysius's. Aloysius asked Lowell if his name was fake, and Lowell said, very proudly, that it was.

"Well done, then," Aloysius said. "I don't think, though, that you've made the grade yet, Bryan Ferry. I almost called you Rod Stewart; I'm sure you are that unutterably big of a wanker. Just leave me the fuck alone, you muck-wallowing, ascotted artiste, and let me watch my telly. Artistes always make me run straight to the loo. And *whot* is that accent? Are you the roommate?" he asked. That question was for me.

I believe I nodded.

"Bring us another lager, then," he said.

Had Fergus been in this situation, he would now have been shivering in a fetal position in the bathtub. Lowell took a different approach: It looked as if he were preparing to coldcock the world's foremost punk-rock singer. I asked what my being the roommate had to do with an ability to bring him another lager.

"It means you know where the lager *is*. Thought it would be rude to help meself."

Lowell paraded over to my bedroom and slammed the door. Aloysius Canker laughed robustly at something on the bee show and pointed. I, defiled, debased, brought him a beer.

"Thanks, luv," he said. "Means a lot to us."

I asked him why he was here.

"Didn't mean to withhold information, dearie," he said. "Emily ran out to buy you a little gift. Can I ask you a question now? My turn. Do you think I have a handsome profile?" He moved into a side view, angling his chin high. In the background, the TV beekeeper looked like an astronaut.

Lowell was in my room, lying on the mattress, staring up at the ceiling. I asked him if it was true he'd changed his name. He said it was. He'd had a lot of pain in his life, he told me, followed by a statement I didn't understand about how he was "the son who was never given anything." Then he asked if I would lie with him, if I could lie in the crook of his beautiful arm. Later, I put my head on his chest and listened to its ancient living sea.

8 July

I don't know if I've technically quit Van Pelt's, but I'm definitely not showing up anymore. This morning, Lowell and I were in my room and he was talking about how he'd "maintained a steadfast resistance to drawing lessons." He said, "My mind is on God and the Renaissance, not on *Gray's Anatomy*!" This seemed like a very funny thing for him to say, and we both started laughing. He told me how much he liked to see me laugh. "I don't think I've ever even seen my fucking mother laugh once," he said.

He seized a hunk of my hair, petted it, then put it into his mouth.

Later, I was in the living room, fooling around with the sketch pad, drawing Grunt. Lowell was sitting next to me on the couch, watching. Scrumpy, who came out of the kitchen with a bowl of spaghetti Bolognese (his specialty), started yelling about how he wanted to see Lowell draw. (Actually, he said, "Let's give the pouncy girl over there a go at it.") His hair spikes cast a dinosaur shadow on the wall. He said if he was sharing a flat with the art crowd, he was owed some *art*, wasn't he?

First Lowell complained that there wasn't enough good light in the living room. Then it was "The paper is far too cheap to use"; then it was "Scrumpy, go out and buy me a new charcoal pencil."

To which, Scrumpy gave Lowell the international symbol for Up Yours.

(And oh yeah: No mention was made of Aloysius Canker's visit last night, mainly because I don't know what Scrumpy knows, or is supposed to know.)

Lowell asked Grunt to stop with her ghastly squirming. Grunt responded by saying that if Lowell made her look disgusting, he was a fucking dead man. Then Lowell called them both "dissolute ruffians." Silence for a few seconds as he tried to concentrate on the sketch. He quickly became very purple-faced and absorbed, and I wouldn't have been surprised if his head had just popped right off. I imagined the terrible champagne-cork sound that would have accompanied the decapitation.

Scrumpy was digging at the sole of his boot with a matchbook. "Are you from underneath the sea?" he asked Lowell. Then Scrumpy announced that Lowell had the dodgiest accent he'd ever heard.

"Are you from Maryland?" Grunt asked Lowell.

"Um, nooo. I'm from right here in London," Lowell said.

"What *part* of London?" Grunt asked.

"Right down the road . . . but . . . all my travels have gotten my accents all jumbled."

"Do you remember the girl from Maryland, Scrumpy?" asked Grunt. "What was his name? You know the one I'm talking about, with the—" Here, Grunt crouched and made the devil-horn sign. Scrumpy scratched his head between the second and third spike.

Lowell gave his sketch a final look, then flipped the pad shut. Scrumpy asked if he could see.

"Not ready yet," Lowell said, then tucked the notebook underneath his arm and arose. "Thank you for your time, Grunt. Scrumpy. Good-bye." He opened the front door and walked through it.

Scrumpy threw his boot at the door. But Lowell was gone.

And then I went right through that door, too.

Back in his room at Scotto's, on top of his right-footed bed, Lowell asked me to draw a picture of him. Words can't do faces, either, so I don't know how to describe my drawing of his face, other than what he said about it. "It's the first time I've ever known what I look like," he said. Lowell taped the picture over his bed. I saw him cry for the first time tonight. He cried, and looked at me, and held me, and said he'd never lie to me again. We lay together, my head on his chest again, just like last night. I didn't know whose body I was listening to, his or mine.

He's looking at the picture of him again as I write this, again crying.

10

Merit and Wyatt met in college—at the student center. It was the late nineties and Merit was a senior. Wyatt was older—a "Ph.D. candidate" (that's what they called themselves, Merit learned) in statistics, a TA, a husband (although separated), a father, a real adult person with a job, and, most shockingly, a *commuter.* When they met, Merit and another girl were hanging posters for a College Democrats–sponsored speech by Richard Gephardt, an event it would have been quite impossible for Merit to care any less about. She would even have admitted this at the time. She was, preposterously, the College Democrats' vice president of communications that year. She had been interested in this position, which involved little more than hanging posters for the very few College Democrats–related events, only because with it came an on-campus car pass. The Jaguar had come into her life the year before, and obviously she needed to be with it. She had had only a few minor parking lot– and driveway-oriented mishaps at this point, and the Jag was not yet the lemon it would become.

Wyatt, a tall, lean, bespectacled person dressed in a fisherman's knit sweater, carrying the biggest goddamned briefcase Merit had ever seen, came up to the other College Democrat girl and started talking. Just started talking—something that really *wasn't done* all that much, not in Ohio, maybe in New York, or in Texas, California, or even the distant state of Washington, but not in Ohio. He set his briefcase against the wall. Merit initially thought he was trying to sell the girl something. Then she thought he was a military recruiter. Then she understood he was a professor. Merit was curious. She inched over to them and slapped a poster right over the girl's head.

These were the first words Merit heard Wyatt, her future husband, say: "I have a clipping from the *Toronto Globe and Mail,* if it would help you, but it was so extreme that it made me doubt the validity of the ratio, which was that it takes eighteen months for the earth to regenerate the amount of energy it uses in a twelve-month period. Hey, would you mind watching my briefcase, Gail?"

"Um, what?" the girl (whose name was Gail) asked. She wore her hair in braided pigtails. She was from Moline, Illinois.

"I have to run an errand. I'll be back before you know it." And this tall, dweeby person loped off without his briefcase. He walked as if his sphincter were his most developed muscle.

"Who was *that*?" Merit asked.

"Statistics TA," Gail said, looking at the briefcase dumbfoundedly. "That class is *so* not fun."

Gail stood stiffly against the wall, as if having her height measured. She peeled tape off her thumb and watched the briefcase very intently.

"You're taking *statistics*?" Merit asked.

"Yeppers," Gail said, apparently unable to remove her eyes from the briefcase. She remained in that position for about two minutes more. Then she said, "I'm out of here. I have to go to the bathroom."

Merit's response: "Uh, well. Okay, I guess. Sure!"

Merit picked up the briefcase, nestled it between her feet, leaned against the cold wall, and crossed her arms in front of her. She felt like she was on a mission, in the army or something. *Must protect the briefcase. Must protect the briefcase.* She was already worried that she wouldn't know what to do with the briefcase if the stiff didn't return for it soon. Until then she would be the best little briefcase protector ever. Ah, but there he was—after about five minutes that had seemed like thirty—in the distance, approaching her, and his briefcase, at a fast clip. He licked an ice-cream cone. The ice cream was bright green, licked into a perfect sphere. Merit was the kind of person whose ice cream was forever dripping down her arm, so it made sense she was impressed by those who were able to eat their ice cream in a tidy manner. He held the cone up and raised his eyebrows as if to say, Want some? Merit declined, naturally. He asked where Gail was.

"Bathroom," she said. She was afraid he was disappointed.

"I see," he said. "Nature's tug. Unavoidable, really." His smile was so nice! But his glasses were really crooked, weren't they? The natural thing would have been for Merit to straighten them, or at least offer to, but she felt she didn't know him well enough for that. He licked his ice cream. She watched his tongue.

"Ummm, that looks so good," Merit said. "Ice cream is always such a great idea, isn't it?"

"Oh! I wish mine were more shareable. May I possibly—would it be possible to buy you one for your trouble?"

Merit wasn't sure if the nerd whose name she did not yet know was just being polite or what, but she said okay. He grabbed his briefcase by the big ugly plastic handle. He didn't wear a wedding band. Merit was not really in the habit then of looking for wedding rings on people's fingers (nor was she now), but she did notice his lack of one. The briefcase was so heavy that it made him lean slightly to the left.

"So what's in the briefcase or whatever?" Merit asked as they walked, veering through the between-class students. All the male students at her school really did look exactly like Richard Gephardt, she thought. Personally, Merit was a big believer in the between-class nap, so she didn't understand what it was that compelled these people to want to hang out in the student center.

"Documents," he said.

She still didn't know his name. He seemed unused to being next to a girl who could look him in the eye.

"Of course," Merit said.

At the food court in the student center, they stood in line at the ice-cream area, waiting to order, but things were moving awfully slowly up ahead.

"They seem to be having a real problem with the elements of their system up there," he said.

She didn't want to seem rude, so she pretended she was very interested. His glasses were inclined at such an angle so as to make him look insane, which she could already tell he most definitely was not. He was sort of the opposite of insane. She liked that.

"What does that mean, 'elements of a system'?" she asked.

He was hugging the briefcase to his chest.

"Oh!" he said. "Do you really want to know? Not that many people know how exciting systems can be. A system includes activities, but it also includes other elements . . . components, you might say. It might be a physical component, it might be rules or guidelines, or it might be the resources or people, but all the elements of the system are interrelated, and if you remove one of the elements, then the system will cease to function. See, the elements by themselves don't accomplish the function! If you had just a set of rules and procedures lying around, they wouldn't do anything by themselves. It's the interrelationship of the elements that enables the system to accomplish its function! Whatever that function is! Isn't that fascinating?"

He accidentally spat a couple of times onto Merit's cheek. She didn't mind, and she didn't wipe her face. People spat sometimes and did weird things when they felt strongly about something.

"You should sign up for Dr. Ton's class next semester. I won't be assisting him, unfortunately, but I think you might really enjoy it. He's really very good at teaching statistics in a way that's vital and alive and beautiful, even to nonconverts."

No way was she taking a statistics class next semester. No way. She nodded politely, however.

"Anyway, my original belabored point is that Scoops seems to be having problems with the 'people' element of their system."

Merit said Scoops was always slow, so she wasn't surprised.

"If this line ever moves, I think I'll join you with another mint chocolate chip cone. Hey, I'm really enjoying our conversation so far! Can you see what's going on up there?"

"Seems to be a bottleneck at the cash register." Merit had never in her entire life said the word *bottleneck* before. She wondered what this unbelievably nice and dorky and improbably intense man would think of her if she told him that Jenny had done all her math homework for her since fourth grade. Even during Jenny's most desolate and despairing periods, she always managed to help Merit with her homework. "I think I'll get blueberry," Merit said.

"Ah, blueberry!" he said. "My daughter loves the blueberry."

"Your *daughter*?"

"Did you have any of this ice cream?" Wyatt asked. The freezer door was open, and Wyatt *never* left the freezer door open. He was standing over the sink with his ice cream container. "There's a little spoon groove here, but only one, which seems strange. I was wondering if someone took a little nibble in the store." He had a freakishly proprietary relationship with his mint chocolate chip ice cream. The lightbulb in the freezer flickered off and on.

"Yeah, I did, last night, but the texture was weird," Merit said.

"I knew it! I knew there had to be something wrong with it, because it's very unlike you to take only one bite. And what do you mean by that, the 'texture'?"

"I mean the texture or whatever changed. It went from a solid to . . . something that wasn't a solid."

"Ah ha. Do you mean *liquid,* by chance?" He took a bite of the ice cream. He winced just a little.

"There were all these ice crystals in it, Wyatt. I wasn't going to eat it. No *way* was I going to eat it, *sorry.*" Merit removed the ice cream from his hands and closed the freezer. Caroline was banging around upstairs, getting her things together for the weekend. A CD—flutes, possibly Bach—was playing upstairs.

"I think for my next project I'll put a piece of glass on the door of the freezer so you can see the magical freezing process at work," Wyatt said.

He was opening the cabinet door now and removing, one by one, air-fattened plastic Baggies of food, laying them across the white countertop in the straightest line of air-fattened plastic Baggies you'd ever hope to see. Merit knew what he was up to. Inside the Baggies were nuts, trail mix, M&M's, dried apricots, crackers, oatmeal, wheat germ, pumpkin seeds (also called, Merit knew, *pepitas*). There were other items, too. While Merit was aware the plastic Baggie wasn't the most ecologically minded storage system, she did find it to be the most convenient. Wyatt unzipped each Baggie, flattened it.

"You need to start squeezing the air out before you close the bags. Oxidation is the enemy. Remember, Merit."

Merit thanked Wyatt for reminding her.

Oh, he was all worked up tonight, even more than usual. He had just spent a significant amount of time, before the Baggies, before the ice cream, sharpening all their kitchen knives. Merit hadn't even noticed they were in need of sharpening. That was fine, she guessed, but then he insisted she practice chopping for him, for ten whole minutes, maybe more, with each of the newly sharpened knives, fake chopping, chopping nothing, cutting up air, mindful not to let the knife touch the counter-top, because from what he'd witnessed of her technique in the past, he said, he was convinced she would someday, with surgical precision, slice off her finger. She told him she *had* no technique. She told him to relax. Although she did think the whole thing was absolutely, absolutely in-sulting, she forced herself not to yell at him during her practice test. Wy-att's conclusion: Merit's knife handling was not up to snuff. He told her she was now allowed to use the knives only when he was home. "I guess I can do that," she said. But she was lying.

It was Friday, and Wyatt was agitated on Fridays. Merit didn't think he was aware of this.

"Shouldn't Shelley be here by now?" Merit asked.

"She's been getting later and later every week. Have you noticed that?"

He was hunched over the refrigerator's deli drawer. Wyatt and Merit had spent many hours discussing how unfair it was that tall people had to go around perpetually hunched; that the man-made world had been con-structed for people smaller than they was one of the topics on which they'd first bonded.

He removed each "cheese"-containing plastic bag (there was soy cheddar, imitation Gouda; there were others). He unzipped; he squeezed. Shelley was Wyatt's ex-wife, and every Friday night was Shelley Night, the evening she would stop by to pick up Caroline. Merit's general com-ment about Shelley would still be, five years later (if Wyatt ever actually bothered to ask her opinion of his ex-wife): "I just can't get a read on her. I just don't know." She didn't like it when Caroline wasn't around, and weekends were a drag for that reason, although she knew it was selfish to feel that way, because it was so obviously important for Caroline to have a relationship with her mother that it went without saying.

Merit scooped up the Baggies from the counter and returned them to their rightful place. "So what happened today, Wyatt? In the world, I mean. I wasn't paying attention."

And that was true, too. She hadn't been paying attention. They hadn't gotten back to their desks today until 3:30, a group-lunch record.

Randy rode back to work with her (he'd asked if he could "catch a lift" with her, which Merit liked). In the car (the make of which he didn't comment on, thank God), he changed the radio channel without asking, settling on the college radio station (she was embarrassed the tuner wasn't preprogrammed to it). They listened to a live acoustic version of an old and heartbreaking song by Split Enz or possibly Crowded House. Eddie Vedder was singing backup. She recognized Eddie Vedder's voice, and said so. Randy seemed impressed. It was sad, the way Eddie Vedder sang, "And we're strangers here."

"Well, let's see, what happened today? Oh, I know: The Tooting Subordinate was declared all-knowing," said Wyatt.

Oh *no*. Wyatt was back on *that* again. She hadn't even brought up Randy in conversation tonight, had she? But then again, maybe she had. Maybe.

"Hey. So. I've been wondering: Can I cash in my Get Out of Jail Free card the night of Fergus and Lowell's party?"

"Wyatt. We haven't been invited yet."

"They'll invite us, Merit. But *why* you want to be invited is the real question."

Wyatt hated Lowell and Fergus. But it was his opinion of Jenny that really perturbed her. He didn't even seem to find her interesting.

Wyatt removed his glasses and laid them flat on the countertop. Merit decided against reminding him again that Jenny had received her invitation yesterday. Merit hadn't seen Lowell for two years. How sad that she needed a party as an excuse to be in the same room with her own father. And Fergus, too, although Fergus wasn't her father.

"Tap them," Wyatt said.

"I've been doing this for seven years. I think I know how to do this," Merit said.

"A tapping indicates a lack of symmetry, so that's what you should be doing."

"Okay. Fine," she said.

She tapped. There was a sound.

"It's a tedious process, I agree. It looks as if the temple piece is inclined toward the center. Do you see that?"

"I think maybe I should twist them, don't you?" she asked.

"The more they're straightened, the less they fit. Quite the paradox, isn't it? Which I know leads everyone to the conclusion that the problem isn't the glasses, but the accident I had in high school that made my ears asymmetrical."

Rosalita gave a half bark from the living room. She sounded as if she'd been asleep. Merit felt that piercing half bark in her chest. This meant only one thing: Shelley Time. There was the sound of boots pounding up the steps of the Wyatt-built front deck now, the sound of footsteps that meant business.

"Welp, time to go brush my teeth," Wyatt said.

"No *way* are you leaving now."

"I'll be back before you know it. You were right about that ice cream. There was something real funny about it." His glasses were back on, and unusually straight.

Wyatt disappeared, as Wyatt often did on Fridays. The doorbell rang and the dog went bananas. The bottom part of the front window was already steamed up from dog breath. There was also dog slobber. Rosalita kept looking up at Merit, trying to get Merit to confirm her theory that, yes, there was indeed someone at the door. Merit called the dog's name, trying, unsuccessfully, to trill the *R*.

Merit opened the front door just a little bit, then bent over to yank Rosalita back by the collar. She was afraid she was hurting Rosalita, but what other way was there?

"Hello, Shelley!" Merit said.

"Hi there, Merit," Shelley said. "How are you? Hi there, doggy." Merit hated it when people didn't call Rosalita by her name. It was dark outside and she couldn't really see Shelley all that well. She could see, though, from her vantage point, that she had guessed incorrectly about Shelley's footwear: pumps, not boots.

"Oh my God," said Merit. "The light didn't come on out there. I'm so sorry."

"Not a problem," Shelley said.

Merit opened the door all the way, concentrating mainly on holding back Rosalita. She knew Rosalita loved them, but she had to face facts, too: Rosalita was a beagle, and a beagle will absolutely make a break for it at the first available opportunity.

"You could have broken your neck!"

"Not a problem." Shelley wasn't tall, but Merit felt that she had more of a tall-person voice than did Merit, who was an actual tall person. Shelley was a chemist at the tire company Wyatt worked for, and maybe talking to chemists all day, most of whom were probably male, and weird, made your voice go one octave deeper. If you were a woman, that is.

"I hate these stupid lights, but you know how Wyatt is about them."

"Not an issue. Wyatt may be gone, but his spirit lives on in these automatic lights."

"Oh, Wyatt's here, actually. He's just upstairs. Do you want me to get him? I'm sure he'd like to say hi."

"Well, I assumed he was here. . . . His car is in the . . . I was just . . . How are you? How was your week, Merit?"

"I'm good, Shelley! Everything's good! Would you like to come in?" Rosalita was really tugging. Please don't snag her dumpy nude hose. Please don't snag her dumpy nude hose. Merit liked Shelley, and she thought Shelley maybe even liked her, at least a little, but their conversations were not, even all these years later, getting any less pained.

"Hey, why not?" Shelley said. She stepped inside, and Merit let the dog go. Naturally, the dog went straight for Shelley's crotch. Merit pretended not to notice. "Do you know how the kiddo's doing?" Shelley was sort of trying to brush Rosalita away.

"Oh, Caroline's great. She's doing really well," Merit said. "She just wrote a paper on Rousseau this week. Her Kent State for Kids teacher, Mrs. Wurpp, said she was going to keep it to show future classes!"

"No, I mean . . . is she *ready*?" Shelley was not an unattractive woman, but she was, essentially, lipless. Shelley also talked out of the side of her mouth in a way that had always reminded Merit of one of the bigger midgets in the Lollipop Guild—maybe it was the middle one—from *The Wizard of Oz*. She had never mentioned this to Wyatt, or anyone else.

"Oh, right, *right*! Let me check." Merit went to the bottom of the stair steps, made a megaphone with her hands, and called Caroline's name.

Caroline's voice came from upstairs, floating somewhere over, or maybe under, Bach. Water was running. That was Wyatt.

Rosalita was on her hind legs, nipping at Shelley's pocketbook. The overhead light in the foyer turned itself on. Shelley raised her pocketbook above the Rosalita danger zone.

"What's the wattage of these automatic bulbs, Merit?" she asked. "I'm curious."

Merit said she had to admit she had no idea. "The lights," she said, "are Wyatt's thing."

"My guess is that these are fifteen-watt fluorescent bulbs that look like sixty. I'm sure Wyatt installed these in some bizarre, time-consuming way."

Merit was overcome with a wave of melancholy, a brief but intense one, which had to do with many things she didn't understand, and some she did. The main identifiable one: Shelley and Wyatt had been much more suitably matched as a couple than Merit and Wyatt were. Right now, she felt, as she often did, that all she was was a dumb little magazine-working dingdong. The world would get along fine without assholes who sold ad space at magazines. Actually, the world would be much better off without assholes who sold ad space at magazines.

Caroline thumpingly pulled her suitcase downstairs. Rosalita, Merit noted, was elsewhere in the house now, having at some recent point lost interest in Shelley.

"Caroline!" Shelley said.

"Hi, Mom."

The feeling, the same feeling she always had when she heard it: an ache in her chest. To Caroline, Merit was "Merit." Always "Merit."

Caroline dragged the big red suitcase across the linoleum floor. Red scuff marks resulted. Merit didn't care. Caroline and Shelley hugged. Shelley did that rubbing-your-back thing some people sometimes do when they hug you. Merit asked Caroline what was in the suitcase.

"*The Story of Civilization,* by Will and Ariel Durant. I've only got up through *The Age of Voltaire* with me, though."

The books had belonged to Merit's dead grandmother, Jenny's mother, and she thought it was both beautiful and sad that Caroline was finding them of use. Caroline had never gotten to meet Merit's grandmother.

Shelley set the suitcase upright and rolled it toward the door. "I was thinking: pizza tonight?"

Caroline gave Merit a quick little glance that said (Merit thought), Doesn't she know I don't eat pizza anymore? What utter kid's stuff. Caroline was still wearing the red yarn ankle bracelet.

Merit and Caroline hugged briefly. Merit told her to have a good weekend. Merit's other grandmother was still alive, but her relationship with her now consisted of no more than annual birthday and Christmas cards (Lowell's mother still continued to send her a fifty-dollar check for each, although Merit wished she wouldn't). Caroline had never met her, either. Merit often felt guilty about not having any real relationship with her only living grandparent, but Lowell had no relationship with his mother, so neither could she. It was Lowell's show, she felt. All she could do was watch and follow.

The whole front deck rattled as the suitcase bumped down the steps, the outside light came on, and Merit concentrated on the tight little bun on the back of Shelley's head that she imagined biting off.

11

Now here's a mood-dampener: You stroll on into someone's living room and see, set precisely between the two picture windows, a colossal TV. You'd thought, back when you met this handsome person in, say, your Turkish bath, or perhaps at a deadly dinner party (you liked him because he was the only individual there who actually seemed to be having a worse time than you) that maybe you'd made a new friend, that maybe this could be a friend who would stay, but then you pay him a visit and get the house tour, and then there's the centrally positioned TV . . . so, well, you must verily bid that little dream adieu. TVs aren't art, let's recall, and they mustn't be displayed as if they were. If you can swing it financially, all household electronics should ideally be hidden in a separate home-entertainment room. Do yourself a favor and tuck away all the phones, too. Electronics are the enemy. Remember I told you this.

My house has eighteen phones, and eighteen phone booths. Well, they're not really booths so much as hot, dark little nooks carved into the walnut—or mahogany, or tiger maple, or cherry, depending upon the section of the house—walls. I have ten phone nooks in the upstairs bedrooms, four in the upstairs hallways, and four in the downstairs hallways. My favorite phone room is in the downstairs hallway, off the great hall. For the last three days, I'd been hiding in it.

It's the most mysterious of all the phone rooms, and sometimes I like to pretend—half-pretend—that I'm a dauphin and I'm being held prisoner in a tiny, lightless, library-smelling dungeon. I don't want anyone to wreck my small private fantasy, so I keep the door closed. The catch, though, is that this particular nook is insufficiently ventilated, so approximately every twenty minutes I need to get up, and out, and breathe.

At one point on the third afternoon of phone duty, when I was feeling a little rough around the edges, I gently opened the door, glanced to see if anyone was around, and jogged in a sportive manner up and down the hallway. To amuse myself, I tried to leap into the floor's wear marks. I remembered standing over one of the men from the construction outfit years ago as he sanded the indentations into the sandstone. I remembered explaining why the footprints needed to be *closer together,* why they couldn't be placed in a *straight line.* "Look," I said as I walked hither and yon for him, "*This* is how we walk." The footprints he'd already made would have been impossible for anyone under nine feet tall, and anyone who possessed knees, to replicate. He told me he was a professional and that I shouldn't worry. Then he proceeded to place his sanding machine about thirty inches directly in front of the last wear mark. As the sander blasted, I held my ears and (fruitlessly, it turned out) screamed, "Is it not self-evident how humans walk?"

My feet were bare, and the cold stone felt fantastic. Lowell hates it when I go barefoot. I remembered when Merit was young, remembered her jumping from footprint to footprint, and the steely echo of her heartbreaking little-girl shoes. I remembered one of Lowell's parties, when a young male, whose name I've forgotten, took off his pants and sat in each footprint, swinging himself by his arms to each footprint, like a beggar alone and legless on a boardwalk.

Lowell has always been more of a party planner than an artist or a father, by the way, or a husband.

Jenny had not called me yet, nor had Merit.

The classless hack magazine journalist from New York, that Bradley W. Dormer person, had left three messages, asking in each one if he could "crash" the party and interview Lowell.

Ray-Ray had called, too, saying it would "be great" to see Lowell again. Don't know how Ray-Ray heard about the party.

Merit loved hiding in this phone booth when she was a child. Sometimes we'd hide in it together and sing "I'm Getting Myself Ready for You." I taught Merit that song. Her favorite lyrics (which we would scream when we got to them) were "I'll never stoop to onion soup! And pork and beans are taboo!" Years later, when she was in college, she told me she'd heard a recording of the song and realized she'd incorrectly been singing "pork and beans are the boo!" How could I not have known she'd misunderstood the words? Wasn't I listening? I always listened to Merit, listened when she told me what to do with her dolls when we played with them on the floor by Lowell's studio, listened when she told me what we were going to wear in the mornings. And Merit listened to me, too.

She'd never "reached out" to me in the last two years; being a path-of-least-resistance fellow myself, I made no effort, either.

I lifted up the latch. I squeezed through the slender door. My RSVP notebook was open and awaiting me on the red-cushioned bench. The phone's message light was not blinking. I sat down.

It's strange, really, that phones look the same when they're ringing and when they're not. Phones don't move when they ring, which it seems they should. The real pleasure is in watching the red message light go soundlessly on after ten seconds, for example, or maybe after twenty. If the red light doesn't, however, blink on until 120 seconds after the last ring (a 120-second message is the systemwide maximum), all I can say to you is, *Enjoy*. You've got a long-winded one to deal with on the other end.

I wasn't there to answer the phone, naturally. I was there to wait for the red light and to retrieve the voice-mail messages. I hated Lowell for making me do this party, hated him for making me service him and Drisana-Nari, but, if I looked deep into my heart, I could perhaps admit that I was, in fact, rather grateful for something to do. Also, it gave me an excuse to contact a few certain someones.

When he was still working, he told me there were only three people in his life: Jenny, Merit, and me. Before his retirement, Lowell had no need of any people other than us. Now, let's call his promiscuity his SSRI.

I sat back on the hard bench and flipped through my RSVP log/reporter's notebook (two birds with one stone, as it were). I had invited 250 people, and so far I'd received only ninety-two RSVPs. There had been three declines. Two of the three decliners (my chiropractor, Trudy Blumenschein, and my accountant, Phipps Delmonico) both indicated on their voice-mail messages that they had previously planned vacations on the seventeenth of August; the other decliner (Mrs. Wendell S. Ng, a friend from my old book club, back when I still tried to believe in groups) said she had a wedding to attend. That someone would actually choose a wedding over my party was unfathomable to me, but Andrei told me not to worry about it. I told Andrei if I ever found out that Mrs. Wendell S. Ng ended up, on August 17, at the wedding of a coworker or, worse yet, a coworker of her *husband's,* it would *not* be good. I hadn't seen Heather (Mrs. Ng) in years; for months, the book club had been ignoring my pleas for the inclusion on the reading list of novels of a historical nature, and I finally took the hint and stopped showing up. I left a message for her once after that, asking if she'd like to join a Falstaff society I was thinking about creating, but I never heard back. This invitation was her last chance.

The names came largely from Lowell's Principal Akron Guest database. The list was on Lowell's new computer, which I don't know how to use. Andrei helped me, but when he suggested we print mailing labels, I told him to back the fuck off. Later, I asked him to help me download some songs onto my iPod.

I picked up the phone receiver just to make sure it was working. Yes, there was indeed a dial tone. Who created that noise, the dial tone? And if a dial tone is a manufactured sound, if it's not the noise the function must be, can't they make it nicer? Ditto for fax noises. Given that the house has only one phone line (how *else* am I going to keep track of the phone bills?), there's upward of a 70 percent chance that when you pick up the phone, there'll be a guest blah-blahing it up on another extension. I've learned to deal with it, and, happily, I don't really get all that many phone calls anyway. Lowell detests the setup of the house phones, and their one-line nature, and he has, over the course of the last decade, stopped using them. He now has a cell phone, a satellite cell phone, a pager, and a BlackBerry that vibrates in his pocket whenever he receives an E-mail message.

This particular phone room reminded me, in both temperature and smell, of the woman's attic in which I took violin lessons as a boy.

I flipped through the phone-message log (in the back of the notebook; the pretend articles I'm writing for the pretend magazine are in the front). I thought about listening again to a few of my favorite RSVP messages (I'd saved the politest ones), but then I decided against it. The best messages were from twenty to forty seconds in length, and they were not delivered in a tone so pompous as to make me think the message leaver believed it was a big treat for me to get to hear from him (you'd be surprised what some people think). The polite responders also spelled their names, first and last, clearly and slowly. If a callback number was left, it was stated at both the beginning and the end of the message. I had quite a few party-inquiry calls to return, but I didn't feel like it at that moment. Maybe I could drag Andrei out of bed and make him do it. You have no idea, really, how many questions people have had about the party.

It appeared to be the "costume" element that had thrown everyone off. Examples:

Q: "Do we have to wear a costume?" (A: Yes.)
Q: "Do we really have to wear a costume?" (A: YES.)
Q: "Will we look silly if we show up without a costume?" (A: YES, YES.)
Q: "You won't let us in if we don't have a costume?" (A: YES, YES, YES.)

Yes, I definitely thought I'd have Andrei call these people back.

Jenny said once that I was far too emotional to be alive, and I would have to agree, finally, after all these years, that she was right. One of the most hateful things Lowell ever, ever said to me was that it was surprising, given my intolerable nature, that I wasn't an artist. A vile statement on a number of levels, don't you think? The least of which: I *was* an artist, once. That was when I had something to photograph. There are things I wanted to do, you see, but couldn't, things no one knows about me. When Merit was a child, she and I were friends, and I mean *friends,* blood brothers, as peculiar as that sounds, just as her mother and I were once, and I told Merit who I was. I told her how much I worshiped her parents, and how they would never see me as their equals. Merit once said she wanted to *be* me—not be *like* me, *be* me—and I endeavored to make her in my image. But then she went away. She rejected me; she refused me. A few dark years of hating her followed. I hated her for knowing what she knew, but then when I would see her, this gangly, faltering girl, whenever we chose to invite her over, her vast soft eyes, magnified through her eyeglasses, would make me want to bite my lip until it bled. At this point, I wasn't sure she would even remember anything I'd told her about myself. How many years ago was it when Merit would take her faceless dolls into this phone room and lock the door? She'd tilt the red cushion against the wall and make a fort. How old was she now? Thirty? Older? Younger? I didn't know. Merit had talent and grace, but she respected neither. After I saw her play a Mozart piano concerto in a high school recital, I begged her, "At least *apply* to Juilliard." If she had stayed with me, I would have shown her how a life built on inertia isn't one worth living.

I probably would have liked her much better at that moment if she'd already called me.

I'd never before thought that the great hall phone nook smelled like

Mrs. Mickley's attic. She was my violin teacher for five years. Five years of lessons isn't long enough to really be any good at an instrument, particularly if you copied (as I did) the answers from the back of the workbook (at the age of ten, I thought it sensationally savvy of me merely to locate the answer key). Mother, being Mother, insisted that we always be early for practice, so, in a cracking white wicker settee, waiting for my lesson to begin, when I should have been brushing up on "Lightly Row" or "Hot Cross Buns," I'd thumb through Mrs. Mickley's *Modern Maturitys*, and help myself to the Jolly Ranchers in the lead-crystal candy bowl (being so very careful not to let the lid make any sound while raised or lowered), noiselessly opening the wrappers and stashing them into my pockets, my eyes on the back of Mrs. Mickley's white spun-sugar head the whole time, and listening to the kid whose lesson was before mine, and whose playing was always inevitably better than mine, no matter who the kid was. I fainted in that attic because it was hot, and airless, and August. I should have sat down during my lesson when the black stars started clouding my sight, but I didn't. When I came to, Mrs. Mickley was squatting next to me, in her dress, and trying to get my mother's phone number out of me. I told her I was surprised she didn't have it written down somewhere. I could smell Mrs. Mickley's hair spray, could see her underpants and bare knees.

The only light in the phone alcove came from a single bulb in the ceiling, a feeble fifteen-watter. I stared at it, and it didn't even burn my eyes. Throughout the house, I use a special kind of bulb, one that's made to look like a torch flame, although it's not as if it's fooling anyone. Since I built the house, I've single-handedly kept the Ye Olde Colonial Lightbulb Company in Williamsburg, Virginia, in business. Don't you think they should at least send me a Christmas card some year? I remembered when I'd lifted Merit up to this bulb, back when she was small enough to lift.

In my notebook, I flipped to my latest "magazine piece."

WHAT MAKES THE MOST FAMOUS MAN IN THE WORLD RUN?
By "Bradley W. Dormer"

"I'm the luckiest man in the world," Fergus Goodwyn says as he leans back into a luxe tapestry armchair and takes a puff off a long brown cigarette, so exotic-looking it can only have been imported. We are in the library of his famous, impeccably turned-out one-hundred-room Tudor mansion on the coast of Akron, Ohio. On this resplendent summer afternoon, Fergus is taking a break from preparing for one of his legendary parties. It has been called "the house to end all houses," and he has been called "the host to end all hosts." "His parties have become the closest we have to the Algonquin Round Table," says close personal friend Robin Leach in an E-mailed statement. The house has become a virtual *Who's Who* of movers and shakers of this century and last. So it is interesting to note that despite all the exciting hustle and bustle throughout this wondrous house, he is relaxed, at ease, and charming.

Truth be told, I wasn't sure what to expect of Fergus Goodwyn and was indeed a little nervous about meeting him. Why? I'd been trying to get this story for five years and four months.

Arranging this interview was, for the past four months, a tense diplomatic negotiation, and one that made me think getting in to see Kim Jong-il would certainly be easier going than this. It had been a year of calls back and forth between his various publicists, managers, and handlers. There had been delays, reschedulings. ("We're definitely, absolutely, on for your chat with Fergus"; then: "It turns out that Fergus has to entertain the queen that day, so I'm afraid we're going to have to reschedule again," etc., etc.) And then just this afternoon there was the issue of trying to explain myself at the door to the very rude and not very attractive (or fit) butler, Andrei, who I thought was going to drag me back to my white Budget rental car by my tongue. So, five years, four months, fifteen days, and three hours after this quest began, here I finally am, sitting knee-to-knee with the most famous person in the world—famous for all the things he's done, and famous, too, for just being Fergus.

"Let me tell you why I'm so lucky: Someone once said to me, 'Someone like you, Fergus, someone with your intellect, sensitivity, looks, talent, grace, doesn't have to *do* anything; all you have to do is *be*.' Clearly, I didn't take the advice to heart, although I could have."

Exclaims editrix Polly Mellen, "Last year everyone but *everyone* was wearing the Fergus Fright Wig. His hair is so intensely red, as you know, the essence of red, the idea of red. And the way his hair goes all over the place, as if it were thrown about in some ribald tempest, it cancels out every hairstyle that's ever come before it!" Indeed, Fergus has been said to have been single-handedly responsible for making the so-called Freckle Look the must-have face of the season. And then there's the A-OK sign, his trademark gesture. Reuters/Lou Harris polls indicate that the American public can't even seem to remember the time before Fergus made the gesture his own.

"All I did was put my thumb and forefinger together as a response to Barbara Walters's putting her hand on my knee and asking, 'How are you *really?*' That's all I did; flashed A-OK and mugged, looking smack-dab at the camera. It was all so silly. How odd it was, then, to see how that one very unimportant gesture just took off, like a fire to a Christmas tree in April," he says. "To be driven through my neighborhood, or any neighborhood, or to walk through any of my malls and see the people, young, old, rich, poor, flashing one another the A-OK sign, it was . . ." And here he trails off, shaking his head in disbelief.

"It must be a heady thing," I say, "to be that powerful. I mean, that gesture has been around since who knows when."

"Oh sure," he says, elegantly lighting another cigarette.

The TV series *Fergus!* is, still, after almost a decade, number one in the ratings. As you surely know, in *Fergus!* he is the elusive object of desire. Rarely does he appear on the show. We're only ever granted fleeting glimpses of him, of his head, of his hair, of his hat, as his fans chase and chase him—it could be a shot of the carroty hair on a crowded city street, the carroty hair itself possessing so much magic that it can only belong to one person. Even before *Fergus!* became the global sensation it is, who can forget Fergus on the cover of *Time,* in an advanced-yoga pose? Or the Oscar-nominated song, which Fergus himself refused to sing last year on the Academy Award telecast? Or *People's* "Most Beautiful People in the Galaxy" cover, for which Fergus refused to be shot. (Who can forget that miniscandal of the stark white photoless cover of that issue, red banner headline declaiming, "The Sexiest Man Alive Doesn't Want You to See Him"?) Now there is the rumored presidential run, the possibility of which I was sternly instructed by his publicist, Taffy ("like the candy," she said every time she left a message) not to bring up. The consequences were guaranteed to be dire, I was told.

He's taller than I'd imagined, and smells of expensive French-milled soap. He's in his forties but has the disconcertingly lineless face of a fetus. He seems to have been put on earth for us to worship. "People say to me, you have so much, you're so lucky, and I say to them, 'Aaaah, here's what you don't understand; I have so much to *lose.*'" With that, he takes a sip of his priceless port, the liquid clinging to the sides of the glass in a pleasing way.

Fergus's wit is razor-sharp, and as such, he's tremendous company. With little prodding, he launches into savage impressions of Jennifer Lopez, Donald Rumsfeld, and Jay Leno. His funniest impression, though, is of nineteenth-century German philosopher Frederick Nietzsche, the impression that had Larry King laughing until he was, quite literally, crying. I ask Fergus to do it. He cups his right hand (Fergus is right-handed, just like your intrepid scribe) over the perfectly formed area between nose and lip, indicating, I believe, a mustache. "Here's Nietzsche in the morning: 'Das vich does not kill us makes us stronger.' " I laugh uncontrollably. His hand is still over his upper mouth area, mustachelike. He is kind enough to pause, allowing me to regain my composure. When I've gotten myself together, he lets loose another one: "Here's Nietzsche after being kicked by a horse: [pregnant pause] 'Das vich does not kill us makes us stronger.' " The hand is still over the mouth, signifying a mustache. I don't think I've ever laughed harder in my entire life. I'm laughing so hard that I'm in dire need of a Kleenex. The butler, Andrei, trots over to me with one. "Thanks darlingee," I say. I am feeling very comfortable now. I am totally at ease, and I feel like whooping it up, letting it all hang out.

I'm emboldened enough now to ask a probing question, one which turns out to be incautious, and really stupid. "So why do you still live in Akron?"

Fergus slams down his cordial glass of incalculable price and says, "You have no right to say such things. New York, or L.A., or wherever it is you're from, is much more provincial, has much more of a 'small-town mentality' than Akron. You and your *Brown* education, what of it?"

Touché. (My wife and I went to Stanford, but no matter.) It has been said that going tête-à-tête with Fergus Goodwyn is a dangerous proposition. I have gone too far, and have been punished accordingly. I have learned a valuable lesson, and I will tread more carefully for the rest of my visit.

"Whilst Fergus is pure sterling, I certainly wouldn't get on his bad side," says Queen Elizabeth II in a written statement. I think I now know what she means.

I look around uncomfortably and start chattering about the house. "George W. Bush says that it's like the Playboy Mansion, but with class. How would you respond to that?" I ask, fiddling with my Uniball.

"I've never invited *Bush Two* here," Fergus says with a sniff. "Wouldn't *dream* of it. I'd like to know where you're receiving your information."

"Uh," I say.

"Exactly," Fergus says. "Research," he says, tapping on his temple. *"Research."*

When speech fails, at least there's still the house. I compliment him on his taste, which is, in a word, perfection. He's known as the foremost collector of Tudor-era antiques in the world. "What are fancy objects to me?" he says. "My life is rich and full enough without them. Balthus and I saw eye-to-eye on this score: One must be surrounded by beauty in order to be sane."

"Um," I say.

"Yes?" Fergus says. "Speak up, boy. Let's get this bloody thing over with."

"So, do you . . . *work out?*" I ask. I'm finding myself overwhelmed by his biceps, which, I've just noticed, are making excellent mountains underneath his incredible red silk kimono.

"Never," Fergus says. "Never, never, never. I've been blessed with a terrific metabolism."

"Come on," I say, incredulous. "Not a little trot on the old treadmill? I know from my Nexis search that you have an Olympic-size pool, tennis courts, a croquet lawn. You never partake?"

"For the guests," he says, "for the *guests.*"

I feel foolish for having thought for one second that he'd do something for himself, rather than for others.

Fergus's selflessness is legendary. Says friend Maya Angelou, "I always say to Fergus, 'You're too hard on yourself. If you could only see what we see in you, how lovable and wondrous a creation you are, then, finally, you'd get the happiness you deserve. You must rise up, rise up, rise up.' "

I ask if I can feel that bicep.

"You may."

Fergus rolls back the sleeve of his antique kimono, flexes. I touch. Think Mr. Olympia-era Schwarzenegger, think Rambo-era Stallone.

"You're not *so* hideous-looking, you know," says Fergus, peering deep into my eyes. Just at that moment, a gong is struck, signaling the start of lunch. I will always wonder what might have happened next had it not been for that gong.

I follow Fergus to the dining room. I know now what Peter Martins meant when he hailed Fergus's "precision of line," and said, "To see him walk across the room is to be devastated."

The dining room is all dark wood and candelabras. On the walls hang strange but nevertheless extraordinary paintings. This is Fergus's famous *Canterbury Tales* cycle, and no one except those who are invited to On Ne Peut Pas Vivre Seul has ever seen these portraits. My eyes are literally popping out of my head.

"Lunch is served," says Andrei, in a tuxedo now. He dramatically removes each silver lid over each plate.

"We only eat *spa food*," Fergus says. "Hope you like *spa food*." For the life of me, I don't know why he's emphasizing the words *spa food*. There must indeed be some hidden meaning in them. We dig into the low-cal, but nevertheless delectable, feast.

"Is this cumin?" I ask.

"It is," Fergus says with a twinkle in his limpid eyes, which are as clear and deep as Narcissus's pools.

"So where's Lowell?" I can't help but ask. I've been trying to restrain myself, but I've decided that I can't keep it inside any longer.

The Lowell/Fergus romance, as we have learned in the last few months, when it was outed in *Fergus!: The Unauthorized Biography,* is the stuff of legend, a true Graves/Riding romance from the first. The Akron wedding three months ago for one thousand of their closest friends was "more chic, and much droller, than the Black and White Ball ever was," Marissa Berenson says. For their honeymoon, Fergus bought Lowell seven Pacific Islands, now renamed the Fergus Islands. The TV commercials for them have become ubiquitous. ("I never conceived of it as a package-tour destination," harrumphs Fergus). We also learned of Lowell's unpleasant divorce from his wife, and the child left behind.

"Oh, I have him locked up in the dungeon," Fergus says, and blows delicately on his spoonful of soup.

I'm taken aback. "What?" I exclaim, thinking I've surely misheard him.

"I have him locked up in the basement, so no one else can have him. He's mine, all mine." he says. He leans over. He smells delightful. "I'm kidding. He's in the kitchen. Actually, he just prepared the pumpkin mushroom soup you're presently enjoying. Let's get him in here, shall we?" Fergus rings the crystal bell on the table and calls, "Lowly Worm! Come on out here, sweet thing. Don't be shy."

When I ask him about Lowell's former marriage, which was, as we all know, to Fergus's high school chum Jenny Meatyard, Fergus says, "There will be no public record of my opinion of *that*." A Nexis search yielded this statement made by Fergus several weeks ago: "Their relationship was a mangy old worm-ridden mutt that needed to be put out of its misery."

As if right on cue, the mysterious Lowell Haven shuffles in, wearing an apron that says WELL SEASONED BUT STILL COOKIN' and a chef's hat. He looks older than I'd imagined, and shorter, and fatter. Not to be indelicate, but any fool could see that Fergus is very much the better-looking of the two.

"Oh, lovey, did you call me? I got here as fast as I could," Lowell says, rushing over to Fergus and running his finger across Fergus's ridiculously well-defined cheekbone.

"Oh Lowell. I just wanted to show you off." They hug, then Lowell sits on Fergus's lap. They curl into each other. Clearly very much in love, clearly not needing me. They are wound around each other like one body. "Look at you," Fergus says to Lowell. "You're so small and so awfully, *awfully* good."

With a wink, Lowell says, "Anytime we're out of bed is wasted time indeed." Suddenly, I am able to comprehend the dynamic of their relationship. And it's clear who's the alpha dog. This is Fergus's relationship, and Lowell is something Fergus owns, like all the other priceless objects in this dream house. It is a relationship that will go on forever, as does all unrequited love. Fergus, you see, doesn't love Lowell back.

"You should go get ready," Lowell says. "We're due to see the prince soon."

"The real prince?" I ask aloud, unable to contain myself.

"He comes to see us from time to time. He's swooping in for the party, the dear soul. I said we'd go out and meet his motorcade."

"Dash off and get ready, you," Fergus says to Lowell.

"Will you miss me horribly?" Lowell asks.

"As much as it's possible to miss something that's not dead," Fergus says.

I've learned that Fergus the man is pure gold, on both a personal and professional level. Fergus Goodwyn, the man whom Andy Warhol called "so great," waves good-bye from his Jaguar and flashes me his trademarked A-OK sign. As the tinted window goes up, he says, "I'll call you. I'd so very much love to have you at one of our parties." And the Jaguar speeds off to collect its royal cargo, leaving me in the dust.

The call to the party, I fear, may never come.

As you've been warned, I'm not the best writer.

The phone rang four times, then stopped. I flipped to the RSVP section of my notebook. After the last ring, I depressed the timer button on my watch. One never knows if the caller has hung up or has left a message until the red light flashes. This time, the light appeared after 23.38 seconds (according to my Cartier, a long-ago gift from Lowell, and still so accurate the Greenwich Mean Time people really should set their clocks according to it). That was a good length for a message to be, I thought: 23.38 seconds. I had a whole mental list of the people from whom I wanted to hear, starting with Merit and Nostrils (whose name is, I've learned, Preston Lympany), or maybe Nostrils and Merit, if I wanted to be really honest with myself, and ending, I supposed, with Jenny.

I picked up the receiver. I clutched my pen.

Female voices on the phone, on another extension, speaking words.

". . . and so then I go, 'You are totally fucking with me, Karl.' "

"It's just so good you said that. Seriously."

"I know! And then this other guy kept calling the mint jelly 'lime jelly.' "

"So stupid. There's no such thing."

"I know. Who would think it was lime jelly?"

"What, is that like the new thing: lime jelly on lamb? So disgusting."

"Totally disgusting."

I knew I was doing wrong by listening in, but I couldn't help it. It was just too tempting. I thought perhaps I recognized one of the female voices, but I wasn't entirely certain. I racked my vehement brain, trying to remember if in the whirlpool I'd spoken with Drisana-Nari about jellies. I hadn't seen her since then. (And I *certainly* didn't know anyone named *Karl*.)

"I mean, it's *green*."

"I know. But it's that real fakey kind of green."

"Popsicle green."

"Candy green."

"Easter grass, you know what I mean?"

"But what, so anything that's that exact green has be 'lime'?"

"It's oppressive thinking, when you think about it."

"I know. I would call him an 'oppressive thinker,' *definitely*."

Were they talking about me? I knew I'd better figure this out soon, because I didn't know how much more of this I could take. I was less sure now it *was* Drisana-Nari.

"Do you hear someone breathing?"

"What?"

"Do you hear someone maybe breathing on the phone? Shhh. Be quiet."

"It's more like wheezing than breathing, isn't it? Are the lines crossed?"

Oooopsie!

Back when there were phones with actual hooks, it was much easier to eavesdrop. One would have to depress the hook tenderly, very tenderly—the slower and gentler the return of receiver to cradle, the better; one would have to spend minutes, literally, hanging up the phone to achieve the coveted silent hang-up. But this isn't an option now, in the era of the cordless phone. I punched the talk button (which, in this instance, meant no talk). It beeped when I hit it, but there was nothing I could do about that.

The red message light was winking at me. I was brave and picked up the receiver. Dial tone! I must have scared the fuzzy bunnies away. That hadn't been Drisana-Nari's voice, I felt sure now, although I didn't think another woman was staying with us. This was the message:

"Fergus, Lowell . . . get off of there. Trevor's cat is . . . wiping his ass on my keyboard. . . . Trevor gave me a male cat. . . . you know how he feels about male animals. . . . *Go!* Are you listening to this message yourselves, or are you having someone else do it? I have to be a pro about it, in that case. George Clooney here, calling about your party, which I *will* attend. Thanks so much for inviting me. Oh, and Trevor sends his regrets, because he'll be at the hair-trade show in Las Vegas. Love to you both and a special hi to Fergus. All best. It's not George Clooney, if you haven't figured that out yet. It's Preston. Preston Lympany! Bye!"

"Nostrils!" Well, well.

And guess where he said my name? You got it: *first.*

I listened to the message again, and thought I could detect a slight italicization of my name, an emphasis, a beat, a pulse.

Query: Do you think if Preston Lympany moved in with me, he'd bring his forty-two-inch flat-screen TV? How much "rounding up" does one need to do if one "likes someone"? What if, for instance, he has no interest in medieval history? What if he has no real aesthetic to speak of? What if, as I now know, there are only three books in his house in Dahmer country, and those books (*Listen to the Warm, The People's Princess,* and

Glamorama) are kept beside the toilet? What if he's a lovely person, but when you, for fun, tell him he resembles George Clooney, he gets a little more excited than you think he should and, well, runs with it? What if he reads magazines and believes them, and what if he watches TV and believes it? What if his TV has 700 channels and he says (as he did while drinking a low-carb beer from a can and watching channel 405), "I'm always so *busy*"? But what if you think he is of generous heart and noble spirit, nobler by far than yours (or certainly Lowell's), and what if you have a hunch that you and he could be quite a team, so long as he keeps his distance?

The prospect made me giddy.

I could build a cottage in back of the house, for him and his TV, and perhaps one night every two or three weeks I could knock on his door, and he would open it, and he would step out into the blue vapor and he would take my hand, and he, Preston Lympany, would say to me, "Concentrate."

12

Wyatt was in the backyard, dragging a very large panel of cedar board from the deck over to the pig enclosure. Wyatt had recently mentioned something about how he'd wanted to make the walls of the pigpen higher; when Merit had asked him if this new project had anything to do with the fact that he didn't want to see the pig from the kitchen window, he'd just kissed her and told her not to worry about it. Sometimes Merit really hated how he was about Arabella.

Merit was barefooted and walking toward Wyatt with a rubber-banded bundle of mail (Merit continued to think they received more mail than anyone else she'd ever met—except for, of course, Lowell). She had found, while down at the mailbox, an invitation: *the* invitation. It had been sandwiched between Wyatt's *Consumer Reports* and his *Journal of Applied Statistics*. The envelope had been addressed by Fergus, in green fountain pen. Fergus's handwriting, Merit had now decided, was ever more troubling than Randy's. It was addressed to "Ms. Merit Haven." Wyatt's name was absent.

The return address was:

The Havens
On Ne Peut Pas Vivre Seul
Le Quartier de la Vieille Ville
AKRON

Merit, unlike Jenny, didn't get a red wax seal.

"AHHHHHHHHHHHHHH!" Wyatt shouted, and let the cedar panel flap down onto the soft grass. The panel didn't make much of a sound. He shook his left hand vigorously. Merit ran to him because there was no other option. "Wyatt, *damn it. Damn it,* Wyatt," Wyatt said. When he got really mad at himself, he referred to himself in the third person.

"Let me see, let me *see,*" Merit said. Although Merit didn't like this solution, the ground seemed to be the only place to put the mail. The invitation was on top of the bundle, outside the rubber band.

"God FUCKING damn it, Wyatt," he said, squeezing his hand. Wyatt only swore on the rarest of occasions. This must have been bad.

"Give it here. Let me see," Merit said. He was unwilling to surrender his hand. "Help me out here. Do I need to get bandages, gauze, what?" The invitation had gotten itself detached from the rest of the mail. Merit kicked it in back of her a little more so he wouldn't step on it.

"No, it's okay. It's. . . . Whew. I'm okay. Hurts. I'm fine. Go *fuck* me." He was absolutely determined not to let her see his hand. He rubbed it like crazy.

"Here. Give your hand here."

"Don't touch it. Don't touch it!"

"I won't touch it."

"Don't touch it."

"And I'm looking for what, exactly?"

"Are you touching it? You're touching it."

"Wyatt, am I looking at this tiny little splinter on your thumb?"

He opened one eye, then the other.

"Wyatt!"

"Is it real bad?"

"Wyatt Ash, you are just such a big fucking baby!" she said. "I'll try to get it out. Come inside."

"*Try?*"

"It might break apart, it's so small," she said. "Come inside."

"Are you going to hurt me?"

One of Randy's favorite things to say at work, uttered whenever he got off the phone with a weenie-type client of Merit's, was, "What a wank." She liked that. Wyatt wasn't the best with wounds, his or anyone else's. About two years ago, for example, Merit had come home for lunch and sliced open her index finger while opening a can of diet organic cat food for Admiral Edwina Simmons. She had followed orders, had acted according to the Plan, which was to call Wyatt at the office as soon she or Caroline had suffered any kind of injury, no matter how minor. When Wyatt arrived home ten minutes later—so breathless and out of sorts that *he* was the one who'd needed to be attended to—Merit was doing an intermediate-level Ashtanga yoga tape. She was posing in the savasana position (also called, Merit knew, "corpse pose") when Wyatt came into the bedroom. He screamed. (Had he thought she was *dead*?) Although she told him her finger didn't hurt that much, Wyatt insisted he drive her to the emergency room. They had just backed out of the driveway when she decided to peel back the paper towel swaddling her finger and show Wyatt how small the cut was. She waved the finger in front of Wyatt, who made a noise Merit had never heard before in her life and hoped never to hear again, then promptly conked out. The car accelerated, careening directly for the fantastically well-groomed front lawn of their Arabella-hating neighbors, Dr. and Mrs. Mitchell. Merit yanked back the emergency brake. (That she actually *thought* to use the emergency brake impressed Wyatt, and then everyone else who heard the story afterward, a lot more than she thought it should have.) The car jerked to a stop. Wyatt came to with an out-of-it *"Huh? What's it?"* Mrs. Mitchell, who not only detested Arabella but had never engaged Caroline in conversation, came running out the front door of her pukey nineties-constructed "Victorian" house, shouting, "Good Lord! Oh my *good Lord*!" Mrs. Mitchell was no more than forty, but she was always seen, whether in her yard or at the store, in an old-lady housecoat, which is the same idea as an apron, but really just so much worse. Merit's finger had started bleeding again, and Mrs. Mitchell insisted Merit take her wet dish towel (Mrs. Mitchell had come outside with the dish towel slung over her shoulder), then jogged back into the house for a glass of water and an ice pack for Wyatt. Since this accident, Merit suspected Wyatt avoided working outside whenever Mrs. Mitchell was in her yard. She had never asked him if this were true.

"Can you come out here with the tweezers?" Wyatt asked. "I need to sit down for a minute. *Rest.*" He staggered a few feet, then oofed down on the grass, rear end smack-dab on the day's mail. "Hey, what am I sitting on?"

She slid the invitation out from under Wyatt's rear. How could such a nonexistent ass have done, in no time flat, that kind of damage to such thick, unharmable-looking paper?

"Is that the newspaper? Why did you bring the paper out?"

Merit told him it was an invitation to a party.

That party.

"Boy, this day just gets better and better. Can you do me a favor and just bring the tweezers outside, Merit? Please?"

For God's sake. She said she would. The invitation was crumpled. She tried to smooth it out, but it did no good. Maybe she could entomb it between the pages of the volume of *The Story of Civilization* Caroline was reading. Or maybe she'd put it in Jenny's 1976 journal. She could also use the 1977, 1980, 1984, and 1985 journals, of course. (Merit would have taken more, but Jenny came storming out of the house and yelled at her to get away from the box.) Merit was only able to read the journals in small chunks. Her cheeks burned whenever she read them. When she'd get to the point at which her whole face burned, she'd stop reading and take the dog out for a brisk walk.

The invitation was important because she hadn't been invited to a party of Lowell's (or anyone else's) for quite some time. She was still flummoxed by the "Mr. and Mr. Lowell Haven" part. The party wouldn't be good for Jenny's mental and emotional wellbeing, although she would go anyway. It was a better idea for Jenny and Lowell to be without each other. It was a better idea for them to be rudderless and alone. The seventeenth of August was exactly two weeks away, and Merit really wished she'd had a little more advance notice. She felt her pulse in her throat at the thought of Lowell and lies and the party. Lowell had never once mentioned David Hockney to Merit. Or Josephine Baker. She felt her heart in her head now.

The party was too soon.

She ducked underneath Rosalita's dog run. Rosalita was not presently attached to it, and her rope hung plangently down. The dog run was a thick steel cord, and a rope attached to a pulley, that ran exactly down the middle of their backyard. It was suspended at seventy-two inches (Wyatt said). She couldn't figure out why Wyatt hadn't made the metal cord a few inches higher—they were both large people, after all. The length of the rope was exactly the distance from the metal cord to the Mitchell property line. Wyatt was yelling at himself again, inspecting his hand. Merit slid open the glass door to the family room and bounded toward the bathroom. She felt bigger now and brawnier, which is often what another person's mishap will do for you.

She had never known there even *was* an inspiration for Fergus's house, her home from ages four to eight. She was aware even then, in her kid brain, that their living situation was fragile, doomed to be merely transitory. They'd moved there because they had no money. Also, Merit suspected they, Jenny and Lowell, liked how it looked to the world at large (like the world *cared,* Merit now thought), that this shacking up with Fergus was the fantastically "bohemian" thing to do. And in the house, in the secret studio, whose secret hallway was accessed by pressing a faux copy of *Nicholas Nickleby,* Jenny and Lowell were so inseparable, Fergus referred to them as "Jewell," as if they were one person. Merit wondered if Fergus remembered his name for them. Merit still knew exactly what it felt like to be a kid, and she found it interesting how other adults didn't seem to remember how smart you were when you were small. However, she did miss one vital fact: She didn't, as a child, know what she would later learn about the paintings.

As a child, she found it difficult to sleep in the house. Her room there was darker than any room she'd ever been in before or since. (She'd wished, even then, that Fergus would have given her the option of decorating the room herself.) Lowell, Jenny, and Fergus would take turns tucking her into the canopied bed, which was so high, she had to use a little walnut step ladder to get into it, then kiss her head and draw the terrifying bed curtains closed. As soon as the bedroom door shut, she would spring up, rip the bed curtains open, and dive underneath the bedspread again. As the hours passed and the room lightened, which, happily, it always did, Merit would become increasingly emboldened, inching the bedspread down to her open eyes. What she would invariably see, though, was worse than the dark. Within the folds and pleats of the fabric above her, she could make out, very clearly and distinctly, a human hand. The long index finger of that hand was curled toward her, beckoning. It was a feminine hand, its nails red claws.

When she was seven or so, she would sometimes sleep in Fergus's bed. She still remembered exactly—exactly, to this day (she could imitate it, and had)—what Fergus's snore sounded like. It didn't take her long to figure out that if she kicked Fergus in the shins, the snoring would stop. Only for a while, though.

The house had a carousel, and a harp, and terrifying suits of armor, and a big gold gong, and a stage on which to twirl, and a pool you could sink to the bottom of and listen to your heart, and there were these beautiful emus outside. There were always some strangers who seemed interested to meet her. Merit remembered this one big bearded guy in a wheelchair who always seemed to be playing pinball downstairs. He took Merit and Fergus sailing on Lake Erie once, on his motorboat. She couldn't remember, looking back on it, whether the guy had been in his wheelchair while in the captain's chair or not. She remembered a woman, of roughly baby-sitter age, she recalled thinking then, who was an artist working in something she called "light sculpture," which, as far as Merit understood, seemed to involve taking about five hundred of those amusement park–issued thin plastic tubes that have some kind of glow-in-the-dark substance inside them and knotting them up into a huge ball. Merit remembered another woman—she couldn't remember her face, but she did remember what she'd said—who told her, "Pendleton was my generation's Jordache" and "*genuine* means 'fake'; so whenever you hear someone on TV say something is 'genuine,' you know what they mean is 'fake.'" Merit was probably five or six years old at the time, and she'd believed *genuine* and *fake* were synonyms until she was about twelve. She remembered how Fergus's extremely nice housekeeper, Fatima Valdez (who still came to the house three times a week, or at least she still did as of Merit's last visit, two years ago), would cook her beloved childhood meal: extra-wide egg noodles, prepared with half a stick of butter and lots of salt, then topped with a hearty sprinkling of sliced dill pickles. Fergus would always join Merit for this meal.

Merit, incidentally, went to grades two through seven with Fatima's son, Chuck, who once won second place in the sixth-grade science fair for his project on sheep organs (as in heart, liver, kidney, spleen, taken from an actual slaughtered sheep), which he'd displayed on, in Merit's memory, a cookie sheet. She vaguely remembered the story about an older Valdez sibling, a med student at NEOUCOM, somehow getting the sheep organs for Chuck, and she remembered thinking then, for the first time, something like, Nepotism pays. Should you choose to use it. Which Merit never had.

At Merit's seventh birthday party, one girl brought cookies in the shape of the number seven. Merit didn't remember this girl's name, but she could still hear her voice, and the loathing there, when the girl stepped inside the house for the first (and last) time with the plate of pink-frosted cookies and said, "Merit's got monaaaayyyyy." The girl stretched out the last syllable in an adult-sounding, righteous-sista way, and Merit still remembered what she'd thought then, in her seven-year-old-brain: The girl's assertion was plagiarized, heard elsewhere about someone else, used as her own. Merit and Fergus both wore rhinestone tiaras that day. Merit's favorite outfit in 1984 involved a lavender sweater vest and a navy blue straight-bottom knit tie. Merit ended up wearing a dress on her birthday, but Fergus wore *his* lavender sweater vest and navy blue straight-bottom knit tie. Looking back on it now, Fergus must have been disappointed to see the dress; she and Fergus often wore matching clothes that year, the year before she moved. At the party, she went around telling everyone the house was hers. There was a little girl guest who cried (rule number one: At every kid birthday party, there will always be a little girl guest who cries), sucked her thumb, and whimpered that she wanted to go home. Merit informed the little thumb-sucking sobber she'd better shut the hell up, because she was lucky to be there. Fergus bent down and whispered to her that lovely Cole Porter used euphemisms in his songs instead of bad words, so shouldn't she? Merit played a game in the red music room to see who could bang the gong the loudest, and yelled at everyone when she lost. Fergus stood in the corner of the music room, hands over his ears, his tiara aslant. On the piano, Merit plinked out the treble clef of a highly simplified little Mozart tune she'd just started to learn. (She did not yet know the tune was "Voi Che Sapete" from *The Marriage of Figaro*.) She had invited a boy from her class named Floyd. Floyd, it was known throughout school, had lice, and several of the bitchier female guests informed her that she shouldn't have invited him. Floyd tried to disassemble one of the suits of armor, with the hope, clearly, of getting inside. Everyone was scared of all the paintings of Lowell, and some little kid asked her if the man in the pictures was dead. Merit remembered Lowell, in his French cuffs, telling the kids how to draw a flower. (She still thought he was the artist then.) Merit remembered notifying everyone her flower was the best. Lowell smiled at her, beautifully, and said she sounded as arrogant as her mother. But Merit *did* think her birthday flower was the best, and it probably actually *was*, because she *was* the most talented artist in school, she sometimes thought.

She had occasionally nurtured thoughts that she was, or could be, a talent, too. Or at least maybe a mini one. But then she realized she was just being delusional.

Everybody used to tell her she'd been very talented at music, but they weren't telling the truth.

Merit would show Wyatt the invitation later. The envelopeless invitation was placed on the mail table in the hallway, heavy plasticky glasses case on top (sharing a home with so many animals really drove home the point that anything that fell to the floor could, and would, be eaten). She shredded the envelope, wondered whatever happened to Fawn Hall, and disposed of the pieces in the kitchen garbage can. Wyatt, seen through the kitchen window, seemed to be trying to extract the splinter with his bare right hand. The air conditioner was on, and, although Wyatt had recently installed a new Whisper Quiet system, she was unable to tell if he was still making noises outside.

With the second hand of her cheapie watch, she timed her sprint up the stairs: three seconds something, which was pathetically above her personal best of two something. At the top of the steps, Merit waited a few beats for the light to come on. It didn't. She waved her hands. Still nothing. She felt for the light switch. A piece of tape was slapped over it.

The automatic light in the bathroom worked at least. Peering in the medicine cabinet mirror, Merit zeroed in on a reflection: the light switch by the door. Another piece of tape. Merit turned around and looked at the light switch for real, yanked the tape off, rolled it into a sticky pill, and shot it into the toilet. *This* was how Wyatt chose to spend his Saturday? Making high walls to hide pigs behind, and taping light switches that didn't work anyway? She washed the tape gunk from her hands and rooted around in the medicine cabinet for the tweezers. The medicine cabinet held many products, and not all of them Merit's. Wyatt was massively brand-specific about toothpaste, soap, shaving cream, and deodorant because brands other than the Wyatt-approved ones caused breakouts. She located the tweezers behind an amber-colored prescription bottle of Wyatt's. (His million-year-old dermatologist continued prescribing two different kinds of antibiotics for his acne.) The tweezers were rusty, and she dipped them in rubbing alcohol. She found the Bactine and Excedrin. She took those, too.

Would one of the feather masks she'd bought in New Orleans a few years ago be good enough for her to wear to the party? She'd bought them on the off chance that a Halloween party or costume ball or something might someday come along. You certainly had to be an optimistic person to think that a costume ball might ever present itself in your future. Merit liked that. Another piece of Scotch tape on the light switch by the sliding glass door.

Wyatt was back at dragging the wood panel across the backyard.

"I brought first-aid supplies!"

"Oh, thanks, sweetie, but I think old Iron Wyatt got it out himself."

Upon further consideration, if Merit were to show up at the party in a three-dollar feather mask, she'd probably really be letting Lowell, and Fergus, down. They'd expect something creative.

"What can I say? It takes a lot to fell your old Iron Wyatt."

"Can we at least. . . . *disinfect* or something?"

"No, I'm fine. I have a new project for you. Want to hear it?"

She ditched the Bactine, Excedrin, and tweezers, dropping them onto the grass. The bundle of mail was still there. She said she wasn't sure she wanted to hear about her involvement in a new project of his, but shoot.

"How would you like to help me research a new fan for Arabella?"

Merit made no reply.

"We need to buy a bigger fan. I'm thinking the size of one at a ski slope. I can almost guarantee that we'll have to drive up to Cleveland to buy one. Maybe you can help me find out where to get it."

"Wyatt, did you tape up the light switches so I wouldn't touch them?"

"Well. *Naturally,* I still have the on-off-switch *set* to *on,* Merit. Now, I know you think a big new fan will be cumbersome, but it would be mounted up off the ground and out of sight. . . . That's not only an aesthetic decision, you know; it's also to circulate the air."

"Wyatt, you're trying to make it so I don't touch the light switches. I *know* you are. Admit it!"

"Merit, what are you talking about? Here. Look at my thumb."

He held the thumb out. It was indeed pink. But *come on.*

Merit asked how he got it out.

"With my teeth," Wyatt said. "Let me show you where I want to mount the new fan. You tell me what you think." With his uninjured hand, Wyatt opened the latch to Arabella's house. "See, over *here.* I'd build the motor frame off to this side, with a belt connected to a pulley behind it. You don't have to worry at all. You wouldn't even see it."

Arabella was asleep on her bed, snoring. A patch of sunlight fell on her right tusk. Merit loved the pig so much that she wanted to grunt whenever she saw her. Her hooves were like high heels. Like all good animal parents, Merit tried hard not to rate her babies in order of preference . . . but it was so awfully hard not to. Although she'd never told anyone this, the pig and the rabbit were her favorites. Or the rabbit and the pig, depending on her mood. Both such unlikely creatures! Merit had tried to do a sketch of Arabella once, a couple of years ago, but it turned out to be a disaster. She wasn't a talented enough artist to get at the spark in Arabella's eye; only a real talent could capture an animal's exiled essence.

Jenny would have been great at drawing Arabella. Merit had come close to asking her to draw Arabella once, for Caroline's birthday last year, but she couldn't bring herself to do it. Jenny hadn't drawn anything for five years.

That was Merit's fault, too.

13

11 July

A rainstorm stewed. I wanted to tell him, wanted to tell Lowell everything, but I couldn't, because you can never tell someone everything, because there would be nothing left to tell. Tonight, a boom of thunder. I dug into my bag for my gloves, although I knew they couldn't protect me. For the first time, I know nothing can protect me, nothing, not even Lowell . . . and Lowell's what I must be protected from. Can you feel yourself becoming another sort of person? I became someone else this evening. Should I be scared by that? If so, I'm not. I became a person who loved everything tonight: the rain and the black and the rattling hearselike taxis and the trench coats and the self-interested umbrellas that thought nothing of knocking us out of their way and the yowling traffic and the places on my body Lowell has been and the druggist and the punks and the shivering people we passed who have suffered, who suffer, who continue: I loved them. Will we suffer? Will we be able to lead polite and tolerably pleasant existences now that we know what we know?

Lowell canopied his black jacket over me and we held each other and ran through the rain. It's tragicomic, anything I write down now. I shouldn't be old enough to say, Life all comes down to one question: How much time? I shouldn't be on that schedule yet. But I am, today. Time: with Lowell. Lowell and I slid into the taxi, and he took my gloved hands into his and peeled off my wet, wrinkled glove, held it until it was no longer cold, and said, "This is what your hands will look like when you're very old, my dear." Lowell has taken presence of me. I love him. Unforeseen.

12 July

What it feels like when the air has been drawn from your lungs, when you have no breath left. Lowell sat for me, and I made pictures of him all day long.

13 July

The grocery store with Lowell. To be together, and alive, amid such plenty! At the Safeways supermarket. I climbed into the cart and Lowell pushed me down the aisles, throwing boxes and bottles up in the air in perfect arcs. I, in my cart, caught them. Back at Scotto's, I drew more pictures of Lowell, unsigned, because, as Lowell says, scholars agree that studies should have no signature. There must be more pictures, more Lowells! How did I live before? Life up to Lowell—a trance. We laugh now about how "off-beam" (as Lowell says) my initial impression of him was. Lowell says he fell in love with me, in part, because of my reluctance. I think I must have feared him, as anything that can have power over us is to be feared. He says I was his longest holdout.

The mystic coincidence of our meeting here, in London! Perhaps fate isn't as unlikely as I've thought.

14 July

Lowell is going around London with my sketches, telling everybody what a genius I am. Lowell says, rightly, that we ought to cash in now on our extreme youth and beauty and talent and whatnot. To be the recipient of such bottomless devotion! Unprecedented sensation! Lowell's room at Scotto's house is wallpapered with him, with me; my drawings and watercolors of him. But what pale impersonations the pictures are when weighed against the real Lowell. He is near me now in this room, his power tugging me toward him.

This evening, we were in Scotto's greenhouse. How fine Lowell looked in his goldfish-pink shirt, the sun setting violet behind him. We were drinking tea. Lowell watched me drink and told me he wanted to kiss me toe by toe. The leaves in my cup swished and drifted like sand. He told me he wanted to make me happy and asked how he could do that. He told me I was the most miraculous being he'd ever encountered and that he wanted the universe to know about it, about *me.*

He said he wanted to host a gallery opening for me.

He clapped three times and shouted, "Scotto!"

From unlocatably far off in the vast house came the distant rattle-snake muffle of our old drunk duke: "Yesssss, my dear?"

Lowell yelled, "You're going to have a party for Jens in a few days, yeah? We shall present my portraits to the world!"

Scotto's voice: "Let me come into the sssssolarium! I can't make out one devilish word you're sssssssaying!"

I was sitting on Lowell's lap when Scotto, in the room now, asked if he were "interrupting ssssssomething." I could see the outline of Scotto's distended belly button through his Prussian blue charmeuse robe.

Lowell told Scotto that he wanted him to host a party for us at his gallery. Scotto said, "Pastels and watercolors and ssssstudies aren't, in the main, *acceptable* works for a gallery opening, my ssssssweet."

"But this will be to show *Jenny* off," Lowell said. "Tell me what you want me to do, Scotto, to convince you. I'll appear entirely in the nude at the party, if that's what it takes."

"Nude?" Scotto asked.

"I wish I were joking," Lowell said.

"Name a date," Scotto said.

"I'll give you two days," said Lowell. "We're geniuses, and geniuses can't be kept waiting, of course."

My heart is doing queasy cartwheels!

15 July

This afternoon, Scotto elephanted up the stairs, batted at Lowell's door, and gasped that the "disssssstaff division" had a telephone call. I kissed Lowell, skipped downstairs to the phone. It was Dad. He said Fergus's father is sick. Fergus, Dad said, is in trouble. I'm illish-feeling again.

18 July

Gallery opening. We didn't sell anything. I shouldn't have had so much champagne and gin last night. And now I must convince Lowell to move from Scotto's house.

The evening, in miniature:

At 4:00 p.m., Lowell, Scotto, and I heaved into the backseat of Scotto's chauffered Rolls-Royce. (Now would be the place to insert a fat joke about that senile old liar Scotto, but I'm not that kind of person anymore; even hangoverish, I am Love, yes, even to Scotto.) In the car last night on the way to the gallery, I asked how I should handle myself, as I'd never had an art opening before. Lowell kissed me on the nose and said there were three rules for such an event: Be unassuming. Don't take any credit. And don't interfere. Scotto said that seemed like good advice for everyone. Lowell laughed and said he hoped he would be grown-up enough to listen to his own wise counsel. As soon as we got to the gallery, Lowell fetched me a gin and tonic and told me not to worry about *anything*, that he'd handle all the nasty little details, that I should just drink, drink, drink, and relax. He went to work arranging our pictures on the white walls. He brought me another cocktail. When the string quartet arrived, I was pretty far gone, and by the time the party started at 7:00, I was positively blotto.

The only significant memory from last night? The guests were just beginning to arrive. They handed their dripping Burberry coats to the tuxedoed staff and were offered, from an in-transit tray, a gin and tonic or a champagne. Dry, and with a drink in their hands, they started settling into my pictures. Lowell and I watched them look, and they really looked. (But then why didn't anyone buy anything?) Lowell turned to me, put my drink on the floor, clasped my hands together and brought them to his heart, and exclaimed with giddiness and with triumph, "Oh, Jens. You've made me what I want to be!" Then he whispered into my ear, "I love you so much that I'm afraid, my dear, I'm just going to have to call you 'Me'!"

And what other, far less important, memories do I have from last night? I believe I made my fist into a hand puppet and asked someone (talking, I'm afraid, through the hand puppet) whose above-the-neck area is now a blur what talents were necessary to be a puppeteer. This person replied, "A facility with string," and I stamped my pointy boot twice and shouted, "Not a *marionette,* stupid! A *hand puppet!*" Someone came up to me and said, "The boy in the pictures looks so *lifelike*." (Not much of a compliment, I think.) And someone else said, "This evening cost Scotto twenty thousand pounds; you're fucking him, I presume?" I'm afraid I responded in what I very soon learned was an unladylike fashion. I didn't yet know Scotto was shuffling around, wheezing at people that Lowell was the artist.

About an hour into the party, Lowell and I were still standing side by side. He plucked a gin from the tray, handed it to me. I drank it. I must have made a quite horrid face, because an older man (he was wearing overalls, and I tend to avoid grown men in overalls) sauntered over to me and said, "It's not a *sipping* drink, love; you've got to swallow it in one gulp, like *this*." He gulped, and Lowell and I watched him. Then the man walked away. Lowell stage-whispered, "That's *Theodore Goalting*, Jenny." I admitted I had no idea who Theodore Goalting was; apparently, he had been a very famous painter in the fifties. "Hold that thought, you gorgeous genius, you" Lowell said to me. "I should go and introduce myself. He was *lovely*. Just stay there; I'll be back momentarily."

Another silver tray came around, and I traded my empty glass for a full one. I stood there drinking and overheard a very upsetting conversation. I don't recall the speakers' bodies, but I know they were men.

"What a pretty model!"

"He is pretty, isn't he? Is he the chappie talking to Theodore? He's the artist, too, isn't he?"

"Yes, Scotto told me the boy's a *self-portraitist*. *Just* what we need more of."

"I do enjoy the theme: a shrine of self."

"Would that we all had such shrine-worthy selves!"

"Is that a nose job, do you think?"

"Notice how the skin throbs in the light in that one? Notice the ecstatic treatment of his own flesh? It's positively Catholic."

"Scotto predicts the boy will win the Turner someday."

"Scotto is beyond vulgar. Who would say such a thing about a child?"

"How old is he anyway?"

"He's seventy next month. Want to reckon that won't be a birthday with a party?"

"The boy, numbskull."

"Scotto won't give us a figure, but he has hinted that whatever he's doing with him is pleasingly illegal."

"How glad I am I've not had my supper yet; it would have just come up the other way. That one over there: The blue background is rather caustic, wouldn't you say?"

"How did he achieve such a scathing blue with watercolor?"

"Horrendous."

"Dreadful."

"Is the boy *really* ready to show, do you think? *Watercolors?*"

"Scotto's an utter charlatan; I've told you that."

"Did I tell you what Tibor de Nagy said about him?"

"Only about a hundred times. Are you and Tibor lovers? One more drink, then, shall we?"

"I tremendously respect Tibor, you know. But we must speak with Scotto one last time."

"Oh, must we? I'm rather inclined not to. I'm so, so exhausted. They forced me to journey out to *Twickenham Green* this afternoon."

"Miss, might we trouble you to bring us two more kir royales?"

Oh, what a rage I was in! How many other people had Scotto lied to? I've been brooding about this constantly, but Lowell says I shouldn't brood, that Scotto's senile, and not terribly bright on top of it. (I think Lowell's being too generous: Scotto lied because he hates me.) If only we'd sold a painting! If only more than one person had said nice things to me! What did the rest of them think about my work? Did they hate it, too? Does everybody hate me and what I do?

Is it wrong to say that my joy last night derived from drinking and watching Lowell?

Lowell took Theodore Goalting by the elbow and escorted him to *Lowell Number Three* (the offending watercolor with the blue background, which I personally find more milky, actually, than caustic . . . I've never heard anyone say anything negative about my work before. What if they're right? What if I *am* no good?). Lowell and Theodore were talking and laughing. Talking and laughing: What more is there to life? Lowell laughed and slapped his knee in delight. I watched Lowell for what seemed like hours, wanting to concentrate on his pull. Time with Lowell: I am greedy for it. I wish he hadn't left me alone last night, because it's such exquisite happiness standing near to my Lowell, my Me. To have a child, yes, with Lowell. I think I understand now.

14

Were all men like this? Did they all have a special room in the house where they went to hide? Wyatt had not emerged from his study yet today. Merit knocked on the door. The plastic mask was making her eyelids sweat. She was wearing her detested contacts.

"Yes, Merit," Wyatt said.

Merit entered.

"Hi!" she said.

Wyatt's desk was the least cluttered desk in show business. It was an organizational miracle, a TV talk-show desk, a prop desk, a sham desk, on which no real work ever happened. On it were, among a couple other things, a green-shaded banker's lamp, Wyatt's laptop, and four yellow mechanical pencils set in an anal-retentive line. Hanging on the wall over the desk was a brass plaque engraved with his motto IN GOD WE TRUST. ALL OTHERS MUST USE DATA. ("Statistician humor," he'd said when he brought the plaque home.)

Wyatt was enormously caught up in whatever was on the screen. His long neck was jutted toward the computer in a birdlike fashion. He was doing some kind of Internet search, and Merit clunked in closer to see exactly what the topic was.

"Do you think this would be a good costume to wear to Lowell and Fergus's party?" A feather tickled her forehead and she thought she could smell weird toxic feather dye, although she might have just been imagining it.

The chair squeaked as Wyatt leaned back in it. He swiveled around. He was expressionless, and Merit saw in his expressionlessness, as she sometimes saw when he was in a terrible mood, intimations of the constipated German farmer stock from which he was descended. He rubbed his chin.

"Did you get that in New Orleans?"

She had.

He was silent for a few seconds. He took his glasses off and made a minor readjustment of the nose pads. He rubbed his eyes. He said, "Jesus Christ, sweetie. Get it *together.*"

She kept her mask on, although Wyatt definitely thought she looked stupid in it. She was waiting to see how long it would take him to say something about her clogs. Wyatt didn't like people wearing shoes in the house. Which made sanitary sense, she guessed, but did he need to be such a dictator about it?

Dictator was too harsh a word.

"You're thinking about this party just a little too much," Wyatt said. The subject of his Internet search was "left side of head hurts."

Merit said that a costume party took a lot of preparation, and that if he thought he was going to go dressed merely as "Guy in a Suit" (Wyatt's Halloween standard, as in, "Hey, I'm Guy in a Suit!"), he was so very mistaken.

"Merit, you're not actually going to make me go to this, are you?"

"Oh, you're going, mister."

"If you asked me what my own idea of hell was, I'm pretty sure I'd s—"

"Oh, thanks. You're saying this about my family? *Nice.*"

Wyatt revolved toward the computer screen, leaned back in his chair, head tilted toward the ceiling, and sighed.

"Are you ever going to go through that stack of mail in the hallway?" He seemed to be directing this question toward the motion-activated overhead light. "You've got unopened mail from the Reagan administration out there. It's driving me nuts."

Merit replied that she would organize the mail at the first available opportunity.

"All your animals need baths. It's hell on my allergies. The dog is filthy, the rabbit's chewing through the plastic in the bedroom, and I've been taking care of the pig for days. Let's not let everything here fall apart."

Merit said she'd probably have some more time tomorrow.

There was a bottle of beer on his desk. It was 3:00 p.m.

"What is *wrong* with you, Merit? Are you paying *any* attention at all? You're kind of disappointing me here."

There was the word again. She was "disappointing" him. She was, as she always was, a "disappointment"—to everyone. Last year, after she told Wyatt she hadn't gotten a raise for the third straight year, he said her job was "really turning out disappointingly" and maybe she should think about starting to look for a new one. Merit responded by maturely pounding her fists on the bed; when he came over to her, she pounded her fists on his chest, then tried to push him away. She had messed around with someone else that afternoon, and afterward, she had fallen asleep underneath her desk, with her door open. She still wasn't sure if anyone had seen her. She hated that Wyatt couldn't sense then what she'd done a few hours before.

"Oh, I'm sorry I'm not *perfect,*" she said now. "I'm *so* sorry I'm letting you down, Daddy."

When she slammed the study door, she noticed the DO NOT DISTURB sign swinging on the knob. Wyatt had stolen the tag from the door of their room at the Ritz-Carlton, Kapalua, Maui, Hawaii, when they were there on their honeymoon; she and Wyatt hadn't been convinced that pinching a plastic DO NOT DISTURB sign from a six-hundred-dollar-a-night honeymoon suite (paid for by Lowell and Fergus) was technically stealing, although the hotel disagreed and had sent them a bill for twenty dollars. She hadn't seen the sign when she'd entered the room.

Merit fled the house because she needed to flee the house. She was horrified by her slip.

In good weather, in good traffic (there was always more weather than traffic in Akron), the drive to her gym in the valley took fifteen minutes. It was, chiefly, a meathead gym, but what wasn't? She strolled into the lobby, mad at Wyatt, semimad at Lowell, mad about all the ways they were similar (only superficially were they different, apparently). The guy at the front desk made a gun with his thumb and index finger and pointed it at her. She gave him the first two digits of her five-digit membership number, but he cut her off and said, "I believe I know it, madam."

Jenny had told Merit once that Lowell had said he was disappointed in her. He wished she'd "put more effort" into her piano lessons, and everything else. It still seemed sadistic to Merit that Jenny had relayed this comment.

Randy belonged to this gym, too. She'd seen him here only once, but there was always the off chance of an encounter.

Upstairs, on the stretch mat, a one-sided tussle was in progress—a man in a wife beater–type tank top (a tank top that wasn't doing all that much to conceal the fact that the guy had breasts, actual titties, B cups at the very least) called a woman an "annoying bitch." Which the woman, who didn't even look up from her downward-facing-dog stretch, probably was (even from an ass view, Merit knew who this woman was, and she had to admit she had never gotten such a great vibe from her), but which

Merit found an inappropriate public proclamation. Merit, looking in the mirror, gave the man the evil eye. He either didn't notice or care.

Also in the mirror: a guy from her high school, doing squats on the Smith Machine (Merit had become a gym rat recently and now embarrassingly knew the names of some of the machines). His name was Justin, and he wasn't jacked at all. He was wearing white shorts. Once a tennis fag, always a tennis fag, she thought. Merit had heard he was a plastic surgeon in Hudson. Made sense. He was the person who had informed her, when he sat behind her in seventh-grade Ohio History class (he was one of those kids who constantly jiggled his feet on the book rack underneath your desk), that a girl could have an attractive face or an attractive body, but usually not both. Up until that point, it had been news to Merit that people were thought of in terms of face versus body. In Ohio history class, he had also warned her about something else, something potentially even more troubling. She didn't want to talk to Justin now, or ever.

Merit suspected she was probably the only gym member who didn't appreciate the recent installation of plasma-screen TVs at the head of each treadmill. Actually, she actively loathed the presence of the TVs, and took it upon herself to turn off the ones in front of unused treadmills. Her need to do this bordered on a compulsion, and compulsions concerned her. Look what they did to her mother. And Fergus. Oh, and Lowell.

And Wyatt.

On the treadmill, she started her warm-up at 5.5 mph. Her intention was to run seven miles. Merit ran seven or eight miles five times a week. She was thinking now that she wouldn't go to Lowell's costume party. Her absence would hurt him. She knew that. Let him be hurt.

Ooospie! As Fergus says, or used to say (it had been a long time). There, in the smeary mirror in front of her, on the elliptical machine behind her, was someone who looked a whole lot like Randy. Except this guy was wearing a baseball cap. Randy would *never* wear a baseball cap. Not really his look. The guy was bopping to a tune on his headphones. His eyes were closed, and he was beating on invisible drums. The baseball cap said COCKS. It was definitely Randy. Merit looked away.

She had slipped a couple of times during her marriage. *Slipped*—not the best word choice. The unadorned fact of her marital slippage shamed her deeply, and she had told no one about it. She would never tell anyone about it. And, yes, it terrified her how she clung to these two flings, how she nurtured them, worked on them, buffed each's memory as if it were a prized blue marble and she a toothless, bridge-dwelling hag who cackled and held the marble because it was hers and kept it warm and polished it until it was the shiniest thing.

Randy was squinting at her reflection now, trying to figure out if that was her. No escape now. She waved at him. He smiled, and there were his braces, and he waved back. He continued his drumming. The rhythm was unchanged. Speed metal.

The first slip was with a twenty-year-old server at the Rainbow Villa, a health-food restaurant downtown where she sometimes went for lunch. The palms of his hands were orange—all the carrot juice he drank, he said. The second one was a fellow student in her once-a-week continuing-education nighttime sculpture class at Akron U. She didn't want to talk about their names. The first one liked to smoke pot and listen to music and fool around (there's really not much else to do when you're stoned—there's music, and there's fooling around, and that's pretty much it, as far as Merit could tell). These activities occurred about two days a week, for a month and a half, on her lunch break. The second, a twenty-three-year-old aspiring sculptor/personal essayist, was, for reasons beyond Merit, impressed by her job as an account manager at a regional magazine, and he was deluded enough to think that she possessed the ability to get his essays under the noses of appropriate editors at various worthless yet forbidding nationally distributed magazines she really had nothing to do with; he made her read, comment on, rewrite, and help submit approximately twenty first-person on-spec essays. The subject of about half of the essays: a cross-country road trip he'd taken with his brother the year before. The subject of the most memorable piece: the night he and his brother had had sex with the same girl in a tent at Burning Man. He had a lot of good qualities, though, one of which was his extraordinary memory for song track numbers on CDs.

Merit hadn't actually done much to correct his misunderstanding that she was a very connected person, looking back on it.

Randy climbed down off the elliptical machine. He was now ambling bowleggedly in her direction. He was holding a magazine. His eyes were fixed on a treadmill TV, not on her. His headphones were still on.

"Yo," he said. "Yo, yo, yo, yo, *yo.*" He approached the treadmill zone, pointing at her, her body. He wasn't winded.

"Yo yoself," Merit said. Yikes. Merit enjoyed the ha-has, but she was aware that she herself was not funny. She knew funny, but funny she was assuredly not.

"You're not going anywhere on that thing, you know."

She slapped the cumbersome red stop button. She made a mental note that she had run 2.36 miles; heart rate only a measly 137. To be continued.

"What's going on, boss lady? A little Sunday-afternoon run on the treadmill?"

His headphones were still on, and Merit was unclear if he was listening to her or his music, or what. She braced her hands on the treadmill's control panel. She was already sweating, and this was just the warm-up.

"What are you doing here, Randy? I've never seen you here." Merit was telling a fib now, fibbing in the same way her whole family winningly fibbed, the same way that drove her crazy. (But, man, was playing dumb ever effective.)

"Oh, you know how it is, Mrs. Ash. Sometimes I just need to come here and work off some steam."

Merit clambered down from the treadmill. He'd never called her "Mrs. Ash" before.

"Well, *good*," she said, and nodded like a supportive auntie. She was only a few years older than Randy, but often she felt about a million years older. She was twelve years younger than Wyatt, and sometimes, but not often, she thought about what that was like for him . . . if it was actually like anything. Wyatt seemed not to think about things like age.

"Hey," Randy said. "I saw you here once before. Remember when we talked? You had some kind of car issue and your husband had to drop you off, and he went around the gym looking for you in dress shoes that made a lot of noise and a shirt that had a lot of pens in the pocket."

"Oh yeah," Merit said. How could she forget? "It's all coming back to me now."

"Are you having a swell weekend?" he asked. "Lots of Ash family fun?"

A woman who, curiously for a gym setting, wore complicated shoulder-brushing earrings asked Merit if she was still using the treadmill. Merit shook her head. The woman mounted the machine. "Great weekend. Thanks for asking. . . . Although Caroline, my . . . my husband's daughter hasn't . . . How are *you*?"

"Eh, you know. Pretty cool, I guess, but this girl I've been sort of hanging out with . . . well, it's too fucked-up to go into right now."

"Is this the fashion student at Kent State?"

"Hey. You've got an awesome memory! No, this is a totally different girl."

"Oh, so this is the former girlfriend you're sort of sometimes still seeing?" She was prying now, and everybody knows that the world does not like a prier.

"Nope, totally different girl. Not the ex."

She didn't care for it when people referred to other people as "the ex" or "my ex"; she found *ex* a nasty word, an ugly word, but she realized this was just a personal tic.

"It's hard for me to keep track of all your ladies, Randy, honestly." She really should, she realized, make it seem as if she were paying less attention to the busy details of the romantic life of one Tooting Subordinate.

"Check it out. It's cool; it's relaxed. Everybody's happy. No hard feelings." His baseball cap cast a shadow on his face. His eyes were not really visible.

"Are your headphones actually on, Randy?"

"I got the volume turned way down. Is it bugging you to look at them?"

Merit said that it was not. The woman who had usurped her treadmill was walking, not running. What was the point of walking on a treadmill? Go outside and walk!

"Hey, so I got this magazine from the rack or whatever," Randy said. She looked at it now. It was the archrival of the magazine at which Merit and Randy were employed, and it was, alas, the more successful of the two. "Success" in Merit's (and Randy's?) line of work meant number of advertising pages. "Check it out," he said.

He flipped. Uh-oh. She was looking at a front-of-the-book spread from a particularly unbudgeable potential client. That meant this other magazine had finally broken this client's business; thus, Merit, whose job was, in part, to break automotive business, was screwed. (She thought it was funny that she worked as a manager of automotive and liquor accounts; it actually really was fairly comical, when you stopped to think about it.)

"Somebody needs to tell editorial they need to do more shit in the magazine about cars," Randy said.

It came as somewhat of a shocker that Randy was paying attention to the ad pages of other magazines versus their own. Maybe Randy was more ambitious than people gave him credit for.

"I think they have a really aggressive team over there," Merit said.

Aggressive team?

Randy removed his headphones, then his cap. His hair was completely, unfairly, beautiful. He shook it like a girl. Merit's sculptor/essayist friend had had Randy hair.

"Well, I'll let you get back to your run now. And hey," he said as he touched Merit's skin directly above the belly button, "nice tummy."

Merit hit the steering wheel. She was sitting in her car in the gym parking lot and was beating herself up for being the kind of female boss whose younger male assistant felt that stroking (and there'd definitely, *definitely,* been a second or two of stroke action) an area of her physical person fell within the realm of socially acceptable behavior. She hit the steering wheel again. It *was* her fault, wasn't it, for not being scary enough, or intimidating, or bosslike? The problem, obviously, was that she was too fucking nice. That's what Wyatt and Jenny had told her repeatedly: "You're too nice, Merit." In college, for instance, whenever she did laundry in the basement of her dorm, and whenever the timing and dryer availability were such that she would be required to remove some phantom person's clothes and sheets and towels from a dryer that had just finished its cycle, she would fold, as assuredly as a professional, that phantom's clothes, sheets, and towels and organize them in the waiting plastic basket by item type. Mostly people just dumped the other person's clothes into their basket and ran, whistling, back to their rooms. (She'd even paired *socks* together.) Merit remembered the birthdays of everyone who had ever been important to her, and sent these people birthday cards, and she always came back from her vacations with little gifts for everyone in her office, and when she, Caroline, and Wyatt went to Paris for their big vacation a few months ago, she'd bought everyone at work (and that was fifteen people) hand-tooled leather journals that had cost anywhere from twenty (Ronnie's and Claudia's) to sixty (Randy's) Euros each. And she *had* been too nice, to Randy particularly—she'd tried, professionally speaking, to encourage him in ways in which he didn't deserve to be encouraged (she'd even let him take full credit for the vodka business, and he had had nothing to do with it). And she occasionally gave him cash—out of her own pocket, because assistants were not given expense accounts—to take a few clients out to lunch, and, although no actual business had actually seemed to come out of it, she'd let him have her American Express number and with it sent him to the auto show in New York at the Javits Center. And she had never once corrected or even brought to his attention the weird spelling problems on his phone-message E-mails (Merit had been crowned 1991 Summit County Spelling Bee Champion, but she'd lost in the first round of state competition to the nettlesome *pusillanimous*), and she typed her own letters herself, because how could she possibly let his "Merit"-signed letters out into the world? She'd sent him an E-mail once with the subject line "You're Going Places!" She was famous as an assistant-indulger. When Sabine, her pre-Randy assistant, had quit last year, each ad/sales department assistant, every single one, had tiptoed into her office to inquire as to whether she might possibly consider him/her for the vacant job, saying his/her current boss didn't know anything about this inquiry and it would be so amazing if she didn't tell anyone anything, and she hadn't. She was the kind of boss who had framed photographs of dead pets in her office. Merit knew she would have been the kind of college professor (not that she was an expert in anything or had anything to teach, or that she had really even liked school when she was a student) who would smoke a ton of weed with her students, and give them her home number, and hang out with them in bars at the pathetic age of fifty, and get too bizarrely emotionally involved with each kid in her class, and tell them to do the absolute opposite of what she had done in her life. "Look at me; now *run* in the other direction," she could hear herself saying. "Wow, man; that's one cool older chick" would be the students' response. She had allowed the working relationship between Randy and herself to become too casual and undefined. Previously, she had preferred her assistants to be female, for females tended to have more respect for established systems of power, it seemed to her. Now authorityless, Merit would be forced to pay for her deviation from the course.

The Jaguar started on the fifth ignition crank.

Justin, that guy from her school who was squatting forty pounds (she could squat a hundred) on the Smith Machine, had told her back in seventh-grade Ohio History class that all girls grew up to marry their fathers.

When they'd lived at Fergus's house, Merit remembered, during the last year, Jenny sometimes talked to Lowell in a baby voice. Even then, Merit couldn't tolerate the voice, or the question the voice sometimes asked Lowell. The question was "Do you hate me?" Lowell always seemed very upset whenever the question was posed. Merit didn't understand how Jenny could possibly think Lowell hated her. She remembered often being lifted by Lowell during that era, and held in the middle of an embrace between Jenny and him. Merit had loved being held within her parents like that, but even back then, she'd worried that they didn't need her there. They were mostly locked in their studio, without her. Jenny and Lowell seemed to need only Jenny and Lowell.

During the horrible baby-voice year, Jenny would often come into Merit's room late at night (when Merit wasn't sleeping with Fergus), climb up the little walnut ladder, and burrow next to Merit in the canopied bed. Jenny never had to open the curtains to Merit's bed, because they were already open. These nights, Jenny would awaken Merit by squeezing her, Jenny's wet and suffering breath on Merit's neck. Merit still, more than two decades later, couldn't sleep if another person (meaning Wyatt) was in any way touching her. She knew this was abnormal and sad.

Merit couldn't ever remember calling Lowell "Daddy."

Once when Lowell was visiting Merit at her new house, Merit rode on a seesaw at the playground across the street. Lowell didn't ride the seesaw with her, but he stood at the opposite end of it, pumping it with his arm. He wore a French-cuffed shirt and a purple ascot. He pushed the seesaw and asked Merit why she didn't call him "Daddy" anymore. So she must have called him "Daddy" before that, at least sometimes.

Because if girls grew up to marry their fathers, that would mean Merit was Jenny.

15

When I suggested to Andrei he pose as my secretary and make the call to Preston Lympany, I wasn't sure whether I was going to get an earful or not. In April, I'd made the mistake of giving Andrei a box of Godiva chocolates for National Secretary's Day. When offered to him, he grimaced limply at the card, opened the gold box, selected a red foil–wrapped heart-shaped milk chocolate, chewed, swallowed, and denounced himself a "bad boy," stating this meant an extra fifteen minutes of cardio the next morning. I naïvely thought he'd gotten a kick out of the winsome joke, but then I heard from other people staying with us that he was deeply offended by the gesture and had told them I needed a reality check. I myself cannot hear Andrei uttering "reality check," but you know how imprecise gossip can be. So when I proposed the idea this morning, I braced myself for the worst.

I found him in my library, sacked out on my tufted couch, ogling my TV, my remote control in his hand. My mah-jongg set was strewn on my original Gothic Revival (c. 1843) gaming table. I asked him what he was doing.

"This is *Braveheart*. I am watching the action sequences from it, *Fergus*." And here he hit the rewind. Andrei claims he's from Rio, but I have my doubts. He came here to study with Lowell, and is, in addition, a poet manqué. I've never seen one painting or one poem, but I did once overhear Lowell say Andrei was shy about showing his work around.

"I like it when he does this," Andrei said. I cannot give you details about the scene on the television; I wasn't paying attention, because I noted the trick bookcase was slightly ajar, revealing the secret passageway behind.

"I don't know how you're going to react to the following question," I said. I thought I saw a shadow moving on the cherry passageway wall. The passageway leads to Lowell's studio. No human being has set foot in Lowell's studio for five years. I was tense for a number of reasons.

"If you are buying, Fergus, I am flying."

Stupidly, *paying* Andrei to make the call hadn't yet occurred to me.

"I'll give you a hundred dollars if you'll do me a very small favor," I said.

Andrei gave me a supercilious little glance, chucked the remote control, and rubbed his sweaty thumb and fingers together like an Uzbek rug merchant.

I upped the fee to two hundred dollars and explained what I wanted him to do. He didn't blink, but then again, he never does. We practiced the conversation—Andrei as my secretary, F.B.G. as Mr. Nostrils Preston Lympany—by the library's inglenook. Forty minutes later, satisfied we'd covered all possible conversational permutations, and satisfied, too, no one was lurking in the secret passageway, I led Andrei downstairs and pushed him into my phone room.

I begged him to break it to me gently if Preston Lympany declined my invitation to come over and look at magazines; I begged Andrei to lie, actually, if Preston Lympany rejected me: "Tell me he's stricken with walking pneumonia, or whooping cough, or a particularly virulent strand of asthmatic bronchitis," I said. "I'd rather believe he's dying than know the truth about what he thinks about me." Andrei picked up the handset, then said he'd decided to change his fee to three hundred dollars.

As there wasn't enough room in the phone alcove for both of us, I had to stand outside, directing the conversation. It went like this:

"Hello, Preston?" Andrei said.

Nooooo! I pantomimed. Think secretary, not friend! We had *gone over this* during our *rehearsal* by the *inglenook*.

"I am Fergus Goodwyn's personal assistant. He has asked me to give you a ring."

That was better. Andrei nodded in agreement with whatever it was Preston Lympany said. He gave me the thumbs-up sign. I gave him an A-OK.

"I will! I will tell him that!"

He put his hand over the handset, mouthed something to me. The conversation was over about ten seconds later. He hung up and informed me Preston would be stopping by in twenty minutes.

I had had no shower this morning, no shave, no visit to the WC at all, in fact, no run, no protein shake, no coral calcium capsules. I was, in short, in no state for visitors. Also, I didn't know if I had enough magazines.

"You are welcome, Fergus," he said. "Now where is my money?"

"Would Donald Trump take an appointment on such short notice? It's absurd. It makes me look bad." I told him he was relieved from any further secretarial duties.

Andrei, who had been wearing the same leather vest for the last five days, sneered at me and asked in a very rude way if I had "anything *else* to do this morning."

I admitted I did not, then, giving his vest the once-over, asked if he was intending on joining a motorcycle gang.

"The pockets are great," he said, showing all his teeth. His lower cuspids are cat fangs. "They are the perfect size for subway tokens."

I asked what metropolitan subway system he was riding these days, because Akron, Ohio, as far as I recalled, did not presently have, nor would ever have, a subway line.

He said the side pockets were just the right size for a quarter, too.

I asked why he needed a quarter when he owned a cell phone, which I was fairly certain he did, because, if I was not mistaken, had I not written him a check for last month's bill?

I was, frankly, surprised how poorly I was responding to the notion of Preston Lympany's sudden visit.

I hustled downstairs, threw off my maroon dressing gown, and slithered into the whirlpool. Whenever I'm in the market for an accelerated bath, I head right to the whirlpool. Let's not think about the sanitary implications.

Abbreviated wash completed, I patted myself with my robe, stuck out my tongue at the hideous late-stage Lowell self-portrait screaming at me from the opposite wall, and dashed back upstairs. In my bathroom, I applied one layer of roll-on deodorant, dried my underarm area with Lowell's hair dryer, applied another layer, dried with Lowell's hair dryer, then repeated this sequence ten more times. I flossed my teeth, teased what was left of my hair, shaved my neck, checked ear holes for any stray hairs, and squirted myself with Lowell's Milanese cologne. A button had fallen off my shirt with the beautiful fretwork, the label cut into my neck on my other favorite shirt (Lowell has said it makes me look like a Mennonite, but I still like it), there was a stain on my good white pants, and my black silk shorts must have shrunk at the dry cleaners. Clothes: always trying to beat you. Maybe I would present this as a conversational topic with Preston Lympany.

Although Andrei never made it as far as this during the call, the premise of the get-together with Preston Lympany, was, as I had conceived of it, to be this: We would "read" magazines together for party ideas. Preston is a real pop-culture fanatic, I have learned. As I was attempting to sew the button on my shirt (I pricked myself with the needle twice, wiping the blood on my thigh both times), I remembered again the big hitch in the plan.

I pressed the button on the intercom for the library, hoping Andrei was back at *Braveheart* again. I very much doubted he was elsewhere. How right I was.

"Fergus?" said the intercom.

"I need magazines." The blood had turned copper on my leg. The pathos of being human is sometimes too much to endure, depending on one's mood. "He's going to be here in three minutes."

He waited a few seconds. I prepared myself to be hit up for more cash. "I will leave now. May I drive your car, Fergus?"

"Of course," I said. "But be back soon. And no home-decorating magazines. *Southern Country Living* almost made me have a stroke last time."

Through the stained-glass window in my bedroom, I watched Preston Lympany shamble up my gravel driveway. My first impulse, when I see someone outside, is to duck behind my red Jacobean settee and hope they'll just go away.

I left him waiting only ten minutes. He was in the foyer when I went to fetch him. He was sitting on the bench underneath Lowell's King Arthur portrait, and in his lap was a paper shopping bag. Whenever there's a shopping bag in front of me, I've just *got* to know what's in it. We cheek-kissed. He's about five eleven, and he looked fantastic. I asked about the bag.

"It's *so* good to see you, Fergus. You look great! I brought cupcakes, cigarettes, a bottle of sparkling water . . . and an extra added surprise."

(The surprise turned out to be a blimp eraser, but that was not revealed until later.)

We had discussed cupcakes last week at his house. I was touched he remembered the conversation.

"I've never seen a ring in a lion's mouth," he said.

I was trying to direct him out of the foyer, but he was loitering in front of Lowell as Arthur. There is no lion in this painting, only a shirtless, black-eyed Lowell. I was confused. "Beg pardon?" I asked.

"On the door outside," he said. "The knocker. It's really, I don't know, *sexual*. It's like a gag ball. I wasn't sure I was at the right house." Now I knew Preston Lympany was no mastermind, and I knew his last visit had been under somewhat more intoxicated circumstances, but I really hoped he wasn't *that* dumb. How could he have forgotten my house?

"Is he here?" he asked. He was still looking at the painting.

"Who?" I asked. I was afraid he was still talking about the lion. I really didn't want Preston Lympany to turn out to be a hula girl vis-à-vis brainpower.

"Him," he said. " 'The painter. Lowell Haven.' "

"Is that a quote from something?" I asked as I tried to lure him through the door into the great hall. "A magazine puff piece perhaps, from the old days? Don't know where he is, actually."

But hula girls can be smart, too, the little voice scolded.

"We don't care for him, really," he said. His paintingward gaze was as steely as diplomat's. "Do you mind me saying that?"

"Not at all!" I said. "You do know Lowell painted from my photographs, don't you?"

"Really?" Preston Lympany asked. "He was very rude to a friend of ours. I've never forgotten it." And here he slung his arm around my shoulder, just as if we were pals, old pals who had so many good stories to tell.

I hoped he hadn't meant it when he said "ours."

Here's how great I felt, at first, with Preston Lympany: I ate three of the six cupcakes in five minutes. Here's how comfortable he was, or seemed to be, with me: He lit a cigarette without asking. We were sitting knee-to-knee on the west terrace, under the most loathsome gargoyle, the one with the Brando nose. This gargoyle juts out from the house on a horizontal neck; I find it frightening. Our chairs were directed toward the daffodil field and, beyond it, the pond. I knew the cigarette meant bad things for my asthma—a few parties ago, when I was a little too relaxed about letting people smoke, my asthma was so bad afterward, I had to sleep outside in a tent for three nights.

I wasn't letting myself think about the consequences then, though, with Preston Lympany.

"Can you believe they say she didn't have plastic surgery?"

He was scrutinizing a photograph in a movie-land magazine. Now is the place to reveal that I didn't really think all that much of Andrei's periodical selections, although I did take responsibility for not having given him enough direction before I sent him off. I had at that moment decided food magazines were the only tolerable glossies, and I was happy about the one he'd bought.

"I'll believe anything," I said. "Genetics. Look at Lowell."

He inserted another cigarette into his mouth. "Someone told me that you can have the crappiest genetics and work out like a maniac and never eat the bun and still be fat," he said. The cigarette was long, brown, thin. I recognized it.

"I used to smoke those," I said.

Now "used to smoke" was maybe plumping up my relationship with the cigarettes somewhat: I'd bought one pack of them once, when I was in high school. Jenny, viciously, called them "pimp cigarettes"; such an insult was, at that shaky time of life, enough to humiliate me out of smoking them, and everything else, for good.

"I wasn't aware that particular brand still existed."

The smoke tusked out of his proud nostrils. I imagined how his hands would smell: smoke and heat.

"Trevor gets them for me when he goes to Mexico."

"Ah," I said, feeling something I preferred not to give a name to. "How is old *Yellow Hair*?"

"Ooooh, he'd be so mad if he heard you say that! He does the color himself every other Tuesday night."

I hoped Preston Lympany's hands, if I touched them, wouldn't be cupcake-sticky, despite the fact he'd had no cupcake.

"That's a line from Joyce: 'Lean out your window, yellow hair.' "

"It's about Rapunzel?"

I was unsure whether it *was* Joyce now. I was feeling insecure in every possible way. I hoped Preston Lympany didn't notice.

"Did I tell you that Trevor's . . . looking forward to the . . . *party*?" he asked experimentally. "He was going to go to Las Vegas, and that's also the weekend of his parents' fiftieth, but he wanted to come to your party instead."

My lungs were constricting. I sneezed thrice, shallowly, into my cupcake napkin.

"Grand," I said.

What did I feel? Deceived? Unloved? Ashamed because I had no right to be in pain? Terrified I was becoming some kind of mewling delusional basket case, sobbing on the side of I-271 in March sleet?

"Do you like this table setting?" he asked, angling his magazine toward me, as if this were story time—he the governess and I the little boy. I still remember how teachers would always flip the page before we'd gotten a really good look at the picture. "It's from a baby shower at Melanie Griffith's. Maybe you can do something like that. It says here the place cards are chocolate!"

"Excuse me for a minute," I said. "I'm moving out of the sunlight."

I dragged my farthingale chair across the terrace. I parked myself underneath the purple summer awning outside of the window to the great hall.

I was faking it in the shade, pretending to enjoy a picture of a browned scallop in *Gourmet* magazine. I could sense Preston Lympany looking back at me, then turning away. I rubbed my thighs, pretending I was working in sunscreen I'd not applied back in the house. The sepia blood was there to stay.

Preston Lympany waved his arms in the sunlight, asked me a question about the cupcakes' durability. Although I'm debilitatingly near-sighted and wouldn't have been able to see his eyes from that distance anyway, I wished he weren't wearing sunglasses.

He asked the question again. "Should I bring the cupcakes over there, Fergus? I'm afraid they're going to melt!"

I couldn't find it in myself to be mean. I told him if he wanted to scoot his chair over, that would be nice.

He folded the magazine and tucked it into the back of his jeans. He carried the cupcake box and dragged the chair, which screeched like a Strindbergian matron. He set the box down, hoisted the chair up over his head, displaying biceps, triceps, and that front deltoid some fantastically in-shape people have (he was wearing a tank top). He set the chair down next to me.

The way he had positioned his chair made it feel as if we were riding a bus. We sat that way, side by side, looking out at the pond, like a couple who'd known each other since we were each diapered and dimpled fifteen-pounders. I would have offered him a toothpick if I'd had one.

"Your house is amazing."

"Thanks," I said. "But Hepplewhite is so much more my style nowadays. Let that be a lesson to you."

"Yeah, but the *details* . . . Hey, is Manikin Pis the inspiration for that fountain?"

He was contemplating the statue in the center of the reflecting pool: the dauphin, who wees in gentle, soothing drops.

I get scared when someone tells me something I don't know, and I'd never heard of this "Pis" thing before. "There is no inspiration for it, I'm afraid. I got it at Krim's Garden Supply on State Road," I said. "It was deeply discounted."

We were silent for a few minutes. I could hear my cells dividing. A turning magazine page was a deafening *rrrrrip*. The reflecting pool mirrored the black statue, the peonies in their green planters, the trees, the sun, the sky. I'd waded in that pool before, with Merit, but that was years ago.

Preston Lympany lit another cigarette and asked how the party preparations were going.

I said we'd received a few calls from some castoffs—those who hadn't gotten invitations, those who wouldn't be getting invitations—wondering if theirs had gotten lost in the mail. I do not return such phone calls, I told Preston Lympany. I kept my eyes on the magazine, as if what I had in front of me were a terribly pressing matter.

A black squirrel scrambled onto the terrace and frightened away two starlings. Preston Lympany tapped his cigarette ashes onto the mossy bricks. I wished I'd brought a hat.

"They should do an article about *you*," he said. He pointed to the magazine with his cigarette. I was afraid I was going to sneeze.

"Who?" I asked.

"This magazine," he said. "Any magazine."

"Really?" I asked.

"Sure," he said.

"Well," I said, getting my Kleenex ready, "I think I'd need a publicist first."

"Really?" he asked. He pushed his aviator sunglasses to the top of his head. He was young, about Merit's age. This was the first time I hadn't seen him without at least one glittery ring.

"Besides, I don't really have anything to promote," I said.

"Bless you," he said. (I had sneezed.)

"Publicists: the enemy and the savior."

"Wasn't Lowell in this magazine once?"

Despite my wriggling, my shorts were too tight to fit the sodden Kleenex into.

"Maybe," I said. I started clawing at the Kleenex.

"I've always thought you have a lot more charisma than Lowell," he said. He fiddled with the ball on his lighter. "The first time I saw you, I thought two things: He's from somewhere else. And *he's* the source of Lowell's creativity."

I kept right on clawing the Kleenex. Lint, which wastes no time, had swiftly found its way to my black silk shorts.

"Lowell's just the manufactured center of attention," Preston Lympany said. "You're the real focal point, Fergus."

The only other person who'd ever dared to see me for what I am was Merit. Only Merit, and now Preston Lympany, understood.

"Excuse me a moment."

I rose and strolled, barefooted, over to the intercom on the side of the house. I shakily brushed the ivy away and pressed the button for the library.

"Fergus?" the intercom asked.

"Can you be a honey, Andrei, and bring me a lint roller?"

Andrei said he could do that. He was being stunningly agreeable today, really. Maybe it was the money.

Preston Lympany, still sitting in his chair, put his sunglasses back on. I pressed the button again. "And a hat!"

Once, when I was on the stage in the music room, choreographing the dance for "I'm Getting Myself Ready for You" (I was stuck on the lyric "And besides which, I want you to holler 'hooray!' / When first you see me in my so-to-speak"), Merit said to me, "You're funny! I want to be you when I grow up, Uncle Fergus."

"Be like me?" I asked.

"No," she said, "*be* you, Uncle Fergus."

I've never told this to anyone. But Preston Lympany would listen if I told him; I knew he would.

I peeked inside the cupcake box once I'd sat back down. The chocolate icing had slid off the top of one of my moist delicious friends. I thought that I really should eat at least one, or possibly two, before they melted away.

"Butler," I said, meaning Andrei, in case Preston Lympany cared.

"So how rich *are* you, Fergus?" Preston Lympany asked.

"Oh, I'm good with my money, and Akron is cheap, so looks can be deceiving . . . but I used to be even richer," I said, picking out another cupcake from the remaining three, "before Lowell got his own money."

"Let *me* be your patron," I said to Jenny over twenty years ago. "Let *me* be your benefactor." My offer was, eventually, accepted. Jenny, Lowell, and Merit were living in New York then. Lowell's career went magnificently well in New York (although he and Jenny still had no money), but Jenny, whenever we spoke on the phone during those years, often seemed resentful and unhappy about Lowell's success. *Restless* was a word that often came up in our conversations. One time, I asked her about her own art, but she wouldn't answer directly, and saying instead how she was stewing about everything all the time and wanted to be someplace where the people were "recognizably human." ("Well, move back home to Akron!" I said.) The main happiness in her life then was Lowell. She called me one morning when Merit was an infant, dizzy and euphoric at 8:00 a.m. (and 8:00 a.m. was as early for me then as it is now). She told me she'd been up all night watching Lowell sleep. He held an endless fascination for her, she said, although he was "a very damaged person." A very damaged person! I thought. I suppose you could say I fell in love with Lowell because of Jenny.

And when they all lived here, we were happy. Lowell was the first person in my life who'd ever encouraged me about my photographs. We quickly became collaborators. I built him a studio, and he worked, and Jenny followed him, and Merit and I became one. And *I* was happy. That's how our little lives eddied pleasantly along until Jenny and Merit left us.

After they were gone, I wrote down a dozen questions about them for my Ouija board. It seemed to me the only way I could understand what they had done. Lowell and I sat in the darkened, candle-lit music room, facing each other, our knees tantalizingly close. For every question Lowell asked (Lowell was always the medium, back when we still played macabre games), the board had the same answer: GIRLS GONE. BOYS MANY TEARS. To this day, Lowell promises he hadn't been deliberately pushing the planchette.

But eventually, Merit and Jenny began coming back to the house (Jenny more than Merit), and Lowell and I got back to work again. We may not have been as happy as we'd been before, not yet, but we found strength in one another. I remember what it was like to go up to people at parties and introduce myself as "Lowell Haven's muse." Most people, I found, believed me, although anyone who even perfunctorily knew thing one about Lowell's work would surely have been aware that Lowell Haven's muse had always and only been Lowell Haven. It was fun making people believe I was a minor celebrity (Lowell, in fact, always encouraged me to lie about that), and I would bustle home, all atremble from having made such a splash at a party, and I would press down on the phony *Nicolas Nickleby,* and the phony bookcase would *always* revolve open, and Lowell would emerge after a minute or two from his mystery studio (access to which was strictly denied to anyone, even to Castelli when he came to visit, and Sonnabend before him, even to the person who owned the studio and the house that contained it), a paintbrush tucked behind his ear so elegantly, so offhandedly, that it looked like a prop, and I would recount my evening's adventures, and he would listen and he would say, "Tell me about it, Fergus; tell me *everything.*" And I would.

We became the couple you see at Kroger, so cheery as to be nauseating, Lowell pushing the cart, me crouching in the basket, Lowell throwing supermarket products to me. We were two delighted, handsome adults playing catch. And we would stay in the bedroom for days, and I had to have his great room door widened so we could fit his wing-footed bed through, and I built the carousel for him, Jenny, and Merit, and I bought the emus for them, too, and in the springtime, when we went out for a walk after dinner, Lowell would caution me to be careful of the puddles, and he showed me his Goyas at the Prado, and whisked me to the National Gallery of Art, and we revisited the Gold Flacon, the restaurant where we, accompanied by Jenny, had met (I thought the place was called the Gold Falcon until our trip back), the restaurant where he first called me "distracting" (I would hear him describe me this way again, many more times), and we went to Documenta 7, 8, and 9 together (and I didn't even mind going to awful Kassel, Germany, because I was with him), and he told me everything he knew, and he showed me who he was.

Once, he peeled off my gloves and said of my cold hands, "This is what your hands will look like when you're very old, my dear," and he wrote me letters, and I felt exultant and blood-filled, and I loved Lowell's daughter as if she were my own, and I even still loved Jenny, and I loved everything that was his as if it were mine. I loved his shedded hairs on the floor tiles, and his paintings, and his French-cuffed shirts after he'd worn them, and his fluttering lungs.

I loved him as if he were me.

And Lowell loved *me*, too. How much? So much that he called me "Me."

It is difficult—but necessary, I'm afraid—to remind yourself what you had before is never coming back.

And it was only after Jenny and Merit left that he finally told me who he was, that he had dreams of empire that only *I* could help him achieve. He didn't have enough talent on his own, he said. When he made me promise I'd never tell anyone, I said mischievously, "You certainly must trust me."

"Oh, I trust you enormously, Fergus," he said, "more than I've ever trusted anyone, in fact." How smug I felt! How very smug. I was so desperate to believe his flattery that I wouldn't let myself see his declaration was not about me at all; it was meant to be a renunciation of Jenny, directed to the universe, not to me. And it wasn't true.

The way one goes over things in one's head, the same dead things, over and over.

"Do you want me to read your horoscope?" Preston Lympany asked.

"I'm a tough case," I said, "being a 'cusp' man myself. Pisces-Aries."

"My mom is a Pisces," he said. The Brando gargoyle cast a shadow over Preston Lympany's right boot. The shadow meant: noon. Lowell would have approved of the boots.

"Fantastic," I said. "I love mothers."

"Which do I look under? Pisces or Aries?"

"Depends which has the better horoscope, doesn't it? *Cusp* is an atrocious word, isn't it, Preston? I'm sorry you had to hear it."

"Yeah!" he said. "It *is* pretty bad."

Andrei hadn't yet arrived with the lint roller. I tried covering my downy lap with my *Gourmet*.

"What's *your* least-favorite word, Preston?"

"I don't know. I'd have to think about it," he said. "*Cusp* maybe? I don't know. What's yours?" He peered (or at least I think he did) at me through his opaque superhero glasses.

"Saatchi," I said.

"Oh," Preston Lympany said. "*Right.*"

We were silent again. Lowell maintains that he stopped painting because he'd become "obsolete." He used that word on me, too. Five years ago, when Lowell finally became rich and sold off much of his work, he told me *I* was obsolete. I was now obsolete to him.

Preston Lympany read the Pisces horoscope, followed by Aries. I told him I chose Aries today because it seemed more agreeable to me, given present circumstances.

"I'd like to revise my least-favorite word," I said. "I'll go with *obsolescence.*"

He crossed his cowboy boots at the ankles, and I had the sudden, and probably incorrect, suspicion he was wearing lifts. He clasped his hands behind his head and leaned back toward the open sky.

"What's that noise?" he asked.

"What noise?"

"Don't you hear it?"

"No."

"That."

"Ah," I said.

"It sounds like a really big fan."

"Not from Akron?"

"Steubenville," he said. "Originally."

Preston Lympany's description of the sound of the blimp was a well-chosen one, I thought. The thing really does sound like an enormous sky-mounted industrial fan. And there the blimp indeed was, coming into view, up over the line of poplars, a weightless gray whale creeping through the sea green sky.

"That reminds me!" he said, and bounced over to the flapping grocery bag at the other end of the terrace. With the bag in hand, he bounded back to me. I decided he wasn't, in fact, wearing lifts. The crunching of the bag as he dug into it was louder than the blimp's engine. "I forgot I had Pellegrino . . . and *this*!"

And here Preston Lympany presented a thumb-sized baby blue eraser in the very shape of Akron's own blimp. His smile was a merry smile. His nostrils twinkled.

"Well, *I'll be*," I said. "Consider the odds."

He held the eraser up to the sky and, behind his sunglasses, squeezed (I think I saw this) one eye shut. "The eraser's bigger than the real blimp!" he said.

"Perspective," I replied.

"Here," he said. "I brought this for you. We were talking last week about the Soap Box Derby and the blimp, so I thought you'd think this was cute!"

We had talked about the Soap Box Derby last week, it's true, and the blimp. What I hadn't told Preston Lympany then was how Lowell bought Merit and me a Soap Box Derby car once, and a child driver to go with it. We won the race that year; the child driver kept the scholarship. What I hadn't told him then was that Lowell once rented the blimp—there were only three then (there's a whole fleet these days)—and a pilot for me for a weekend, many weekends ago.

Then Preston Lympany leaned over to me and did something I'll never forget. He touched my cheek with the eraser, then gently dragged it downward. He traced the eraser over my lips. It tickled as if it were his own finger.

He put the eraser in the palm of my hand, wrapped my fingers around it, held his hand there. The eraser was gummy. I wanted to smell it, but I didn't. I already knew what rubber smelled like.

The genuine blimp was directly over us now, and on its belly were words in lights: REMEMBER TO CHECK YOUR TIRE PRESSURE.

"Public service announcement," said Preston Lympany. He was still holding my hand.

"After the little incident a few years ago with the other company, they started a public safety campaign," I said. I wasn't really listening to myself. Walking down memory lane with my phantom Lowell seemed more honest to me than sitting on my terrace, watching the blimp with another, even if the other was a sweet man who smoked too many pimp cigarettes and liked me and read the horoscope sections of magazines and held my hand, and who liked me.

"The blimp seems superslow and low-budget," he said, removing his hand from mine.

"Interesting you say that. In late '99, they debuted a blimp with a turboprop engine, which, as it came into its mooring, jammed and then floated directly into a copse of trees. I believe that was around the time, if I'm remembering correctly, that the company was removed from the Dow Jones 30. *Not* a good time for Akron."

What I didn't tell Preston Lympany was that if Hollywood ever finally does call me and I'm asked to cry spontaneously for the big scene, I'll think of the heartrending whir of the blimp. Whenever my mother would hear it, she'd holler up to me in my room, and I'd put down my toys or my books and sprint out into the yard. And there we'd stand, on our front lawn, my mother and I, holding hands, listening and watching as the blimp floated low and slowly, slowly away from us.

And when Lowell, Jenny, and Merit first lived here, we'd pop open the champagne whenever the blimp made an appearance. (Merit would get a Shirley Temple.) This was in the early eighties, when nobody else in Akron had much to celebrate, other than Devo. We weren't thinking about anyone else, though, then.

"Do you know," I asked Preston Lympany, "that Lowell doesn't even know how ticklish I am? All my mother had to do was wiggle her index finger in the air, and I'd fall onto the floor in a twitching heap." I was feeling sorry for myself now; I was letting my self-pity get the better of me, but I couldn't help it. I couldn't stop it, not now. I wanted his hand back. The blimp was moving northward over my grounds. In about four minutes, it would be over my neighbors' (much less big) yard. I've never met these particular neighbors, but Lowell has said they were lovely.

"How *mean*," Preston Lympany said. He was thumbing through my

Gourmet, which was apparently no longer on my lap. "It makes you wonder: Does *Lowell* have a mother?"

Funny how things change, isn't it? Nowadays, the blimp overhead was a nonevent. I wasn't sure who was staying with us, but I knew there were at least a few guests; not one of them came outside to see what there was to see.

"Oh," I said, trying very hard to hold it together, trying not to yell at Preston Lympany for missing the point, trying not to stick the baby blue blimp eraser into my mouth, which had just then presented itself as an attractive activity, "he has a mother. Believe me, he has a mother."

16

Contrary to conventional wisdom, Merit actually liked Mondays. Caroline was at home then, Wyatt was in a better mood, and the weekend's chores had been completed. It was a lie, Merit thought, that weekends were fun. Where was all the fun? Merit didn't know. She worried that maybe she was the only person in the whole world whose weekends were not thrill-packed. She did the laundry; she worked out at the gym; she cleaned the house; she went grocery shopping; she set two places at the table instead of three. These things needed to be done, did they not? Merit did them.

Merit didn't care for the expression "gifted and talented" because it made people who weren't in the program feel bad. She wondered if the term was Ohio public school–specific. In the mornings, she and Wyatt took turns driving Caroline to her summer school "gifted and talented" day camp. Today, Monday, was Merit's day. During the drive to Kent State, she and Caroline talked mostly about what Caroline had read over the weekend. Caroline said she was disappointed because she'd only been able to get up through the Roman Empire in *The Story of Civilization*; that she had been torn this weekend, as she always seemed to be torn now, because she wanted to spend time with her mom but also wanted to read. "The weekends are the only uninterrupted reading time I've *got,*" she said, reaching for the air conditioning vent on the passenger's side and directing it away from her. Merit suggested that Caroline explain to her mom how important reading time was to her, and maybe ask for a few undisturbed hours each weekend day.

Caroline asked Merit what *booty* meant, exactly, in the context of the Roman Empire. Merit said she thought it meant money, gold, treasure, things like that, and Caroline asked if she were right in thinking that *booty* didn't mean sex. Merit said she thought that was right. Caroline mentioned that she'd like to rent *I, Claudius,* possibly tonight if Merit had the time. Merit said she'd only seen parts of *I, Claudius,* but that in the parts she'd seen, John Hurt's performance had really made a big impression on her. Merit expressed concern that she'd never noticed a copy of *I, Claudius* on the shelf at the local Blockbuster, although it was true she hadn't really been looking. Caroline said that if Blockbuster did carry *I, Claudius,* it would probably be in the TV section, and Merit admitted that she'd never once looked in that particular area of the store.

Merit pulled into the parking lot and asked Caroline if she had her protein-shake box and her PowerBar and her water and her banana and her Rubbermaid container with the kale and barley and tofu, and Caroline said, "Yes, Merit, thanks," and stepped out of the car.

The Jag stalled twice as Merit attempted to pull out of the parking lot. Looking in the rearview mirror, she could see Caroline standing on the sidewalk, motionless, clutching the straps of her backpack to her shoulders. Merit turned around in her seat and waved to Caroline. Caroline's arms were so skinny. Merit couldn't handle it. She loved Caroline more than anyone, including Caroline, probably knew. She knew it was crazy, but she thought of Caroline as her own daughter.

The car stalled five times on the way to the office. Accidentally, Merit ran one red light, made two rolling stops, swerved into oncoming traffic while trying to avoid a pop can, and somehow stopped in the middle of railroad tracks precisely as the flashing red gate descended. She had to back the car through the little space between the closed gates. Merit had never been so great at backing up, especially not when it needed to be done quickly. She was a better and more attentive driver when someone else was in the car. She knew this.

Was she was looking forward to seeing Randy this morning? She couldn't tell. She spent an enjoyable minute or two thinking about firing him. Although touching your boss's stomach for a second or two at a gym was probably not a fireable offense. Inappropriate, yes; fireable, no. Plus, could a tooting subordinate sexually harass his *boss?*

In bed last night, Merit had thought about that touch.

Merit's magazine's offices were in a building with a dentist, an orthodontist, and a driving school. The hallway of the building smelled like cleaning solvent and teeth. The outside door said EAST AVENUE INDUS-TRIAL PARK. That was the door Merit opened.

Randy was already at his desk. He was the first person at work. Eight-ten for Randy was a first in her memory; mostly Randy was a 10:00–11:40 guy (which Merit would have been, too, if she'd had a boss like Merit). The stupid headphones were on. Never too early in the day for headphones! Randy gestured to her as she walked past his cube, but he didn't look up from his computer screen. The gesture was a heavy-metal sign of some kind, raised pinkie and thumb. It was less easy to be mad at someone when you were in the same room with that person, wasn't it? It was not outside the realm of possibility that Randy had shown up early just so he could see her.

Claudia was in the central assistants' area, emptying a small garbage can into a much bigger wheeled garbage can. In its overlit, exposed awfulness, the cubicle zone had always felt to Merit a lot like a Jerry Lewis telethon phone bank. At her office door, Merit waved to Claudia. Claudia waved back. The times they had spoken, when Merit got in early enough, she felt weird about it afterward. She'd never really paid much attention to Claudia in high school . . . although it was true Merit had never paid attention to *anyone* in high school. Whenever she saw Claudia, she was reminded how small-hearted she had been then (and still sometimes was), how easy it had been (and was) for her to ignore everything she felt she could choose to ignore.

"Hey, Merit. Look who's in early today."

"Hey, Claudia! This probably isn't early for you! *You* probably get up at *four* or something."

Merit opened her door. Claudia wiped her hands on the abdomen region of her pale blue smock. She had choppy blond hair and pinky powdery skin.

"You're close," she said. "Five. We've got two other jobs before this one." Claudia's husband's job in the office seemed to involve one task: polishing the floor—very, very slowly—with a big noisy buffer that was taller than he was. Merit didn't know if the buffer belonged to them or to the office. The husband didn't appear to be around today.

"Five!" Merit said. "Wow!"

Merit's office smelled like Lysol. Her trash can was empty. She liked that her office was one of the first ones Claudia cleaned in the morning. It was funny, but before Claudia started working there a couple of years ago,

Merit had never really given much thought to how much trash she made at the office daily. And she believed she made more trash than anyone there. Since Claudia, Merit had also become very conscious of the quality of her garbage. She now wrapped plum pits and gum in paper towels, drank the last cold, awful, sweet swallow of her coffee before pitching the cup, remembered not to dump several pounds of pennies in her office trash can, etc. She was uncomfortable with the idea of having another woman clean up her mess, especially if that woman was someone from her high school. Even if they hadn't been in any of the same classes.

Merit continued standing in her doorway, locking, unlocking the bolt, locking, unlocking. "Have you heard about Krissy?" she asked Claudia. Krissy was just a girl from their high school. Merit had recently gotten some thirdhand information about her. Merit and Claudia really had only high school in common; there wasn't all that much else for them to talk about.

Claudia squirted some Lysol onto a towel and wiped down an assistant's phone with it. "She's pregnant again. Kid number four, husband number two."

"I know! How do some people have the time? I was going to ask if you'd heard that."

"Well, we talk every week."

"Every week? The only person I talk to every week is my mother."

Lysol bottle and rag in her front smock pocket, Claudia rolled the garbage can out of the assistants' area, heading in the direction of Rebecca's office.

"You and Krissy were never *friends,* were you?"

It was possible, looking back on it, that Claudia had ignored Merit in high school, not the other way around.

"Hey. What's up?"

The Tooting Subordinate was standing at her door. He was wearing shorts, flip-flops, and a black Iron Maiden T-shirt. He looked extremely dumb and hot. Rebecca had previously said things to Merit about how Randy's dress code wouldn't even be tolerated in other workplaces on Casual Fridays. Merit had to figure out a nice way to tell Randy she thought it would be a good idea for him to stay seated today and lay as low as possible.

"*Love* the outfit," Merit said. And she did, too. Merit and her unfortunate burnout weakness. Back when she was in school, a couple of the cuter burnouts (although not Micah) had worn this exact T-shirt. A classic, as far as band T-shirts went. Eddie, Iron Maiden's massively cheesy yet still somehow weirdly cool skeleton mascot, "ripping it up" (as they say) on the bass.

Randy had really shapely ankles.

"Hey, I'd be wearing a belly shirt, but some of us aren't blessed with what I like to call 'Merit abs.' It was hard for me to come up to you yesterday, because the guy on the elliptical machine next to me said something about how your pants looked like they were ready to split down the middle. I thought, If that happens, I've got the best possible view."

A widening, an opening, of her nether regions. A pulse down there, hot and greedy.

"So, you already got a voice-mail message this morning from your lunch date today or whatever," Randy said. Was he tapping his fingernails on the metal door frame, or was that her head rattling? Here was a scary thought: Something Randy'd said *about her* had turned her on.

"What?" Merit said.

It was like getting aroused by looking at yourself in the mirror. And, yes, she was aroused. She couldn't have sex right now, or ever, with Randy, and she didn't want to masturbate, but she did know that something large and eager and not necessarily even Randy-attached needed to find its way deep into her pussy very soon.

"I listened to your messages this morning, and this chick you're supposed to have lunch with called to confirm. She left a message over the weekend."

"Why [a stern throat clearing] are you listening to my voice-mail [a lesser throat clearing] messages, Randy?" she asked.

"Burning the old midnight oil, you know?" He was flip-flopping toward her now. That's why they call them "flip-flops," Merit thought hazily.

"How did you know my . . . password, Randy?" She was confused right now, disoriented.

"Uh . . . dunno."

"I have a lunch today, then." Randy was now standing on Merit's side of her desk, which was not an appropriate place for him to be. It was like walking behind a cash register, except different. She knew she would blush if she looked at him, so she pretended to read an E-mail.

"Yeah, you do. With that brandy chick. The one that keeps sending us free brandy samples. That's today. She left her cell number."

"Oh, *today*? I totally spaced." She was almost mouth level with Randy's crotch. Only one (or possibly two, if Randy was wearing underwear, which she guessed he probably was not) layers of fabric separated Merit from Randy's cock. Morning sex was, in Merit's opinion, the best kind of sex. The way you'd float on it all day.

"Do you want me to cancel it?"

"I never schedule lunches on Mondays, so . . ." she said. Merit never scheduled lunches ever, actually. Randy seemed to have kind of an erection, visible through his shorts.

"I'll cancel it."

Randy leaned down over Merit. They were cheek-to-cheek now. Merit was terrified he was going to kiss her, although she might have been misinterpreting the signs. She was very bad at telling when someone was putting the moves on her, and she had sometimes humiliatingly thought people were hitting on her when they weren't.

"Why don't you tell her I can't . . . and . . . *you* can. . . . Yeah. . . . Why don't *you* go instead?" The whole scene fluttered like a slow dream.

Randy put his chin on top of her head. "I *could*," he said.

"Why don't you?" Merit asked. She wheeled her chair back. Randy's chin went away. She stood languidly up, stepped away from him.

"Why don't I?" Randy asked.

Merit bent over her bag, shamelessly flipped up the back of her skirt, and made him snatch a gander at her ass. She was wearing a flimsy summer skirt. It really was unconscionable. She knew herself well enough to know how close she was to dropping to all fours, offering herself to him that way. If Merit decided to, they would, in about three seconds, be fucking.

She could hear Claudia rolling her big wheeled garbage can in the direction of Rebecca's office.

Merit gathered her skirt, opened her wallet, and pulled her American Express card from its slot. She brushed his hand when she gave it to him. "On *me*," she said, and led the Tooting Subordinate (who presently had her credit card in his possession) right out the door.

As a child, Merit had never exactly been a church regular, her attendance being Jenny-stipulated only on Christmas Eve. Merit never got why

Christmas Eve service at the Unitarian Universalist church was so important to Jenny. Jenny had once—but only once—told Merit she was an atheist. When Merit was eleven, she attended, much to Jenny's disapproval, a weeklong evangelical summer day camp (she was recruited by a girl who lived down the street). At home after the last day of camp, Merit showed Jenny the clothespin giraffe she'd made that day. Jenny shook her head and said, "Doesn't it seem a little bit secular to make a child do a *craft* [how she spat that word] at Christian camp? And I'm an atheist!"

Christmas propelled this particular UU chapter, and probably every other one, too, into a spectacular multiple-personality-disorder tizzy. There was an Advent wreath, a menorah, and, in later years, a weird candelabra thing for, Jenny said, Kwanzaa. Every year, some older hammy congregant would inevitably read either " 'Twas the Night Before Christmas," or, more to Merit's liking, *The Velveteen Rabbit* (Merit was a sucker for any rabbit-oriented subject matter). One year, everybody sang "Kumbaya" and "Hark! The Herald Angels Sing." The next year, or maybe it was the year after that, "Grandma Got Run Over By a Reindeer" and "Hark! The Herald Angels Sing."

Merit had wanted to elope, but Wyatt didn't think that would send quite the right message to Caroline. Merit could see his point. When Merit told Fergus Wyatt was making them get married in Akron, Fergus *pleaded* with her to let them throw the wedding at his house. The idea appealed to Merit, in a way, mostly because Fergus said he'd take care of everything. He'd already chosen their colors (bluey pink and jade) and their flowers (peonies: "big blowsy-dame flowers," he'd said, "just like you and your mother!"), when Lowell called her, two months before the wedding, and said he was afraid he'd be unable to have Jenny at his house. He said that he'd felt blindfolded lately, and that each day was like walking in night "as black as blood," with no one to guide him. He said he'd been sad, and "completely knackered," but that he couldn't explain it any more than that. Merit knew the truth: He couldn't be around Jenny because she'd finally stopped painting him. Yes, thanks to Merit, Jenny had gotten her dignity back. And also thanks to Merit, everyone in her family was sad—or sadder.

Merit and Wyatt were married at the Unitarian Universalist church.

During Merit and Wyatt's one So You Want to Get Married meeting in the church office (the inside of which seemed to have been inspired by a ski lodge), they told the young new minister they intended to have the quickest wedding ceremony on record. As in Vegas quick. The minister said that wasn't the first time she'd heard that—this was, after all, a UU church. The minister kept telling Merit and Wyatt that she wasn't from Akron, and that she was planning to go to Yale University or Yale College or whatever and earn her Divinity Ph.D. It seemed very important for Merit and Wyatt to understand this. Merit, after having been given the same information about six times, muttered, not as under her breath as she apparently thought, "Like we *care.*" The minister said, "Ex*cuse* me?" Wyatt took Merit's hand and gently pinched it. A gentle pinch was Wyatt's eccentric nonverbal cue for the pinchee to stop whatever it was she was doing.

During her walk down the aisle, arm in arm with her father, Merit forgot how she was supposed to behave, and she unfashionably grinned and waved to those in the congregation whom she knew, and she knew everyone (it *was* her wedding, after all). Jenny and Fergus were seated several rows apart, much to Merit's relief. She did something she wasn't supposed to do then: She smiled immensely and waved hi across the stage to Caroline, who was eight and blond and in a blue terry-cloth dress and holding daffodils, and who, Merit feared, hated her. As Caroline gazed unsmilingly up to the rustic cedar beams, Merit knew she had some work to do.

The subject of Merit's closed-door Internet search was "What is sexual harassment?" Merit was pretty sure Randy's behavior didn't constitute the term's legal description, but, in a way, she hoped it sort of did. She was looking for some loophole. If Randy were sexually harassing her, then she'd be the victim, which meant, didn't it, she'd be in the clear? Even if maybe she had accidentally hiked up her skirt for the perpetrator's (and, more to the point, for her own) stimulation?

What, like she was actually going to sue Randy?

Merit thought: Okay, she was finally going to be honest with herself. She wanted to have a (brief) sexual encounter with Randy. But she couldn't herself be the instigator of the fling. Merit felt this made sense. She was, after all, an honorable woman.

Because those guys who'd spread her apart, those guys who had guided her mouth to their erect penises and said, as both had, "I made that for you," didn't mean it. Merit wasn't stupid. But Wyatt meant it. Wyatt was the one who meant it.

And it was she who had ended both previous slippages. When she stopped them, she didn't once cry, which seemed like something you really should do when you'd decided to dispose of a certain person. *I knew you, and now I choose not to.* It was sad, or it should have been. She sent them away, and away they went. When she told the sculptor/personal essayist that she would no longer be spending twice-weekly lunch hours with him or the occasional twenty minutes after work, he said, "Okay." She said she was so sorry for "hurting" him, and that he was being so admirably big about it (it was she who got melodramatically on her knees then and took his goateed face in her hand), and he said, "It's cool," and she said she'd still be more than happy to continue to read his personal essays, because she had liked the latest one (yet another offering from the cycle that recounted, in tremendous detail, his drive across country with his brother), especially that part in it about how standing on a corner in Winslow, Arizona, was the fulfillment of a lifelong dream, because dreams were important, but she reminded him that this meant his enormous sculptor's hand with its frank ringed fingers would no longer be allowed inside her vagina (she actually said this; she was quite out of her mind and exhausted on this lunch hour). Then he directed his eyes behind her (Merit thinking, for a half-pleasant second, he was too distraught to look at her face) and said definitively, "*Cloister.*" She touched his weird goatee and said, "I know. I have to be alone with my husband now." His monkey brown eyes were still focused in the same place. Merit turned. On the windowsill behind her was an empty water bottle—brand: Cloister.

Nobody fought for her. Nobody had *ever* fought for her. Not even her own father.

She was being pathetic again, and how she despised that part of herself. The problem was a fairly simple one, wasn't it? She believed that because she hadn't had all that many interesting experiences in her life, she was owed some now. She was *owed* some fun. Merit sincerely felt this to be true.

Randy was still not back at his cubicle at 3:10. Merit stood in the hallway, peering into his empty work area. She knew she shouldn't worry, but still. She was, she generally believed, often a pessimistic individual, and when she began to worry, when the "doom loop" (as a therapist to whom she went an impressive four times called it) reared its rancid head, *look out.* The doom loop could not be reasoned with. No one else's brain in her family, except for Fergus's (and Fergus wasn't part of her family) operated this way.

Merit had these fleeting thoughts: Randy's been killed (because of me), Randy's killed himself (because of me), Randy's quit and is never coming back (because of me), and, finally, Randy's having sex with his (my) lunch date, the brandy chick (because of me). The last possibility was, to Merit, the most troubling. Merit couldn't remember ever having met this brandy woman, although she had sounded a little too congenial in her previous voice-mail messages, and had, Merit remembered, the sexy voice belonging to a very specific kind of peppy, winner-type person, who would naturally be a marketing manager at a liquor company, and who would have breast implants, and who would live in New York City, and who had never had a boring day in her life, and whose family actually gave her money, and whose family wasn't insane, whose uncle wasn't Fergus, whose father wasn't a homosexual and a liar, whose mother had some self-respect, and who would, during one blow-off out-of-town lunch date, put her salon-manicured hands onto the thigh of the assistant who worked for her client at the unimportant magazine.

Now was maybe a good time for Merit to remind herself that not everyone was as unprofessional as sh—

"Hey there. 'Sup?" Randy tossed his bulging messenger bag underneath his desk. The bag's flap wasn't latched shut, and Merit saw what she recognized to be a yellow plastic Tower Records bag peeping up. The only Tower Records in the area was way up in Cleveland.

"Randy! Hi! I was just . . . Your desk . . . I was wondering . . . How'd it go?"

"Huh?" Randy scratched his head through his amazing hair. Randy dust came detached from his enthralling Randy body and rose up through the fluorescent light. He was not looking at her.

"Was she great? Was she nice? Did you sell her thirty pages?"

"Oh. She was awesome." He slid into his chair, considered his computer screen, and made a lot of noise with his mouse. Merit was hurt, just a little bit, that he didn't want to stand next to her.

"Where did you go?"

"Uh, just that place—what's it called? The one with the ribs."

"Damon's? You took her to Damon's? Did she like it?"

"Yeah. She said this thing about not having ribs in wherever. New York."

"So you really got some good work done at lunch, then?" He really should have given her back her credit card by this point, but Merit felt that she couldn't ask him for it yet. It was important that Randy felt she trusted him. Merit noticed men's necks, and she noticed Randy's. She imagined her tongue on it. She didn't understand why he wouldn't look her in the eye.

"Yeah. She said hi. She was like, 'Tell Merit I said hi.' " She felt she was making him uncomfortable.

Merit really didn't think she'd ever met this woman, but maybe she was wrong. If Randy hadn't given her her credit card back in an hour, then she would ask. "That's nice that she said that," Merit said. "I always liked her."

Randy pounded his mouse on his desk. The workdays often found Randy pounding his mouse, or shaking it, or slapping it violently. The ball inside always seemed to be causing problems, as if it, too, were conspiring against hot, dumb Randy.

With her office door closed again, she squeaked back in her leatherette desk chair, spread her legs, and braced her feet up on opposite sides of the desk. What she did then was shaming, deeply shaming, and was one of the most mortifying things she'd ever done. She had this terrible suspicion that all her coworkers were outside, watching her through a hole in the door or wall, and laughing. Her desk faced the door. She barely had to touch herself. After she took care of what she needed to take care of, she turned on her under-the-desk space heater and spread her legs for that, too. She developed a heat rash on her panty hose–less legs and tried to rub it away. She hadn't had sex with anyone but Wyatt for seven years. You couldn't really count the other two guys. Plus, did the orange-palmed server at the Rainbow Villa really even count as a *sexual relationship?* They were just bath buddies, really.

It was 4:00, and Merit hadn't done a lick of work yet today. She wasn't worried, though, because it was August and nothing happened in August. About thirty or forty E-mails awaited, all from people she didn't want to hear from . . . except for this one from Randy, sent not two minutes ago. This one had a red exclamation mark mood stamp. "I FUCKED UP! ! ! ! ! !" (Randy was very fond of the E-mail mood stamp) was its subject line.

Hey, Merit. I need to tell you something big. Its bad and I'm sorry about that. I didn't go take out that "Brandi" (ha-ha) lady for lunch today. I lied to you about that. I've been feeling like I been really letting you down a lot lately and what happened was I went out and bought you some things, presents, to show my appreciacion (smile) but that meant I spaced on lunch. I can not explain it. I had it in my head earlier in the day to buy these things. Yes I know we talked about the lunch before but my mind was on other things (: and . . . Well what can I say but I fucked up? I hope you can find it in your heart to forgive me. I know I feel extra shitty about the whole escapade (sp?). Well I guess I better go now. Please when you come out don't scream at me. Sorry for taking up so much of your time.

With ultra admiration,

Randall (your biggest fan)

When Merit emerged from her office and rounded the corner to the cubicle, the Tooting Subordinate's head was in his hands. "Randy?" Merit asked. She was standing over him now.

"I'm sorry. I'm really fucked-up right now. I got *no* sleep last night. I know that's no excuse," Randy said.

"Gee, Randy," Merit said. "What's going on with you?"

"I know. I'm an asswipe. I promise I'll never sully your name and reputation like that."

"Just don't lie to me, okay?" He was crying, Merit thought, or had been. Rebecca's assistant, Karen, floated by them, holding a stack of papers. She pretended she wasn't listening.

"Scout's honor," Randy said. He refused to look at her. She felt terrible. It was really her fault—she shouldn't have sent him off to do *her* goddamned job. Maybe this was karma payback time.

Merit dropped to her knees and stroked his hair, just like a mom (of sorts). "It's fine," she said. "Just promise me that you'll never lie to me again?"

"There's something really wrong with me today. Do you think maybe, if it's not too much trouble, you could drive me back to my place?" Randy asked, and cupped his hand over Merit's right breast.

17

Today: What to say or think about it? What have I learned about Lowell? And what do I do with this knowledge? This evening, Lowell was circling his bed like a shark, doing some calculations. He was trying to figure out how to get his bed on the plane to New York. We're leaving in two days, although now two days seems too far away. Or does it seem too soon? I've been feeling jittery and anxious since Lowell and I decided to move to New York . . . although I naturally agree that opportunities must be pounced on when they present themselves. It's all happened so fast. When Lowell told me Andy Warhol admired my pictures (thank you, Theodore Goalting), and intends to make us belles of the New York ball, we agreed that we must go. So what, then, accounts for my nauseous last-day-senior-year feeling? (On the last day of school in May, after the bell rang announcing the end of the last high school class we'd ever have and we all ran outside, I sat in my car with Fergus and sobbed. I was inconsolable, and I didn't even *like* school. It was just that everything had become the *past,* so suddenly. I sobbed in the hot car, while everyone else shouted and honked their horns and flung their folders toward the sky. Fergus touched my arm and said, "We'll never be back here. Even this parking lot is dead to us now.") And again, I feel that a vital, if brief, phase of my life has come to an end. How can you not be sad when you know something's never coming back?

But I didn't want Lowell to know I was half-gloomy about leaving London, not tonight. As he circumnavigated his bed, I sat on the floor and absentmindedly rubbed at one of his bed's gold feet. Lowell asked me not to rub too hard please because he was afraid the gold might come off. Up until that point, I'd thought the feet on Lowell's bed were real gold. Then Lowell said he loved me very much, sat down on the floor, and wrapped himself around me. I inhaled him and he inhaled me. I felt tranquil and full-hearted again, and no longer melancholy or scared. Then Lowell and I had sex on the floor, our first of two times tonight.

But I'm terrified again now—about everything. Lowell is sleeping fitfully next to me. The walls of Lowell's room here are barren and Lowell-less. They have been for two days. He packed my oil paintings as soon as we decided to move.

After we had sex the first time tonight, Lowell got dressed and said he needed to go downstairs and talk to Scotto. Scotto hasn't, apparently, been taking the news of Lowell's departure well (although I wouldn't know; he's avoided me since my art opening). I was alone in Lowell's room and thinking about how poor my handling of light is in many of the new pictures. If you have no light, you have no art. When I point out the problems to Lowell, he says I'm wrong, but all I can see is an inventory of weaknesses. When Lowell and I were on the floor, I'd noticed the big portfolio underneath the bed. It struck me as an odd place for it to be, but only slightly.

Alone in the room, I slid the cold leatherette portfolio across the floor. I unzipped it. When I saw it on the first picture, the picture I had painted of Lowell's face, I thought it was a joke. Then I turned to the next picture of Lowell, then the next. Feverishly, I flipped through the whole book. It was on every single painting—in the bottom right corner.

Although I don't remember, I must have screamed Lowell's name, because he erupted into the room soon after that, saying, What's wrong? What's wrong? But I didn't have to tell him. He looked down at the open portfolio.

He collapsed to the floor and threw himself around me.

His mouth was on my cheek. "Oh Me. Oh Me Me Me," he said. My cheek was wet from his tears. I wasn't the one crying, not yet.

"My Me, my beautiful Me," he said in scarcely a whisper. He sounded like a little boy. He looked like a little boy. He was rocking me now. I've only seen the one picture of Lowell when he was a child, playing on the beach. He says that's the only picture he has from his childhood. Lowell says he has no past, no life before me.

His hands were on my body now, down below, searching for the place.

"I'm nothing," he gasped hopelessly, his face buried in my hair. He was weeping real tears. "I'm *nothing*."

I said he needed to tell me *why*.

"Can't you *see?* I want us to be one person. We *are* one person, Me." His hands had found the place.

He inhaled the breath from my lungs, then whispered, "Me? There's something greater we can create than mere pictures. Let's have a child."

On the bottom right corner of my paintings was a signature: "Lowell Haven."

18

A miserable-looking kid hobbled out of the orthodontist's office. His mustache zone was spider-furred, which meant he was roughly Caroline's age. Merit wondered if Caroline knew him, and, if she did, if he was nice. There was some shuffled confusion about who got to go down the four steps to the front door first, but Merit took charge, followed single file by the kid from the orthodontist's office—the terrible torture thing called "headgear" stretching his furry lip out in such a sad way—and, at the rear, Randy. Merit held the door for both of them. Neither looked her in the eye as he passed, but Randy did, she thought, semiburble, "Thanks." Whatever the cleaning solvent in the office building hallway was, she could taste it on the back of her tongue. The word *orthodontist* made her think of birds.

In the parking lot, the kid clambered into the shotgun side of a van waiting in the handicapped space. Merit didn't notice a handicapped sticker on the back plate. Randy's car was at a weird angle two lanes, or aisles, across. She wondered if she should offer to drive him home in his own, as Wyatt would say, vehicle. Randy was the owner of a redneck seventies-era half car/half truck—color: white. In the middle of the rear window was a small American flag decal, which, she presumed, had come with the car. Merit had always assumed he'd selected a white used car/truck because he clearly thought such a curio was funny.

She decided not to ask if he wanted her to drive his vehicle.

She didn't know exactly where Randy lived. She asked him if he wanted to go the "scenic route" or the "fast one," and Randy said he didn't care. She told him he'd have to navigate when they got close to his place, but he didn't say anything, just kept staring out the dirty window. She turned on the radio, and wondered if maybe they would kiss later; he punched the radio off, and Merit was temporarily shattered by the thought they wouldn't. He drooped forward like a sunflower who'd seen better days, head sunk forlornly into his hands. Fergus, she remembered, had sat like that once, on a flight to London, a trip he'd given her as a college graduation gift—*not* that when she'd opened the card containing the ticket she could have guessed Fergus was planning on going *with her*. During the entire flight, his head was in his hands, elbows propped on the coffee-ringed tray table. For six-plus hours, he clutched his red hair and made these bottomless groaning sounds. From that day forward, this particular body language had always tended to make Merit feel tremendously unconfident about whatever situation was at hand.

It was possible Randy was having a migraine, or maybe he was tired or depressed. Maybe he was overwhelmed by the fact that his boss was driving him back to his house, and that there was indeed kind of a possibility that she might come inside. She wanted to smell the back of his neck, that most protruding vertebra.

She waited until she was totally lost to ask him. She was in a scary neighborhood then, kids hanging out on porches, all that. He gave her approximate directions ("I don't know street names," he said, "only like landmarks and shit"), but, after forty minutes (later, on the futon, Randy told her he did the drive to work in ten), and only one stalling of the car (on Memorial Parkway; Randy seemed oblivious), she found his house. She thought she should escort him to the door at least, like a proper friend.

Neither said anything. They climbed the rickety white steps leading up to his apartment. He lived in the remodeled attic of an old blue house. The steps were outside and seemed clearly secondary and fire-escape-y. Merit was sure there had to be another set of stairs inside, and she wondered for a moment if he was sneaking her in . . . but whom would he be hiding her from?

The white door atop the fire escape had lots of scuff marks on it. He kicked it with his flip-flops and, at the threshold, parted the hanging beads for her.

What did his apartment smell like? Incense? Patchouli? Beer? Cigarette smoke? Pot? Pungent combination of all five? *College.* That was the smell. Oh, and another question: What in God's name was she doing here?

Randy flopped down on the futon. Merit stood by the door and played with the beads. She was thinking about how to get out.

"I don't know if I told you, but I've been getting these un-fucking-believable headaches lately. In the car, I was like, Am I going to yak? I've had to pull over before."

"Oh my God, Randy. That's terrible."

"Yeah, no shit."

"Do you want some water or something?"

"Nah. I'm better now, though. I was freaking myself out that I had a brain tumor. I think it's probably stress."

Merit was calming down now. She was trying to focus on the room, the ceiling of which was slanted. She stepped away from the door (she knew this wasn't such a good move), ducked her head. The center of the room was the only area in which she'd be able to stand up to her full height. She hunched toward it. If she and Wyatt lived here, they'd be scooting around on their knees.

"Wow, Randy," Merit said. "Love the place." A purple-and-blue Indian-type tapestry was haphazardly tacked up over the window. In front of the window was a mannequin—Styrofoam, it looked like, and black. Rivulets of red and yellow melted wax dripped down its head to its torso—evidence that Randy, presumably, had stood above the mannequin at one point, pouring scalding wax onto its head.

"I saw a homemade crack pipe right on the sidewalk outside my door a few days ago. The neighborhood's going right down the crapper. It's totally sad."

"I'm amazed! How did you know it was a crack pipe?"

"Because that's what it was, dude: a *crack pipe*. Homemade. Tylenol bottle."

Merit barely knew what a Tylenol bottle looked like, much less a crack pipe, and she was impressed by Randy's savoir faire. She got a better look at the wax-dripped mannequin. Taped onto its feet was a piece of white paper, which read SLY AND THE FAMILY STONE! The handwriting (in red Magic Marker) wasn't Randy's.

"I'm getting you some water," she said. "Then I should go."

"Hey, you know what? You're the best. You know that? Driving me home and everything, I'm mean, after the way I fucked up today?"

She said she was glad to help. En route to the kitchen, she smacked her head on the stupid slanted ceiling. She didn't think he heard the embarrassing thud.

"I don't really drink water, so I don't have that many cups. Just pour some in that peanut butter jar that's out there."

Merit did as she was told. Her head throbbed, and she despised herself for dawdling here in Randy's apartment. She couldn't really even tell if he wanted her there anyway.

She slouched over to him. He was lying on his back, a hand draped over his eyes like a debauched plantation mistress. There was a new addition to the picture now: A big orange cat was coiled on his belly.

"Ooooh! I didn't know you had a *cat*," Merit said.

She was hovering over him now. Had there been a bowl of cat food on the kitchen floor? It wasn't like Merit to miss evidence of a household pet. This is how little she knew Randy: *She didn't even know he had a cat.*

"Merit, meet Hux. Hux, meet Merit." Randy's mouth barely moved as he spoke. The hand was still shielding the (minimal, Merit thought) light.

"Huxley?" asked Merit.

"Huxtable," said Randy.

He elevated himself and held his hand out for the Peter Pan jar. The cat gave him a perturbed, tooth-baring meow. Merit thrust the jar toward Randy. She, Wyatt, and Caroline ate only natural peanut butter, and Randy's consumption of this particular processed-food product concerned her for a moment.

"Hi there, Hux. Real nice to meet you." Merit took the cat's white right paw, shook it, felt for claws, and delighted to find Hux's were still intact. She probably would have had to leave right then if she'd discovered Randy was a cat declawer. She sat on the floor and petted her. (Merit automatically assumed all unfamiliar animals were female.) The cat was still on Randy's stomach. Her hand was now conveniently close to Randy's johnson.

She hoped Randy wouldn't take her interest in his cat the wrong way, because once, in the car after a party at the house of one of Wyatt's coworkers, Wyatt had informed her it had been "poor form," the way she had rolled around with the dog on the floor, especially when everyone else ("all the other adults" was how he'd put it) was seated on the couch. This had been one of the few cocktail parties Merit and Wyatt had ever been invited to. Cocktail parties weren't all that big in Akron. Merit had been excited when she saw the word *crudités* on the invitation, but at the party she had looked all over for a plate of those pretty little pastel-colored bite-size marzipan cakes that look like tiny presents. On the credenza was a plate of Brie, some crackers and pita wedges, a bowl of spinach dip, and a platter of cherry tomatoes and small peeled carrots like the ones she fed her rabbit, but, sadly, no crudités. Later, Merit and Wyatt figured out that she had confused crudité with petits fours. Wyatt told her this was probably a common mistake.

"Hey, Merit," Randy said, "I have something to tell you."

He removed her hand from the cat's head, squeezed it. He bent into her and rubbed his nose on her cheek. On the slanted wall across from her was a Radiohead poster. Merit wasn't really thinking about it. She was sure he could hear her heart, see it move through her dress.

During the course of the next two hours, Merit found out certain things. After she had stripped Randy of his Iron Maiden T-shirt, she discovered that he had really sensitive nipples. He told her this was often the case with guys who smoked a lot of pot, which, he assured her, he did. She learned that kissing someone with braces wasn't weird at all. She realized Randy didn't yet understand there are few benefits, when you're messing around with another person, in saying, "I heard she tells people that I still call her all the time and hang up, but that is *so* not true." She learned Randy was one of these people who talked more or less the entire time. He talked about his route to work, he talked about his migraines, he talked about a German class he'd taken in college, he talked about the sexual likes and dislikes of someone named Libby, he talked about his trip to Tower Records in Cleveland that very afternoon, and he talked about Phish. When Merit lifted her head up and said, "Phish? What was the point?" Randy said, "*That was* the point, man. There *was* no point." She learned that other people weren't like Wyatt. She remembered now what they were like in college, and what they did, the way each guy, when he was down there, looked like he had a goofy Hitler mustache (insofar as anything that reminded a person of Hitler could be goofy), the way each would experiment with how much of his forearm he could fit inside her. She learned that Randy didn't care when she accidentally knocked over his Peter Pan jar of water. She learned that she didn't want to see Randy's face. She learned this didn't seem to bother him. She learned he was more than happy to oblige when she suggested he get behind her, keeping one hand exactly where it was, that would be great, she told him, and then give her the other hand so she could put his fingers in her mouth. She learned that everything she asked for, she received. She also asked for a trip to the bathtub. She got that, too.

"Hey. I remember two sentences from my German class. Want to hear them?"

They were in the bathtub. Randy was on the bottom; Merit was straddling him. His fingers had been in the same place for about an hour and a half. "Shoot," she said.

"*Das ist mein Einfart.*"

She said she had no idea what an "*Einfart*" was, but whatever it was, it didn't sound very nice.

"It means 'garage.' Here's the other one: *Das ist mein Shield.*"

"Ooooh," Merit said. The "Ooooh" wasn't for the shield. She wanted Randy everywhere—in her pussy, in her mouth, and in the place you weren't ever allowed to talk about, ever.

"*Shield* is the same in both languages."

Merit was surprised by how good she felt. She wasn't dazed or sad. She knew precisely what she was doing. She was, after all, the boss. It was funny, because with Wyatt . . . well, with Wyatt, there was always this issue of control. Although she had never really thought about this until he, Wyatt, brought it up. Last month, they'd visited a carnival, and the two of them, Wyatt and Merit, went on this ride together. It was called the Berry-Go-Round or something. Each two-seater car was like this big strawberry, and inside each strawberry was this wheel you were supposed to twist. You twisted the wheel, the strawberry spun like crazy; you didn't twist the wheel, strawberry no spin. Merit didn't understand the mechanics of how the thing worked, and didn't care. Inside their personal strawberry, it was like *The Hunt for Red October,* Wyatt said later. Wyatt kept trying to crouch over the wheel—Merit thought, Neanderthal protecting his food supply—but she kept knocking him away. She pulled the wheel as far as it would go to one side, then the other. She enjoyed repeating this move over and over. The strawberry spun and Wyatt screamed, "Let me stabilize it; let me stabilize it!" The ride was much too short, and Merit, when it was over, was a big show-off, jumping right off the strawberry, forgoing the little retractable stepladder. She didn't even notice that Wyatt was still inside the (now-stationary) strawberry until she was outside of the Berry-Go-Round gate. He was dizzy for the rest of the night, he said when they were at home, when he'd finally starting talking to her again.

Then he said, "You always need to be in control, don't you? You'll never not be a Haven, Merit."

So this was all to say that she was fully in control of the situation with Randy.

"We're not having sex," said Merit, "so don't even . . ." She suddenly didn't know how to finish that sentence. "We're not having sex."

Randy squinted. "I really thought you were going to say, 'Don't even go there' for a split second." He slid in closer to her, kissed her. The kiss was hot and wet and open, and it lingered.

She considered Randy, very much liking what she saw. You always pretty much knew what someone was going to look like naked, didn't you? What you were confronted with after the shorts and the Iron Maiden T-shirt came off was never really a big shocker. If she were a better artist—like her mother, say—she could have, just a few short hours ago, before they'd gotten naked, drawn a picture of Randy as she imagined him. That theoretical drawing, Merit was proud to report, would have been entirely anatomically correct.

There were two wall hangings in the bathroom. One was a sepia-toned map with the following flowing type at the bottom: ENGLAND REQUIRES THAT EVERY GOOD MAN DO HIS DUTY. There was also a warped Fat Elvis poster. An aquamarine Post-it note hung on the poster's right bottom corner. It read IF THE KING CAN DIE ON THE CAN, YOU CAN TOO!!! And it wasn't Randy's freakish handwriting. Plus, Randy would have messed up the *too* usage, opting instead for *two* or, more likely, *to*.

"Did you have a roommate?"

"I guess you could call it that. That girl I told you about. Melody."

Why was it that even though Merit didn't love Randy, she nevertheless felt bitten in half? And why did everything seem to bite her in half these days?

"You mentioned someone else. What was the name?"

"Nah. Libby? We're just friends. She's like *a guy*. She lived here, too."

"Who is she? Melody? Is this the fashion student?"

"Can we like not talk about this? It's kind of private. She still has to come over and pick up her rosemary plant and her towels and her fucking needlepoint pillows and all her shitty DVDs. It's like *Ghost* and *How to Lose a Guy in 10 Days*. I'm like, Do I need this crappy shit around here? If I want that, I can just go over to my sister's in Shaker. Don't think I haven't sat around and been like, Hmm, I should really load all her crud, including Hux, chuck it all in a box or whatever, and go and drive my ass over to Kent and throw it all on her lawn."

"Oh! Hux is hers?"

"She told everyone that I was calling her all the time and hanging up. She told my buddy Cooper that I was stalking her or whatever. She's *insane*. Next time I see her, you can *bet* that I'm calling her out."

"I can't believe she left her *animal*. What kind of person—"

"It'll be four and a half months next Tuesday. I'm like, Get over it. Hey, wanna smoke some weed?"

Merit said she really should check back in at work.

"Work?"

"Yeah. *Work.*"

Randy laughed. Merit laughed. They both laughed and laughed. They dried each other with Melody's—or maybe Libby's—awful yellow towels, and, naked, smoked pot from a bong, and continued laughing about how funny it all really was.

Blockbuster wasn't easy for her to deal with. It was always far from Merit's favorite stop anyway, then add being stoned, and sore (both of which were secrets), on top of that. This was their third stop at an Akron-area Blockbuster. The girl at the cash register at the last place had sent them here, having promised this location did, according to the computer, have a copy of *I, Claudius.* All three of the Blockbusters were playing the same abrasive *The Scoop in Hollywood!* tape on their ceiling-mounted monitors. Good news: They did carry *I, Claudius;* bad news: they only had episodes seven through nine. Merit expressed her disappointment, and Caroline said she really didn't mind beginning the *I, Claudius* experience in the middle. Merit said maybe they could find episodes one through three, four through six, and ten through thirteen on eBay. The kid at the cash register acted in a dickish manner because Merit's Blockbuster card had been "issued from another location." Merit said, "You've got to be kidding" and "Oh, *come on,*" several times, and while not perhaps a terrifically sophisticated argumentative technique, it did turn out to be persuasive enough to get him to relent finally and rent her the DVD.

By the time she was on the interstate, she was thinking about Randy, and his skin.

"How long do we have this until?" Caroline asked.

"I think the box said three days. So that would be Thursday."

"That's good. Because then I don't have to rush and I can watch one episode a day. How long is each episode?"

"An hour, I think."

Something was banging around under the hood of the car. Merit tried to ignore it. They were in the old-people's lane, the classy Jaguar speedometer at an old-people's fifty; she remembered what a cautious driver she used to be when, in her pre-Wyatt college years, she used to drive stoned. She hoped Randy never drove stoned. She realized they hadn't discussed how he was going to get to work tomorrow.

"That's good, because I can watch one after dinner."

"Sounds like a plan," Merit said.

The banging was now difficult to ignore. Merit could feel Caroline's eyes on her face.

"Is your hair wet?"

"No."

"It looks like your hair's wet."

"It's sweat."

"That's *sweat*?"

"Remember when your dad said I was the sweatiest woman he ever met?" Oh, weak, Merit H. Ash. Pitiably weak! And to bring Wyatt, your husband, your number-one friend in the world, into your alibi!

Caroline fiddled with the lever underneath her seat. She and the seat jerked forward. Was Merit ashamed of herself? Oh yes, she was.

"I can't wait until I can drive."

Merit had accidentally been forty minutes late in picking Caroline up tonight. Caroline was, Merit knew, mad at her. And you know what? Caroline had every right to be mad at her: When Merit had finally skidded into the empty basketball court at the Kent State gym, stinking, she feared, of weed and Randy (Randy's weird Randy DNA really pretty much all over her), Caroline was sitting in the corner, atop a big blue Physioball, underlining passages in her book with a pink Hi-Liter. Wyatt didn't like her marking up their books; Merit encouraged it.

"Yes," Merit said. "Driving is important." She was feeling exceptionally stoned right now.

"How much did the DVD cost?" Caroline asked.

"To rent?"

"Um, yeah."

"It was like four dollars."

"Well, I'd be more than happy to pay you for it, Merit!"

Caroline had started proposing to pay for stuff recently. Wyatt and Merit had talked about this new development, and they had agreed not to take her money when offered (it was all *their* money anyway—her allowance came, obviously, from the central Ash hopper).

"That's sweet of you." Merit's head was making a lot of unpleasant sounds. According to the rearview mirror, about ten cars were bumpered up in back of her. Naturally, she was being tailgated. Caroline unzipped her backpack. Did Caroline actually *own* a wallet? Merit couldn't remember.

"Do you have change for a twenty?" Caroline asked.

The knocking in the engine was now beginning to scare Merit.

"Sweetie, keep the money." Years ago, someone had told Merit a terrible story about a cat that crawled up in the hood of a car, and what became of that cat when the car started. "Maybe you can buy me a frozen yogurt or something."

Caroline said okay.

It wasn't possible, was it, that Hux had gotten up in the car?

"So guess what? My art teacher had us draw self-portraits in class. She talked about Lowell. It was really interesting. I was going to tell you before, but then I forgot. We weren't allowed to look in a mirror."

"Really? What did she say?"

"About what?"

"About Lowell."

"Well, she didn't only talk about *Lowell*. She talked about John Currin and some other people—Lucian—I don't know how to pronounce that—Freud. And then she showed some slides of some of Lowell's stuff—things that I've seen pictures of before."

"What did she say about him?"

Merit felt a loss right now, the same terrible loss she felt whenever she dragged Caroline into the game. But she couldn't help herself.

"She said he helped some movement—I forget what she called it—reach its potential, but that he was too obsessed with himself and too macho for her taste, but that it was probably a crime to say that in Akron."

"I've never heard him called 'macho' before," said Merit. She was waking up a little bit now and was very concerned that she had turned Randy's cat into a sausage. "Did you tell anybody he was your"—what was he, exactly, to Caroline?—"stepgrandfather?"

Caroline was wiping something from her hand onto the seat. "No," she said.

"Oh," said Merit.

As soon as she got back home, she would call Randy, who would reassure her Hux was fine.

"Merit?"

"Yes, Caroline?"

"Have you ever heard of any artists who were women?"

"Sure," said Merit. "Tons."

"Who?"

Now was not really the best time to test Merit's smarts.

"Edie Brickell?" Merit said.

Caroline unzipped her backpack. Then she zipped it again, upzipped it, zipped and unzipped. It was still making Merit crazy that she wasn't able to picture Caroline's wallet. What does a thirteen-year-old need a wallet for anyway?

"We'll look in that art book tonight."

"Merit, why aren't there any women artists?" Caroline asked.

Wait: Randy still hadn't given Merit back her credit card.

"Maybe because women have too much guilt?" suggested Merit.

"Merit?" Caroline asked. "Is it true what my teacher said about how artists have to be good liars?"

When Merit pulled into the driveway, Wyatt was wobbling around up on a step stool in the empty garage. He was doing something with pliers and the garage-door opener. His Toyota was at the bottom of the driveway, and Merit parked in front of it, which seemed to be where he wanted her to park.

"Hey there!" Merit shouted.

Wyatt waved with his pliers.

"Hi, Dad. We got *I, Claudius!* Episodes seven through nine!" said Caroline. She jiggled the handle, making sure, as she always did, the car door was locked. Wyatt always did this, too. Her backpack thumped as she ran through the yard, headed, presumably, for Arabella's house.

"As you wish, Caroline," said Wyatt. Merit wondered what BBC miniseries he'd gotten that line from. He looked at Merit, then did a double take. He pursed his lips. "Is your hair wet?"

"No," said Merit.

"Did you come from the gym?"

Merit said, truthfully, she had not.

Wyatt went back to twisting whatever he was twisting in the garage-door-opener. He was wearing his old glasses, his embarrassing granny glasses. They were always crooked, too.

"Soooo, aren't you going to ask me what I'm doing? Aren't you curious, just a little bit?"

Merit crouched in the driveway, examined the area underneath the car. Something was dripping from the engine, but something was always dripping from the engine.

"Can I ask you why you're wearing your old glasses?" She didn't look back at him.

"In case they somehow get knocked off up here. . . . Well, I'll just *tell* you what I'm doing, then. I'm installing a sound-activated garage-door opener!" She couldn't tell whether the puddle on the driveway was Hux-blood-colored or not. "I'm sort of making this up as I go along, so we'll have to consider this a bold new experiment."

The puddle looked like oil, but she wasn't totally sure.

"Why don't you just use a motion detector, Wyatt, like everywhere else in the house?"

"Because then our garage door would open for any joker who stands in front of it and waves his arms! No, no, *no*: What we're working on here is a garage-door opener that opens when you honk your horn. We'll have to create a code, a series of beeps. Then we can practice it together."

She thought about opening the hood of the car, then decided to stick with her original arrangement, which was to call Randy. "Sounds like a plan."

"I still don't know how you can lose all these garage-door openers. You don't ever take them out of the car, do you?"

Merit asked Wyatt what in the heck she would be doing with a garage-door opener outside of the car.

The whole summer, Wyatt had repeatedly asked Merit to throw out all the junk, as he called it, on the shelves. All of it was Caroline's, and most of it predated Merit—a Slip 'N Slide, a Barbie yacht, a croquet set, and a box of Nerf balls. For three months, Merit had been rejecting Wyatt's garage-cleanup requests. As far as Merit could tell, the croquet set had never been removed from its box. Here was a humorous image: *Randy* playing croquet.

"You seem very hyper. Did you have a good day?" Merit asked.

"Nothing to write home about, really. Although Gregg put his car keys in someone else's briefcase. I had to drive him home."

Now would have been the obvious time to make a comment about the weird symmetry of events today; Merit, too, had driven a coworker home. She didn't, however, mention this unusual coincidence.

"Wow. What's the story with Gregg?" she asked. Gregg was the guy who'd had the crudité party. She liked Gregg not only because he had a great dog but also because Wyatt had told her that after the party Gregg had said he and his wife thought Merit and Wyatt were the best couple there.

"I think the job's running him ragged, between us. Hey, did you know that Caroline did a 'designed experiment' this evening, when she called both of us?"

Merit understood the cue. She inquired as to what, exactly, a "designed experiment" was. She was underneath the garage-door-opener mechanism now, looking up at Wyatt. He was wearing her garden gloves.

He explained what a "designed experiment" was, although Merit wasn't listening. When he leapt off the stepladder, though, she started listening again.

"*What* is wrong with your eyes, sweetie? Your pupils look *huge*."

He came toward her. She backed up.

"You should go look at yourself in the mirror on the car," Wyatt said. The way his hands, in Merit's canvas gloves, were raised made him look like a burn victim, or a monster, or an accidental murderer (*See this blood; look upon what I've done!*). "I think maybe you should go lie down."

Merit backed into something on the shelf. That something turned out to be the box of Nerf balls. The box fell onto the floor, and the balls rolled from the garage down the driveway. A yellow-and-black Nerf soccer ball bounced soundlessly into the silent street. "I think maybe I should go lie down."

"You should definitely lie down."

She felt, suddenly, inexplicably, exceptionally aroused. Maybe it was the gloves.

"Will you come with me, Wyatt? I have something to tell you."

Wyatt never liked to mess around before bedtime on weekdays. Their bedroom was separated from Caroline's bedroom by three rooms—Wyatt's study, the guest room, and the upstairs bathroom—but, even so, they couldn't have sex if there were any possibility that Caroline was awake, and upstairs. In the bedroom, Merit told Wyatt what was going to happen. He locked the door, checked the knob twice.

They got going, and Merit was concentrating on getting off without Randy thoughts, which she was pretty close to doing, when Caroline, who had always, up until that point, seemed to avoid their bedroom, knocked on the door.

"Merit? Are you in there? I have that book for you, the art book."

"Caroline, Je-*sus* Christ," said Wyatt. "Get away from the door! How many times have I told you *never* to knock on our door when it's *closed*?"

"I just wanted to show you this thing in the book. Are you coming downstairs soon?"

"Yeah," Merit said. "We'll be downstairs soon."

"I don't see anyone with the first name Edie in the book. Maybe I'm not spelling it right."

"I'll be downstairs really soon, Caroline," Merit said.

"Hey, Merit," Wyatt whispered. "I love you."

"Hey, Wyatt," Merit said. "You, too."

Merit didn't support the idea of ranking people like that. She had bought the book, an anthology called *The Five Hundred Greatest Artists of the Twentieth Century,* because she always bought books about Lowell. She bought them, she half-felt, to punish herself. There was never any mention of Jenny in these books. Or of Merit.

The entry on Lowell was longer than most of the others. Lowell's item was also set off in a special box. The book, which was seven years old, had cost seventy-five dollars when it was new. It had been printed in England, so some words in the entries had weird spellings. Merit had looked for the book a few times in used bookstores, and she'd found it once, for seventeen dollars. This book ranked Lowell number 228 out of 500, which had always seemed to her an okay number to be—not quite good, not quite bad, just about in the middle. Out of 500, 228 was sort of like the Ohio of numbers. Merit had never heard of many of the artists who ranked 229 to 500, but she would have been the first to tell you she didn't really know very much about art.

Jenny wouldn't stop talking about this book when it came out. Merit wondered why she cared so much about some stupid editor's opinions. Rivers was ranked before Lowell; so, too, Basquiat and Bleckner. *Haring,* even (although he was, by all accounts, a wonderful human being). Schnabel, she said, was one of the few "of my generation" whose existence she could tolerate. That Jenny thought in terms of "my generation" had always seemed weird to Merit; artists shouldn't think of themselves as part of any kind of group, although Merit realized if she were an actual artist herself, she might have a different opinion about that. Jenny *absolutely detested* Cy Twombly's work. You did not want to get Jenny going about Cy Twombly. Merit had often wondered if Jenny had somewhat fixed ideas about the kind of art she deemed acceptable.

Right after the publication of this anthology, Jenny had called Merit at school—several times a day, for several days in a row, for several weeks—to bitch about it. Merit could still see the chalkboard on the outside of her bedroom door in her first and only apartment, her roommate's bubble writing announcing "Your MOTHER called. Call her ASAP." ASAP was underlined four times. During those weeks, the roommate had kept a running tally on the board of the number of times Jenny had called.

But they're *hacks,*" Jenny screamed into the phone one night; and "They're only illustrators"; and later, "They're commercial artists; they should be selling ads." The last time they had ever spoken about this book, Merit had just come back from one of her early dates with Wyatt (having not yet told him any choicer familial nuggets for fear they might scare him away). The board's phone tally had two more ticks. Merit had been a little bit drunk (two beers at dinner; she hoped this Wyatt guy didn't think she was a lush). "Misunderstood and despised, as always," Jenny said. "I'm a better artist, at least in as far as my technique is concerned, than all of them *combined.*" Merit told Jenny to get a life and made her promise to shut up about the stupid book.

Caroline, who knew none of the big book's complex history, was lying on the floor of the family room, flipping through it. *I, Claudius* was playing on the TV, and John Hurt as Caligula was misbehaving charismatically, but Caroline was more interested in the book.

"I found Georgia O'Keeffe," Caroline said. "Mary Cassatt."

"I never liked either of those. Flowers and babies. *Next.*" Wyatt had appeared. The motion-activated light on the end table came on as he stepped down into the sunken family room.

"Where did *you* come from?" Merit asked. She had left Wyatt passed out on the bed, and she had figured, although it was only 7:45 now, he was a goner for the rest of the night.

"Yoko Ono?" he asked.

"She has the best name: Yoko Ono," Caroline said. "I think I saw her in here. I think I read about her. Is it 'Fluxus'?"

"What number is she?" asked Merit.

Merit had never told anyone this, but during finals week her senior year, she'd kept the book on her desk, opened to Lowell's page. She could still recite the paragraph about him.

Never appearing as himself in his work, the enigmatic artist Lowell Haven has painted over five hundred self-portraits. Each self-portrait is a performance, which has led his critics to suggest his work can appear dangerously self-indulgent. But in Haven's best-known work, we may see a mirror for our own self-indulgence as a society. Haven, much like the pop star Madonna, who has cited Haven as an influence, re-creates himself in every new work. A maestro of brushwork, and one of his era's few "painterly" painters, Haven produced lush, lavish, and straightforward early self-portraits, known for their brooding intensity and the subject's/artist's striking looks. They bring to mind the work of such figures as Goya, although to compare anyone to Goya is to be absurdly hubristic. A protégé of the late Andy Warhol (and represented by Warhol's legendary dealer, Leo Castelli), Haven became more commercially successful as his self-portraits became more detailed, turning, in the mid-eighties into large tableaux projects. In this phase of his career, each portrait became an extravagant stage set, in which the artist depicted himself in costume, often as figures from literature; his full-scale series of paintings of Lowell as King Arthur and Lowell as characters from *The Canterbury Tales* are not available to collectors. In the years that followed, Haven became interested in male archetypes and the portrayal of masculine identity in contemporary culture. His art from this period attempted, it has been suggested, to ask the question, What is a man? In the late eighties, an uproar took place when a retrospective of his work was banned by the city of Cincinnati, Ohio. Works such as *Lowell Copulating with Hole in Roxy Bathroom Stall; Lowell with Cohiba Cigar As Pacifier and Ralph Lauren Polo Shirt;* and *Lowell Naked in Room with Empty Containers of Procter and Gamble Products* were deemed unfit for public display; the Cincinnati Series, as it was later called, was bought by the advertising firm of Saatchi and Saatchi for, it was reported in the *Financial Times,* tens of millions of dollars. His other significant collector is the famous Count Panza of Milan. Haven's later work has been increasingly abstract and difficult to categorise. An Englishman by birth, little is known about Haven's life, and, in his work, he takes pains to appear sexually ambiguous. Presently, he resides in the "Rust Belt" American town of Akron, Iowa. In the words of Haven, in one of his few interviews, "My only project is anyone's only project: myself."

Birthdate: London, England, 1955

See also Balthus, Cindy Sherman, Robert Longo, Bas Jan Ader.

"Four hundred and fifty-two," said Caroline.

"Did you look at Lowell's entry yet?" asked Merit.

"Oh, no," Wyatt said. "You're not talking about *that* again, are you?"

"Yeah, but I think they missed something big," said Caroline.

"What'd they miss?" Merit asked. Whenever Merit felt nervous, as she did now, she imagined sucking on her own hair. If she'd been alone, she would have done that. She didn't know where this impulse came from. She'd been much younger than Caroline when she found out the truth.

"They missed what?" Wyatt asked. "That they say he's from London? That he's a pathological liar? That he lives with a clinically depressed psychopath in the Temple of Dendur?"

"They missed that his paintings are so *hilarious*," said Caroline.

When Merit was eight, shortly after Jenny and Merit moved into their house, she sneaked into Jenny's room because she'd wanted to play with Jenny's jewelry. She was never allowed in there unsupervised. Merit had a can of pop with her, and a bag of pretzels. Jenny's pink room smelled of hot nutty paint. In the middle of the room was a wet canvas, lying across two towel racks like a rug. Three dark, indistinguishable seated figures were in the painting. Merit was leaning over it, trying to get a better look at it, when she accidentally spilled the pop on the painting.

She was trying to wipe it off with her shirt when Jenny came in.

"What are you doing?" Jenny yelled. "Get away from there!"

The soda seemed to be eating through the painting. Jenny yanked Merit away and shook her.

"*Destroyer!*" she screamed. "You little destroyer!"

"Why do you have Dad's painting here?" Merit asked. "This is *Dad's* painting."

And then Jenny did something she'd never done before, or since: She hit Merit across the face.

The soda can crashed to the floor. Merit fled to her room (remarkably, she was still holding on to the pretzel bag) and locked herself inside. She sat alone in her bolted room, remaining on the floor for the rest of the night. She didn't cry. She wanted to stop thinking. So she occupied herself by methodically licking the salt off of every single pretzel in the bag. After she'd done that, she placed each licked pretzel upon her blue Trapper Keeper. After every one had been licked, she tilted the Trapper Keeper and let the pretzels slide back into the empty bag.

Merit had never before hated her mother. She'd never before hated anything. But that night, she was filled, for the first time, with hate.

For several hours afterward, Jenny knocked and knocked on Merit's door. Eventually, she stopped knocking. But she did not, would not, leave.

"Oh God, I'm sorry," Jenny said. "Oh God, I'm sorry, I'm so sorry, pumpkin. It's just that I didn't want you to find out what liars we were. Dad and I are liars. We lied to you. I'm sorry. I'm *sorry.*"

And it built, the hate Merit felt that night. Merit let herself feel it, until it was almost unendurable. The desk lamp in her bedroom did not go out. She sat on the floor until dawn and thought, for the first time, about what she was capable of.

Merit didn't come out of her room until the morning. Jenny was asleep on the floor in front of her door. And Merit stepped over her, went downstairs, and poured herself a bowl of cereal.

Someday very soon, Merit would have to tell Caroline. Throughout their marriage, Wyatt had made it very clear he would not be implicated in the lie. Caroline would be disappointed in Merit, and in Merit's whole family. And she would know, finally, what Merit was: a liar.

Merit couldn't find her cell phone anywhere, so when Wyatt was out walking the dog, she called Randy from Wyatt's study. (His number was, for some reason, written on the back of a Saks receipt that Merit found in a drawer.) She had to keep the call quick, because what if Caroline picked up the receiver in her bedroom? When Randy answered, he sounded as if he'd been asleep, but everybody who ever called Merit at work and talked to Randy commented that he sounded as if he'd been asleep. She didn't bother with small talk, asking immediately if Hux was there. He dropped something, shouted, "Fucking piece of *shit*" to the thing that dropped, and said Hux was fine, that he'd been sitting around on his (*his?* Merit thought) ass all night, biting his paw. Merit said she was glad to hear it, then asked Randy if he had a ride to work tomorrow morning. He paused. He said he was fine but that he had to go because he had to keep the line clear for Cooper, who was supposed to call. She thought about asking why he didn't have call waiting, and also asking him about her AmEx card, but she asked about neither, just said good-bye. She hung up the phone, went outside and fed the pig, and played with the cat and the rabbit. She was sad now, not debilitatingly sad, just a touch melancholy, really, because who was she? A seller of ad space, a person who didn't really have anything to look forward to, or dread, other than a party, a sexual-harasser of assistants, a *liar*? A liar who'd been brought into the world to cover up a lie? She'd probably never see Randy again anyway. He'd probably quit tomorrow and she'd never see him again. Her mother had been lured into having a child to cover up a lie. *This* was who Merit's mother was. This was who her *father* was.

Wyatt was still up when she got into bed. The rabbit was under the bed, chewing on a box. Eight months ago, the box had contained a five-page personal essay by her sculptor/essayist friend about his adventures trying to teach his brother how to drive a car with a stick shift. Merit couldn't remember what had happened to the essay; nor could she remember why her once-special friend had sent it to her in an L. L. Bean shirt box; nor could she remember why what remained of the box was now underneath her bed. He had always signed the notes accompanying his personal essays "Love." That had really bugged Merit. Who needs to be reminded all the time that everyone—even a temporary special friend—is a liar?

It wasn't quite right that she'd been born to cover up a lie, actually. Merit had been created to sustain a lie. Which was somehow much worse.

19

17 January 1977

Sometimes I think my pregnancy was intended as a way to relinquish control. I think a lot about how nice it will be to have a baby and take a temporary break from all my weedlike striving. To give in fully to one's femaleness: nothing ahead but the complacency of being a woman.

Sorry in there, little baby. If you're a girl, may you not grow to have such a malevolent and self-destructive brain.

The real reason it will be wonderful to have a baby: The child will be half Lowell. Almost too immense to ponder!

But constant worries about money, worries about where we'll live when the baby's born. Next week, when Desmond (our new patron) is out of the hospital, we'll be homeless again. There is no talk yet of where we'll go next. Lowell says Desmond told him red carpets will be rolled out for us extremely, extremely soon. Lowell says, "What's going to happen next is preordained." Lately, I've been staying home and working. We had a bad couple of months when we first moved to New York, but now all the insanity—what he did to my paintings—is behind us. I now understand Lowell's extreme need for recognition. But, unlike Fergus, Lowell assumes that recognition is a divine right. (It still makes no sense to me: Why do they *need* outside recognition?) "Painting me is just the beginning," Lowell says, "consider yourself my *creator*." I think I'd probably do anything to keep Lowell *Lowell*. It's better now, because Lowell is out constantly, meeting collectors and dealers. He says he adores feeling useful when he's not sitting for me, and, as I loathe being social in New York, this arrangement works out nicely. (Why is everyone here so chic and dumb? How do they manage to be both uninteresting *and* uninterested? London was fun. New York isn't.)

But tonight I broke form and went to a party with Lowell. Andy Warhol, about whom I've been hearing so much recently, was there. You know what? Not impressed. Toward the end of the evening, Lowell left me and went into another room. I overheard people in the room talking, saying how everything, everyone was "so great." At one point, above the human noise, Lowell said, "That we ended up here, in Elsa's fabulous apartment, with *Andy*, well, it seems almost *mystically planned*. Wouldn't you agree, Jenny?" (When I once asked Lowell how he made his voice into a weapon, he said, "Unfetter the consonants; augment the vowels.") Andy and I were the only people in the dining room. We were both eye-balling the Goya on the wall. Elsa, the party's hostess, was so wealthy (so I'd been told) that I made the mistake of assuming the Goya was real. "Isn't it great?" he asked me of the etching. His voice was high-pitched and breathy. He took a gulp of red wine and wiped his mouth on his sleeve.

The Goya, which I'd seen in books before, is an etching called *Hasta la Muerte*, number fifty-five from the *Caprichos* series, I believe. In it, a ghoulish old woman sits in front of a mirror at a dressing table, making adjustments to her flouncy hat. She seems less distressed about her ghastly reflected image than Goya seems to think she should be. It's always struck me as a deeply misogynistic work. (How it pains me to say that about my hero! But I must always remember what Mom told me about never underestimating how much men hate women.) Andy said, "You know, I think this is a *copy*." He took off his glasses. He said it was a copy of a copy, actually. I wanted to get a better look, so I charged toward the picture, accidentally colliding with Andy's wineglass, knocking it out of his quivering pale-skinned hands. Red wine on the white shag rug.

"Oh dear," Andy said.

Elsa was going to murder him, he said. She'd never invite him to a party of hers again. I went to the kitchen for some paper towels. When I came back, he was gone.

In the cab home, Lowell talked about what qualities he thought made an artist "great," then interrupted himself in the middle of a sentence and asked me if I thought he had any theatrical talent.

18 January

Fergus called. He said he needed me, said I was the only person he could really talk to. He'd forgotten I was pregnant. When I reminded him, he asked, "Does the father know?"

Fergus's father's case is terminal.

20

EMULATING FERGUS
By "Bradley W. Dormer"

So was I shocked when I got the invitation to Fergus Goodwyn's costume ball? You bet I was. As far as I understood it, our parting had not been good. I had not heard from him after my article appeared in these pages last year, and my multitudinous phone calls to his publicist, Taffy, then to his new publicist, Bucki ("The man changes publicists as often as Luther Vandross changes pant sizes," confided one veteran celebrity wrangler), went unanswered.

I had just returned, soaking, from lunch when I got the invitation to the party. Oh, sure, I know what you're thinking: Here's a guy who enjoys his expense-account three-saki, three-salmon-caviar-roll lunches. But let it be known that the freewheeling three-hundred-dollar lunches of the past are but a distant memory, at least in my organization. For the past hour, I had been gnawing at a prosciutto/mozzarella/pesto sandwich on an impossibly hard ciabatta roll. Across the booth was a Janus-faced movie studio publicist. We were lunching at an upscale delicatessen. There was no wine list; that was how bad times were. Although the rain was coming down in sheets, I got out of my lunch appointment as fast as I could, without ordering a cappuccino. I had no umbrella. There were no cabs. In my Thomas Pink shirt and Ferragamo loafers, I splashed back to my office. Battered inside-out umbrellas littered the sidewalks like so much plunder from Neptune.

Upon my return, I was, needless to say, a mess. My assistant brought out a Frette towel from my editor in chief's office and dried me off with it. When I finally sat down at my desk, somewhat less wet, I noticed an ecru invitation gleaming in my otherwise-empty in-box. The heft of the high-rag paper, the costliness of it, the elegance of the calligraphy could only mean one person: Fergus.

There was no return address, but the postmark was stamped Akron, Ohio. How I worshiped that postmark.

I couldn't help myself. I ripped into the invitation.

I was being invited to a party at Fergus Goodwyn's in a fortnight's time! I closed my door and danced a jig in my tiny wet Ferragamos. I would see Fergus very soon, on August 17! And he hadn't hated me, or my piece about him last year!

Apparently, I had packed my suitcase too full. Waiting in the baggage-claim area at Cleveland Hopkins International Airport, I was confronted with a disturbing sight: My bag was open, and upside down, its contents scattered on the conveyor belt! Not knowing what to expect on this trip, I had brought two dozen pairs of underwear, despite the fact I was just staying for two days. A nice woman named Bev (whose ex-husband, I learned, was a professional emu farmer residing points west) scrambled up on to the moving belt and helped me gather up all my things. Tumbling down the revolving conveyor belt like that, I realized with horror the bulk of what I'd brought: underwear and party costumes. Did I get a lot of strange looks from the folks in the baggage claim at Cleveland Hopkins Airport? You bet I did.

"Do you party?" Bev asked me, surveying my curious possessions, which were now bundled by our feet. She applied cherry-flavored Chap-Stick and smacked her lips lasciviously. Her highlights weren't terribly well maintained.

I gulped, tossed my Fergus wig, plastic snake, and underwear into my oversized suitcase, slammed it shut, and scurried over to the car-rental counter.

Once in my hotel room, I popped open my bag. Several important costume items were missing, revolving, presumably, on baggage-claim carousel number three at Cleveland Hopkins Airport. One of my wings was gone, although my horse head was still there; a one-winged Pegasus does not, nor should not, satisfy. There were only two fake snakes, out of an original seven, for my Medusa head. I held the two up to my head and examined what I saw in the mirror. Unacceptable, Brad, I thought, unacceptable.

I twirled the Fergus wig around on my finger. I smoothed my actual hair down and put the wig on. In front of the full-length mirror in my room at the hotel at Quaker Square (I'd never slept in a converted grain silo before!), I considered things. Maybe it was just wishful thinking, but, with the wig on, and with all the weight I'd lost lately, and with my recent obsession with physical fitness and new nightime grooming regimen, I really actually did look like him. My handheld mirror hadn't gone missing, and thank God for that.

At the beginning, I was alone. I parked in the enormous, manicured, impeccable front lawn of his glorious brick and stained-glass Tudor mansion, underneath a white canopied tent, around the perimeter of which white *Midsummer Night's Dream* lights twinkled. I was fifteen minutes early. I had brought a flask. Inside the flask was J&B. I guzzled half of it, alone and quaking in my midsize rental car. I had not yet bobby-pinned the wig on.

I couldn't get over how glamorous and luxurious the cars parked under the canopy were! There were Rolls-Royces, Ferraris, Lamborghinis, and even a DeLorean! It's a very specific feeling, car-shame, and I'd never felt it anywhere but in Los Angeles, where I often visit. I was not expecting to feel that special car-shame feeling in Akron, but, as Fergus has reminded us, unexpected things can, and do, happen, in Akron, Ohio.

An older but well maintained Jaguar puttered in next to me. Out stepped a tall yet lusterless man in glasses. He looked statistics-professor boring. An equally tall dark-haired young woman, attractive despite her glasses, in a Marian the Librarian way, stepped out of the other side, and a teenaged girl stepped out of the back. The girl was definitely too old to be their daughter. I hid my flask between my knees. The woman in the glasses gazed into my rental car, then shot me a quizzical but not unfriendly look. She had a kind face. I gave her one of my biggest Bradley smiles. She waved at me and motioned for me to roll down the window. The car was a 2002 Taurus, and thus had no manual roll-down handle. I started the car and pressed the button for the window.

"Hey! You could have just opened the door," the woman in the glasses shouted, laughing over the noise of the motor.

I turned the car off. The Tudor mansion in front of me sprawled out like a Shakespearean dream. The turrets, the minarets, the towers, the ivy: a dream I just wanted to crawl inside of and die within. Inside that house was Fergus.

"Isn't this great?" the woman asked me again. "Doesn't his house look amazing?" She wasn't wearing a costume, nor was her colorless, Dockers-wearing stiff of a husband. The pretty blond teenager sported a pink princess dress, complete with rhinestone tiara and scepter.

I stuck my hand out of the window to be shaken. The woman bent over and shook (I got a good look at her rack that way). I explained who I was, and what I was doing there. The bobby pins in my pockets were poking my thighs. I hoped my Fergus wig wasn't getting crushed in my briefcase in the backseat.

"I'm so glad to meet you, Bradley! I've been looking forward to this day for my whole entire life. Fergus is, you know, basically my father. Maybe you can write about that?"

"Not a bad idea," I said. My tape recorder was in the briefcase, too.

"Fergus gave me drawing lessons once," piped up the pipsqueak. "He's the coolest single guy in the universe. Also the nicest. When I grow up, I want to be him."

"Be like him, you mean," the nerdy-looking fellow said. "Although I hope you don't mean that, either."

"No," said the girl, "*be* him."

The nerdy-looking fellow convulsed. His lips were covered in foam.

"Wyatt doesn't like Fergus because he's jealous of him," said the woman. "All I know is that Fergus is my hero, and without him, I'm nothing."

"I'm nothing, too!" chimed in the teen.

"Hey, Brad, are you walking in now?" asked the bespectacled, uncostumed woman, who wore battered Levi's and leather clogs. "Maybe we can go in together!"

I needed to do two important things: attach my Fergus wig and reacquaint myself with my flask.

"I'm afraid I need a little time to prepare, folks. But see you inside!"

The little nontraditional family took its leave. The man clearly had a broom handle rammed up his ass. I was concerned about how'd he fare in this crowd.

I'm afraid my pinning job in the car wasn't the most professional-looking; I employed about thirty inexpertly hidden bobby pins. Reflected in the rearview mirror, the pins flashed within the nether regions of my wig like stainless-steel sutures. I smiled at myself. I hate my teeth. I grabbed hold of my wig and tried to move it around. It did not budge. (The pins were indeed ugly, but did they do the trick? Oh, they did.)

I went "La la la la laaaaaa!" into my microcassette recorder. I rewound, played, then covered my ears and closed my eyes. The worst part of being a reporter is listening to all your sycophantic yes-man interviews, your tinny, terrified voice in them, your slavish willingness to agree with everything your subject says, just so he'll like you, just so you can get what you need from him. Just so you can get a good story.

With my wig on my head and my flask in my sock, I started making my way up the long driveway. The microcassette recorder was in the side pocket of my black Gucci pants. I was concerned about the bulge. *Sleekness,* Bradley, I could hear Fergus say. Above and beyond all else: *sleekness.* I took the recorder out of my pocket and started talking into it.

"I am walking up the driveway now, looking at the great lawn leading up to Fergus's house. The house fills me with such a special kind of joy that I want to leap and run up to the door. But I don't, because I'm pretty drunk already. The grounds are located on fifty-two acres of lush northeast Ohio rolling hills and they're rolling out all around me. Okay, I'm getting closer now, I'm staring at the house. It's strange, but it looks as if it's throbbing. It looks alive, and it's as if I can feel its beating heart. Also, remember to write about how the grounds are as magnificent as the house itself is. Hawthorne trees, apple orchard to my right, weeping forsythia over there—is that the elliptical garden I read about? Remember to check out later tonight. Balm of Gilead, Good King Henry, mead-owsweet, a witch's herb garden. I'm coming up to the entranceway now. That very fat and ugly butler I remember from last year, Andrei, is guarding the door like some hideous Cerberus. Andrei and I just made eye contact. I'm backing up. Okay. I'm ducking behind the pink rhododendron. I'm drinking some more from my flask. More later. Sign-ing off."

I spat behind the rhododendron. I placed a Listerine breath strip on my tongue and approached the gate for the second time.

"And you are?" the ghastly Andrei said. I jammed my microcassette recorder back into my pocket. The breath strip turned to glue on my tongue.

I stated my name and credentials. The bobby pins were stabbing my scalp. I didn't care for the way he was looking at my wig.

"I have never heard of that magazine," he said.

I just knew he had terrible taste in magazines, and I was relieved, in a way, he had never heard of the one you hold in your demographically coveted hands right now. You should be glad, too.

"But I was invited!" I screeched. "Fergus invited me!"

"Oh. Well, in that case, sir, please come in! Fergus is—how do you say it?—the sun in my sky. For Fergus, I will do *anything*."

The foyer was empty, but from beyond, within the great hall, I could hear the bustling sounds of merriment. Once inside the foyer, I found myself standing in front of the glorious self-portraits of Fergus as Arthur, king of the Britons. In these paintings, he is, to quote the poet, "god-sized." He is indeed the golden boy, the sun shining down in exquisite rays through his tempest-tossed russet hair. Fergus has caught himself in just the mo-ment before he pries the sword in the stone loose—one leg is propped up on the stone, and the other braces itself on the ground. In the painting, his flexing calf muscles bulge and ripple sexily. What a very great artist he is! And Fergusian Arthur stares intensely not at the sword, or the stone, but out at the viewer, conveying such self-belief and such ferocity that he makes this one particular art fan, at least, question the very valid-ity of his manhood.

Which reminded me I had been planning to read "Preiddeu Annwfn," so as to impress Fergus with my knowledge of Celtic lore, but I had just remembered I had forgotten all about that machination.

The butler, Andrei, wearing a bizarre Harley-Davidson leather vest, was back, and noted that I was looking hard at the Fergus-as-Arthur painting.

"Excalibur is an impressive sword, yes?" said Andrei.

Excalibur was *not* the name of the Sword in the Stone, but I did not correct him. He was my own personal Morgan le Fay, but yet there was nothing to fear. I took a sip from the flask, fluffed my wig, and raised the wrought-iron latch on the door. I entered the din of the great hall.

The celebrities! The costumes! Each costume with which I was greeted was more beautiful and more lavish than the next. Henry Kissinger was there, with a wire cage suspended around his midsection, and his beautiful wife, socialite Nancy Kissinger, was costumed as a predecapitated Marie Antoinette, complete with powdered wig and décolleté-boosting gown. As I made my way toward them through the glamorous crowd (I was heading for the bar, actually, not for them), I could see Frau Kissinger was wearing a long necklace, the pendant of which was a three-tiered hand-painted enamel Limoges cake.

"So what are you supposed to be?" I asked the former secretary of state as I passed.

"I'm *weal*," Kissinger said. "Fergus drew the *cow*." He pointed into the cage that bisected his ample tuxedoed torso. Taped to his chest was a dazzling little drawing of a baby calf, sketched by none other than the maestro himself.

At the bar, I ordered a J&B on the rocks from the magazine-gorgeous male bartender. My cocktail was served in a sterling silver (I hope it was *sterling silver* and not *pewter*!) goblet. I took out my microcassette recorder and whispered into it again.

"I'm at the bar right now, and I'm looking across this room, through this amazing, amazing crowd. A majestic stag's head is mounted above the huge fireplace. In the minstrels' balcony high above me, a madrigal band plays charming tunes. Italian, it sounds like, possibly Monteverdi. The Juilliard-trained musicians look like extras from *Much Ado About Nothing*. In the middle of the great hall is a table, on which sits an ice sculpture in the shape of Fergus's delicately formed head. There are waiters, men as beguiling as the spawn from Uranus's severed penis and the sea, serving mouthwatering hors d'oeuvres of shrimp and such. I see movie heartthrob Ben Affleck in the distance. He's dressed as a beefsteak tomato, and he's chatting up a buxom lady friend. Prince William is wearing a kilt. My wig is starting to itch and I'm afraid I'm now a conspicuous presence here, muttering like some creep into my microcassette recorder. I'm starting to feel really not right. I've counted about six people in Fergus wigs now. I guess my getup isn't as original as I thought a few hours ago. Signing off."

I grappled with my microcassette recorder and asked the Redford look-alike behind the bar to refill my silver chalice, no rocks this time. The Fergus heads were all clustered in a busy, buzzing bunch now, over by the Fergus ice sculpture. Affleck, Prince William, the Kissingers, and Jerry Hall (dressed, it seemed, as Mae West) were all milling around, too. They were smiling and whispering and glancing pensively in the same direction.

It could only mean one thing: Fergus.

I hid my microcassette recorder, clutched my goblet, and made my approach. The red rug underneath my feet felt very luxurious and costly indeed.

"Oh, thank you, thank you. . . . I know. . . . You're too kind! . . . Oh, please. Flattery will get you nowhere, Henry."

The voice did sound uncannily like the hilarious Dustin Hoffman impression of Fergus during the closing credits of *Goodwyn!: The Documentary*. It had been a year since I'd heard, in person, Fergus's resonant, captivating voice, about which Penelope Moyer, voice coach to the stars, says, "The tone is richer than Orson Welles's even. And the pitch is possibly greater than Olivier's."

All the Fergus heads were bobbing as if they were buoys or blow-jobbers. Zombies, I thought, every last one of them. Prince William had that special horsey look of the aristocracy. He kept elbowing Fergus, sharing some kind of in-the-know joke. Keep on milking him, Wills, I thought. Suddenly, I came up with a way, a clever yet most frightening way, to separate myself from the obsequious Fergus wanna-be pack!

I wedged myself into the inner circle, bracing myself for whatever would come next. What would he look like? I wondered. How would he have changed in the year since I'd seen him?

"No, Jerry, you're not being mean at all. Do go on. Henry *is* horrid," Fergus said. He came into view now. He looked, in a word, astonishing. And mysterious. Very, very mysterious. In his right hand he held a black lacquered stick, atop of which was a black silken eye mask, which tragically covered the top half of his amazing face. How I wanted to pry off the mask and gape at that face! We were wearing the same outfit: next season's black Prada shirt and black Gucci pants. But Fergus wore his clothes with such elegance and panache that my Prada shirt and Gucci pants might as well have been bridge-line items.

Suddenly, a middle-aged woman who looked middle-aged and sorely in need of an aesthetic overhaul from our magazine's own makeover column "Help Me, Dr. Rhonda!" butted rudely into our little glamour pocket of the great hall.

"Another drink?" she brayed. "Anyone, anyone?"

"Jenny," Fergus said. "Not '*another* drink,' my dear. Say, 'May I offer anyone *a* drink?' "

The unstylish woman in pleated tweed slacks looked down sheepishly at her unpolished brogues. "Oh, I do apologize, Mr. Goodwyn."

"Well then," Fergus said, "off with you now!"

The shabbily dressed woman listed shamefacedly away, and Fergus drew our high-profile huddle closer together. It was unsettling not to be privy to the joyous mobility of Fergus's facial expressions, due to the opacity of the mask.

"She's an old friend from high school who's lately fallen on hard times. Jenny needed the work tonight, but let's not let on I've told you this. I've tried to help her as best I can. It's . . . it's so *hard* to be me sometimes." His luscious bee-stung lower lip trembled with sexy emotion.

There was a lull in the conversation. My opportunity had presented itself. I pounced on it.

"Fergus went to high school, just like everyone else!" I said excitedly. I wondered what we looked like to the other watchers. Was gazing at us like gazing into some fabulous mirror?

More importantly, I wondered what I looked like to him. The mask made it impossible to tell what he was thinking, insofar as you can ever tell what another person is thinking.

"Yes?" he said quizzically. There was ice (metaphorical ice, of course) in his eyes, which were visible through the eyeholes of the mask. "And you are?"

"I'm *you*! Or, more to the point, I'm the *story* I wrote about you last year!"

Fergus stroked the cheekbone of his mask. "I'm afraid I don't know what you're talking about, sir." I watched his lips move.

"I'm the story! 'What Makes the Most Famous Man in the World Run?'! That's me!"

Ben Affleck, in his stuffed tomato suit, looked stupefied. I looked much more like Fergus than the Roman-nosed Fergus-wig guy twitching next to Affleck.

"I'm sorry," Fergus said very gently, very politely, "but I've never seen you before in my life.

I ran out of the commotion in the great hall, in search of a bathroom. I ran past two life-size self-portraits of Fergus donning Shakespearean garb. Finally in the bathroom, I ripped off my wig. Bobby pins jutted out chaotically from my hair like antennae from spaceships. So Fergus had forgotten about my story. In her more chilling moments, my wife likes to say magazines are as disposable, as expendable and forgettable as any woman is. I was taking a full account of the Bradley situation in the mirror now. I looked like a clown postshow. Violently, I tugged out each bobby pin, one by one, and threw each in the sink with a bobby pinnish *ting*. The party dinned on outside. The party did indeed continue. It's a good dress rehearsal for death, reminding yourself that the party goes on without you. This is what it's like to be alone, I thought. This is what it's like.

21

The blimp floated by yesterday. Then Preston Lympany's cell phone, in his front pocket, rang and rang. Initially, he ignored it, but when the sound became unignorable (he had his ringer set to the first few notes of "People Are Strange"), he slipped the phone out of the pocket ("God, who keeps *calling* me?" he asked as he unfolded it, and I really believed he felt as exasperated as he sounded) and noted, expressionlessly, the name and number on his unit's caller ID.

Someone else wanted Preston Lympany, and was making the point relentlessly. I bit into cupcake number four and tried not to think about how Preston Lympany's existence had nothing to do with mine. There were forces, inevitable forces, that would remove him from me, and I didn't allow myself to contemplate them. The phone went off again, and the realization came to me I was going to eat every single cupcake in the box.

Preston Lympany apologized, then answered the call.

"I left a message for you that I was at Fergus's," he said into his cute silvertone phone. I licked the icing off the top of my fifth cupcake. "God, your phone's the worst. I don't know why you're still on that plan."

I tried to be polite and not eavesdrop. Leaves, brown ones, floated on top of the reflecting pond.

"Trevor says 'Hi,' Fergus," he said.

"Hello, *Trevor,*" I said.

They were my first fallen leaves of the season. It was sad to see them, but August is always sad that way. I had to remember to collect them from the pond before the party, although I didn't think we had any kind of long-handled net.

"I'm telling you, cats *do* that sometimes. It's like they're tripping. They see things in the air, they freak out."

Preston Lympany had had about ten cigarettes, and I could smell them in my hair (Andrei never did come with that hat). I was still, at this point, able to breathe, somewhat.

"All right, all right. I'll come home," he said. "You, too. Bye." He folded his phone. He sighed. "The cat's having some kind of issue. Trevor says he's got this crazy look in his eye, and he's doing this lockjaw thing and can't close his mouth."

"Oh," I said. I knew what "You, too" was the response for. "I'm very sad to hear that."

"It happens a couple times a year. Trevor's just never home alone with Thurston like I am all the time, so he doesn't know what the hell he's doing." The cigarette pack was on his lap. He dug into it. "I'll have one more; then I guess I should go. I wish I could say longer."

"Well, this has been nice, hasn't it?" I wanted to collapse onto the mossy bricks, crawl over to him, grab hold of his boot, cling to it. I wanted to touch *him* with the eraser this time. "We'll see each other soon enough. . . . And thanks awfully much for the suggestion about the chocolate place cards!"

He lit his cigarette and breathed it in. He would not look at me, nor did he touch me again. "Fergus?" Preston Lympany asked, "why are you so good to me?"

You know how the movie or the book always ends at the party, before the next day's cleanup scene? That's not very realistic, now is it? Every encounter leaves its trash, remember. Preston Lympany left our twosome; I ate cupcake number six, then gathered up the empty box, the unopened bottle of Pellegrino, and the magazines and deposited them in the shopping bag his hand had held. I collected a couple of cigarette butts, but I gave up after about the third one. The baby blue blimp eraser was on the farthingale chair he had sat in. I brought that eraser to my lips. The upholstery was still warm—from him. That ashy streak on the crimson damask was from me.

I had just washed my hands in the kitchen sink when that special old strangled feeling returned. I should have known better than to let Preston Lympany smoke his eleven brown cigarettes yesterday.

In the kitchen, I dried my hands with a dishcloth. I was thinking about how I have this habit of smelling my hands immediately after I've washed them (which I did this time, too), when the attack came on. My lungs were no longer two big happy inflating/deflating balloons; they had become weepy, fungusy multipocketed sponges, and they were trying to kill me.

It felt as if a cravat had been tightened around my neck by someone whose notions of how to tie neckwear were formed by the most sadistic headmaster on the block. I sat on the island in the kitchen. I put my head between my bare legs and concentrated. My shorts were tighter in that position, and I heard (and felt) the lining inside them split. I remembered I'd stashed an inhaler in one of the island's drawers for situations like this. I scooted down the countertop, rummaged around (in a very frantic way, actually, also upside down) in the chaotic utility drawer, where I found my beautiful blue inhaler—a similar blue, really, to Preston's blimp eraser—next to the pizza cutter. I removed the cap, brought the thing to my mouth, and sucked as single-mindedly as my lungs would let me. I felt a little better. I shook the inhaler, flipped up the tab, and sucked again.

I was almost okay then, okay enough, in fact (although still not great), to hobble downstairs for my tent. Nighttime was a long way off, but I already needed to prepare. I'd had practice at this.

I hadn't been in the basement since the last wheezy retrieval of my tent, which was after our last big party (Lowell's birthday, at which Lowell gave his own birthday toast himself). The basement also contains some of Lowell's unsold work. I know that someday, when I'm dead, I'll be publicly vilified—by strangers who are, at the moment, infants or not even yet born—for not tending to Lowell's art (minor as these pieces are) with a little more TLC. Lowell told me once, during a cleaning frenzy one white-skied winterish morning half a decade ago, to "get the stuff out of my blasted sight." He amassed the undesirables outside his studio. I dealt with them. In Lowell's mind, if there's no public desire for something, it's *nothing*. It never even existed.

The unsalable paintings are imitations of imitations—studies from the *Naked Akron* series and *Lowell Crucified with Cow Crucified Next to Him,* and sketches for paintings that never came to fruition, such as *Death of Lowell As Martin Luther King, Jr.,* and *Lowell As Salome and Head of Lowell as John the Baptist on Platter.* The finished paintings there are *Lowell Throwing Elephant Dung on Lowell As Lowell in Calvin Klein Ad, Lowell and Flag, Lowell and Brillo Box, Lowell As Warhol's Monroe,* and *Lowell's Family, or: Lowell As Father, Mother, and Daughter.* The latter one is from 1985, and Lowell has said it's the worst painting he ever did. The canvases and sketchbooks are propped against a damp brick north-side wall.

It had been years since I'd peeked under the black sheet covering Lowell's artwork. I shook my inhaler, gasped, and pulled that black sheet back.

I didn't have enough breath in me to scream. I was confronted with *Lowell's Family, or: Lowell As Father, Mother, and Daughter.*

I hate this painting, too, but for my own reasons. The three cement-colored semiabstract figures in the painting have always made me think of those ghostly Easter Island statues, but Lowell has always maintained that wasn't the intended reference. The cantilevered-browed family is seated on a bench, arms entwined, the small Lowell in the middle, big Lowells (one in a vague outline of a dress, the other wearing a hazy necktie—Merit sometimes wore a knitted necktie then) on either side. I took the photographs that inspired this, too: Lowell, flanked by Merit and Jenny, outside on my Chippendale bench. That was the day I saved Harry Bailey Two from choking to death. That was also the day Jenny fired this question to me as she tore out of the gaming room: "Fergus, do you remember if I've ever been sane?" I reached for her, wanting to keep her with me, wanting to comfort her, but she was already out the door, out of my reach. Jenny and Merit only lasted another couple months in the little home we had created for ourselves.

I also dislike this picture because it is further evidence Lowell does not, nor has not, considered me a member of his family.

The tent was folded in a box on a shelf.

The basement also contains my photo albums, my pictures of Lowell. This is the real reason I can't go there.

The tent is construction-cone orange. My parents used it twice—once for our camping trip to Burr Oak, and the other time for our trip to Salt Fork. I was a child then. My mother and father still existed. Although it is (at best) a couple-size tent, all three of us squeezed inside it together, each of us podlike in his or her green slippery sleeping bag. Dad slept by the "door"; Mom at the "window" end. I was in the middle. The tent still smells like fishing tackle and mildew. That's how it smelled then, too, all those years ago.

For Bastille Day just this year, Lowell gave me a new two-thousand-dollar self-installing inflatable tent. (I know the price because I had Andrei return it to Hammacher Schlemmer.) Lowell has insisted for decades the old tent is actually making my respiratory problems worse, but he's wrong. "*Akron*'s making me sick," I tell him. "It's *Akron.*" But he's never listened. I thanked Lowell, quite sincerely, in fact, for the gift, both in person and in an E-mail. With my refund, I ordered a new silicone-coated sleeping bag, a portable battery-powered dehumidifier, a dozen shuttlecocks, and a bank-breaking wooden model of a 1954 Mercedes (an "impulse" buy, really, and one I now regret).

Of what is dust made? Human skin, insect corpses, particulate matter from tires.

My night last night, in the tent, in the mummy bag, had been vastly better than it would have been back in the house. Last night, in preparation for sleep, I'd zipped closed both the door and window flaps. No Akron dust could get in that way. I woke up only once. My trusty inhaler had been stationed within arm's reach; so, too, my VapoRub. I hadn't needed them, as it turned out, but if I had, it would have been trouble: I was zippered into the mummy bag up to my nose. It was too tight for me to move. My cell phone, whose number I still haven't learned, was also in the tent, in case of an emergency, as well as a bottle of water, the dehumidifier, raisins, a tube of Bactroban Cream (just in case), and a box of Kleenex. Also, there were magazines.

I wasn't yet awake enough to tell what hour of the morning it was.

"Ferrrrrrgus?"

I wasn't presentable. Movement was, at that point, impossible. I was facing away from the door flap and couldn't see him.

"Lowell?"

"What the devil are you doing in here? You look like Tutankhamen. I couldn't find you *anywhere* this morning."

I wriggled within my green bag like a pupa. Some part of my clothing appeared to be stuck in the zipper, but I didn't know which part. I didn't want him to see me, not like this. "You were looking?" I asked.

"Oh, Fergus. You look as if you need a bit of help there. May I?"

As Lowell lowered himself inside, his clothing made contact with the tent. By the angle and quality of light through the pinpricks overhead, I guessed it was now about 10:30 a.m. It sounded as if Lowell were still in his robe.

The tent being only three feet high, he would have to come over to me on his knees, or crawl on his stomach.

I couldn't move as gracefully as I would have liked (in fact, I couldn't move at all), so I was only able to see his tanned busy fingers on my sleeping bag's zipper. Beautiful fingers.

"Fergus, good Lord; you've got your hair in the zipper, too. Don't move now. Was it a serious one, the attack?"

Like a nurse propping up an invalid for his electrifying daily spoonful of chicken broth, Lowell slid a hand underneath my head. The other hand went at the zipper. Beautiful hand. Toxic dust fluttered in a thin pillar of light. I was seized by the exceedingly horrifying thought that I might start to cry.

"Lowell?"

"I wish you would have told me you were going to be spending the night outside. It's tremendously unsettling, you know, not having you at the house. . . . Good God, is there any ventilation in here at all? . . . I cannot understand how you can sleep here . . . when I know for a fact that your mother used to warn you all about the 'turtle headache' phenomenon. Is this sort of another antimother minirebellion of yours?"

"It was *your* mother who said that, I think, Lowell."

His hand—still unlined, although more veined now than previously—glowed dark in the tent, almost red. It stopped its nonprogress up the zipper. The other hand was no longer under my head. "*Fuck,*" Lowell said. "It *was?*"

"I remember you mentioned that once when we were staying at Count Panza's villa in Varese. We slept in that small canopied bed, and you couldn't breathe, either. Lowell?"

He began tugging gingerly on the zipper again. I was able to see the first few inches of his forearm now. The muscles worked. There was no sleeve, no French cuff.

"Fergus, my memory absolutely terrifies me. Sometimes I think I can't even remember who I am."

"Lowell?"

"You'll tell me when I finally do go full-on senile, won't you? I mean, you *would* tell me, yeah?"

"You're not going senile; all of us blot out certain events. Lowell? Can I ask you a question?"

"Certainly, Fergus."

"Do you know that tires are made from petroleum, butyl polymers, chloroform, methylene chloride, trichloroethylene, and carbon black fillers?"

"Yessssss. I did know that, Fergus. We must have read the same article, although I certainly couldn't remember one of those chemical's names, the little beasts. And was it that eighty percent of the dust we breathe comes from tires? A fairly Akronian statistic, I thought. Can we go outside and talk about this? I need to discuss some other things, as well."

"Lowell?"

"Voilà!" Lowell said as he burst through the catch in the zipper. "Chrysalis!" On his knees, he maneuvered around the length of the sleeping bag (knocking over my inhaler and unopened bottle of water, but taking care, it seemed, not to squish me with his knees). He unzipped the whole thing for me. He was barefooted and dressed in the silk saffron-hued pajama bottoms I'd bought for him and, shockingly, a white T-shirt.

I had been freed.

Lowell, on his knees, hovered over me. In the tent's light, he shone pumpkin, as if in a convection oven. I probably did, too, although I couldn't see myself. I sat up. The green sleeping bag slid down to my waist.

"Feeling better?" he asked.

I felt as if I were choking again, but for other reasons.

"I'm sick, Lowell," I said. "Not right now, but generally."

"You look hot. Are you hot?"

"Yes, Lowell," I said. "And cold, too."

"I worry about you, Fergus, truly I do."

"Do you remember when you said I wasn't long for this world, Lowell?"

"Sounds like something I'd say, doesn't it? Let's talk about the *party*." Lowell, at the foot of my green sleeping bag, crossed his legs like a Turk. I took this to be a sign he intended to stay awhile. I felt happy about that. I know how much he hates my tent.

"The party?" I said.

"Yes, the party. Now, my sense is that you're not delegating as many responsibilities as you should be. This troubles me." The bottoms of Lowell's feet were dirtless. Mine, however, were somewhat muckier. I hid my feet in the folds of my sleeping bag, hoping he hadn't seen them.

"Oh, everything's really completely under control," I said. I was, of course, lying. I hadn't even begun to think about my costume.

"Let's begin with the basics, shall we? I haven't even seen the guest list. How many affirmative RSVPs have we at this point?"

"Tons," I said. "A couple hundred?"

That wasn't true.

"Good. Heard anything from Merit?"

"Yes," I said, "I have. She's a yes."

"Good. No guests, right? She's not bringing the Automaton, is she?"

"She left a very brief message. She didn't say anything about . . . *him.*"

Merit's message had been only eleven seconds long. I'd timed it the fifth time I listened to it.

"Thank God. I've met rubber bands with more charisma. Have any notable persons RSVP'd?"

"Depends what you mean by that," I said.

"If you have to ask, my dear, I'm afraid I must take that to mean no. Ah, not like the old days, is it? At any rate, I think we still need someone at the door, regardless. Whom would you suggest?"

"Well," I said. The answer to that question seemed to be self-evident. "I was thinking . . . *Andrei?*" Naturally, Andrei would be at the door, because Andrei was always at the door.

"That's actually what I came to talk to you about, Fergus."

Lowell opened my container of VapoRub and sniffed opulently, as if it were a 1990 Romanée-Conti. Do you want to know what's really sad? For a moment there, but only for a moment, I thought Lowell had inhaled so deeply of my VapoRub because . . . Oh, never mind.

"Andrei's like crabgrass or a plague sore or a pop-up ad," I said. "He's just *around*. Plus, I think he really likes standing by the door." I was surprised to hear myself semidefending Andrei. I knew what this meant.

Lowell, jar in one hand, lid in the other, gazed at me. The whites of his eyes were orange. Everything was orange. He smiled. His teeth were orange, his orange/black hair backswept. He looked as if he were posing for an ad. I remembered something I'd read (and reread about a million times) about him in a magazine profile: "Lowell Haven seems to have an innate sense of when the cameras are clicking."

"What do you think of Andrei? I mean, really, Fergus? Let's talk now."

The VapoRubbed tent now smelled like a TB ward. The tent smelled, I'm afraid, like me, only more so.

I didn't know what to say. So I said nothing. Had I been in a better mood—had I, in fact, been another person entirely—I might have had something to say. I was not, however, in a good mood. I was still, lamentably, myself.

"Look now, don't you rather think Andrei has been, to put it mildly, taking supreme advantage of our generosity? He's become so offensively at home here these last few months. This morning, I looked out of our window, and there he was, wading around in my Wellingtons in the reflecting pool. I think he was collecting leaves. With my butterfly net! And just last week, he did some watering outside, which, okay, I'm sure he thought he was helping us by doing, but then afterward, he didn't even coil the hose properly. I know you think these gripes seem petty—Fergus, ooooh, I can see the judgment oozing out of your every pink pore—but . . . he's so shallow, don't you think? What can one talk about with that . . . man? Nothing! He has no interests, no talent. He's thoroughly self-involved—I think there's a Jungian term for it, but I can't recall it right now. He sits around in the library watching our television at all hours. . . . I apologize for rambling away like this, Fergus, but it's something to which I've lately given a tre*men*dous amount of thought. You need to get rid of him."

Fergus: Lowell's hatchet man.

I didn't really know all that much about Andrei, but I was fairly sure he didn't have anywhere else to go. I didn't think I had any real feelings for him, because you cannot have any real feelings for someone if you've never told that person anything . . . and I'd assuredly never told Andrei much of anything at all. He'd been an entertainment to us, as indeed we'd been to him. And one can find entertainment anywhere, anywhere.

"But Lowell," I said. "I don't know if I—"

"You'll find a way, Fergus," Lowell said. "You always have."

"But Lowell," I said. "Andrei makes such good . . . drinks."

"He couldn't make a maggot, Fergus."

"But Lowell," I said. "He's so *good* to me."

"Ah. Always about you, isn't it, Fergus? God, there isn't enough oxygen in here for the both of us. Forgive me, but I've got to skedaddle before I go belly-up myself." Lowell screwed the VapoRub cap back on and handed the jar to me. He clasped my other hand, planted on it a soft kiss. He hadn't given me a real kiss for years. His eyelashes swiped my hand. He said, "I just thought of something now. It was a line I read once, in a letter, although I don't know whom by. 'Should there be other summers, you would perhaps come.' "

And on his knees, he glided toward the door, away from me.

"Sad thing to say, really. Don't know why I just thought of that. Odd the way the brain works, don't you think?" His voice: distanter and distanter.

Again, I felt strangulated. Again, I couldn't breathe. I lay back in my sleeping bag and opened the VapoRub tub. I lifted up my shirt and slathered the stuff on my chest. How it stung. That little scalding we cannot know the reason for.

Lowell called from outside the tent: "I'm pleased to hear the party preparations are going so well! You promise to signal if you want me to do anything, yeah?"

Yes, Lowell, I said. Sure will.

"When you're feeling up to it, come join us in the kitchen. Drisana-Nari's teaching me to make a rustic country breakfast for the three of us, just the way they do in old Pittsburgh, Pennsylvania."

Oh, I said. How lovely.

"And Fergus? She told me the blimp was out yesterday, by the way."

It was, I said. Oh, it was.

"I wish you would have called to me, but Drisana-Nari said you seemed to be rather busy outside. I was pleased she noticed, because I'm afraid I've inflated her worth in some other essential ways. So you were with that handsome young man, were you? The smoker from my dinner party?"

But, I said.

"Don't worry, Fergus; I forgive you."

But. Oh my Lowell.

"You always underestimate me don't you? You *think* I don't know what you've been up to? Preston Lympany cannot come to my party, either; he will not be there. Understood? See you inside, my dove."

I'd lost him again. The tent blazed its orange into my closed eyes. Above me, I pretended, was a fire. And now he was determined to make me lose Preston Lympany. I kept my eyes closed and felt for my phone in the orange emptiness.

I found it.

I'd looked at the number I was about to dial so many times over the course of the last five years, I had it memorized. The number was from his letterhead. Someone must have been looking out for me, because I pecked out the digits perfectly on the first try.

"Hello," I said into my extremely small phone. "I'm Lowell Haven's personal secretary. Is Mr. Bradley W. Dormer available?"

I wondered if the girl on the other end could tell I was talking to her with my eyes closed. I tried to breathe. I thought about how human lungs simply weren't made to withstand it all; they just weren't.

"Not in yet? May I leave this message, in that case? Mr. Haven has asked me to call Mr. Dormer and invite him to a little costume ball we're having on Saturday."

In a few short days, the ruse would be up.

Should there be other summers, you would perhaps come? There's a larger, sadder story somewhere in there, I think, Lowell. Should you dare to look for it, dear friend.

22

Rebecca's office was huge, but it had only five chairs (not including Rebecca's). Eleven people (including Randy) went to the remarkably listless weekly production meetings there. That meant six people (unless someone was on vacation) always stood. Randy was not, in the meetings, a stander. Merit, by virtue of her horrible fucked-up habit of being late for everything in her entire life, was.

Merit knew it was pathetic, how she'd just kind of sneak up and lurk by Rebecca's door five to nine minutes after the start of the Wednesday meeting, hoping no one would notice her.

Randy hadn't shown up for work yet. It was 11:37. Yesterday, Merit and Randy didn't speak. They both pretended, in an extremely lame and childish way, Merit thought, that nothing had happened between them. Which, in a way, nothing had.

Merit was kind of more outside Rebecca's office now than inside, really. Rebecca's assistant's little dorm room–size refrigerator whirred warmly by Merit's shins. The window off to the side of Rebecca's desk looked out onto the parking lot. In that parking lot was Randy's car/truck/whatever, although Merit, from her angle, was unable to see it. The "vehicle" had not moved since Monday morning, and that troubled Merit. This meant Randy had gotten to and from work yesterday by some other means, a fact that could possibly signal the reentry of the mysterious Melody (or maybe even Libby) into his life.

Merit was trying to reassure herself that a guy named Steve was the one giving Randy rides. She didn't know if Randy actually knew anyone named Steve (didn't *everybody* know a guy named Steve?), but she hoped he did.

Not only was Randy's weekly attendance at the meeting not required; it was not even really approved of. Randy went to the meeting because Merit was somehow able to persuade Rebecca his presence was absolutely essential. "But he handles so many of my accounts!" Merit once said to Rebecca, and then really wished she hadn't.

Actually, to be honest, Randy's attendance at the meeting was barely even tolerated.

Randy's sole contribution to the proceedings came about once every six weeks or so, when he'd again suggest somebody in ad/sales go and tell them down in editorial to do a story about Eminem. "If they ever want to get any music advertisers, then they have to do some shit in there about music," he'd say, or words along those lines. Eminem was from Detroit, he would remind them, as if Detroit and Akron were the same thing. They were not. Merit's magazine (circulation: 160,000) only ran Ohio-appropriate stories.

Rebecca was running down that week's lineup of accounts, asking the appropriate ad manager about that account's status. Mostly, the account managers always just lied and said everything was cool. Luckily for Merit, the automotive/liquor/tobacco accounts were always among the last on Rebecca's treacherous lineup sheet. The meetings typically lasted anywhere from fifteen to forty-five minutes.

"Have you closed the Dillards account yet?" Rebecca asked.

"Closed it yesterday," said Todd, the "luxury goods" manager. His title made Merit laugh when she thought about it, which wasn't often. Todd always sat in the middle of Rebecca's black leatherette couch during these meetings. He was two years older than Merit, had four kids, looked vaguely, Merit thought, like a juvenile Vladimir Putin, and had these weird clear, buggy, thyroidic eyes. She couldn't, from her vantage point, see Todd, or anyone except Rebecca, who was looking awfully empowered there at her big glass desk.

Someone coughed: a man. Strangely, Merit couldn't identify the person it came from.

"Run down the real estate accounts for me."

"Well, we've got Century Twenty-one and Coldwell Banker, and St—"

During these meetings Merit always tried to make the best use of her time by thinking about something else. Right now, she was trying not to think about Randy.

Last night, Merit had told Caroline that maybe they could wrap a white sheet around her or something and she could go the party as Caligula. Caroline said that would make her look like some dumb drunk girl at a Beta house toga party. Merit wondered how Caroline knew the name of a fraternity at her young age, although she didn't ask her. Merit said maybe they could shake a jar of Tabasco sauce or Red Hot on the toga, as a sort of blood stand-in. Caroline seemed to like that idea.

Wyatt was still threatening nonattendance. Merit hadn't, and wouldn't, tell him his name wasn't on the envelope. He didn't seem to approve of Caroline as Caligula.

Merit was still thinking maybe something bird-oriented for herself (the masks from New Orleans continued to be on her mind). But she was so tall and awkward and squawky herself, she was afraid if she wore one of those masks, she might look like Big Bird (a mass-culture reference Merit enjoyed), or possibly Papagena (high-culture one).

The front door in the reception area (which contained four blue plastic chairs, discards from the orthodontist's office down the hall) slammed shut. The sound of frantic flip-flopped feet flip-flopping toward their desk. Something was thrown down. Something was banged around. Flip-flopping again, getting closer. Breathing. Breathing. Flip-flops stopped. Breathing. A hand on Merit's shoulder. A Randy hand brushing Merit's hair back.

"Hey, Merit," he whispered into her ear. It took Randy breath to make you realize how cold your ear really was. "What'd I miss?"

Randy was kind of a psycho, Merit thought. The way he'd acted all cold with her yesterday, and then this touchy-feely stuff right now. Merit already preferred today to yesterday.

She cupped her hand over her mouth and grazed his ear with that hand. She told him he hadn't missed much, making sure she was close enough to let him smell her hair.

"Tina's car was totally fucked. I had to hitch a ride here."

Rebecca gave them a "Nobody talks in my classroom" glare. Merit half-knew he was lying about the hitchhiking, but she preferred not to focus on that: Who the hell was Tina?

"What've you got there?" Randy whispered, and put a finger exactly where her nipple would have been had her purple Clairefontaine notebook (the paper of choice among French schoolchildren) not been there.

"In case I need to, you know, take notes."

"Gimme that," he said, no longer whispering. He slid the notebook out from her crossed arms and snatched the pen from her hand. Rebecca seemed to be trying to ignore them.

He opened to a random blank page and started writing something. His expression indicated Merit should get herself ready to be seriously wowed.

Merit wondered who was sitting in Randy's self-appointed spot on the couch next to the KGB-agent-in-training-looking Todd, although she didn't care enough to poke her head in and see. It was weird how everybody sat (or stood) in exactly the same place at every Wednesday meeting, but Merit supposed she had to chalk that up to human nature.

Randy grinned at her, braces glinting. He handed back her notebook. He'd written, "This is Merit's notebook, who nobody likes!" His braces flickered impishly. Why couldn't she just kiss him right there? Why wasn't that allowed? "This notebook belongs to Merit, whom nobody likes!" would have been a much better sentence . . . but who was she to correct Randy's grammar like that? His shirt was on backward—no, not backward, but inside out. It was a black shirt, white stitches on the outside, thus imparting a certain insouciant dash to what was an otherwise standard-issue Gap T-shirt.

"Merit, what's going on with Bacardi?"

"Yo, Merit," Randy said. "Wake the fuck up."

"What?" Merit asked.

"What's going on with Bacardi?" Rebecca asked again.

"It's totally done," Merit said. She almost said "Nothing" in response to Rebecca's query, but something, thank God, prevented that.

"Hennessey?"

"It's *so* done," Merit said.

"Tires?"

"Just closed them," Merit said.

"Okay. Any other problems anyone wants to bring up?"

Randy was still smiling at her, and Merit liked that. His were not the costly near-invisible Tom Cruise accessory braces; they were the old-school heavy metal rack-and-screw kind. She suspected Randy had had braces for a really long time—like maybe since when he was a kid—but had been really bad about wearing his headgear and rubber bands and things.

A series of coughs—this time from a female employee.

"No?" Rebecca asked. "Everybody go bye-bye now."

The assistants always seemed so pissed when all the senior (minus Randy) ad/sales people would trudge single file past the assistants' desks as they left the Wednesday meeting. Merit had come to think of the march back to her office at roughly noon on Wednesdays as the Walk of Shame. The oxygen got sucked out of that part of the office during the Walk of Shame, and Merit just knew the assistants were sending one another these snitty little E-mails, typing things like, "Why does stupid asshole Randy get to go to the meetings when we don't?" Merit had told the (non-Randy) assistants over and over again that they had no reason to be pissed Randy attended the Wednesday meetings and they did not; they were actually really lucky they didn't have to go, Merit told them, and mouthed Rebecca's company line about how there were too many people in the update meetings anyway. But she knew that was not the real reason. So did they.

Randy let Merit walk in front of him during during the Walk of Shame, and Merit thought that was because he wanted to watch her. Back at her office, she thanked Randy for the funny thing—she hoped it was supposed to be funny, she said; she hoped it wasn't the truth—he'd written in her notebook. She thought about asking him if he wanted to grab some lunch, but she didn't.

She closed her door (not all the way—she didn't want Randy to think she was mad at him), situated herself at her desk, and did an Internet search on something she'd read about that morning in the paper. In Australia, a blind kangaroo had saved a man's life; disappointingly, the paper had had no picture of the kangaroo. Merit needed to find one. The search results came up, Merit clicked on a couple of sites, finally found a picture. It looked like a really, really big rabbit. A pet kangaroo would be interesting . . . but if she took a kangaroo home as a pet, she would definitely want her to live inside the house—maybe not in the bedroom with the rabbit or anything, maybe more like the garage—but Wyatt would almost surely insist on keeping her outside. Merit could already see this was a conflict in the making. She still didn't have a real clear idea how big kangaroos were, and she realized this was maybe something she needed to research. She had just finished typing "kangaroos as pets" when someone (she hoped Randy) knocked on her door.

"Hey, baby. How's it going? Can I come in?"

"Hi Alanna! It's good. It's *good!* Come on in."

Alanna never really stopped by Merit's office all that much to chat, but whenever she did, Merit would think afterward, What a good egg, and would wonder why she'd been so lazy about getting to know her.

Alanna propped her foot up on the visitor's chair across from Merit's desk and did this bouncy stretching thing. Her haircut was more *pageboy* than *Stephanopoulos* today. "You got your AmEx stolen, right?"

"Uh," Merit said.

"They just called me, because yesterday and this morning there were all these changes from Music World and ComputerLand in Montrose on your corporate AmEx. Some stuff in Cleveland Heights. Tower Records. I said, No way, that's not Merit."

"My credit card?" Merit asked. A Nixonesque hot flash. "Wow. I thought I just had it yesterday. Geez, let me look."

Alanna, foot still on the chair, straightened her leg and bent forward and touched the toes of her black tennis shoes. "Your back ever get stiff like mine does, or is this just God's way of punishing me?"

Merit was up now, on the floor, going through her purse. "Boy, mine, too. Remember when there was this big plan to buy us all ergonomic chairs? That seems like a lifetime ago, doesn't it?"

"I still don't understand why *Randy* got an ergonomic chair. What's up with that?"

"Back problems," Merit said, although she wasn't listening to herself.

"You don't lock your door when you get up to use the can, right?"

Merit clicked open her wallet, hiding her face as best she could from Alanna.

"I should have Rebecca send around a memo about that. They think the cleaning service is stealing stuff from people's offices and desks. Todd had his CD player stolen from his desk last week, and some CDs. He said they also took the fountain pen he had since he was in high school. They took Rebecca's mug, too. You didn't hear about that?"

"God," Merit said. "It doesn't seem to be in here. *Weird.*"

The cleaning staff meant Claudia and her husband.

"Cool. I'll have them cancel and reissue a new one. Do you usually leave your pocketbook out there in the middle of the floor like that?" Merit did the brave thing and looked at Alanna, who was audibly cracking her neck. She was one of these small, fidgety athletic-type people who, whenever you were talking to them, seemed to be engaged in some sort of minor self-administered body-realignment procedure.

"Well, I—"

Alanna made an *ach* sound as her leg came down from the chair. "I'm sure one of the cleaning people stole it. I'll get it dealt with. They charged about three thousand bucks, you know that? Thanks, baby. Is that a new picture on your desk?"

The framed picture had been on Merit's desk for about two years, but Alanna rarely visited down here. It was understandable the photo had never registered with her.

Merit hoped she wasn't going to get Claudia into trouble.

"That's my rabbit—well, one of them."

"Cute! My dog chases rabbits. How old is it?"

"Oh, well, Basil's dead. I mean, she died."

"Shit. Sorry about that. I hope a dog wasn't, you know, involved."

"No, no. It was natural causes."

"So, you want your door closed, right?"

"You can just— Can you just shut it? But just a little bit! Thanks!"

"Ciao, baby."

"Thanks, Alanna! Bye!"

Merit was really hoping she wasn't going to get Claudia into trouble.

She felt sickened in the way she often felt sickened when she knew something calamitous was about to happen. There was a time once when she thought life would someday make sense to her. It was funny, in a way, to think about that time before Jenny's diaries. She had, of course, known the bald facts of her parents' lives, but she hadn't really chosen to understand the complications.

And she had grown up to have a malevolent and self-destructive brain: her mother's curse.

Merit could fire Randy, of course. Everyone in her office would applaud such a move, after all. But then would she have to tell Rebecca and Alanna and everyone else how she'd totally fucked up? How she'd given Randy her corporate card in a gesture of what she presently understood to be truly staggering brainlessness? Oh, Merit was a very confused person right about now, on just about every level.

Merit had never fired anyone in her life. But she couldn't fire someone, especially not Randy. They'd exchanged body fluids! Plus, was she maybe a little in love with him? No, wait. She definitely was not in love with him.

Randy was checking out real estate listings on his computer. She asked him if he had any stamps, although she didn't need any.

He tilted his head back, displaying a very lickable Adam's apple, from which sprouted one lone brown hair. She found she wasn't mad at him.

"Dunno. Wanna look through my drawer?"

He rolled back and gestured decorously toward the open drawer in a way that was probably meant to remind Merit of that Nolan Miller–wearing, letter-turning chick from *Wheel of Fortune,* whose name she couldn't remember right now. The drawer contained about three thousand staples, loose ones. Had Randy actually broken apart all those rows of staples himself? She sunk her hand into the staple drawer.

"Oh shit. I forgot I did that in that drawer last week. They're in here," he said, then bent over (plumber's crack), opened the bottom drawer, and came up with a fistful of first-class U.S. stamps.

"Are these the current stamps?"

"Yeahhhhh. Why?"

"I don't know. I just thought stamps were up to fifty cents now. Seems like they go up every week."

"God. You are *really* out of it, Merit. You've been totally stressed lately. Are you okay?" Randy's voice was in no way lowered, but it was lunchtime, so it wasn't like anybody was there.

"Me?" Merit asked. "I'm *fine.*" The way that came out sounded very clenched and antiorgasmic and housewifely. "I'm fine. *Seriously.*" That sounded even worse.

"That's why I wrote that thing on your notebook back there. You seemed so flipped out."

Merit's hand was now coated in a sticky, stapley, lead-pencil grime. She listened to the sound of her fingernails making little agitated *tappy-tap-tap* sounds on the plywoody partition of Randy's cubicle. She really hoped she was going to be brave enough to bring up the little matter of Randy's stealing her corporate card and charging, oh, about three thousand dollars to it.

"Should we talk about this?" Randy asked. He stood and, like a coach, placed both firm Randy hands on her shoulders. She'd never really noticed before how much taller she was. "If you want it this way, look: What happened totally didn't happen. If that's what's freaking you out, you have my word of honor as a loyal citizen: *What happened didn't happen.*"

Were migraines contagious? Merit seemed to have caught Randy's from two days ago. "Oh, that's not it. It's just that there's this . . . party."

Merit hoped Randy wasn't hurt to hear he didn't even rate, not at that particular moment, on her list of concerns. No, wait. She hoped he was hurt, just a little bit, about that.

"A party?" Randy asked. "That's what this is about? Parties are such stupid horse shit. Who gives two fucks about a party?"

This really illuminated the fundamental difference between the two of them, didn't it? The very concept of a theoretical party didn't fill Randy with a nauseous dread.

"But you don't understand," Merit said. She couldn't, couldn't, *couldn't* let Randy see her cry. "I can't have them all in one room."

Randy stroked her back, but in a nonsexual way, which both relieved and disappointed her. She wondered if he could feel her bra strap. Maybe he, too, was disgusted by the concept of a weak-willed woman on the verge of tears. "Is your *husband* going? To the party?"

Merit was crying now, for real. She didn't cry often, but when she did: epic.

"Of course he's going. He's my *husband*."

The concentrated furor with which she affirmed Wyatt's attendance surprised her.

Randy actually hugged her. She cried, reassured herself no one else was around, and cried some more. He smelled like Randy.

"Hey, don't shoot the messenger; I'm just asking. Do you maybe want to get something to eat? I'm star-ar-arving. I could totally go for one of these Italian subs at Valario's."

"Do you know, Randy, do you have any idea," Merit said, talking into his shirt, "do you know that—" Thank goodness the shirt was black, because she was doing terrible, terrible things to it. She was going to ask him if he knew how salami was made. But she couldn't.

Merit used to lie and say she was a veterinarian. She discovered once, when threatening the department manager of the local pet store she visited at least weekly with legal action, a vet's complaints are taken much more seriously than those of a nonvet. The department manager was a skinny young guy with a patchy beard; his crucifix pendant hung outside his blue Yappy Hour smock. He'd had a tragic, Wyattesque acne problem in his youth, Merit could tell. She told him his store's treatment of rabbits was despicable and that he should be ashamed of himself. Three adult-size rabbits were quaking together in a cage made for one; the wire cage cut the rabbits' feet (which were unpadded, unlike a dog's feet or a cat's); there was no evidence of any timothy hay, and no timothy meant instant death from gut stasis; there was only one water bottle, and it was empty; and when she stuck her fingers into the cage and examined the rabbits' mouths, she found two of the three rabbit friends' front teeth were in desperate need of filing.

For all the interest he displayed in her list of grievances, he might as well have been studying an astrological chart. At first, that is.

"And let me add," Merit said, "I'm a *vet*."

The department manager blinked three times, tugged at his crucifix, and stood up straighter, the way people do when they're confronted with a person of importance. Merit was pretty sure she wasn't imagining this.

"You think I can't shut you down?" Merit asked. She was so proud of her nerve. One of her proudest moments ever, in fact. "A single call from me to the Animal Welfare Board, and I guarantee you, you *will* be shut down."

Merit never did make that call to the Animal Welfare Board, but she went back to that same Yappy Hour location twenty-four hours later and found each rabbit in her own newspaper-lined cage, her own water bottle hooked into her cage's side. There was still no timothy hay, and Merit forgot about checking their teeth again.

She'd run into the department manager a few times after that, and one of those times, about a month after the incident, he called her, in a way that didn't sound sarcastic at all, "Doctor."

After that, she'd had this plan about going to every pet store in the northeast Ohio region as a sort of rabbit freedom fighter. She'd hit about six stores last year, all within the Yappy Hour chain, posing as a vet in each one. But she hadn't gotten it together to liberate any rabbits yet this year, although the rabbits of the world needed her, she felt, this year as much as any.

Randy wouldn't let her take her car; she was too upset to drive, he said. Valario's was in the strip mall that contained the site of Merit's original cranium-swelling lie: "I'm a *vet*. You *think* I can't shut you down? Think again, little man." Randy did not know this. As he negotiated into the parking space, she reached into her wallet for a five and was reminded again of the matter of the purloined AmEx. She didn't feel right bringing it up then.

It wasn't a winter month, so Merit had no Kleenex in her bag. Randy had been inside the sub shop for about five minutes when Merit opened the glove compartment in the slim hope of finding something to wipe her nose with. She snooped around in there (maps and a tire gauge) and was appalled to find herself wondering if she was half-looking for a condom, or possibly some other evidence of Randy's non-Merit sexual life. Horrifyingly, a screw pinged down on the rubber mat as she slammed the glove compartment shut.

She was hunched over, fingers going over the extremely dirty mat (this was not an unfamiliar thing for her to do—it felt exactly like looking for an earring back, something else she often dropped), when the driver's side door screeched open. Hot air and the smell of thirty-year-old vinyl.

"What're you doing down there, boss?"

Merit popped back up. Head rush. If she hadn't already been sitting, she would have had to find a chair.

Randy folded himself into the car and pulled two subs out from the bag. Each was wrapped in white butcher paper.

"Man, you don't look so good. You need sustenance. Here. Catch."

Merit made a spazy attempt at a grab, missed. Her sub (tomato and cheese, unless Randy had messed that up) hit the floor. She retrieved her lunch from the mat, dusted it off. The little screw was embedded (along with tire-colored soot and tiny pebbles) in a wet spot on the sub's wrapper.

"Never played catch when you were little?" Randy asked.

Jenny or Lowell (or *Fergus*) playing catch? Merit brushed the little screw off the butcher paper. "I can't imagine a situation where *catch* would have even really been a possibility when I was a kid," she said.

"What's that mean?"

"I don't know. It's weird."

"You're from Akron, right?"

"Can't deny that."

"Not *so* weird, then. . . . Oh, yeah: They said they couldn't make your sub without mayo. I told them to put olive oil on it, like you said, but they gave me an extremely hard time. They used to be much cooler in there."

Randy unwrapped his sandwich, balled up the wrapper, and tossed it to the floor of his car/truck. (Caruk? Merit thought. Trucar?) He had indeed ordered the Italian sub, and it was every bit as piggy as Merit had predicted. Merit unwrapped, too. He'd gotten the tomato and cheese part right at least. She asked Randy for a napkin, then waited until he was in the middle of a very ambitious bite to blow her nose into it. It was rude, but there was, at the moment, no other option. Randy didn't notice anyway.

After his bite had been successfully swallowed and washed down with ginger ale sipped through a straw (had Merit been in a different mood, she would have been amused to discover he was both a ginger ale guy *and* a straw guy), he opened his jaggedly gnawed remainder of sub and rolled a piece of ham into a pink piggy tube, which he directed at Merit's closed mouth. The fellatial implications were not lost on her.

"No likey?" he asked.

Merit shook her head (a little too truculently, she felt).

"I was just joking. God. What is it with you today?" He popped the end of the tight nasty little ham roll between his teeth. The way he held it dandyishly there reminded Merit, for a moment, of a rose. Remarkably, no food was stuck in his braces.

Merit was annoyed by Randy's presumption of . . . what? Intimacy? Equality?

The cheese and tomato sub smell was making her sick. She asked Randy for the paper bag, tucked the sub back in it. Her plan was to put the sub in Rebecca's assistant's fridge, take it home with her at the end of the day; maybe all three of them, Merit, Wyatt, and Caroline, could split it as a carb-heavy predinner appetizer (although any trace of mayo would naturally have to be wiped away). Maybe she'd want to eat by dinnertime.

She forgot what she was doing and accidentally disposed of the napkin she'd used as a Kleenex, stuffing it in the paper bag with the unwrapped sandwich.

"Remind me I owe you two bucks. It's *cheap* when you don't get meat."

AmEx.

"Randy?"

"See that pet store over there?" Randy asked, pointing, mouth again full. "They have these little mini albino frogs that look like little men, the way they swim in their tanks. It's totally wild. You know what I'm talking about? Those little white underwater frogs that look like naked men?"

Merit said she usually just headed right for the rabbit section.

"What time you got? You wanna go in there and check them out real fast? Me and Cooper used to get baked and come over here and stare at them. It's the craziest thing. Once I remember standing there for an hour and staring at them, and freaking out because I swore to God I thought they were actual humans who got shrunk."

The smell of pork products now. Merit had to get out of there immediately. She tried to unroll the window, but it wouldn't go down.

"What, are they like this?" Merit made an O with her hand and showed Randy. The O was about the size of a kiwifruit.

"Nah, fuck man, these guys are little. They're like—" Randy did the same move with his hand, but his O was pea-size. He squinted at Merit through it.

"Oh, I get it. They're like tadpoles." As soon as Merit said that, she realized she probably meant sea horses.

"Sorry to disappoint you, Merit, but I think they're actually a little bigger than sperm."

"You know what they call a group of frogs?"

Randy was right: The albino aquatic dwarf frogs *did* look like little tiny men.

"I don't know," Merit said. "A school?"

"A 'school'? A *'school'*? That's hilarious!"

It was hard to say how many were in the tank. Twenty? Thirty? They were each about an inch long (back in the car, Randy had really exaggerated their smallness), and it was impossible to get a fast head count. Pink eyes, ghostly skin. Merit thought about Randy's question quite seriously for a few seconds, then said she was embarrassed to admit she had no idea.

"An army. Didn't you ever learn that a group of frogs is called an 'army'?"

"An *army*? How weird. Geez. I don't think I ever knew that."

"Maybe it's more like something *guys* would know. I asked my sister that question once, too, and she didn't know, either. I take it your parents raised you in a very girlie way. It's like, you know, you're not girlie now, but I can see how you used to be *super*girlie."

Merit had never really thought of her parents as raising her in a much of anything way. It often seemed to her that her chief function for Jenny, Lowell, and Fergus was as a watcher. At the dinner table at Fergus's house when Merit was small, all three of them would chatter simultaneously about themselves. Merit would sit quietly and stare at the *Canterbury Tales* pictures on the wall. In the portraits, Lowell would watch Merit, evaluatingly, as the real Lowell ignored her, trying flamboyantly to outtalk Jenny and Fergus instead. Merit would writhe on her towel and imagine Lowell as the Wife of Bath rebuking her, something the real Lowell never, never did: Merit, the picture would say. You're a stupid little girl. You're stupid and you're silent. What a disappointment you are.

At family mealtime, the seat of Merit's chair would always be covered with a towel, placed there by Fergus. Even though Fergus had a lot fewer spills than Merit did, he gave himself a towel to sit on, too. Fergus's matching towel wasn't there simply to make her feel unalone. Fergus, throughout Merit's childhood with him, would often try to copy her, sometimes in very peculiar ways.

Once, in the music room, when they were dancing to a Cole Porter song, Fergus told Merit he wanted to "be her."

"You want to be like me, Uncle Fergus?" Merit asked.

"No," Fergus said, gliding his finger down her cheek. "*Be* you."

Randy tapped at the glass aquarium. He waved to the little frogs. Fascinating creatures. Muscles moving underneath transparent skin. So beneath their pride to be kept in a tank with blue pebbles the color of toilet bowl cleaner and a plastic violin-playing skeleton. Even—especially—albino frogs have their dignities, Merit knew. One little guy did a one-armed push-off of that idiotic skeleton.

"Do you know that when a frog leaps, it's like the equivalent of you or I jumping a hundred feet?" Randy asked.

It really was sad, wasn't it, how very little Merit knew, or cared, about the planet's nonmammals? "Wow," she said. She couldn't tell if each frog hand had four toes or five. "Hey, do you think my cat would eat these guys if I got some?"

"Not if he wants to look you in the eye again he won't."

" 'She'," Merit said.

"Are you really going to buy some? That's awesome! Then I can come over and get high and watch them in your house."

Yeah, Merit thought. That would work.

"How much are these suckers?" Randy asked, snaking around, in need of some Yappy Hour assistance. Merit looked at her watch. It was 12:58, and lunchtime at Merit's workplace unspokenly ended in two minutes.

Merit had been unaware how many products there were out there for the home-aquarium owner. You had your heating equipment, your siphons, vacuums, tank sealants, electric thermometers (Wyatt would approve of those), isolation tanks (the sound of which sounded terribly poetic to Merit's ears). *Fuck.* Merit's department manager friend was standing over in the aquarium-ornament section, arms crossed, chest puffed exaggeratedly up. There really is no scene so harrowing, Merit thought, as the professionally desperate person who really thinks he's lucked into some big-time authority. Merit wondered if they got their blue Yappy Hour smocks for free or if they paid for them or what. Randy waved both arms at him. The department manager tugged at what appeared to be a hangnail. Merit wondered how that was for Randy, having people pretend not to see him all the time.

Randy waved again, and the department manager glanced over at Randy, then at Merit, and nodded, sort of. Merit was suddenly, for reasons she didn't understand, terrified he'd remember her.

The department manager flicked what Merit imagined to be a bit of skin onto the floor and strolled on over to them. He was not in a hurry; he seemed to be whistling. Merit looked away. She tried to appear very interested in the plastic aquarium ornaments over where the department manager had just stood. It was weird, when you thought about it, that there was that much of a demand for so many different kinds of these things: skulls, gargoyles, pagodas, sunken ships, buried treasure chests, mermaids, windmills, lighthouses, a Roman ruin, a skeleton at a wheel, a scuba-suited diver examining a giant purple clam, little signs that said NO SKINNY-DIPPING and MERMAIDS WANTED.

There was also a cheesy Tudor castle that looked exactly like Fergus and Lowell's house.

Randy and the store manager were talking now. Merit wasn't listening. The placement of the turrets and minarets, or whatever they were called, on the plastic house was exactly like the ones at On Ne Peut Pas Vivre Seul (whose name Merit still couldn't pronounce). She preferred to call it (hearing it in her head in an accent a lot like Lowell's) One Cannot Live Alone.

"No shit, man!" Randy said. "I didn't know they could live that long."

The department manager checked Merit out (although she wasn't the one talking) as if she were someone he couldn't place, someone from high school, or maybe possibly even a lesser celebrity.

"What do they eat?" Randy asked.

"Bloodworms. Baby lobster cockroaches."

"Awesome!" Randy said.

"Whole aisle of stuff over there. Brine shrimp, too. Beef hearts."

"Ewwwww," Merit said, sounding much more like a third grader than a real live vet.

The department manager still had, a year later, that same crucifix necklace, still had the same Snickers bar–type skin. She felt a little bit queasy again, and was now, for the first time, deeply mortified by her year-old lie. She really hoped he wouldn't remember her.

"How big do they get?" Randy asked.

"Not that much bigger than they already are right in that tank there."

"How can you tell the difference between a boy and a girl?" Merit asked. "Male" and "female" would have sounded much more vetlike, although she was sure now that the store manager didn't remember her from last year.

"You're so funny," Randy said. "God, you don't know *anything* about animals, do you?"

"The females are always larger." The department manager's eyes were all blood-vesselly and unsmooth.

"How much are they?" Merit asked.

He pointed to the yellow price sticker on the tank. "Seven dollars apiece. If you buy three, I'll give you one for free."

"Three's maybe . . . too many," Merit said.

"Okay, but that's a thirty-three and a third percent discount."

"*Shit,* Merit. I need to talk to you. Did I give you back your credit card from Monday?" Randy went for his back pocket. Merit couldn't tell if he was reaching for his wallet in the fake way cheap people do when they have no actual intention of paying for lunch or if it was for real.

"I don't *know,*" she said. "I don't . . . *think* you did."

The move to retrieve the wallet was aborted. Randy squinted and clutched his curly and very beautiful (now that she was able to look at him again) hair. "Mother fuck. I just had this like visualization. I think I accidentally left it at Tower Records."

The store manager's weird grin made Merit feel she'd just given him something he really wanted. Not sex, but something worse somehow. He got this sort of visionary flash in his eye, as if revelation-struck. "Hey," he said, shaking his finger at her, "I know who *you* are."

"Remember when I told you I was going to buy some shit at Tower Records as research for this music story I wanted to pitch them in editorial? I know I'm a douche for using your credit card there, but you told me once when I said I was thinking of starting to pitch stories to editorial that I could use it if it was for research or whatever. Well, I was just hit with this recovered memory that I left it there, at the cash register at Tower Records in Cleveland. How whacked is that?"

"Hey," the department manager said, "I remember *you.*"

"Please, please, please. What can I do to make it so that you don't shit-can me for the credit card? I'll get down on golden kneepads and beg. I'll wash your car for you. You can spank me. I'll go down on you every day in your office. . . . Oh, whoops, I'm sorry. . . . I mean I *won't* go down on you every day in your office. *Please.*"

The department manager was smiling and flaunting, like the Joker, all his back teeth. The frogs were tiny space travelers, clawing their way upward. The water was so still, it looked like air.

"Sir," said Merit, "may I please have twenty of those albino frogs?"

Merit's keys were not in her bag. She'd either left them back in her office (best-case scenario) or in her car (total worst-case scenario). She'd accidentally locked her keys in her car a few times before, of course. . . . Actually, to be honest, the last time, she'd officially locked them in her *trunk*. It had happened about three months ago. She'd parked the Jag way back in the lot at Kroger (in crowded lots, Merit, who was not a talented parker, knew it best to get as far away from the other cars as possible), where she was about to do her weekly shopping. Her rattan produce bag was in the trunk. The very second the trunk banged shut, she thought, *Shit, my keys.* When she called Wyatt on her cell phone, he said he'd be right there. She waited for him, leaning against the hood of her car like a naughty cheerleader in a fifties movie. It was one of the first warm days of the year, and she felt the sun on her face and wished she had a cigarette, although she didn't smoke, except maybe for a funny cigarette sometimes. When Wyatt pulled up ten minutes later in his Toyota, he asked her where all the shopping bags were. She told him she hadn't gone inside yet, then added it was good, in a way, how this had worked out, because she could use some help. Wyatt started yelling at her, saying how she needed to be more careful with her keys (and everything else), how she really did seem to have great difficulty with focusing on the thing that was right in front of her. Merit knew this was all displaced anxiety, though; Wyatt just hated to go grocery shopping.

She therefore really hoped her keys were on top of her desk at work, shining underneath the cancerous fluorescent.

It was 1:39 and they, Randy and Merit, were idling in her driveway, right in front of the closed garage door.

"Well, how the fuck are we going to get in, then?" Randy asked.

When she had decided to purchase four (her department manager friend said she'd need a two-hundred-gallon tank for twenty frogs, so she settled on four) albino aquatic dwarf frogs, Merit had been unaware she would be required to buy a whole aquarium system (a pump, heater, some kind of aeration tubing/valve thing), as well as an aquarium hood with a light tube inside it, a feeder to mount to the hood, a silk plant, frog food, frog immune-system booster, mulch, a humidity gauge, a thermometer, a water-test kit, and a bag of tricolored gravel (the kind whose pieces were too big for the frogs to eat). These items were contained in four yellow Yappy Hour bags in the backseat. Merit was holding the frantic plastic gallon-size Yappy Hour bag of darting frogs. The weird plastic model of what she was now pretty sure was Fergus and Lowell's house was in her lap. It didn't weigh much. She hadn't known which thing to look at when they were driving home: the frogs or the model house. The house actually even had a little tiny banner over the front doorway that said, or at least she thought it did (the letters were very small, and she needed a new prescription for her glasses), ON NE PEUT PAS VIVRE SEUL. The paint job on the house was pretty bad. She had not told Randy why she had bought such an aquarium ornament, nor had he asked.

Merit explained it was quite a lucky coincidence, because Wyatt had actually just yesterday rigged up this new garage-door-opener system that didn't require a key.

"Your horn works, right?" she asked.

"Fucking-A my horn works. What, is your husband like some kind of wizardman?"

"He'd be flattered to hear you say that," she said. "He *is* very handy."

Merit and Wyatt had just practiced the code last night, while sitting in the driveway in his car. He said he'd change the code to something more complicated, and thereby more secure, as soon as he was convinced Merit had this one down.

Merit excused herself and leaned over and honked the recently rehearsed code on Randy's horn. Two short beeps and one long one. She found she had put her hand on his quite ravishing bare thigh (his shorts were pretty short—running shorts, really) as she did so.

"So now I know the big secret Ash family code," he said as he shifted out of park. He laughed; a B-movie villain was the reference. He seemed to be ignoring the hand. They lurched into the garage, right into Wyatt's space. The Fergus/Lowell house slid down Merit's lap and dangled between her knees and the glove compartment.

"No, wait! You can't park in the garage. Pull back out! Pull back out! We're just going to be here for a second. We're just going to drop all this stuff off and go!"

Randy switched off the ignition. He looked at her straight on, taking her face in. What did he see? She heard birds, a distant train. All the longing and hunger she'd ever felt was at that moment contained in that train whistle.

"I said, *Pull* back *out.*"

"Nope," Randy said. She took her hand away, and he slid down in his seat (the resulting noise was not, alas, unlike a junior high boy's gag armpit fart), shoving his keys into his pocket. "I like it here already."

"Randy!"

The light inside the garage turned itself off.

"I'm just kidding. I was trying to freak you out. We'll get out of here in a second. I'm sure Rebecca's all wondering where the bad kids are."

He reached into the backseat (he wore no seat belt—if, in fact, his side even had one) and grabbed two Yappy Hour bags. He reached into one and started studying, or pretend-studying, the receipt. He shrugged at the receipt and made an expression so contemptuous, it seemed to say, Hey, what are you going to do? Receipts are always stupid that way. He crumpled it up and disposed of it in the Yappy Hour bag it had come from. Merit was watching him. He readjusted his shorts, and then, without any contemplative time at all, leaned over and licked her neck.

Merit set the plastic house back squarely on her lap. She held on to it. She thrust her thumb through the house's little main door. Two fingers were in a window. She transferred the frog bag to her right hand and let herself be licked.

Merit had never really experienced a tongue quite so probing. And while she couldn't imagine that doing what he was doing to her ear was something Randy actually enjoyed, the zeal with which he went at it certainly was convincing. Merit's eyes were open, and she was considering the plastic mansion. She realized she didn't even know how many windows were in the real house's main tower. She was moaning a little bit, and this wasn't even necessarily a moaning situation. She sunk lower and lower into the seat, moving with Randy's tongue. There wasn't enough room to spread her knees as far as she needed to. The four frogs—two male, two female—might or might have been aware that the plastic house had fallen to the floor. Each of the four little creatures within the twist-tied Yappy Hour bag had a heart and a brain. Strange to think about. For all Merit could feel, the bag might as well not have held them at all.

The next part happened very quickly. With one hand (frogs in the other), Merit unzipped her jeans, then pulled them down over her hips. She took Randy's hand and guided it into the place. Her actions, frankly, surprised her. Watching his hand go inside and out like that was, she thought, ridiculously exciting to watch. She didn't care if he thought so or not (although she did wonder if the frogs bothered him). Her feet were straddling the plastic mansion. The plastic mansion was probably making one big mess of the tomato and cheese sub.

Wyatt was *not* going to be happy about those frogs.

Merit needed to research if tiny aquatic frogs and a very large cat could coexist in the same room. But for now, she didn't want to risk it. She and Randy were in Merit and Wyatt's bedroom because there was no other catless place in the house. There was, of course, the guest room, but Merit didn't like it there because that's where she hid all of the wedding presents she hated but didn't have the heart to throw away, and then there was Wyatt's study, which she wasn't even allowed in. The plan was to shoo the cat away and close the door, then set up the frogs in their aquarium and zip back to work. It was 2:19, and she didn't have time to read the instructions on the aquarium box. She commanded Randy to go fill the tank with water from the master bathroom's sink while she cleared a place on Wyatt's already mostly clutterless dresser.

On top of Wyatt's dresser were the two ties he intended to wear for the remaining days of the week (every Sunday night, Wyatt laid out five ties in a neat row on his dresser top), his old college mug (filled with pocket change), and a tape measure. Merit pushed everything off to the side and flopped the frog bag down. It bulged in such a way that it looked like her idea of a breast implant, except with four frogs in it. You'd have to be a pretty stupid person to want to sew two plastic bags into your chest, Merit thought. A mirror with a Wyatt-made pine frame hung above the dresser. Merit observed her reflection. She looked like hell. A sooty mascara stripe (which had, presumably, been there since before Yappy Hour) trailed down to her jaw.

The plastic Fergus/Lowell house was on the bed (she'd cleaned the mayonnaisey sub goop from it in the kitchen sink); inspecting it now, she wondered if it might be too big to fit into the aquarium. The dog—or maybe it was the cat—scratched at the bedroom door.

Water splashed onto Wyatt's ties when Randy, very incautiously, set the aquarium down. She unwound the bag's red twist tie, upended the bag, and dumped the frogs into their new home. She watched them. Did they remember the blue pebbles and the skeleton fiddler? Were they lonely for them?

"So this is where it all happens, huh?" Randy was over on Merit and Wyatt's king-size bed, lying on his back. Flip-flops still on, he scissored his arms and legs. If settings, and seasons, were different, he would have been making a snow angel. "So this is where it all goes down?"

Merit had never before realized there were many different ways to feel cold. She felt them all, at once.

"You've got to get off my bed."

"Why?"

"Please get off my bed."

He stopped moving. "What*ever.*"

"Please."

"What, I'm not good enough to be in your fucking bed now?"

"Oh Randy. *Please.*"

She thought, Fear makes us do things. Everything was making her cry today.

"Oh my God, I'm sorry. Please don't cry. Please don't cry again, Merit."

Her hands were covering her eyes now. Peering through her fingers, she could see the shape, blurred around the edges, moving toward her.

He peeled her fingers from her face one by one. For a moment, Merit wished he would say, "Let *me* cry for you," but he did not. What he did say was this: " 'My insecurities could eat me alive.' Do you know what that's from?"

She knew she would suffer, but she would not be afraid. Her parents were afraid, had always been afraid, but she would not be. "No," she said. "I don't."

"It's from 'Hailie's Song.' I cry whenever I listen to it. I'll burn you a copy of it on this new computer I just got." He was forced to stand on tiptoe to reach her. "Would you accept that gift from me?"

Merit said she would. His tongue was on her cheek. It was moving.

"And did your husband ever do this for you? Lick your tears?"

Merit said he had.

She didn't know how they got to the floor—she didn't know who led, who followed. They were on the floor now, on the floor of the house Wyatt had built, on the knot rag rug she and Wyatt had bought together in Amish country. Randy's cock was in her hand now, which was one of the lesser places it needed to be.

Underneath his belly button were two surgical scars, side by side, two dashes, each maybe two inches long. Merit said she hadn't noticed them last time, although she immediately feared this admission sounded insensitive. She asked what they were from. He said he had an operation when he was a little boy, said he could still remember when the scars were pink, when they were as wide as he was. It was insane to think about how small you used to be, he said. Merit cupped his heavy testicles in her hand, asked how it felt. She said she remembered lying in the unfamiliar bathtub at her mother's new house—the house they moved to after her mother had tried to remove herself from her father, although her mother ended up going back to her father again and again (Merit didn't tell Randy the reason)—and thinking, For as long as I can lie in this bathtub without bending my knees, I am still a child. She thought this every time she took a bath, she said. Randy's clothes were off now, and Merit's, too. His fingers were moving inside her. It was in fourth grade, she said, when she was taking a nighttime bath after swim-team practice, when she could no longer lie down in the tub. Her mother was in her bedroom/studio, painting a picture of Merit's father, when Merit, wet and naked, exploded in with the scary news. Her mother, she said, kissed her and told her she was an odd little person, then said she sometimes wondered if Merit were really a small adult playing the part of a child. "It's weird," Merit told Randy. "When I was ten, I was emotionally fifty; when I'm fifty, I'm sure I'll be emotionally ten." Merit said she remembered informing her father on the phone maybe a day or two later that she was no longer a child, and she remembered the congratulatory gifts he and his boyfriend sent: an ostrich-eyelash paintbrush and an adult-size blouse (whose historical significance she didn't understand until much later), designed by Chanel for Cocteau's production of *Antigone*.

" 'But you're not large enough to use these yet. Wait, Merit,' the letter accompanying the presents said. '*Wait.*' "

Randy's penis was in her mouth now. After a few minutes, she took a break and asked him how it felt.

"Did you say your father's 'boyfriend'?"

Merit looked into his face and said she didn't remember saying that, but maybe she had.

"Way to set the mood," he said.

Again, it was as it had been on Monday: She didn't want to see him. This had never happened to her before with a man.

She said she wasn't sure this was a normal thing to want or to say, but she wanted him to blindfold her and fuck her all the way up to her throat.

Randy said he'd be happy to arrange that.

Randy, in his extremely erect state, followed Merit's instructions. He visited Wyatt's dresser and fetched the old brown paisley Countess Mara tie. She folded her glasses and placed them safely away from the rug. When Merit was ready, she told him to blindfold her with the tie. Was it the water from the tank that made the tie wet and cold, or was it something else? She would not be afraid. He asked her how dark it was, and she said she couldn't tell. He asked if she was going to keep her eyes open or closed, and she said she didn't know yet. He bit her nipple, hard, and asked if she was still a child. Oh yes, she said, she was. And so with both hands, she spread herself wide and let him in.

23

22 December 1980

My day, by the hours: nine to twelve (addressing Christmas cards, making two meals for Merit) felt like five minutes; twelve to four (working on a new project behind the closed bedroom door) felt like an hour; four to five (watching the clock) felt like a week; five to now: unplaceable time. I've begun looking forward to five o'clock so I can start drinking again. Tremors of anxiety when I'm not drinking. What does this mean? I've spilled wine on every piece of furniture in our new host Tamsin's apartment. Must stop drinking as soon as I finish *Lowell/Not Lowell*. Constant concern about Merit in this apartment, this death universe of glass. When I can't watch her, I strap her into her booster seat.

Fergus called at 6:30. I was sufficiently drunk by then. He hasn't been well or strong since his father died. He keeps begging us to move into his new house with him; you'll have your own *wing,* he says. Lowell continues to be very curious about the house. Fergus said he'd send us new pictures and blueprints. His neediness has become inexhaustible.

Dinner tonight. Merit was amusing herself by pounding her fish sticks onto her tray. "Codfish!" she said. "Codfish, codfish, codfish!" Lowell, who was also drinking this evening, told her not to say *codfish,* that it was *so* like an American to force stature on something so humble. Then he looked at me sheepishly, apologized, and said sometimes he forgets who it is he's talking to. He's been feeling very ragged and sad in anticipation of his mother's visit tomorrow. Fergus still can't believe I haven't met her yet.

Merit licked her tray's fish mash and asked us what she was like when she was a baby. I told her she was the same, but smaller. Lowell said he couldn't remember.

Will I forget what she's like now? In fifteen years, will I have to flip back through these pages to remind myself what my daughter was like when she was three? I will not let myself forget; I will not.

Lowell followed me when I was getting Merit ready for bed; he talked about how our little game was the only thing keeping him sane. He hates the people who buy our paintings, because all they can ever be is owners; they are not creators, and for this we must scorn them.

"The superiority of knowing," he said as he staggered into Merit's room. "The Pyrenees are no more!"

I asked Lowell what he was talking about.

Louis XIV.

"Where's the superiority in knowing about a charade?" I asked. I told Merit to pick out the nightgown she wanted to wear.

Lowell said we were together in this, joined in the "mystery."

For the rest of the night, he was very quiet and sullen.

"I'm going to kill myself, and her, if she brings her thermos tomorrow," he said. "Although not in that order." He asked me how many dissatisfactions in life constituted a tolerable number.

My choices have somehow become limited. There is no world apart from us. If I am to do this, and I will, all I can do is sink deeper into the chasm of us.

24

Merit hadn't accidentally left her keys in the office after all. This was not good news. When she and Randy got back to the office (at 4:45), she was expecting her keys to be on top of her desk, where she thought she'd left them. Had the office thief swiped those, too? Unless she called Wyatt, the most obvious way home was with Randy. And Randy wasn't an option, not now. She didn't want Randy anywhere near her house ever again. She was thinking about telling Wyatt to change the beep code for the garage door tonight.

Randy asked her if she wanted help looking for her keys (he'd be glad to help her "tear up" her office, he said). She said thanks, but everything was cool.

During the mostly speechless postsex drive back to work, Randy tried twice to reach over and kiss her. Merit said, "Not now" each time. Randy, in a very un-Randy way, came to a full one-one-thousand, two-one-thousand, three-one-thousand halt at each four-way stop they encountered, even when there were no other cars around. Merit suspected he was trying to win some nice-guy points with her, because on the floor in her bedroom, Randy hadn't been a nice guy (but Merit hadn't been a nice gal, either). After they did what they did, they each took their own quick showers. The private showers had been Merit's idea, and Randy had seemed unhappy about it.

She wondered if she could make it through the rest of her life without ever once thinking of sex with Randy again. Merit knew she was on her way to becoming a very mean person.

She would give herself until 5:00 to find her keys. Five o'clock was the earliest Wyatt could conceivably get off work, although Wyatt had in the past made it known his boss took a very dim view of his employees' early departures. Merit didn't locate her keys, but she did unearth, among other items, a date book from 2002, in which she hadn't written one thing (slow year), a nine-month-old invoice for fifteen hundred dollars from someone who'd done some freelance work on a promotional event on

Lake Erie (she wondered why the guy had never called to bug her about his money—very unlike a freelancer), and about ten birth-control pill cards that weren't empty but should have been (each card had at least two, and some up to five, erratically located tiny green pills in it; Merit was never as fastidious about birth control as the more responsible and mature citizens of the world were).

Wyatt, when she called him at 5:00 on the schnozzle, chose not to emit the big sigh to which he was entitled. He said he'd be right there. Merit asked him ("just double-checking," she said) if he had a key to her car on his chain. He was silent for a few seconds, then asked her how unsystematic she thought he *was*. She hung up the phone, then immediately realized she hadn't told him something important. She called him back. "Don't come into the office, okay?" she asked. "Just wait in the car if I'm not outside; I'll be right there."

"Okeydoke," he said. "But you do know this means the Tooting Subordinate and I won't be able to chat, don't you? Do give him my regards, though."

Merit shut down her computer without checking her E-mails, stood up from her desk without listening to her voice-mail messages. She turned off the light, shut the door, and said good-bye to Randy.

She waited outside by the back exit. There had really been no reason for her to return to work this afternoon. She probably just should have stayed home after she and Randy had fucked three times. Merit took a full-bodied breath. She was a child, and children loved the smell of August. Even the air in the parking lot smelled very deep and ripe and slow. She tasted the air.

Merit closed her eyes and decided she wouldn't open them until she felt Wyatt pulling into the parking lot. She would open her eyes *before* she heard the car. She hoped she and Wyatt shared that much of a connection. She sometimes thought they did. She thought so right now.

If the wind was blowing in the right direction, you could hear the river sounds of the cars on the distant interstate.

She was thinking about what she'd done, but she wasn't thinking about it. She was also thinking about one of Jenny's unsold paintings: *Lowell's Murder.*

A thought: What if she could only love horrible things?

She did feel Wyatt's approach before she heard his car. She opened her eyes. Wyatt puttered neatly around the corner, both hands securely on the wheel of his spotless blue Toyota. She ran toward his car (which was, un-like Merit's, unblemished by rust splotches, hail dents, or key scratches). The driver's window descended. He held a key between his long fingers. She took it, thanked him, and clomped toward her car.

"Hey, don't I even get a kiss?" he asked.

Merit turned and walked back to Wyatt's car. She bent over into the blast of climate-controlled air, kissed Wyatt on his bald spot, and asked him if he would wait up for her, so they wouldn't get separated when they were driving. She instantly wondered why she thought she needed to follow him home; she knew where she was going. He said he'd be with her half the trip, but then he'd have to turn off and pick up Caroline. The way he looked at her made her think he thought she was losing what was left of her mind.

Merit's Jag started okay. He flipped on his right turn signal before they even left the parking lot. Merit already knew which way to turn.

Following him felt very much like a driving test. She knew she was being monitored from up front, so she tried to be an extra-subtle and extra-slow driver. *So* subtle and slow, in fact, she accidentally let a couple of cars weave in front of her. It was sad those cars didn't know she and Wyatt were together. But didn't they seem together?

Wyatt, seen from behind, in his car, was unknown to her. This, she thought, is what my husband looks like as a stranger: He is an old but well-maintained (200,000-plus miles) Toyota Cressida hatchback (whose brake lights were illuminated pretty much constantly), cautious at stop-lights and turn signal–happy, containing the balding back of a head of a middle-aged Caucasian male. You couldn't even tell how tall he was in there. Wyatt, like Merit, had freakishly long legs and a normal-size torso (hence her adolescent nickname "Spider"; Wyatt, as far as she knew, had never had a nickname). Neither of them ever really appeared particularly tall when sitting.

The first time Jenny met Wyatt, Jenny told her she thought Merit and Wyatt looked like siblings. Jenny appeared not to remember that she'd said the same thing about two other guys Merit had brought home, one early in college, and one in high school.

Her cell phone rang: Wyatt, reminding her they'd now have to part. They were parked at a stoplight, and looking at him, she couldn't even tell he was on the phone. He was as inactive as an artifact.

"Bye," Merit said. "You, too."

He turned one way; she turned the other. She was home in five minutes. She did the special beep, honked the Wyatt-created code. The door opened, the light came on, and she parked her car on her designated side.

Wyatt and Shelley had lived together in this house for two years before they got divorced, so Merit's parking space had presumably once been Shelley's. Merit had never really asked if this were true, but she thought so, since Wyatt wasn't a guy who'd ever willingly switch to the other side of the garage. Merit used to think it was weird Wyatt never wanted to move from the house where he'd lived a whole separate existence before her arrival, but she'd finally given up trying to talk to him about real estate three years ago this coming Christmas.

Merit, in her clogs, stepped over the fresh iridescent oil or whatever it was puddled on Wyatt's side. That fluid was from Randy's vehicle. Her own car spewed lots of fluids, too, but she didn't know if her car's fluids looked the same as Randy's car's. This was, however, something Wyatt would know, and notice. Also, Wyatt had, bizarrely, parked in the driveway a few times in the last week. She backed her Jag out and reparked it, this time in Wyatt's space. There were now a few new hot drops of something where her car had just been.

She was in the shower when they came home. Wyatt knocked on the bathroom door and waited for Merit's response. She gave it. The doorknob turned. Cold air. The door closed.

"Honey, why did you park on my side of the garage?" Wyatt's voice echoed as if in a fallout shelter.

Merit realized she probably should have anticipated this question and come up with a plausible response. She had instead spent the last twenty minutes thinking about when she and Randy had, not two hours ago, fucked on the rug in her bedroom, then not on the rug, then on the rug again.

"What? I parked on *your side* of the garage?"

The air was clammy, already breathed. Wyatt had told her many times before it wasn't good for her to take such hot showers.

"Yes, Merit," Wyatt said. He sounded as if he was standing far away. "You did."

"Spooky."

"Did you *forget* which side is yours?"

Merit said she was so hot and spaced-out that she guessed she'd forgotten what she was doing.

"Gosh, are you okay?"

"Oh yeah," Merit said. "I'm fine."

"When you get out, can we talk about something?"

"Can we talk about something?" was not a question you wanted to hear your husband ask, especially not now. Did he know? He didn't know.

"Are you going to yell at me about the car?"

"It's funny you should say that, actually, but, no, this has nothing to do with the car. Well, it does, in a way, I suppose, but only tangentially. You didn't put the mat down? *Honey.* There's water all over the place."

"Water?" Merit asked, as if that would clear up this issue.

"All the towels are wet. Why are all the towels wet?"

"This is my second shower. The first one didn't, you know, *take.*"

"You've experienced this before—a shower that doesn't 'take.' It's all the lotions and unguents you use. That's my hypothesis at least. See you in my study."

For the fourth time during her shower, Merit squirted shampoo into her left hand.

Fifteen minutes later, Wyatt still hadn't said anything about the four tiny frogs. Merit and Wyatt were sitting together at his desk. He clicked his mechanical pencil. A wet white towel was turbaned on top of Merit's head.

"So. Let's talk. I've been waiting for the right opportunity to bring this up. We've been having a statistically significant couple of months here, Merit."

A piece of paper was facedown on the tidy pine desk he had built when he was married to Shelley. *Click* went the pencil. The lead filament said *Hellothere! Click.* The lead filament went *Oopsgottago.*

"The turning point was your trip to Kroger in May. Do you remember that? When you locked your keys in the trunk?"

Merit observed the reflection of his pumping thumb on the yellow mechanical pencil in the IN GOD WE TRUST. ALL OTHERS MUST USE DATA plaque over his desk. The desk was over a decade old, but it still smelled like shellac; the whole room did. She didn't like this room. Copies of his *Journal of Applied Statistics* were ordered on the bookshelves by date.

She said she did recall the key incident at Kroger.

"Up until that point, you'd been losing—or, to be fair, *misplacing*—approximately one item per week. I'm not even counting today's Event as an Event, by the way. No intangibles. After May fourteenth, the date of the Kroger Event, you started losing two, *three* items per week. My little secret is that I've been plotting the number of Events."

He had a very pleasantly shaped thumb. Some people had really gross little thumbs, but not Wyatt.

"The average since Kroger has been one point three four. But this week, you've lost *six* things that I know of. I think it's important that we talk about this. Are you aware of anything that's changed lately?"

Merit looked at her own thumbs. They were nicely shaped, too. Their thumb structures were very similar, actually, hers and Wyatt's.

With horror, she remembered again what Jenny had said about the two of them looking like brother and sister. Once, at the dining room table, when Jenny was helping Merit with her eighth-grade geometry homework, Jenny stopped in the middle of a proof and told Merit that most people usually ended up marrying themselves.

"Are you aware of any abnormalities in your behavior?"

" 'Abnormalities'? Wyatt!"

Merit could see the ghost of Wyatt-plotted dots on the paper. It was some kind of chart or graph. He had still not turned it over.

"Now don't get upset, sweetie. We can control these things; it's just a matter of figuring out what cause or combination of causes we're dealing with here. This week, have you been getting enough sleep, for instance? Are you drinking wine at dinner? What's going on at work? I'm worried about you, Merit."

The phones downstairs and in their bedroom rang four times. Neither Merit nor Wyatt made a move to answer them. The machine picked up. Wyatt's voice on the outgoing message.

"Where's Caroline?" Merit asked.

"I think she's out back with the pig."

The caller didn't leave a message.

"Hey," Merit said, "should you change the code on the garage-door opener?"

"You're right, but why do you say that?"

"I don't know. It just seems kind of too easy. Like it's the first code anyone would try. Maybe you should change it to something really complicated."

"Excellent point. I was thinking of changing it soon anyway. So you still haven't told me what's wrong. What's changed?"

"Nothing has changed, Wyatt," Merit said, although she didn't mean it. "Nothing at all."

Why did the book say you had to let bottles of tap water stand for at least twenty-four hours before you filled the tank with them? And what did "bottles of tap water" mean? What if you were using tap water from your bathroom sink? Maybe it was a typo and the book really meant "bottles of *springwater.*" She probably should have looked at the book before. The results were generally never good when she winged it. For Merit, preparation was essential.

The frogs were still very much alive, so she hadn't fucked up that much yet.

It was actually good she'd bought the weird miniature Fergus house, she learned in the book. The little frogs would enjoy the house because it would get them closer to the water's surface—they could hang out on the roof, mosey on up and get a gulp of air, then come back down for some more roof sitting. Merit thought that sounded like a pretty good life. (Hey, that sounded like *Fergus's* life.) Someone told her once that looking at animals lowered your blood pressure. She believed that. One of the girl frogs was squatting in the glass bottom of the tank (the bottom of the tank should by now have been covered with the tricolored gravel Merit had bought before she'd had sex three times with a man who wasn't her husband). The squatting frog's arms were out in front of her like a little organist's. The frog moved and kicked up one leg, a cancan. Such a good little entertainer: Look at her, putting on a show for Merit. *Hello, my ragtime gaaaaal!* Merit had always named each of her animals by instinct. The first name that came to her (she couldn't help it; it just *felt right*): Fergus.

Merit didn't remember the first time she'd met Fergus. (Fergus, like the house, had just suddenly been *there.*) Merit mostly remembered how, from the ages of four to eight, she would sit outside Jenny and Lowell's studio, playing in the dark and hidden hallway that smelled of hot paint and turpentine. She was never allowed in the studio with them, and neither was Fergus.

Whenever Merit would lie on the hallway floor, Fergus would find her and lie down next to her. He wanted to join in on her private fun.

"It's us against Jewell," he said. "If they don't need us, we won't need them, either."

She only kind of liked it when he was there, though. Even then, she knew she'd rather be alone. She didn't like having to tell Fergus what to have his doll do and say. Even then, Merit didn't understand why you would want to let someone else into a fantasy you yourself had created.

They dressed her dolls in that torch-lit cherry-walled hallway. A lot of the early designs were simple toga numbers made by twisting Lowell's handkerchiefs around the dolls' plexuses. The doll clothes soon became more elaborate; eventually, little pastel pom-pom balls, glitter, glue, ostrich feathers, wallpaper swatches, and a stapler came into the picture. Along with their new extravagant fashion designs, Fergus suggested an improvement of the dolls' faces was in order. So Merit and Fergus used black Crayola markers to lengthen the dolls' eyelashes and red Crayola markers to rubyize their lips.

In the hallway after school one dreary second-grade afternoon, Fergus gave Merit a manicure. The dolls were in her lap and she was waiting like an invalid for her nails to dry. Most of the dolls had newly glamorous pink Crayola cheeks and blue Crayola eye shadow (two shades too dark, Merit already knew). But Fergus had taken a marker and given one of the dolls, Constanza (named by Merit), a thick black scar (with stitching) on her right cheek, and two black X's over her eyes. Fergus said something about how he'd been in a bad mood the day before. He saturated a cotton ball with nail-polish remover. He daubed at Constanza's face with it, and the eye patch and scar disappeared.

"Can you just do that?" Merit asked. "Take away what you did?"

"Of course, darling," Fergus said. "Everything is temporary. *Watch.*"

Fergus swabbed more furiously at Constanza's face with the cotton ball, and her whole face came off.

"It's better this way, because we can remake her. We can make her prettier. We can draw her to look more like you. Or *me!*"

It seemed incredible to Merit at the time that doll manufacturers hadn't been prescient enough to imagine little girls would eventually figure out what nail-polish remover did to a face, and hadn't taken measures to prevent such desecrations.

When Merit's nails had dried, she gently (careful not to mess up her manicure) daubed at each of her dolls' faces with those sodden cotton balls. Fergus cheered her on.

And so when Lowell and Jenny were on the other side of the door, painting faces, Merit and Fergus, sitting on the floor outside their studio like banished lovers, erased them. Merit had been beginning to learn piano then, but it didn't count as anything important. Her first art was the art of removal.

Merit kept the secret until the second semester of her junior year in college. She worried about herself in those days. She'd become a very unhappy person. She couldn't trust anyone with the truth, and therefore had no friends. She seemed unable to maintain any kind of relationship (with a boy or with a girl) for more than about two months. Her days up until that point had been filled with thoughts of escape; whatever relationship she was in, she would soon fantasize about fleeing. (They hadn't known her anyway, so how could she *not* have tired of them?) And whenever anyone dared to assume they knew her, she would leave them.

As she was rushing to her Women's Studies class (Merit was always at least ten minutes late for all her classes) on the day she told her secret, she passed a girl she'd been friends with—and had blown off—the year before. The former friend was walking across the quad with another girl. When the former friend saw Merit approaching, she tugged on the other girl's North Face windbreaker, and mouthed, "That's *her*." The girls stopped walking and hugged. When Merit passed them (her hands trembling), the North Face girl said, just loud enough so Merit could hear, "She's a total bitch, honey. I told you to forget about her."

In class, Merit felt sticky and viscous. Her hands felt swollen and unbendable, the way they had felt when she'd had high fevers as a child. The topic that particular class period was "Behind Every Great Man Is a Great Woman." They'd been discussing Bill and Hillary, a topic Merit was much less interested in than Lowell and Jenny, so she raised her hand and shakily, haltingly told the class what she had to tell. The eating-disorder girl who'd bawled during the in-class reading of "Daddy" started bawling again. Everyone, even the two weird, spiny, dateless, sensitive-type guys in the class, was horrified and demanded to know why Merit hadn't exposed her father to the world as the hideous fraud he was. The teacher (with whom Merit would later become close) brought up the idea of all of them driving to Jenny's house in Akron in a righteous Women's Studies caravan and staging an intervention.

Back in her dorm room, Merit called Jenny and told her what she had done.

Jenny's response wasn't the one Merit had braced herself for: "Well, had anyone *heard* of us?"

"No, Mother," Merit said. "But that's not the point."

"Well, you can't possibly take them seriously, then, can you? I *knew* you should have gone to Oberlin."

25

I knew where to look, of course, given there are only so many medieval-ists in northeast Ohio. It didn't take that much effort to find my wander-ing minstrels, swordsmen, harpists, jugglers, mimes, fire-eaters, jousters, and serving lads and wenches. I had almost done everything that needed to be done, and I still had one day left. Seating chart: finis. Bartenders: A-OK. Chocolate place cards: arriving from Paris by FedEx this after-noon. Bikini waxing: survived. I had some folks mowing the grounds this morning, trimming, grooming. One of the only loose ends left: I was still thinking about setting up a giant farkle board on the front lawn. But I needed to find someone who knew how to play farkle first.

I suppose I could have been a little bit clearer on the phone yesterday about the caterer's duty, though. I needed them only for *passed* hors d'ouevres, so I really should have said, "Mrs. Valdez will be preparing the *meal*. She'll be working on modern updates of my favorite period dishes; you good people just worry about the *appies*."

From my bedroom window this morning, I watched as the tan Wind-sor Castle Caterers van moved silently into my driveway. (Why is it that nothing ever seems real when viewed through glass?) A girl of college age bounded youthfully out of the driver's side and soundlessly slid open the van's side door (on which was painted a charming picture of the castle's famous flagged round tower). I watched as she pulled a white apron on over her head and twisted her Botticelli hair into a horse tail. I knew I was in trouble when I saw the cart, then the umpteen aluminum-foiled tin platters on top of it. Then the ginormous wicker basket, which I knew contained utensils and napkins. This wasn't my first time hiring this outfit, and I understood what I was in for.

I pressed the button on the intercom to Andrei's room, the room that used to be Merit's. "Fergus?" he asked. "I was not fully awake." Andrei is a late sleeper, too. I like this about him. I told him to get up off his tuffet and help me set up our caterer friend.

"But the party is not until *tomorrow,* correct?" he asked. *That* didn't sound like the stress-free Andrei I knew. It was 10:30 a.m. The party would be starting in thirty-four hours. How long did he really think it would take him to get into his costume?

When I told him he would need to hide his face tomorrow (and put the kibosh on the vest), he was reactionless.

"Taste test," I reassured him. "It's typical in the catering world. And we *know* you're always hungry."

He thanked me, said he'd be right down, and signed off.

This may surprise you, but I've decided to ask him if he wants to move into Merit's room *permanently.* Shocked? Stunned? And do you know what? I'm even thinking about redecorating.

Never had I actually told Andrei that Merit had lived there when she was a poppet, never had I told him I still, twenty years later, couldn't bring myself to redo the room from her era. Strangely, he'd never asked me why a pinkish Barbie Dream House sat collecting dust in the corner of that room, although I'd found most people who stayed there didn't ask that question, either. I'd come to think the Barbie Dream House seemed a little too widowish a gesture, too much like keeping your dead husband's briefcase in the same spot by the front door for twenty years, the same spot where, on his last night, he let it fall one last time.

I have Merit sitting to my left tomorrow. I think she'll be pleased.

I let Andrei and the caterer arrange themselves downstairs. At 10:50, I followed the food smells to the dining room. Andrei (in the vest again) had established himself at the head of the table. They had my silver Sheffield candelabrum going and had helped themselves to my Hildegard of Bingen dessert plates. Where *had* I hidden those? I hadn't seen them for years. There were dozens of the little plates speckled around Andrei, each piled with a steaming heap of food that demanded fork, knife, and/ or spoon. The scene did not look appetizery at all.

The girl was serving (with a rubber spatula) Andrei a shriveled hunk of poached salmon. She was left-handed. I like left-handers, always have.

"Found the oven, I see," I said.

"Mr. Goodwyn?" the girl asked. She thunked the salmony spatula down on my naked oak, sans coaster, but I wasn't concerned. I had bigger fish to fry. "He said we should start without you."

Andrei slurped a spoonful of tomato soup from a puce bowl that wasn't mine. On the left side of his nutmeg-toned face was a pillow crease, lingering evidence of a thorny late morning. He might not have known much about me, but I didn't know much about him, either.

"You were right to do so, honeybun. How's the soup, Andrei?" I asked.

"Good," he said between mouthfuls. He looked as if he were enjoying himself. " 'Two tomato.' "

The girl asked me if she could dish me out a bowl. I said no thanks. I've used this catering firm before, and their food is exceptionally mediocre, but who cares? They've got a great name and a classy van.

"Although I *am* curious," I said. "Is your soup here made with two tomatoes, or two different *varieties* of tomato? Does 'two tomato' refer to the number or the category?"

With her left hand, she unclipped her barrette, smoothed her red hair, and reclipped it again.

"I'm not sure," she said. "I'll have to ask Lance."

"Ah," I said. "Well, let's call this Lance and ask him!"

Andrei was now slicing a sickly porpoise-colored bratwurst with one of the caterers' butter knives. He hadn't finished his soup. I was worried about him. He was poor. I knew that. I wondered how poor he really was.

"Um. Okay," the girl said. I didn't know this Lance person, but I thought he sounded exacting and therefore worth getting to know.

"I like this American sausage," Andrei said. "Very, very good."

"Um, can I use your phone?" the girl asked. "I left my cell phone in the van."

My favorite phone nook was as far away from us as the van was. I didn't want her to leave just yet, not when we were starting to get to know each other. "Let's call Lance later. Tell me, Rachel, have you any finger food?" A shiny chrome name tag was pinned to her white apron. The reflected fire from my candelabrum flicked on that chrome.

She looked at Andrei, who was still chewing, not being any help at all. He stared ponderingly at the little plate of bratwurst, masticating, unblinking.

"Bratwurst can be finger food if you put it on a toothpick," she said.

It was not a good suggestion, but she was trying to be helpful, and I liked that.

"Thanks," I said, "but not going to fly with this crowd."

"We have this breaded eggplant thing," she said.

"Anything a little less challenging?" I asked.

A tiny potato fell off Andrei's spoon and onto his lap. I didn't want him to think I'd seen.

"Do you want to try this pepper-fried calamari?" she asked. I wondered if she was poor, too. Everyone around me has always been poor, and I've never known what to do about it. "You dip it in this Mae Ploy sauce." She indicated a white cardboard container.

I speared a tentacle with one of her company's flimsy forks. I dunked it in the viscous red sauce and crunched.

"*Mmmm*," I said. "Let's get about a hundred platters of *that*."

A little carbon-copy notepad appeared from somewhere, and on it she wrote, "100 CALAMARIES." I used to want people to think I was left-handed myself, and I'd transfer fork or pencil to my left hand whenever I felt the need to take an affected pause in meal or test. I was always impressed by the southpaw's otherness and wondered in school how they did it, watching as they navigated around the notebook's spiral coil.

"Our prime rib is really popular, too," she said. "We can do that on a toothpick if you want."

"Thanks," I said. "But we've got the dinner menu set. We're having a madrigal dinner tomorrow, you see, dear, and I don't *think* you want to bother with the arrangements for five hundred stags and oxen, hais, peacocks, frogs, stone soup, whiskey pudding, Lombard pie, pomegranate syrup, and jumbleberries. Consider this my gift to you, actually."

I was exaggerating about the five hundred stags and oxen. Otherwise, though, Mrs. Valdez did have her work cut out for her. I had to remind myself to give her a big old tip tomorrow night.

"Um, we can't do stuff that's off the menu, really," the girl said.

"Is a madrigal not something performed at Christmastime, Fergus?" asked Andrei. He examined a bacon-wrapped bread stick, twisted it around in his fingers, and chomped it in two. He brushed the crumbs from his lap. There was, I realized for probably the first time, something about him that did rather move me.

"Oh, you know me, Andrei," I said. "Always like to mix it up. Who says the wassail cup can come out only for the holidays?"

Preston Lympany would be sitting to my right tomorrow night. Preston Lympany's Yellow Hair would be to the right of him, and that was okay with me. That would be just *fine*.

Tomorrow, Lowell would see how his power had finally been exhausted. There comes, in each life, a moment of truth.

The girl, tossing a salad that looked as if it involved some kind of proscuitto and avocado concoction, said, "Do you want me to call Lance and see if we can do wassail? I know he said we do all these special Christmas things. I just started in May."

"I think we've got the wassail covered, but thanks," I said. The girl and I had the same brand of vulnerable, watery, freckly complexion. I hoped she took the proper precautions. Could she afford effective sunscreen? This was a good girl, I knew. She was, like Merit, a good girl. "I'm grateful for your enthusiasm, you know. It's not often you meet a fellow enthusiast. Tell me, Rachel: How much do you make an hour?"

The girl let her plump and touchingly childish mouth hang open for a few moments. Then she said, "Uh, seven dollars. But I can get overtime."

"Seven dollars!" I exclaimed, as if this were news to me, although I really didn't have any preconceived notion about how much people got paid hourly anyway. She could have just as easily said two dollars or twenty.

I dug into my pocket and withdrew my money-clipped bills. (The etching on the clip: the *On ne peut pas vivre seul* banner.) I peeled back a hundred-dollar bill. I slid it into her apron's front pocket, knowing as I did that her hands were food-slick.

"Whoa. Thank you so much," she said. She seemed to be wondering if she should put the salad tongs down and admire the money; she seemed to be wondering what the polite thing to do was. "But I'm not supposed to . . . Lance would—"

"Nonsense," I said.

She said "supposed to" like "postta." Merit used to say that, too. Jenny would correct her, but Lowell and I wouldn't. Hadn't thought of that for *years*. Have I ever told you how much I loved Merit? That she was once my one true friend? That, until the invitation, I hadn't contacted her in over twenty-six months? The last time was when she and her new family came over for a drawing lesson. It was the first time in three years

Lowell had talked about his art. I thought it was a real turning point for all of us. I was wrong.

Andrei was trying to pretend he hadn't noticed our little transaction. I would give him some cash later. It was the fair thing to do. I didn't want him to feel left out, and he needed money as much as anyone, possibly even more.

"This might seem an unexpected question, Rachel, but you don't happen to know my d——, my st——, Merit Ash, do you?"

The girl had decided to keep hold of the salad tongs and go back to tossing, although are there really *so many* degrees of tossedness? She was a conscientious one. Her apron was cheap, and the hundred-dollar bill was visible through the insubstantial pocket. I thought, Might it be a thoughtful postparty gesture for me to buy the whole catering staff some good heavy twill aprons from Williams-Sonoma? I would write that down in my notebook when I returned to my room.

"I don't think so," she said. "I don't *think* I know her."

"My guess is that she's several years older than you," I said. "And Akron *is* bigger than we tend to think. But I thought, May as well try!"

"Is this Lowell's daughter?" Andrei asked. In his nonleft hand was a wilted spear of white asparagus. He clamped down on it. "Merit?"

"She's mine, too."

"Oh," Andrei said. He was chewing. "Okay."

The asparagus spear, whose tip was now bitten off, drooped down like the forlornest thing. I wanted to pet it, tell it it would be all right, but that wasn't true; its future had already been decided. He was looking for something on the table. A hollandaisey sauce, I wagered. The condemned asparagus was too bland for our zesty Andrei.

"You would have known her as Merit *Haven,* actually, come to think of it," I said.

"Wait," the girl said. "I knew a girl named Merit Haven. My older sister hung out with her when I was in like *grade school.*"

She said "grade school" as if it were an indignity she simply couldn't believe she'd been forced to suffer. I'd felt that way about school, too. I was growing ever fonder of this girl and was thinking about asking her if she wanted to come to the party—as a guest, not as a worker. But now I wanted to know about Merit as the preorthodontia adolescent she'd known.

"I think she was on my sister Missy's swim team," she said.

"She *was* very active in her YWCA swim club!" I said.

For years, I went to most of Merit's home swim meets, both when she lived at my house and when she didn't—alone, or with Lowell, or Jenny—cheering her from the observation deck. She was a brilliant freestyler, but not so great at the turning part. Once, when she was about ten, she hit her head in an ill-executed kick turn. I was there, watching her from above. I slid down the treacherous steps in my leather-soled shoes. In my mania, I wiped out on the wet pool deck. Fell down and went boom. (Banged my noggin, too.) Merit and I laughed and laughed about this coincidence later. Neither injury turned out to be a big deal. She did place last in that race, though.

"What was she like when you knew her?" I asked.

"I just remember this bathing suit I saw her in. It was red and had all these rainbow stripes going down it—like this." She gestured with her salad tong. A tiny piece of proscuitto: airborne. I ducked.

"That's Merit!" I said. I hadn't thought about that suit for decades, but I could recall it vividly now. Actually, she might have been wearing it the day we hit our heads. Funny how the memories just came cascading back when beckoned. When she was younger, she always, during the summer, had a Band-Aid half-fastened slapdash on one of her beautiful long limbs. She used to give me swimming lessons in our pool when we still lived together. "Blow bubbles, then breathe; blow bubbles, then breathe," she would say, her hand on my head. I could never get it right, but she was always so patient about my challenges in the coordination department. I remember everything she ever said as a child, but I can never remember her voice. Sad, how horribly sad . . . But you know what? I was happy, too, because I was going to see her the next day! It had been *two years.* If gravity hadn't had such a firm grip, I would have pranced up and down the dining room's carved wood wall! Back and forth, up and down, back and forth! "*That's* my Merit. What other good stories do you have about her?"

"I don't really remember much else. I don't think I ever talked to her. But I've always remembered that bathing suit. I was like, How cool! I kept telling my mom I wanted one like it."

How fragile are our moments of glee. I was benumbed. Merit lived in this girl's memory as a body in a bathing suit.

"The bathing suit is *all* you remember about her?" I asked. I was talking to someone, a human being to whom Merit was unreal, for whom she existed only in a finite realm, as a moment in time, one image.

"What am I supposed to remember from when I was like *six*?"

"This is true," said Andrei. "I think we should be happy the caterer remembered Lowell's daughter's name in the first place. Do I meet her tomorrow?"

"She's *my* daughter, too," I said.

I was looking at my wall now, looking and thinking. It had taken two men a year to carve it. Whatever happened to that year? (And whatever happened to the men?) I was not going to redecorate Merit's room, I'd decided, not now or ever.

"You can call me Rachel," she said to Andrei. She scooped a plop of what I took to be a kind of duck moose onto one of the Hildegard plates. She slid the plate over to Andrei, who, in preparation for course number 230, polished his spoon clean with his napkin. The napkin went back to his lap. He dipped into the moose.

"I'll introduce you to Merit tomorrow," I said to Andrei.

"Good," he said. "I have always wanted to meet the owner of the clothes in my closet, the dollhouse, the dolls with no faces."

How did Andrei know about Merit? Had I even mentioned her to him?

"Come again?" I asked.

"You have me in the girl's room, Fergus," he said.

"You *noticed* that? No one has *ever* noticed that!"

"It is not possible not to. The room is no problem."

"Oh," I said. "I do want you to meet her tomorrow! I really think you'll get along. You'll like her. Everybody does! What's not to like? You'll see!"

"Good. I cannot look at these paintings while I eat, Fergus."

I nodded sympathetically about the paintings. Andrei was saying everything I wanted to hear this morning, wasn't he? It's always a buzz when someone shows you they've been paying more attention than you'd thought. Maybe I'd seat Andrei closer to me tomorrow than I'd planned.

"I cannot eat my food underneath these paintings. They are very—what is the word, Fergus?—disquieting. They are disquieting."

All of the tins had been emptied onto the plates. The girl popped a brussels sprout into her mouth. There wasn't much left for her to do until cleanup time.

"Take a load off, Rachel," I said. "Go ahead and sit down. Go ahead."

She sat. Lowell as the Reeve gritted his teeth at me. That was a good example of Lowell's depth of understanding of human complexity: a taste for revenge = gritted teeth.

"About the paintings," I said. "Have you noticed how in every single one Lowell wasn't able to individuate any character, but rather only classify it?"

Andrei shrugged. He licked the pureed duck off of his spoon, front and back. He checked to make sure he didn't have any duck on his bare elbow. (He didn't.) The girl glanced up at the paintings. To see these canvases anew: What must they look like? Staged gimmickry? That was my guess.

"Yeah, it's like there are no *people* in those pictures," the girl said. "Just *costumes.*"

"Lowell," Andrei said, courteously dabbing at his mouth with his napkin, "is not interested in people."

"Oh Andrei!" I said. I wanted to kiss him. I'd never really known he had anything to say, anything rigorous or true. To *think* he used to be my foil! (Or *whatever* he was.)

I extracted a reproduction Glastonbury chair from the table and hauled it over to my intelligent and sophisticated friend Andrei. Before I sat down, I refamiliarized myself with my money clip. I had six hundred dollars left. I would need to send Andrei out to the ATM before the party. I'd have to write that down in my "To Do" list in my notebook, too, when I went upstairs.

Andrei mentally undressed my money clip. He couldn't, even in a positive, up-with-people mood, have guessed each of the bills was a hundred. I smiled at him and unskinned one of those lovely hundreds. Discreetly, I folded it up and nestled it in his lap. He deserved this token. He deserved even more than this, in fact, much more.

"Fergus?" he said as he unfolded the bill. "Fergus!" He held it up to the candlelight. Did he really think . . . Did *I* seem like . . . What sorts of cheap fakers and parasites had he been associating with?

"It's *real*," I said. "*Trust me.*"

"But why?" he asked. "Thank you, Fergus. But why?"

"What do you think of *Lowell,* Andrei?" I asked. "Tell me. What's your opinion? Let's *talk.*"

"Lowell?" he asked. "Lowell is like his paintings. He has no dimension. He is dimensionless, Fergus."

"Andrei!" I said, digging into my money clip again. "You're as shrewd as an Aztec priest."

I shoved another hundred at him.

"Thank you, Fergus," he said. I'd never seen him smile such a real smile before. What causes chalky teeth? A high childhood fever? So Andrei had been a child, just like everyone else? And he'd had a fever? Oh! I gave him another hundred.

"Lowell is all vanity," he said.

"All wanton vanity," I said.

I giggled, then Andrei giggled, and then we both giggled together. I slapped my knee and giggled some more. I handed over the remaining three hundred-dollar bills.

"Don't tell *Lowell* I gave this to you," I said, laughing, letting my happy tears fall.

"Lowell?" Andrei asked. "I have not talked to Lowell for *two weeks!*"

"Aren't *you* the lucky one."

We busted up again. We laughed and laughed. Too many happy tears to count.

"Did you know . . . did you know, Andrei, that Lowell's from *Akron?*"

"Ha!" Andrei spluttered, "I have heard this rumor!"

"And do you know that tomorrow I have him sitting next to his ex-wife and a magazine reporter?"

"Ha!"

" 'Ha' is right!" I said. "I can't wait until the magazine reporter meets *me.*"

Andrei stopped laughing.

"Consider me Lowell's Bernie Taupin."

He learned back and fanned himself with his three hundreds.

"Watch and enjoy tomorrow, my friend! *Watch and enjoy.*"

I took some deep breaths and tried to settle down.

"You must be stuffed," I said.

"No," he replied. "Not really."

"Um, excuse me for interrupting, but I need to get back and give Lance the menu for tomorrow night. Can we go over it?"

The girl! I had forgotten all about the girl!

She was still sitting down, scraping wax from the table with her pink fingernail. "Dear Lord, Rachel," I said. "I'm so sorry! We get distracted sometimes. Listen: Were you planning to work at our masque tomorrow?"

"Well, yeah," she said. "I wouldn't be here right now otherw—"

"Why don't I pay you, out of my own pocket, double what you'd be paid tomorrow? And you come to the party as a guest."

"Whoa. That is so completely nice. But I still have to get someone to cover for me."

"Oh, you'll find someone to cover for you. And you can bring your *boyfriend*," I said. "I'm sure you have a boyfriend."

"I guess I could ask this girl Claudia. She's always asking to pick up more shifts."

"Fantastic," I said.

"Although I don't have a boyfriend exactly. Is it okay if I bring someone else?"

"We're terrifically open-minded here," I said. "Some might even say to an eccentric degree. Bring whomever you'd like. And do call Claudia to cover. That's an order! May I help you clean up?"

Andrei audibly pushed his chair into the table, yawned, and stretched. He examined the cash wad in his bronzed hand.

"Fergus," he said, "I cannot take your money."

"Pish posh," I said. "It's yours."

"For what?" he asked. "Why, Fergus?"

"Do you have anywhere I can throw all this away?" the girl asked. She was crumpling aluminum foil into ragged ugly balls.

"I'll get you some garbage bags. Andrei: just take it."

"It does not feel right to me. What has changed, Fergus? Something has changed."

"Don't be silly, Andrei."

"Something has changed. Do you have anything I can do for the money?"

"You're my guest," I said. "And I love my guests. And I love you. I love you, Andrei."

"Fergus?" Andrei asked. "What is wrong with you?"

"Forget about what I said before about wearing a mask tomorrow, Andrei. You should go bare-faced *and* wear that wonderful vest."

"But you told me Lowell did not want to see my face." He elongated and slenderized himself and jammed the cash into the front pocket of his tight black jeans. "I still do not know how to take this."

"Be naked. Be bare-faced. The more recognizable, the better. *Listen* to your old Uncle Fergus now."

"I have no ideas now. All of my ideas are face-covering. What are you going to be tomorrow?"

"What am I going as?" I asked, laughing triumphantly. "What am *I* going as?" I galloped over to the girl, set down her unholy Reynolds Wrap ball (grown now to the size of an adult-human head) on the table, and took her freckled hands in mine. I led her in the waltz I alone heard. I administered a raspberry to Lowell as the Pardoner. His quest was just so comically hopeless.

"What do you think I'm going to be, darling? It's fairly obvious, is it not?"

I did, by the way, notice Andrei didn't say he loved me back. And do you know what? I didn't even mind.

26

17 June 1984

I couldn't hear anyone else today through my screams of self-pity. Oh, look at me, living back in Akron, on Fergus's dole. I'm not, I have never been, an independent person. Am I a failure at twenty-six? Is there any way out of the situation we've created for ourselves? Who is my mate? Are the paintings my mate? I'm feeling such desperate nostalgia for the people we were in London, New York even, and I didn't think we were happy then. Who *were* we when we moved here three years ago? It all seemed a mad adventure then, but, even then, I knew I didn't want adventure. All I ever wanted was to live in a monastery. My only little dream had been to be alone and work, but I'm never alone and I'm working disgracefully little. The stuff I'm doing now is terrible. All I can do is try to improve my technique. I can't do emotions anymore.

And it *was* fun, for a while at least. I was working so well here, at Fergus's house, for the first two years. I still knew how to concentrate; my thoughts were still of interest to me. And it wasn't *all* work, not in the beginning. Fergus taught us how to play croquet, and Merit and I went for rides on the carousel after dinner, and Lowell and I had loving, fervent intercourse in the studio. It was just this Easter that Fergus, in his giant blue rabbit costume, hosted an Easter-egg hunt for us. Easter wasn't so long ago. What happened? Where did Easter go?

Lowell is asleep here on the studio couch right now. Merit and Fergus are outside, clawing on the door. Today, Lowell got obscenely drunk and talked about how lost he'd become, and how with every new accolade and reward, he feels more hopeless.

"Would I still exist if you weren't here to paint me?" he asked. Then he asked, "Do you hate me?" and fell asleep.

I should have been selfish, like a man.

18 June

This was all that was required to get us past the gate at the company park today: "I'm in research and development," Lowell said to the guard; "I'm afraid I've forgotten my employee identification badge today."

After the guard waved us through, Fergus, in the passenger's seat, said, "Boy, you *sure* can sling it, can't you?" The giddiness, the sickening awe in Fergus's voice. I can barely bring myself to look at that pink eager-beaver face anymore. I almost can't believe those years of phone calls from New York (when I was trying to get Fergus to warm up to Lowell) actually happened. I looked at one of my journals from 1979 this morning, and found this: "When I told Fergus that I smelled Lowell's sweaters in his drawer every day, he said, 'If you love him, I love him, too.' " Maybe that should have been a red flag already.

I was sad all morning, after I reminded myself how I used to smell Lowell's sweaters because they smelled like him.

The carless lot where Lowell parked Fergus's car wasn't asphalt, although it preformed a brave simulacrum of it.

"Why's it squishy?" Merit asked as she hopped out of Fergus's Jaguar.

"*Tires,*" Lowell and Fergus said in unison.

What I learned today: Men, even men like Lowell and Fergus, know things about tires.

At the lodge, I bought Merit a fried bluegill sandwich while Lowell and Fergus studied, or pretended they were studying, the display case of fishing bobbers in the entrance of the cafeteria.

I asked Merit if she wanted tartar sauce. She said she did, and I ripped into the tough little packet, smeared the stuff onto her sandwich with a plastic knife (the serrated knife made rake-in-a-sand-trap grooves on the bun) at the Fixin's Bar. The second *i* in the hand-lettered sign was upside down, the *B* backward; the sign artist had been trying hard for that bumpkinish flair, unfortunately. I offered the sandwich to Merit, who took a nibble. Then, with no physical signal where the action was heading, she spit the bite out all over the floor. I helped myself to some paper napkins and ordered her another sandwich, this time with no Fixin's Bar stopover.

She ate it. We left the cafeteria. Lowell and Fergus were at the boat-rental counter, haggling with the blond kid in the booth about a driver's license. Lowell was wearing his purple poet shirt. Fergus was now in a wide-brimmed black felt hat. I was again reminded he's the only one among the three of us who has a license, although he hadn't brought it with him today.

"Ah, be a sport and forgo the nasty old driver's license," Lowell said to the boat-rental kid. "I know you're a *sport.*" Lowell's red snake tongue arrowed out of his mouth, alighted on his lips, disappeared.

The kid said maybe he could break the rules for us just this once. He stared at Lowell because Lowell demanded it.

Quiescent Fergus finally spoke up and told the kid we wanted to rent two boats for two hours, which seemed to me one boat too many and an hour and forty-five minutes too long.

The kid asked what kind of boat we wanted. There was a lot of wasted peripheral space on his long face—his features were all bunched up along his face's axis.

"Canoe?" Fergus asked.

"Oh, splurge for a *yacht,* Fergus," Lowell said, and pouted.

"Uh," the kid said. "We only have pontoons, kayaks, canoes, and pedal boats."

"Nothing more exotic?" Lowell asked.

The kid was being toyed with. He looked at me for help.

"Two canoes," I said definitively.

Fergus paid. The kid thunked four orange life vests over the Formica counter. The vests' metal clasps scratched the countertop. I could smell the vest fungus from where I was standing. Lowell told the kid he didn't need his vest ("Oh, but many thanks anyway"), but Fergus stepped in and said in that case, he'd like to use Lowell's vest, too, in addition to his own, if he didn't mind. Lowell said why no, he didn't mind. Fergus took the two vests, and I took two, one big one and one little one.

Lowell and Fergus had already let the back porch's screen door flap shut—the metal hook on the door swinging desolately—and were already outside and gamboling over the green toward the dock when I realized Merit wasn't behind me. I retraced my steps and found her standing on the toes of her sneakered feet back at the boat-rental booth. She was staring at the counter. The booth was empty. The kid was gone. The countertop was milk-colored, specks of gold threaded throughout.

I asked her what on the countertop was so absorbing.

"Mommy," she said, "you can see faces in there, too. The *gold*! It makes *faces.*"

She's been seeing faces everywhere lately, in everything. On the ride over to the lake, she had observed that the grilles of the oncoming cars looked like faces. During her bath last night, Fergus said, she'd told him the tub's knobs were eyes, the spigot a nose, and the drain a mouth.

"Why do they make things with faces?" she asked.

"Because it makes people feel better," I said. "Your dad and Fergus are already down in their boat. We should go down to meet them."

"That's *dumb*. Why do *faces* make people feel better?"

"Because people like to see themselves in things that have nothing to do with them," I said.

Lowell was perched like a grasshopper, stationing the canoe against the dock. Fergus daintily stuck his toe into the canoe, as if dipping his sandaled foot into hot soup. His life vest was on. The water at the lake is five feet at its deepest point, although Fergus could probably manage to drown in a bathtub. What was he going to do with Lowell's life vest? Tie it around his *back*? He tossed the extra vest into the canoe. His camera dangled down from his neck on its strap, banged against the boat.

"Fergus," Lowell said, "watch your camera."

Fergus pressed the camera against his vest. The other hand held on to the hat. (Can't forget about the hat!) He dipped his toe into the boat again.

"I can't!" he said. "I can't get in! It's too wobbly." Flushed and open-mouthed, he looked back at me. Underneath that hat were, I knew, two pleading eyes. "Can you . . . *help me,* Jenny?"

Merit sputtered a private little chuckle.

"Don't laugh, pumpkin," I whispered. "We must never let Fergus see us laughing at him."

Merit said she was sorry, then clammed up. I was afraid she was going to cry. We listed up the swaying dock, hand in hand. I still remember what her hand felt like when she was a baby.

At the end of the dock, I fastened the life vest on her and made sure she was planted in the dock's dead center. I told her to stay put. Lowell shuffled down to the helm of the canoe. I grasped the stern end.

"Ready, Fergie?" Lowell asked.

"You can do it," I said. "You're a big boy now, Fergus."

With a squeal, Fergus tumbled into the boat. Although he doesn't weigh much, and although Lowell and I were holding on tightly to the canoe, it bobbed, sent shock waves. The surrounding red pedal boats danced on the water.

One brown arm braced on the dock, Lowell leapt into the canoe like a cowboy. (*Are* there purple-shirted cowboys?) Merit, standing in her life preserver with a soldierlike rigidity, watched him. She looked as miserable as she does when I stuff her into a snowsuit. She then complained that her vest smelled like worms, which she was right about, then said, "If Daddy isn't wearing one, why should I?" A good question, I thought. I set an example and got myself into my own vest. I secured the canoe. She jumped in, slid onto the seat, and said, "Yeah, but *Daddy's* not wearing *his.*"

"Daddy isn't always right," I said.

Lowell's shirt was already off. He was paddling, bound for the hangar in the distance. Fergus polished his camera lens with his shirt. There were now sunglasses, in addition to the hat. A real photographer wears neither sunglasses nor hat, but that didn't matter. Despite what Fergus wants to think, his pictures won't ever be used for much of anything.

I unwound the wet ropes that held our canoe to the dock. I pushed off, reminded Merit again not to move, and paddled. The light shifted on the water. You know a painting's really bad if its usage of light can be described as "sun-dappled." Anything "sun-dappled" has *got* to go.

I should have been thinking a little less about the damage done by terrible artists and their sun-dapplage and a little more about steering the boat, because we ended up in the exact place where we shouldn't have been, bumping into the floating tire reef by the edge of the lake. The blimp hangar was precisely on the other side of the lake, and Lowell and Fergus were headed trimly toward it. There, in the impossible distance, was one tiny blimp. In front of me, on top of the reef of floating algae-coated tires, were Lesser Yellowlegs, pecking at hunks of bread.

That maternal instinct we've heard so much about told me to turn around.

A bird was at Merit's hand. She was petting it.

"Don't touch them!" I cried to Merit. "They're diseased."

Her other hand was propped up on one of the algae-coated tires.

"And don't touch those goddamnable tires!" I yelled. "They're even germier than the birds!"

I lunged at her, still clutching the oars. Merit stared at me challengingly for a few seconds before dropping that absolutely repellent bread.

"I *like* birds and tires," she said.

"Well," I said, "you're in the right town."

Lowell and Fergus were halfway to the blimp hangar now. Had they even noticed we weren't behind them? Lowell was rowing powerfully. Fergus still had his microscopic ant arm on the brim of his hat. The lake is man-made. Don't be fooled: There is no wind there.

"This boy Craig at camp said that we live in the rubbers capital of the world. He said that 'rubbers' aren't the same thing as 'rubber.' He's the one that goes, 'Guess what? Chicken butt.' "

"Craig certainly sounds as if he's going places," I said. With my red right oar, I pushed at the tires. I'm afraid several of the birds didn't like that and flew away. But how inelegantly they flapped. Couldn't they have done a *little* bit better?

"Can I paddle later?" Merit asked. She sounded as if she had gum in her mouth.

"I don't know about that. It's not as fun as it looks," I said. The pleasure in dipping the oar into the stagnant, filmy water was a delectable, childish one. The red oar came up, dripping a diaphanous green gauze. I dunked the paddle in the water. The skin fluttered and sunk back to its black planet.

"Nothing ever is," Merit said.

Merit sometimes comes up with these statements that sound as if she's been possessed by some world-weary ghost. I turned around. Yup, that was Merit, not Marlene Dietrich, seated on the opposite end of the canoe, wearing a pink tube top and an orange life vest, zealously smacking at a lump of purple gum.

I should have asked Lowell for a quick rowing lesson before we shoved off, because whatever direction I wanted to go, I somehow got pointed exactly the other way. The whole steering thing seemed counter-intuitive, but maybe that was just me.

"You should paint a painting of the birds," Merit said. I had gotten us pointed toward the blimp once again. She'd never talked about me as a painter before. Why *would* she?

"I'm not so good at animals," I said. I didn't tell her I can only paint one subject.

"Can *Dad* draw animals at least?"

"No," I said. "He can't, either."

Maybe I'd feel better about all this if Fergus would just *once* ask why I need to tag along on these photo excursions. It's the hardest part of the arrangement—worse, much worse, than lying to anyone in New York has ever been. Fergus thinks I've become a nobody. A mother, and merely that. An unperson.

Whenever we're about to embark on a new cycle, whenever we're about to have Fergus take the pictures, Lowell and I hold hands and say a little prayer together. Lowell makes us go into Fergus's bedroom to pray—we'll feel closer to him there, he says. We did that together this morning, kneeling on Fergus's red rug in his red bedroom, in the house where he's let us stay, rent-free, these last three years. We asked to be forgiven for what we were about to do. Lowell has said it's like saying a prayer before you eat the animal who has died so that you may live. Fergus has given us grandiloquent shelter, and he provides for us and cares for Merit, Lowell says. Lowell also says the arrangement *isn't* cruel to Fergus, because it's *so* important for him to believe he's part of the mystery.

I silently brood and rage when we're in Fergus's bedroom. But I'm so weak and cowardly that I haven't been able to say to Lowell, "It seems *you've* been spending a lot more time in Fergus's bedroom than *I* have." Next time, I'll say this. I'll say this next time. But oh how I'll hate him if he tells me everything.

Ours were the only two boats on the lake. Lowell and Fergus were almost at the hangar. I was paddling away like a Trojan. As we glided toward them, I could see three beached silver blimps, not one.

Lowell knew I wanted to do a cycle close to home after last winter's Berlin trip. (Not that we necessarily even *had* to go to Berlin to get those pictures, but Lowell, in his meticulousness, insisted, explaining that only *those steps* in *that subway station* would work.) I still don't understand the

Berlin series. Maybe nobody else does, either, because we've sold only two paintings from *Lowell's Concussion: Kicked Down, Falling, Thirty-two Fractures* so far. For the Berlin pictures, Lowell had this idea about dressing up in a business suit and throwing himself down a set of stairs. "The perfect statement about the defeated masculinity of the eighties," he said of the *Lowell's Concussion* cycle. For several frigid days in predawn Berlin, I watched through the blanching glare of the flashbulb as Lowell tumbled again and again down an unpopulated subway station's stairs. I watched, and Fergus took the pictures. Fergus never seemed to notice Lowell looked foam-filled and vast and not like Lowell at all. Lowell wasn't as undefended as the cycle's title suggests, for underneath the fatman-size suit, he'd layered a jockstrap, long underwear, shin pads, knee pads, elbow pads, a bulletproof vest, and two sweaters. Lowell did not have what we artists like to call "movement" in any of Fergus's pictures, and Fergus is crazier than anybody ever gives him credit for if he thinks any of the finished paintings came out of *those*.

For my real studies, I had Lowell fling himself down the back stairs at Fergus's house, unpadded, unprotected.

Lowell and Fergus had landed on the shore. They were looking back toward us, Lowell's hands on his hips, Fergus's hands on the brim of his hat. Did I forget to mention Lowell was wearing leather pants?

"What kind of fish are in this lake?" Merit asked.

I could have said, "Well, your lunch, for one," but I decided not to. I couldn't do that to Merit. "I don't think there are any fish in this lake," I said. "Pollution. Northeast Ohio."

"Is this the lake that burned?'

"That was a river," I said. "And no."

Merit started chomping her gum again.

The silver blimps glimmered like spaceships; Lowell and Fergus their alien, insectoid passengers.

Fergus took off his sandals. He pointed his camera at us. The camera spit out a picture. Fergus flapped it dry, peeked, flapped some more, peeked again.

Through his cupped hands, Lowell, on the shore, shouted, "Hallo there, darlings! Where have you been? We saw you had a bit of a run-in with some tires back there. Are you all right?"

My oar struck sand. Fergus took another picture of us, and I smiled for the camera.

"What do you think of your mother's captaining abilities, Merit?" Fergus hollered.

"I don't know. Okay, I guess." Merit said.

"What have you got there in your mouth, sweetheart?" Fergus asked. He was in the water now, ankle-deep. He stumbled, righted himself, stumbled again.

"*Gum,*" Merit said, chomping even more emphatically now.

"I was afraid you were still chewing your sandwich. *That* didn't look like something I wanted any part of." He clutched the stern of our boat and pulled us up to shore. I hoped his hat wasn't going to fall into the water. "If you get really close, you might see some of your fish sandwich's brothers and sisters in the water."

"*What?*" Merit asked.

"Fergus!" I shouted.

He lifted Merit out of the canoe. "Oh! I didn't mean it as a—"

Barefooted Lowell held out a hand to help me out. I squelched to the shore in my plastic shoes, holding Lowell. Fergus unfastened Merit's life preserver.

"Whole flotilla's out today, Jenny!" Lowell said, meaning the blimps. "I'm really wishing I'd brought another change of clothes with me now. I've decided I *hate* that shirt, so: it's topless for me today! Hands, please, if anyone's offended."

And for the next hour and fifteen minutes, Merit sat in the blimps' rotund shade, plucking at dandelions. I followed Lowell and Fergus, watching Lowell pose. Fergus made me hold each Polaroid after he'd taken it. Fergus: hopeless case. Lowell and I will have to return here tomorrow, and the day after that, and the day after that, for my drawings. I wonder if the boat-rental kid is going to pony up a canoe for us again without a driver's license.

We were gathered around Fergus's dining room table tonight, amid the day's Lowell Polaroids. Fergus's jeweler's glasses gave him an added professional seriousness. Merit was up on her bare knees on a chair whose seat Fergus had covered with a towel, and she was holding a naked, faceless doll to the strewn pictures. Although her doll had no eyes with which to see, she seemed to want it to look at the images of Lowell, too. It's a lie that girls play with dolls to mother them; girls play with dolls to *control* them. There is no mothering, only control. All of us, even the blind doll, were looking at Lowell's pictures, because Lowell must be looked at.

"This one's rather nice," Fergus said. That picture was, like the dozens of others, of Lowell in leather pants, no shirt, the blimps tethered, swollen in the background.

"Yeah, a superb picture of me," Lowell said. "Let's use that one. Thank you, Fergus."

I hoped that was a subtle flicker of amused disgust in Lowell's eyes. I hoped it was.

Two years ago, Fergus memorized *The Canterbury Tales;* after his Christmas Eve recitation of the "Wife of Bath's Tale" in the music room, Lowell said he'd come up with the perfect present for Fergus for Christmas.

Fergus knew the theme of the series, but he never knew we were intending to give all the paintings to *him*. His job was to locate the costumes (he looted the costume shops of every community theater in the area, but he did send each theater a big donation in return). None of the outfits fit very well ("God, actors are so bloody *short*," Lowell said as he tried on the Nun's Priest's habit); the crimson hooded robe was indeed the right idea for the Pardoner, but Fergus had chosen to overlook one small loophole: The Little Red Riding Hood for whom it had been made had obviously been seven years old, and sixty pounds. After the costumes had been tailored and dry-cleaned (Lowell insisted), Fergus took pictures of Lowell. Then Lowell and I disappeared into the studio for six months—Lowell posing for me, posing, just as he had for Fergus.

"I'm getting to be a pretty darn good photographer, don't you think?" Fergus asked.

"You are talented, Fergus," Lowell said, taking Fergus's hand. "You *are*."

Lowell's tone was the one he used to flatter me, back when he used to flatter me. So had he been lying to me, too?

Merit sat her naked doll on the table. Up to that eyeless face she held a Polaroid, as if it were a chalkboard or a TV.

"Daddy? I have a question."

"You and your questions! You're just like your gorgeous mother, with all the questions. What is it, darling?"

"Why wasn't there anyone at the lake today?"

"Because they all got laid off!" Fergus exclaimed victoriously. "Nobody here has jobs anymore!"

"Because it's a *workday,* darling," Lowell said. "And people with less eccentric lives than I, or your mother, or your uncle Fergus, were at *work* today."

"This boy Craig at camp says I'm rich. Am I rich?"

" 'Are *we* rich?' you should have asked," said Fergus. He peered at her through his jeweler's glasses. He couldn't see her, I knew, or anything else.

"Are *we* rich?" Merit asked.

Lowell let go of Fergus's hand and began rearranging the Polaroids on the table.

We're not rich, but we did sell a painting last year for fifteen thousand dollars. Castelli said it was an impressive price for "one so young." Unfortunately, that was the only painting we sold. He says all we need is one major collector, just one. Clearly, it's my art that people don't like. But Lowell thinks the problem is him.

"Why don't you let me do things with you?" Merit asked. "Why did you do things without me today?"

Lowell and Fergus were silent. I told Merit that I was sorry to hear her say that, because she and I had been together all afternoon.

"Merit, darling," Fergus said, too gaily, "do you remember the picture they ran in that magazine last year of your daddy?" There was a black smudge on the tip of his nose. Something about the nose smudge and the jeweler's glasses taken together somehow reminded me of an African tribal mask. "*Interview?* Remember? How could we be anything other than rich if we're in there?"

"Oh!" Lowell cried. "I *adore* that picture of me. You've never seen it, Merit?"

Merit grasped her gruesome doll by the torso and made the thing say no by twisting its head to the right, then left, right, then left. *Squeak squeak, squeak squeak.*

"Fergus," Lowell said, ignoring Merit. I want to kill him whenever he ignores her. "Run upstairs and get that magazine for Merit. It's in the Philippe Model hat box with all the other clippings in Jenny's and my room. I can't believe you've never seen it, darling. I do, I daresay, look *good* in that one."

Fergus plunked his jeweler's glasses down on the table. "I'll be back before you know it," he said. He kissed Merit, then me, then Lowell on the head, then was gone.

Lowell set two pictures in front of him, placing them side by side. He smiled. Maybe someday we'll discover these photographs in some forgotten album. Paintings are not sad—that's why I make them—but photographs are. It's the photographs you've got to watch out for. In the future, these photographs will lacerate us; I know it. With longing and with grief, we'll say to one another, "God, look at how young Lowell was." Fergus's pictures serve one purpose: to punish us.

"Look: Here's what I've been thinking about for the *Akron* series," Lowell said. "Dirigibles, as discussed, in the background, but what about, instead of *one* me naked in front of them, we do a whole *canvas* of *mes*!"

"A canny idea," I said. "We've got to sell these."

"Multiple mes! Who wouldn't buy them? We'll have to make me look especially attractive, though."

I told him that meant he'd have to have Fergus take *nude* pictures of him now. A dream come true, for both of them. When did I start walking in this daze of nullity?

"Alas. The only downside as far as I can see. Jenny, why do you think we aren't selling more?"

"And you're comparing us to whom? Monet? Manet? Toulouse-Lautrec?"

"Jenny?"

"Yes, Lowell?"

"They don't love me."

My love is no longer sufficient. It used to be enough. It used to be the only thing, didn't it, Lowell?

"Merit pumpkin," I said, "what happened to your doll baby's face?"

"*You* love me, yeah?" Lowell asked.

"Are you taking my name in vain again?" It was Fergus. He was back, breathing shallowly. He thinks everyone's always talking about him, when no one ever is. "I hurried as fast as I could to get back to my little family."

Yes, Lowell. I do love you. And, no, Fergus, we're not your family. You, Fergus, have no family.

Fergus took charge of the magazine, holding up the picture of Lowell for us all to feast on. The nose smudge was gone. He had looked in a mirror.

"I love you for bringing the magazine. I *love you* for it, Fergus," Lowell said, and glowered at me.

It would be preferable, actually, if Lowell and I were arguing about money again, as we were a couple months ago. I feel much less desolate when we're at least arguing.

"Oh Lowell," Fergus said. "Merit, come over here and look at your daddy. Don't you love him so much? And to think I hated him when we first met in London!"

Merit rolled out of the chair and trudged over to Fergus. He hoisted her onto his lap and stroked her hair.

The picture is a full-page black-and-white Scuvullo photograph of Lowell. He isn't wearing much. Within the piece, I was again reminded, were no images of our paintings. I hadn't looked at this magazine for a year, although apparently someone *else* had. The pages were torn, taped, coffee-ringed; was that a *jelly* stain? The piece had the inevitable magazinilicious headline: WHAT MAKES LOWELL HAVEN RUN? This is my memory of the piece:

LULU: You look great.

LOWELL: Thank you very kindly.

BUTTERFLY: You really do look great.

LOWELL: Why, I believe I'm blushing.

LULU: What's your secret?

LOWELL: I firmly believe one cannot be happy in life unless one has a focus, and indeed my work is the gravitational center of my life. I also take a fistful of tonsil-size salmon-oil pills every day, and I have been visiting an ashram a time or two a month. A most purifying experience, I've found. Each room at the ashram is so humble as to be almost comic: nothing more than an iron-framed bed and a good stiff mattress. Each morning begins at dawn with three hours of meditation. A breakfast of rice water and raw vegetables follows. I then read Gurdjieff until luncheon.

MARK: Can you tell us the name of the ashram?

LOWELL: I'm afraid I cannot.

MARK: Do you find being so good-looking a challenge? It must be, I mean, you know, a challenge. In some ways at least.

LOWELL: I must tell you I don't really think about my appearance. One cannot look at an image of oneself and think, This is my identity. Most good-looking people, and indeed most artists, are tremendously limited in human terms. I'm as yet undeveloped, a work in progress. But here's what I'm determined to be: limitless.

BUTTERFLY: Yeah, but who wants to look at pictures of ugly people?

LOWELL: "Man is undeveloped," says Gurdjieff.

BUTTERFLY: He didn't say "woman."

MARK: Can you spell that?

LOWELL: G-U-R-D-J-I-E-F-F.

LULU: How tall are you?

LOWELL: Six feet, four inches. A fine height to be, I should say.

BUTTERFLY: I think people should either be very tall or very small. I feel bad for the ones in the middle.

LULU: How much do you weigh?

LOWELL: One hundred and ninety pounds, sir.

LULU: Do you work out?

LOWELL: No, no, no, no! Can you imagine me in a health club, communing with that element? I'm a deadly snob, you know, one of the absolute worst. I read English and studied art at Oxford, where the very idea of a gym is terrifically unheard of.

LULU: Do you like to get presents?

LOWELL: I'm rather more a gift giver at heart, I should say.

MARK: That's interesting. What's the best present you ever gave? I'm curious.

LOWELL: Well, I suppose I could tell you about the objects themselves— a Fabergé clock whose maker's name was in Cyrillic, a Louis XIV *lit de repos,* a silver tea caddy owned by Madame de Pompadour, four Isadore Bonheur goat sculptures—but wouldn't that be so awfully hollow of me? I'm going to say the *Canterbury Tales* pictures I just painted for a dear, dear friend of mine.

MARK: Do I know about those? I don't think I've ever heard of them.

LOWELL: They will never be available to collectors. Never.

BUTTERFLY: I wish that people would give more presents.

MARK: How do you come up with your ideas?

BUTTERFLY: I don't get where ideas come from.

LOWELL: All I can say about that is that I've learned to trust my subconscious. If I think it, well, it's got to be right, hasn't it?

MARK: Would you say, then, that your work is charged with Freudian imagery?

LULU: What?

MARK: Freud. Freudian, uh, imagery.

BUTTERFLY: Wait. I think I met him once. His shirt wasn't laundered well and he was wearing a red tie.

LULU: Marcus Aquinas: Your questions are boring. Lowell: What's your favorite part of sex?

LOWELL: I'd have to go with the climax. Not an inventive answer, but there it is.

BUTTERFLY: Men always say that.

LULU: Is it true you and Aloysius Canker were fuck buddies?

LOWELL: Oh my dear. I heard he'd been going around spreading all sorts of malevolent tittle-tattle. At any rate, this is a personal matter, and I'm certainly not going to discuss it with the likes of you. What I will say is that I do hope he's healthier, mentally healthier, than when I knew him. Poor little thing. I hope to God he's been to a professional.

LULU: Are you married?

LOWELL: After a fashion.

MARK: You have a baby.

LOWELL: Now I must tell you I'm finding this delving into my personal affairs tremendously vexing. All I'll say about that is this: Each relationship has its own contract, and what's suited me in my relationships may not be entirely apposite for someone else. Remember: "Judge not, lest you be judged."

BUTTERFLY: "There are no facts, only interpretations." I've noticed that everyone's getting married lately. I hate that.

LULU: That's because they're conformists. Are you a conformist?

LOWELL: Dear me, no!

BUTTERFLY: I just can't see you changing some baby's diapers. Are you sure it's yours?

LOWELL: Quite sure.

LULU: A few years ago, when everyone started figuring out who you were, everyone was like, "Who's that cute boy with the baby?"

MARK: The baby did add to your mystique.

BUTTERFLY: Living in Acorn or whatever adds to your mystique, too. I heard that you live in a haunted mansion with bats and vampires and that you sleep in a coffin.

LOWELL: That's not too far off.

MARK: Let's talk about artists. Do you think there are too many?

LOWELL: Too many bad ones and not enough good ones. But then again, I'm fascistic regarding the standards I hold artists up to. Happily for the world, though, I do impose the same unyielding standards on myself.

MARK: Don't you find it sad, the way our culture doesn't support artists? I was in Ireland recently, and it's so different. Artists are respected there. They don't even have to pay taxes. What do you think about the state of the artist in America?

LOWELL: Don't think I care for that question. Pretend, in as far as you're able, that you're not a graduate student. Scale back; rephrase. Return to me when you're ready.

MARK: Okay. What's your opinion about how artists are treated in America?

LOWELL: I wouldn't know. Let's find an American and ask him. American artists are for shit. Richter's the only contemporary artist worth my time, and he's not American.

LULU: Do you like rich people?

LOWELL: [checking his watch]: Of course. Wouldn't exist without them, would I? Every artist needs a patron. And don't think for a moment it's not always been this way. It has.

LULU: Do you think that artists should be more famous?

BUTTERFLY: When I saw Andy on *Merv Griffin,* I knew it was the beginning of something, or the end.

MARK: Do they do a preinterview for that show? I've always wondered.

BUTTERFLY: How the fuck would I know?

MARK: I wasn't asking you.

LULU: Well, who were you asking?

MARK: Never mind.

LULU: Sorry. Do you think that artists should be more famous?

LOWELL: No one is ever owed anything.

LULU: Why do you live in Ohio?

BUTTERFLY: You like it because you feel safe there, I bet. I mean spiritually safe, emotionally safe.

LOWELL: I'll submit this to you: New York, or L.A., or wherever it is you're from, is much more provincial, has much more a small-town mentality than Akron.

LULU: Why do you only paint pictures of yourself?

LOWELL: My only project is anyone's project: myself.

MARK: So much of your work has an elegiac quality to it. Why is that?

LOWELL: I wasn't aware of that. I hate to think you've noticed something I haven't. I suppose you could say I'm death-obsessed.

LULU: Who's not?

BUTTERFLY: I'm not.

LULU: Who are you in love with?

LOWELL: Every artist must have a sort of romance with himself, mustn't he?

LULU: What's your personal approach to beauty?

LOWELL: An enormous laugh.

LULU: What is "style"?

LOWELL: Self-belief.

LULU: What do you think are the two greatest inventions?

LOWELL: Erasable pens and Kleenex.

MARK: Do you find it easy to make a living as an artist?

LOWELL: I've not made any big money as of yet, but I'm confident in my abilities, and confident in the future.

MARK: What do you anticipate for yourself in the future?

LOWELL: That it will rise to meet me.

BUTTERFLY: I think you just like being looked at. I never knew that was a talent before. Look at me, in that case! I'm talented, too!

LULU: Would you rather be blind or deaf?

LOWELL: Neither. Although there can be no art without the eye.

MARK: Did you always want to be an artist?

LOWELL: I've always been a peculiar little hooligan. But if your question is "Did I wear a fur boa as a child and prance around with a painter's palette?" the answer is a thunderous no. While I wasn't an artist as a child, I did possess that essential quality for an artist: It wasn't enough for the little girl down the lane to trumpet me. I needed everyone.

LULU: What do you hate?

LOWELL: Tiny, pretentious minds.

MARK: Such as?

LOWELL: Spit and you'll hit one.

LULU: How would you feel if everyone suddenly decided they didn't like you anymore? Like the whole world, I mean.

LOWELL: Why don't you ask me that question again in twenty years? Are we done?

MARK: But I have this whole legal pad of questions.

LOWELL: Thank you for your time. Lovely to meet you all.

BUTTERFLY: Bye!

LULU: Toodles!

BUTTERFLY: There he goes.

LULU: I think this went really well.

MARK: Did it? Are you sure? Do you think Andy will be mad?

"Doesn't Daddy look phenomenal in this picture, Merit?" asked Fergus.

Merit was now on Fergus's lap. He was braiding her hair, and she was braiding her doll's.

"Constanza wants to know what he's wearing in that picture," she said. Constanza is the name of Merit's faceless doll. The magazine was unfolded on the table in front of them.

"It's a loincloth, sweetheart," Fergus said. "Can you say, *loincloth?*"

"Fergus!" I said, "She's not *two.*"

"They grow up so fast, don't they?" Fergus asked.

"I think it's one of the best pictures ever taken of me, don't you?"

"Yes, I think so, Lowell," Fergus said. "I really do think so, and you can imagine how much it hurts me to say this . . . as a photographer myself."

Lowell tousled Fergus's hair. Fergus giggled and kissed Merit's cheek, then the other one. "You look so heroic in that picture, Lowell," he said. "Is this the interview where you say that wonderful thing about how the world is looking for heroes?" Fergus contorted himself and kissed Merit's nose.

"I'm not sure," Lowell said. "I've never read the piece. I've merely admired the picture."

Lowell was lying. He'd read the piece about eight hundred times.

"Merit," I said. "You got a lot of sun today."

Fergus squeezed Merit and said, "Look at you! Your shoulders are the same color as your shirt. Such delicious, kissable-issable shoulders!"

Fergus kissed Merit's bare, tender shoulders.

"A lovely pink, at any rate," Lowell said.

Fergus, his chin on top of Merit's head, clutching her, rocking her, said, "There are only so many honest moments in life, and this is one of them."

"It is," Lowell said. "It is."

"Let's never forget this," Fergus said.

"Let's never," Lowell said. "Let's absolutely never do."

———

I fell asleep last night with a headache. In my dreams, I was haunted with visions of Lowell and Fergus bobbing together on a carousel horse. I don't think I've ever actually seen Fergus on Lowell's lap, but, while asleep, the ache was familiar. I've been cast out of their nascent intimacy. And I'm now finding that I'm doing something I've never done: I'm comparing myself to them. I've never compared myself to other people before. Sometimes I feel that I don't even measure up to them. Not to *Lowell* and *Fergus,* but to Lowell's *fame,* and Fergus's *money.* How absurd! What is happening to my mind? I used to have a mind. I must tell myself that it's best to work on the outside. It's best to work snubbed, in anonymity.

Merit and Fergus ride the carousel together every day—she sits on his lap—but last night, Merit was nowhere in my dreams.

27

Wyatt, in times of crisis, did one of two things: He watched either *Caddyshack* or *Blazing Saddles.* This afternoon (Saturday, *party day*), he lay on the couch in the living room and watched *both* DVDs, in succession. Wyatt was a guy who rarely ever even turned on the TV, except for that Louis Rukeyser show when it used to be on on Fridays, or sometimes if he had a tape from a conference he'd just returned from in maybe Boston. Merit had never seen Wyatt lie on the couch for four hours straight on a Saturday. Late-summer Saturdays were, for Wyatt, scheduled around yard work.

At noon, during the "More beans, Mr. Taggert?" scene (a classic in Wyatt's mind, she knew, but not so much in Merit's—flatulence humor wasn't really her bag), Merit found him on the couch. She asked him what he was doing. He said he couldn't work outside today because it looked like rain. Even before Merit had bought his yellow Gorton's Fisherman slicker, he'd never used the weather as an excuse to avoid outdoor chores. Summers in northeast Ohio were short, and you had to get out there and use them while you could. They were sad, summers here. Merit had always preferred winters, when you had the future to look forward to. In the summer, you had only the future to dread.

At 3:00, it still wasn't raining, although the sky did have an ominous vibe. Wyatt was still on the couch. Merit was worried about him.

"Just so you know, I don't want to go, either," she said.

Merit couldn't tell if he was clutching the remote control, or if his hand had just gotten frozen that way.

The other times (Merit knew of) when he'd watched either *Caddyshack* or *Blazing Saddles*: after their rabbit Basil died; after he got his wisdom teeth taken out (the pinkish blood/spit stains on the couch's sea foam–hued silk accent pillows serving as a constant reminder of that particularly dismal weekend); once at the end of the week Caroline hadn't called from camp (maddeningly, her cell phone had just gone straight to voice mail each time Merit and Wyatt had called her . . . something they'd actually sort of promised not to do while she was away); and once after he'd had lunch with Shelley.

"I know this isn't something I say much," Wyatt said, "but I'm going to need to drink a lot tonight."

Both summers when he was getting his master's, Wyatt worked as Chadwick the Chipmunk at Cedar Point. Merit was unclear whether Chadwick was famous once you got outside of the northeast Ohio region, but she thought he probably had to be. He seemed pretty big.

Ever since Merit was a little tiny northeast Ohioan, the Chadwick character had been burned into her cerebrum. But had she never before seen Chadwick, she might not even have thought he was a chipmunk. She might have thought he was supposed to be someone in blackface. The head's cartoon eyes were arches, black pupils rightward, like a time-frozen Kit Kat clock. The weird below-the-nose region was yellow. Chadwick grinned horribly, baring two buckteeth. A line of black stuffed-animal fur ran in a stripe down the back of the head and stuck up like a Mohawk.

The Chadwick costume was stored in a Mayflower Transit box in the basement. Despite Merit's many requests, Wyatt had never once tried the thing on for her. "How much more humiliation can you expect one little man to take?" he once asked her. It was a poignant question from a poignant person. But it was built on an untrue premise. Wyatt was not, nor had ever been, "little." Not by any stretch. Merit had often wondered, Was there ever, in Cedar Point's history, another six-foot-five-inch Chadwick? And that was without the head.

But because he loved Merit, Wyatt was going to the party as Chadwick's head. She'd asked him to wear it tonight. He'd relented, finally, after five years.

Caroline was Caligula. Merit, because she couldn't find the feather mask and hadn't gotten it together to prepare for a plan B, was nothing.

Wyatt told Merit she'd need to be the evening's designated driver. This was okay by Merit, because she sort of wanted Lowell to see her Jaguar, marred now with its animal-rights bumper sticker, wanted him to saunter outside in his faggoty king costume and his crown and wand or whatever and witness for himself that she still loved this shitty piece of machinery enough to allow it to continue to exist. Although she surely knew *Lowell* certainly wouldn't be paying much attention to her *car* tonight (or to her?). Such a fantasy was, she knew, Haven-like in the extreme.

At 7:00 p.m., Merit ran around the house, making sure the coffeepot was turned off; that no candles were lit (which was stupid, because they didn't even have candles); that the sliding glass door was locked; that no towels or otherwise flammable cloths were hanging over any lamp shades; that the computer was shut down; that the door to the frog/rabbit bedroom was shut (she hadn't done the frog/cat introduction yet); that the animals were fed, petted (not the frogs), and each provided with an extra bowl of water and a bag of dry food (again, not the frogs), just in case. Because what if Merit and Wyatt and Caroline got home late? Or what if they never even got home at all? Merit remembered again that she didn't even have a *will.* She had to get one.

Leaving the animals always made her sad. Whenever she left the house, she said good-bye to them as if it were the last time she'd ever see them. Maybe she wasn't as optimistic an individual as she had previously thought.

Wyatt and Caroline were already waiting for her in the car. The garage door was up. It was raining. Merit was taking the *On ne peut pas vivre seul* aquarium ornament with her tonight. She wanted to show it to Lowell. Or maybe she didn't. She didn't know. She climbed in the driver's seat (her hair tangled, as always, in the shoulder harness), handed Caroline her bag and the aquarium ornament, and asked her to please put them on the back floor.

Caroline stretched to see herself in the rearview mirror. Merit, who knew her toga-wrapping job left more than a little something to be desired, wondered how long the sheet would actually stay up. An hour ago, Caroline had stood in front of the full-length mirror in her room, and Merit had knelt beside her, twisting the white king-size bedsheet (from their bed, not Caroline's) around her. Merit had never been particularly good at girl things, like makeup, or hair, or scarves, and making a toga out of a sheet was like tying one really big hard-to-tie scarf. Caroline had examined Merit's work in her bedroom mirror and said, a bit cruelly, Merit thought, that she was going to be really embarrassed if her "spaghetti straps" showed. Merit had never heard Caroline say "spaghetti straps" before, and she found such evidence of an early sexualization of self upsetting. She needed to find out in which horrible magazine Caroline had read "spaghetti straps," then banish that magazine from her household.

"Sweetie, I can't see to back up," Merit said.

Caroline apologized and slid over behind Wyatt.

Wyatt called this kind of spitty, misty rain a "wet rain." He would refuse to acknowledge "wet rain" was redundant. It was more of a springtime rain than a late-summer rain: the kind of rain you couldn't dry off from and that made you really feel like an Akronite right down to the core.

Merit beeped the new garage-door-closing code. Jenny had once told Merit she considered it "in questionable taste" to live on a cul-de-sac, but Merit, although she hadn't chosen the house, or the street, really liked where they lived.

"Does Lowell have any red paint?" Caroline asked.

"Hmm," Wyatt said. "I don't *think* so, honey. Why don't we ask Merit. Merit, does Lowell have any *paint* lying around his house?"

"Why don't we stop at a store and get you some Tabasco sauce, Caroline?" Merit asked.

Caroline, whom Merit glimpsed in the mirror, was attempting to wind the sheet around her spaghetti strap. Merit felt bad they hadn't had any Tabasco sauce or Red Hot (or ketchup even; they were a low-carb household) back at the house, especially since earlier in the week she had promised Caroline they did. A Caligula toga needed a convincing blood-substitute splatter.

"You're going to *stop?*" Wyatt asked. Stopping meant: deviation from the plan.

"*Wyatt,*" Merit said. "If we're early, you're going to *have* to talk to Lowell and Fergus."

"Oh," Wyatt said. "Let's definitely stop at the BP, then."

"But Lowell still has to have paint, doesn't he? That would be so sad if he threw away all his paint," Caroline said. "I think it would be better to use real paint than some kind of food, because it would look more real that way."

For a second, Merit hoped there would be karaoke at the party.

The windshield wipers were moving together, a dance in which the partners would never meet. Merit turned the speed up, just so she could watch them. They were frantic now. From the time she was small, this was what a pair of windshield wipers were to her: a man and a woman, falling, rising, falling, rising, fleeing, returning, fleeing again, forever apart.

God, she was so corny.

She and Caroline were inside the BP store. The rain on the roof sounded like the background noise on a hundred-year-old recording of Caruso that Merit had heard on the radio once. Merit thought: red nail polish? That would be a vivider red than Red Hot, wouldn't it? She herself wasn't a nail polish-wearer, so had none at home. She raised the possibility of nail polish to Caroline, who seemed to think it was a good idea. The BP store was pretty extensive, and it actually had a little makeup section.

Red nail polish, a bottle of water, and three packs of gum: purchased. (Caroline offered to pay for everything, but Merit wouldn't let her.) Merit prepared the umbrella but waited, for obvious superstitious reasons, until they were outside to open it. (She still, like a child, held her breath whenever she drove past a graveyard, too.) She drew Caroline close and sprinted to the car. She had already opened the back door for Caroline, squeaked into the front seat, shaken out her umbrella, and slammed the door, when she realized Wyatt wasn't there.

He did this sometimes in parking lots, which embarrassed Merit horribly.

He was crouched down at a car by a gas pump; a black umbrella mushroomed over him.

"Is he looking at the tires again?" Caroline asked.

Merit couldn't tell if he was making notations in his Tire Notebook, in which he kept a statistical sampling of the tire brands of random cars in random parking lots. There were Tire Notebooks in the glove compartments of both cars.

Merit asked Caroline if she thought her dad was stalling.

"Definitely. Hey, what does *officious* mean?"

Merit lied and said she wasn't really sure. She asked Caroline why she wanted to know.

"Because that's how he described Lowell and Fergus when we were waiting for you in the garage: 'officious twits.' "

Wyatt *was* writing in a notebook. The rain on the windshield had expunged all evidence of the wipers' previous hard work; there wasn't even the ghost of erasure left anymore.

The last time it had rained, Merit had not yet become an adulterer. (The other two guys didn't matter.) An *adulterer.* Merit tried the word on for size. What did it feel like? Not much. The world didn't look all that much different now than it had before. Funny, really.

"Well that wasn't very nice," Merit said.

28

A good host is like a general. And when things don't go the way a general would prefer, does he *retreat*? Or does he dust off the old contingency plan? Three cheers and a cherry for those who answered the latter; you'll be mailed a certificate suitable for framing. The front lawn's farkle board, which had taken me an entire day to paint, had been washed away by this evening's shower. I had told my first-rate friend Andrei to take a little trip out for some last-minute masking tape (seventy-five rolls at Odd Lots). And so, with a retractable tape measure and a slide rule, I measured out a human farkle board on the music room's floor. Indeed, it *would* make my beautiful floor slightly less pristine, but why *couldn't* we dance and play charades and dash like children under the billowing parachute with the tape on the floor? It was *my* house, and *my* party.

Andrei had also been sent out to withdraw ten thousand dollars for me, in hundreds, and to purchase a parachute.

My income (in stocks and landholdings) last year was $820,000.

Not a fortune by any means (barely middle-class in New York), but it's certainly more than anyone else we know here has. Five years ago, Lowell sold his *Akron* cycle to Mephistopheles (some refer to him as "Mr. Saatchi") for one million dollars. Prior to that, his maximum annual income had been $100,000. That was back in '86, when Panza bought in bulk. Lowell spent it all in four months. His third-most lucrative year: $35,000.

So now you know. (You've been curious, but so polite about asking. And, yes, my financial advisers really are excellent.)

Even before the makeshift farkle board, I'd had a busy, busy day. It seemed, suddenly, sad to me I'd kept all my work hidden, rotting down there where no daylight has ever been. Life is all a matter of confidence, isn't it? From the basement I retrieved all my photo albums (or "portfolios"). Eighteen trips, two to four albums per trip. In the ruckus of the great hall, I sat on the floor and stripped off the pictures one by one, arranged each picture in a stack, and arranged each stack on the floor. I had to scream at the pepped-up workers a couple of times to slow down; their airstreams were making my pictures blow around all over the place.

When Andrei had returned with the tape, I'd asked him to help me make about two thousand little one-inch masking-tape loops.

"But I will not have the time to find the parachute."

"This is more important," I said.

"We are doing tape for the big checkerboard?"

"Farkle," I said, although I knew farkle was a dice game (farkle is what I want it to be). "We'll do that later. This is for something else. Oh, and Andrei?"

"Yes, Fergus?"

"Don't you *dare* think about changing from that vest tonight."

If he only knew how I looked out for him.

Andrei and I were in the dining room, standing barefoot on my chairs, slapping my photographs over the *Canterbury Tales* portraits. We had already covered Lowell's paintings in the foyer, main staircase, great hall, music room, Chinese sitting room, knight's hall, and breakfast room. We'd been at this for three hours already. Andrei was taping over the Pardoner; I got the Wife of Bath.

"Remember," I said. "Every millimeter must be covered." I explained we needed to fit seventeen photographs on each picture. Looped around each finger of both hands were five to seven tape rings. (Look at me! I'm married! Multiple times!)

"Yes, Fergus."

"I'm counting on you, Andrei."

I'd found the Wife's costume, a woman's red velour robe, at a community theater in Defiance, Ohio. The keeper of the costumes told me the robe had been used in a recent production of *Long Day's Journey into Night*. When I told the woman I certainly didn't recall tragic old Mary

Tyrone in a bathrobe, not in any production I'd ever seen, she said, "It wasn't *Mary's* costume."

"Fergus?" Andrei said. "This will damage the paint."

"No, it won't," I said deviously.

Lowell, back when he painted, painted some of the truly ghastliest animals ever to have been put on canvas. The Wife's white horse looks more like a very large rabbit than anything. I had Lowell pose for the pictures on a genuine horsehair rocking horse (from Finland) I'd bought for Merit, so I suppose I hadn't been giving him very much to work with.

"Why are we doing this?" Andrei asked.

"Have you ever heard of throwing a black sheet over all the mirrors in the house when someone dies? Think of it like that," I said.

"Who has died, Fergus? Who is dying?"

The pictures he had taped to the Pardoner weren't very even. I tried not to mind.

"No one," I said. "No one at all."

"Why are we doing this?"

He had asked this question before.

"I'm the artist, Andrei," I said. "I'm the artist, and artists do terribly strange things."

A girl with a choppy blond lesbianic hairdo flurried around the table, arranging foil-covered platters of that delicious pepper-fried calamari. I wondered if she could really manage one hundred plates all by herself. As I had just recently learned, Windsor Castle Caterers has a scandalously tiny staff. I hoped she wouldn't be mad when I told her I had a costume for her to wear.

Some of Lowell as the Pardoner's golden hair was discernible through the spaces in the photographs. Also evident was one of the blood-colored jewels of his staff.

"Fergus?" Andrei asked, "Where is Lowell? Does he know about this? We are damaging the paint."

"Andrei," I said, "don't worry about Lowell. He takes an eon to get ready for a party. Why don't you take a few truckloads of tape and go lay down the farkle board?"

He said it was no problem.

"I already traced it in!" I shouted. "Just follow the chalk!"

My cell phone vibrated in my pocket. I knew who it was: Only one VIP had this number today. As my hands were otherwise occupied, I asked the new caterer girl if she would mind liberating the phone from my pocket. She fished it out. The tape on my fingertips made it such that I had to hold the phone in an unnatural way, as if waiting for my nails to dry. I had never heard his voice before, and it was more masculine, and more midwestern, than I'd wanted it to be.

"Right, then," I said, sounding like Lowell. "I'll be out to meet you at the portcullis in three minutes."

The VIP had arrived. The party had, unofficially, started.

The girl was jabbing colored toothpicks into the calamari. I waved at her, my tape flapping. I would have snapped my fingers if I could have. "Girl!" I said. "You there! You don't have any glue, do you?"

She thought about it for a second, tapping an aquamarine toothpick on my tabletop four times, and said she didn't. I'm too nearsighted to have seen this, but I imagined the tip of the toothpick was now frayed, no good to anybody.

I told her to go into the kitchen and ask Mrs. Valdez if she had any glue. "The more industrial the strength, the better!" I said.

I'd talk to Mr. Dormer for a bit, get him set up with a J&B, then come back and finish my work.

I have three boxes of letters from Bradley W. Dormer in my great room. *Lowell,* as I'll tell Dormer, isn't the story anyway. For the real story, one must look elsewhere.

The person greeting me at my front door was *not* the person I had expected, not after all these centuries' worth of correspondence. Firstly, he was wearing surgical scrubs. I immediately, unfortunately for him, understood this was not a one-night outfit. He looked as if he had slept in his rental car. A white Taurus, I saw now, as predicted.

"Brad Dormer. What's shaking?"

"Fergus Goodwyn," I said, taking his huge manhand, shaking it warmly. "A *surgeon!* Clever costume."

"Ex-wife's," he said. "Radiologist. She took everything else."

Someone had once told me that of all doctors, radiologists have the least education, work the fewest hours, and make the least money. I didn't bring this up.

He stepped into the foyer. It was still raining, softly. The sound of rain, the smell of it, makes you feel fantastically loved, as long as you're inside looking out. I shut the door. His height, I must admit, gave me a certain power over me. Two hundred twenty five pounds, easily. Most long-chinned men I've met choose to succumb to some kind of facial hair, which this chap most certainly did. He seemed a little out of it. Was he overwhelmed that his half-decade-long dream had finally come true? That he was, finally, meeting me, me, *me*?

"So you found our little cottage without too much bother?"

"I feel like I need to sit down," he said, then staggered a few feet and steadied himself against the stack of mail-order boxes. My Cartier told me I had two hours left to figure out where to hide them.

I tugged him by his scrubs, to the bench in the foyer. It was underneath the now-obscured Lowell as King Arthur. He slumped down on the bench without even saying anything about my photographs. Didn't bode well for his reportorial skills, I felt.

"I'm a mess whenever I come back. Last time I was here, the Indians fucked the dog during the '97 World Series."

"Water?" I asked, scraping a glue scab from my index finger.

"Something more alcoholic," he said. He wiped his prominent brow. He was handsome, but in a coarse way. He didn't look much like me at all. "Whiskey?"

Ah *ha*. Just as predicted.

En route to the kitchen, we walked through the dining room. He didn't say anything about my pictures there, either.

In the kitchen, I found us a safe place apart from the clamor. I prepared Mr. Dormer a straight-up highball of room-temperature J&B. (I'd spent seven thousand dollars on top-shelf liquor for tonight.) With a large tattooed right hand, he seized the highball. He drank. I waited about thirty seconds for the alcohol to get to work, but he still seemed as discombobulated as before. I'm afraid I had to hard-ass it; I couldn't wait any longer. I'd already waited for five years.

"So," I said. "Where *do* we start?"

I noted he'd brought no bag with him, no bag that could have contained a microcassette recorder or a reporter's notebook. I hoped I shouldn't take that as a sign he'd arrived here this evening with a prefab agenda.

"Do you want me to get you a notepad, or possibly a microcassette recorder?" I asked.

"Nah," he said. "I have a pen somewhere. Whenever I need to remember something, I just run to the john and write it down on some toilet paper."

"Whatever works," I said. "You're the professional here! I love your tattoo, by the way. The interlocking *C*'s are by no means to be confused with the Chanel logo, I suppose."

I heard myself trying to get him to like me. I knew what I was up to.

"Central State," he said.

"Ah, Wilberforce, Ohio!" I said (Central State is located in Wilberforce). "I know it well." (Lying again.)

He had finished his J&B. I hoped he was tipsy enough to get down to business.

"I need to clear some things up with you, Bradley. I'll need to get photo approval, of course. My unique proportions make me a challenging photo subject, to say the least."

"Hey man, no offense. But no profile subject at my magazine ever gets photo approval."

"Had to ask!" I said. One must know which fits to pitch, and this wasn't one. (He'd called me a "profile subject"! But did he mean it, or was he just playing along?)

"And you'll fax the piece to me once you've written it," I said. "Naturally. For veracity's sake."

"Do I look like the world's biggest sleazebag? You're kind of hurting my feelings here," Dormer said. "Not standard operating procedure, man. Can I use your john?"

"Why don't I get you a notebook and a pen instead," I helpfully suggested. "I need to tell you a bit about the person from whom Lowell gets all his spectacular ideas."

His brown eyes widened avariciously. He suddenly didn't seem so drunk anymore. He was thinking, *My story.*

"I *have* heard some pretty crazy rumors about that," he said.

"Can I say something?" I asked. "And I don't want you to take this the wrong way. But your letters make you seem much more effete."

"Blame J school," he replied.

"Let's pick this up later," I said. "I've got to finish my work right now, I'm afraid."

Always leave them wanting more.

"Do you mind if I smoke?" he asked.

"Actually . . ." I said. I knew I'd pay for this. "*Do.* But limit it to one pack, if you please."

As I said: *Always* leave them wanting more.

Examining myself in the full-length mirror in my great room, I decided I'd never looked better. It took only five minutes to bobby-pin my crown into an unslidable position. (I'd allotted fifteen to twenty.) My hooded, one-button, reversible black velvet cape would help me make quite the drama-filled entrance. The roses had been delivered. But: could one carry a single red rose, a scepter, *and* a thermosed Kahlua and skim? This question had not yet been answered. The cape did a good job hiding the bulges in my trouser pockets—ten thousand dollars in hundreds, divvied up in four pockets. I was risking it by carrying no Kleenex. I had glued all the pictures on top of the remaining public-space Lowell paintings. I'd checked in on Andrei; the farkle board was complete. The calamari was being warmed, and Mrs. Valdez and her work-for-hires had the meal well on its way. The harpist had arrived. He'd been instructed to play only catchy Turlough Carolan tunes. I was tremendously excited about seeing both Merit and Preston Lympany; Jenny and Yellow Hair would test my powers of clemency. I hoped no one would be too disappointed the rain would prevent any nighttime jousting, sword fighting, and/or archery.

I was alive with purpose.

Tonight, I would tell Lowell to leave.

Tonight, I was, finally, everything to Lowell's nothing.

Host Psychology 101: The host is always kindest to the first guests to arrive. They are the ones who guarantee your party won't be a total flop. Even if no one else shows, they at least have. As the host, you think the first arrivals care about you the most; the late arrivals, you always fear, have either been dragged to the party by their spouses or have attended some better party first and have come to yours only because they feel they have to.

Andrei, bare-faced and in his vest, was standing by the door. The clipboard was ready.

The lesbian-hair-cutted caterer circulated with calamari tray number one. An adorable boy theater student from Kent State made the rounds with a silver tray containing the following aqua vitae options: wassail, mead, ale, and milk. For our big-time boozers, I'd had two full bars set up in the great hall, and one in the music room.

I'd made the boy workers wear breeches, a shirt, a jerkin, and a hat; the girls a long skirt, a bodice, and a snood.

The first guest was a Wagnerian woman wearing a black wrap. She had either dyed her hair black or was wearing a wig. Upon seeing me, she kissed my right cheek, then my left cheek, then my right one again. Then she gave me a full-on lip kiss. Her eyes were kohl-rimmed, and she was wearing a thick gold choker (a little too sexy for me to handle at that moment). I told her she looked terrific, and she said, "I think I know this." She complained about the rain, then said, "Vhat a day, Fergus, to have a *party.*" I suspected I'd be hearing a lot of comments along those lines tonight. We chitchatted, me with one eye on the entranceway and the other on Bradley W. Dormer, Contributing Writer. He seemed to be getting very chummy indeed with the lady caterer. When the tray-bearing boy passed, I grabbed Wagner a mead and instructed her to drink it. She did, but she coughed exaggeratedly and proclaimed it "Ach, too sveet." I offered to get her something at the bar, but she said, "So unloving of you, Fergus, to leave an old lady all alone." I tapped my rose on the top of her head and told her we'd go together, in that case. My guess was that she was Elizabeth Taylor as Cleopatra. The fake tracheotomy scar was the giveaway. (It *was* fake, wasn't it?)

Dormer had gotten himself over to the bar, where I caught him placing an order for a Drambuie.

"For Claudia," he said when he saw me.

I was withholding certain information from Dormer until Lowell was around to hear it.

Dormer clutched a Drambuie in one hand and a refilled J&B in the other. The glasses the bartenders had insisted on bringing were really not of the greatest quality. Dormer, smiling bashfully, nodded at Wagner. Wagner couldn't be bothered; she was admiring the *On ne peut pas vivre seul* banners—whose coat of arms I myself had designed—ringing the great hall. (I take them out only for very special occasions.) Although I'd been the one who'd invited her, I didn't know Wagner's name. It was now time to introduce them. Good luck to me!

"Darling! Do you know my good friend Brad Dormer? Brad here is a distinguished journalist. The most distinguished journalist, in fact, of my acquaintance. He's a powerful man, so beware. The most powerful person here tonight, and don't forget it."

Dormer seemed satisfied by my introduction. He rested the Drambuie on the bar and they shook hands. They exchanged pleasantries, but I still didn't get Wagner's name. I wasn't listening, because guess who had emerged? Drisana-Nari.

Remember her?

Lowell: nowhere to be seen.

I hoped the Schiaparelli–pink track suit wasn't Drisana-Nari's idea of a costume. Her feet were bare, her toenails painted the same pink as the track suit.

She waved at me just as if she were an old pal, then picked up the pace. She clearly had something to discuss with me. Everybody wants a piece of the host. For this, he must be prepared.

Drisana-Nari tugged on my cape like a little kid. "I need to talk to you about something," she said. She's smaller even than I am. A power dynamic I'm quite unused to.

Dormer had lost all interest in Frau Wagner, and he greedily leaned into us, Drisana-Nari and me. He was practically drooling. He was thinking, *Scoop?* I know how these reptilian brain stems operate.

"Do you mind if I do a performance art thingy tonight?" she asked, still whispering, as if this were some hot gossip. Dormer could have been a little more discreet about how disappointed he was this conversation would reveal nothing he could use. He took a gulp of J&B and turned his attention elsewhere, surveying the room for, presumably, the caterer.

"Well," I said. "We do have some activities planned. We've got mimes, fire-eaters, jesters, jugglers, a Name the Dragon Contest, a Human Farkle Match, a Parachute Dance. . . . But I don't see why we can't add another attraction."

I realized I didn't actually know if Andrei had found a parachute anywhere.

"Cool. I just didn't want to mess with your vibe. I haven't seen Lowell since the day before yesterday, so I didn't know who else to ask."

There are two kinds of parties here: the kind where Lowell withdraws from the guest of honor beforehand, and the kind where he doesn't. When he withdraws, the guest of honor will, the next day, or the day after, be gone.

"Have *you* seen him?" she asked.

I shook my head, trying to look very soulful and distraught. I had come so far, emotionally speaking. For the first time, I didn't care.

"So *do* entertain us tonight, Drisana-Nari," I said, waving my scepter over her, blessing her. A benediction from a most peculiar king. "Life is shorter than we think."

"Cool!" she said jollily. She was off.

Guests were arriving. Logjammed by the bar was not where the courteous host should be found dallying. Dormer sidled over to me. The interlocking-*C* tattoo on his right hand: it was covering something.

"Hey, Fergus," he said. "Do you mind if I just kind of blanket you for the night?"

" 'Blanket' me?" I asked. "As sort of my . . . *sidekick?*" Funny idea. "How do I explain you to the guests?"

"Do you really think they'll ask? I'm invisible. All us magazine hacks are. It's *you* they're really here to see."

"Good point," I said. I knew from his letters how malignantly charming he could be. "Let's go."

"Is Jenny Meatyard going to be here?" he asked.

I excused myself. I needed a cocktail for my thermos. Dormer trailed me.

"You were childhood friends, right?" he asked.

"You *have* done your research," I said. I sounded like a movie-hawking guest on *Letterman.* "A Kahlua and skim. No ice."

Andrei had told me this particular bartender had been unhappy when informed earlier about the costume. The bartender was not, I couldn't help noticing, wearing his hat. He filled my red thermos halfway with syrupy (and very potent) Kahlua. Dormer was breathing gaspingly. I was trying to ignore him, but I was aware this wasn't the wise approach for me to take. I should, of course, have been taking advantage of this opportunity to set the record straight.

"I'd met Lowell only once before he and Jenny came to live with me," I said. I thanked the hatless bartender for my drink, and poured some into the lid. "Imagine that, Bradley. Jenny and I were only in sporadic contact when she called and asked if they could 'crash' here temporarily. This was in 1981."

I was lying. I'd called her every day. I'd begged her to move here with me. I was alone and she was my lifeline.

"The way I remember things is that I say them to myself over and over again. Nineteen eighty-one. Nineteen eighty-one. Nineteen eighty-one. Got it."

"What does that say about me, Brad? That I just *let them* move in?"

"Heck of a guy," Dormer said. "You're one heck of a guy."

"And later, Lowell wrote me *five* letters a day whenever he'd have to attend to art-world business elsewhere."

"*Art-world* business?"

"And we gave Merit the most glorious childhood here! But then Jenny left and took Merit with her."

Jenny said she didn't approve of my relationship with Merit. Jenny had grown to mistrust me, but she did say it had been so long since she'd been sane that she didn't know what to believe.

"And how did that make you feel?"

"What is this, a therapy session?" I snapped. I sipped. "Are you a trained psychologist?"

"I'm not a 'trained' anything, Mr. Goodwyn."

"Can't you see? I loved them. I loved them. She left because she couldn't live here anymore," I said. "She couldn't live here with *me*."

I noticed I had already drained my entire thermos. I handed it over to the bartender and asked for another. The mime had finally arrived, but he was wearing a striped top, opera hat, and suspenders. This was *not* the costume I'd intended for him. But a host must learn to roll with the punches. If I planned to make it through tonight, I really would have to perk up.

I had an idea that would make both of us, Mr. Dormer and me, feel better.

"I like 'shadowing' better than 'blanketing,' " I said, tossing my cape behind me. I dug into my right front pocket. "So let's say you're 'shadowing' me from now on." I unfolded a hundred. With the hundred in my palm, I shook Dormer's hand. The bill was transferred. What can I say? I'm a thug. He smiled, nodded smugly. Bradley W. Dormer knew what was what.

"You got it. 'Shadowing.' "

He made nicey-nice with the bill.

"And for whom are you working tonight?"

"You don't think I have any standards at all, do you, man?" he asked, easing the money into the pocket of his scrubs. He was, as I knew he would be, one of my people; I can smell a self-loather from a hemisphere away. This would be worth the five years' wait. He apprehended the Drambuie he'd ordered last century for the caterer girl. (Before the evening was over, we would introduce Mr. Dormer to at least stage one of the seven stages of chivalry.)

The caterer was now serving calamari to my podiatrist. My podiatrist seemed to be costumed either as Daddy Warbucks or Mr. Monopoly. I wondered where in Akron he'd found a monocle. His wife's lace-up shoes were clearly podiatrist-approved. She wore a mask, Bourbon Street in origin, I guessed, of blue-and-green peacock feathers.

Although no one was in the music room yet, the harpist there had begun; "Planxty Safaigh" was the tune. Dormer and I made our way to the front of the great hall. The caterer had gotten waylaid by my podiatrist and his wife by the entranceway. The podiatrist was consuming calamari like nobody's business, jettisoning each used toothpick onto my shiny floor. About six inches away from them, the mime was "walking against the wind." The podiatrist and his wife seemed to regard the mime as one would a screaming, pants-down-around-his-ankles psychopath, someone to cross the street to avoid. I personally happen to like mimes.

Dormer and I were walking. He lit a cigarette. Preston Lympany had not yet arrived; neither had Merit, Jenny, or Lowell.

"So what's the real reason Lowell Haven abandoned his painting?" Dormer asked. He took a chug of the Drambuie, a drag of his cigarette. I held my breath until his lungful of exhaled smoke cleared.

"Money," I said, pointing to his hundred-dollar pocket with my wand. "*Money.*"

"If this is going to be a mutually symbiotic relationship, you're going to have to come clean with me."

"All right, then, here's a scrap for you: Lowell's only talent is in getting an audience."

"Not a bad talent to have."

"Mr. Dormer?" I said. We would come back to Lowell later. "What do you think of *photography*?"

"What, like Annie Leibovitz's?"

"Well . . . not *so* much," I said. "But don't you think *that's* the real human art? To know when to shoot? Don't you think timing means more than anything else? Where's the human truth in painting? I ask you."

"Tough questions," he said, and tapped the caterer on the shoulder. He raised the Drambuie glass at her and grinned. The mime mimicked Dormer, tapping a phantom shoulder, raising a phantom glass. The caterer thanked Dormer but said she was "a little busy now." She allowed our smallish group a last shot at the calamari tray, then dispersed herself elsewhere in the room. I think she was trying to impress me, her employer, with her no boozing on the job professionalism. I appreciated that.

Dormer: smoked by the caterer! He tried to look as unresponsive as possible. The mime, however, felt Dormer's pain; his painted face was bunched up in an exaggerated mask of grief. With his gloved hand, the mime wiped away a pretend tear. Dormer was sweating. He drank down the Drambuie and lit another cigarette. I backed away. A few more hundreds from me would help cheer him up. I knew him that well already.

An unpleasant pall had descended over our corner of the room.

"Fergus," my podiatrist said, rocking on his heels like a tycoon, "do you know my wife, Henrietta?"

Henrietta and I shook hands. The mime, now performing "man in a box," had moved over to another thicket of guests: among them the choral director from the UU church where Merit was married and the choral director's husband. Both were in lederhosen and Tyroleans. The third point of the triangle was the man who cuts my lawn. He was not wearing a costume. The choral director caught my eye. I excused myself, rather callously forgetting to invite Dormer to come along.

"Fergus!" the choral director exclaimed. She embraced me. Her husband gave me a big hug, too. The man who cuts my lawn did not hug me, nor did we shake hands.

"Erin go bragh!" said the husband, clinking his beer stein (he'd brought his own beer stein) against my glass. "I love Irish folk songs."

"Tammy! Adam! How nice to see you," I said. "It's been too, *too* long. Say it *hasn't* been since Merit's wedding."

I nodded to the groundskeeper.

"Great party," the Unitarian Universalist church's choral director said. "Is that O'Carolan? On the harp?"

"It is."

Carolan or O'Carolan: both acceptable.

"It would sound really awesome on an acoustic guitar, too," she said.

Dormer examined both his glasses to make sure that they were still sapped. With my red rose, I beckoned to him. He gave me a phony double take, as if he were surprised to see me over here. I knew I probably wouldn't have time to search for it tonight, but I used to have a stethoscope around somewhere. A neck-slung stethoscope would have made all the difference in Mr. Dormer's outfit.

I made sure to introduce Dormer to everyone, except the groundskeeper. I explained who he was, and why he was here.

"That's so interesting you're doing a story about Fergus!" said the choral director.

"Well, I—" said Dormer.

"I have a really good cover model for you," the husband said. "Me!"

"What's the story about?" the choral director asked. "Is it about Fergus's *house?*"

"It's not about—" said Dormer.

"Well, what else could it be about if it's about Fergus?"

"I have a question," the husband said. "Do you get to keep all the clothes in your magazine?"

The fire-eater was now making the rounds, although that's not what alarmed me. Hovering over by the far bar was a swaying ashen figure in an upswept Don King wig (this was his costume). A drink in his trembling hand—even from this distance, I knew how unsteady he was—he assessed the room. He had not yet found what he had come for. Everyone else in the great hall was merely anonymous matter. Everyone else, except for one person, was nothing.

I excused myself. I clicked over to Andrei, my cape undulating behind me.

At the portcullis, Andrei was checking the credentials of an elderly city councilman. The councilman wore a striped 1910-era two-piece bathing suit and a straw skimmer.

"Ray-Ray's here," I hissed.

"Who, Fergus?" Andrei asked.

"*Ray-Ray.*" An inch from my temple, I made three loony-tune circles with my index finger. "Good evening, Walter," I said to the councilman.

"Hello there, Fergus," the councilman said, gesturing Edwardianly with his cane.

"Welcome, Mr. Ingberman. The party is straight between those torches," said Andrei. He had located Walter's name on his clipboarded list.

"Ray-Ray. The tree photographer. He's wearing a fight-promoter wig."

"Ohhhh. I remember him. He was not on the list, but he showed me an invitation."

"Andrei?" I asked.

"Yes, Fergus."

"Has anyone said anything about my King Arthur photographs yet?"

Dormer attached himself to me as soon as I had returned to the great hall. As I felt some backup might be necessary, I didn't mind.

The fire-eater, shirtless and in a Loch Ness–plaid kilt, was getting more attention than the mime. I found this sad. They should get more of our respect, those who work in the art of silence.

"So when do I get to see Lowell?" Dormer whispered.

"How long has the party been going on?" I asked.

"Half an hour."

"It's his party," I said. "He'll be here soon enough."

"Always like the star to make the fashionably late entrance."

"What?" I said. "*I'm* the star."

"*You're* the star?" Dormer asked defensively. "Am I missing something here? Are you Lowell Haven?"

"In a way, yes," I said, "I *am*."

"Good for you," he said.

Mr. Dormer would *not* be receiving any more money from me tonight.

"Ray-Ray!" I said to the spectral figure propped up against the bar. We cheek-kissed. His eyebrows, always on the thick side, looked as if they had been hacked at with a Swiss Army Knife. "How lovely of you to come all the way from the great state of California. Please meet Bradley W. Dormer, Contributing Writer."

"Fergus," the disturbing Ray-Ray said, ignoring horrid Dormer and scuffing in disturbingly close to me. I could smell him. He smelled like a doctor's office. We were nose-to-nose. His nose was cat-cold. "What happened to the pictures?"

I remembered his voice now: utterly without inflection. His eyes were horribly open.

"Poof," I said, waving my wand in the general direction of the paintings. "They're *gone*."

"What do you mean by that?" Dormer asked. "That Lowell's paintings are '*gone*'?"

A pen had materialized from behind Dormer's ear, and a notebook was in his hand now, too. He moved threateningly near to me.

"Now just calm down now, the two of you," I said.

"Fergus?" said a female voice in back of me.

She hadn't even bothered to RSVP to my party, although I knew she'd show. How could she not? There would be no two-headed hydra without her.

She was Pulcinella tonight, incandescent in a sugar-loaf hat, white belted coat, and a black mask. Her eyes were wild. She held what I guessed to be a canvas, covered by a wet black blanket. If I were a magician, I would have whipped that wet blanket right off. (Behind it would have been a caged cougar.) Although I hadn't seen her for years, the old feeling returned.

You've probably guessed this already, but Lowell has always loved her more than he has loved me.

"What," Jenny asked desperately, "did you do to the paintings?"

29

He said he should have been more on the ball and have anticipated she'd react that way to the fumes. It was typical of Wyatt to blame himself in such situations. At the gas station, when he was outside examining other people's tires, Merit took advantage of the Wyattless time in the car and twisted open the nail-polish bottle. It would have been easier to do the paint job if the toga hadn't been attached to Caroline, but there was no *way* Merit was going to unwrap the toga, then wrap it up again, especially not in the rain. Merit reached around in the backseat and sort of tried to daintily paint the polish onto Caroline's toga. The nail-polish wand was cheap, and it buckled, making it impossible for Merit to play around with it at all.

After Merit had made about six spastic red nail polishy streaks, Caroline looked down at Merit's work and said she thought it looked really "stripy and unrealistic." Merit couldn't really disagree.

Merit asked Caroline if she could lean forward and hold her toga out for her. Caroline said okay, and Merit very carefully poured red polish onto it. The result looked gory enough, but Merit, from her position in the front seat, was only able to reach the bottom half of Caroline's toga. *Not* such a good look. The red nail polish on the below-the-belly-button region of the toga looked, Merit felt, menstrual in the extreme.

Wyatt bopped from tire to tire on the Nissan. These statistical samplings of tire brands in parking lots and gas stations *had* to be a violation of some kind of tacit privacy code, Merit thought. He popped up and became involved in a conversation, an amiable-looking one, thank God (sometimes they weren't), with the Nissan's barn-jacketed owner, who was filling his tank. They were, doubtless, talking tires. Merit handed

Caroline the nail polish and told her to do a "Jack the Dripper" on the toga's upper regions. Caroline knew she was talking about Pollock. (It was obvious.) What Merit and Caroline were doing together felt, to Merit, terrifically surreptitious and private and female. Regardless of what the rest of the night would bring, Merit sensed she and Caroline were sharing an important moment together.

She assumed the nail polish would dry in the fifteen minutes it would take for them to get to Lowell and Fergus's house.

Wyatt was jotting something in his notebook. The nail-polish fumes were getting to Merit, but she couldn't roll down the windows because, as everyone knows, you aren't allowed to keep your car running at a gas station. Wyatt and the Nissan man shook hands. Nissan man reached into the pocket of his barn jacket and pulled out something that Merit presumed was a business card.

Caroline said, "Uh-*oh.*"

Merit turned. Caroline displayed the palms of her hands.

"I think I got it on the seat, too," Caroline said. "Just a little bit, though."

Merit told her not to show her dad her hands or to say anything.

"And try real hard not to touch anything, either," Merit said.

Wyatt opened the door on the passenger's side, ducked inside, and flapped his umbrella a few times before retracting it.

"What a nice guy. He used to work in research and development, but he just got laid off. He has the new Waterwisker tires; I was curious about their performance in this weather. . . . *What* is that *smell?*"

Merit and Caroline swapped glances.

Merit started the car and put it in reverse, thinking about how she couldn't really breathe all that much, thinking about how the nail-polish fumes might possibly, just possibly (because they were at a gas station and everything), make the car explode. Then she went all watery and boneless, and, very briefly, blacked out.

Lights off for Merit.

When she came to (2.37 seconds later, by Wyatt's calculation), Wyatt and Caroline were both screaming at her. Her foot was on the gas pedal, but she wasn't going anywhere. The car was making this ugly whirring/grinding sound. Merit had accidentally backed up into the air pump.

Had she been alone, she probably would have just collected whatever emotional resources she had and gotten herself right out of there. But she wasn't alone, not now. The air pump was now sort of leaning, teetering like a baby tooth begging for a good yank.

Wyatt yelled at Merit, then yelled at himself. ("God*damn it, Wyatt*, you *know* you can't leave her alone," he said.) He told Merit they were going to go inside and explain what had happened. Caroline was instructed to wait in the car.

The damage wasn't as bad as Wyatt seemed to think—she'd only busted out the *right* taillight, she said. Wyatt reminded her how much a taillight on such an "old import" would cost. But it was true that the right side of the bumper maybe didn't look all that great. He opened the trunk, then slammed it. It wouldn't latch. Wyatt expressed concern that the emergency supplies were going to get wet now.

When she was inside the store again, Merit noticed something she hadn't ten minutes ago: a dirty halved lemon on a paper napkin by the cash register.

"My *wife* here," Wyatt said to the cashier, stressing the word *wife*, Merit felt, in a mean way, "had a little accident with the air pump out there."

The woman at the cash register didn't seem to be concerned enough to go outside and check out the path of destruction. She picked up the phone behind the counter and left a surprisingly short and vague ("It's Dee-Dee; call me back") message for the store manager.

During the twenty minutes it took for the manager to call back, Merit bought another bottle of water and a pack of cigarettes from the cashier. Merit felt this business transaction really reestablished a sense of normalcy between them; the cashier took Merit's money, dipped her fingertips into the dirty halved lemon, gave Merit her receipt and change, and thanked her, just as if she were a normal old customer, not a fainting-prone fuckup who'd just rammed into her gas station's air pump.

Wyatt didn't say anything about her cigarette purchase.

The manager called. The cashier asked Merit for her insurance card, then disappeared in the back with it. Merit felt the cashier must really trust them if she were letting them watch the store like that. Jenny had told Merit she had a very honest face. Growing up, Merit always felt this was the main reason why her mother had never asked her to model for her. The cashier returned with a photocopy of the insurance card. The card was warm, either from the machine or the cashier's hand.

When she merged onto the highway, Wyatt yelled at himself again for letting what had just happened happen; Caroline, in the rearview mirror, was so at-attention, it looked as if she were waiting for an apple to get shot off her head. Merit thought about reaching around and giving her a tissue, but a tissue would just have gotten stuck to everything anyway. Wyatt kept looking behind him—making sure the trunk didn't pop up, he said. Merit felt forlorn whenever the windshield wipers went away from her. She couldn't help it.

Just as if it were still *her* house, Merit went around the back with Caroline and Wyatt, planning to sneak in through the kitchen. Caroline couldn't touch anything, so Merit held the umbrella for her. Wyatt disapproved of this route, and as the three of them slopped through Fergus and Lowell's backyard, he expressed his concern about how it wasn't really appropriate for them to go in the back way; not only was it *rude;* it was actually legally called *trespassing.*

"Trespassing, ladies," he said. "Trespassing."

Merit reminded him she had grown up here.

Wyatt said her mother might have a contradictory opinion about that.

Merit asked if they could speed it up as they passed the great hall's stained-glass windows. She didn't want anyone in there to see her. There was light inside, and noise, and people.

Outside the kitchen door, underneath the purple awning, Merit and Wyatt collapsed their umbrellas, shook them. There really *was* no good way for Wyatt to carry the decapitated Chadwick or for Merit to carry the aquarium ornament. Merit had a headache. She opened the door and smelled meat, various kinds. She didn't know where they were supposed to put their umbrellas.

They were forty minutes late, and Merit knew that everyone, especially Fergus and her mother, would be mad at her.

Mrs. Valdez was chopping either onions or possibly shallots on a thick wooden block. Merit didn't recognize anyone else in the kitchen, and she tried to tiptoe past without getting caught. She was terrible at both hellos and good-byes and tried to avoid both.

Mrs. Valdez could be an L.B.J.-level tyrant to whomever she had working for her at any particular moment, but she had always been very nice to Merit. When Merit was a kid, she'd gotten it into her head Mrs. Valdez was from Mexico, although now that she thought about it again, she did remember Fergus saying something once about how she sent money back to her family in El Salvador.

Mrs. Valdez saw Merit. She said, "Ooooh, it's my baby!" She put down her knife on the butcher block and bustled toward her.

"Look at you, so beautiful!" she said, squeezing Merit's cheeks.

Merit asked her how she was. She probably hadn't seen Mrs. Valdez since her wedding. She looked great, the same as before.

"Good, mama. You?"

"Good!" Merit said. "I'm *good*! How's Chuck?"

Merit remembered something Mrs. Valdez's then grotesquely preppy (as a sixth grader, he actually put pennies in his penny loafers) son, Chuck, had said to her when they were in junior high school: "I'm as white as you are, Merit. I'm a Caucasian, too." Merit had never known how to take that statement. By high school, Chuck was wearing the same red Che Guevara T-shirt every day.

"Ah, he's okay. In San Francisco."

"Well, *good.*"

Merit introduced Mrs. Valdez to Wyatt and Caroline, although there was a very strong possibility they had already been introduced at Merit and Wyatt's wedding.

Wyatt transferred his Chadwick head to his left hand, so as to be able to shake with the socially correct right. Caroline couldn't shake hands at all, but she gave a cute little nod instead. Merit could now admit the nail polish hadn't been the swiftest idea.

The peacock feathers sticking out of the trash can were not there as a decorative accent.

"Your *daughter*?" Mrs. Valdez asked.

She didn't recognize Caroline from the wedding? And anyway, Merit was only a kid herself when Caroline was born.

"Oh," Merit said, "No. Not really. She's Wyatt's daughter."

"Oh, okay. You had," Mrs. Valdez said, scanning Caroline, "an accident?"

Wyatt answered, yes, that she, meaning Merit, had, unfortunately, had an accident. Mrs. Valdez asked Caroline if she needed a towel, but Caroline said she was okay.

Over by the sink, a young man in a green John Deere shirt and a hair net (required, probably, by Fergus) was hacking at something with a cleaver. On the counter beside him was another pile of peacock feathers.

Merit had to get out of there.

"I'm so glad I saw you, Fatima!" Merit said.

"You, too, mama. Hey, you remember Claudia from your school?"

Merit said she did. She didn't tell Mrs. Valdez that she and Claudia actually worked together—in a way. Merit now remembered Chuck and Claudia had been an item at one point during high school.

"She's here tonight, mamita," Mrs. Valdez said, considering the weird aquarium ornament in Merit's hands.

Caroline had never been in Merit's bedroom here before. That seemed so astonishing to Merit right now. But when was the last time she had even been back in her own room? She couldn't remember. She turned on the light. A *real, working* light switch.

She set down her aquarium house and her umbrella by the door.

Merit's childhood dollhouse was still in one corner of the room; her horsehair rocking horse sat in the other corner. Merit had never seen an openmouthed rocking horse except for this one, certainly not one with such lifelike teeth. She had never before thought that they probably *were* real teeth.

Someone was staying here, in her room. A white fleece robe lay on one side of her laddered bed. On the other side of the bed was a person-size indentation. It was a feather mattress (if, in fact, Fergus had kept the same mattress she had slept on twenty years ago); everything that touched it left a mark. Did the man keep the red curtains of the canopy bed open at night, too, just as Merit had done? And it *was* a man who was staying here—Merit could feel that. On top of Merit's dresser was a bottle of cologne, an orange, a wallet, and a Bible.

She felt sort of guilty and weird about being in this room that was no longer hers. Downstairs: party sounds, a Celtic lament on a harp. But not *too* guilty and weird to open the coffin-size carved wooden chest at the foot of her bed.

Her toys were still in her toy chest: a Lite-Brite, a box of Fashion Plates, Lincoln Logs, pom-poms in the University of Akron's colors, stuffed animals, her Madame ventriloquist puppet (Madame's gown was no longer the screaming blue it had once been), and three naked, and faceless, Barbies.

Everything in the room remained untouched. Lowell and Fergus had left her room just the way it had been when she'd lived there.

When she and Jenny moved out, Jenny wouldn't let her take the toys, clothes, and books Fergus had bought for her. They couldn't continue taking things from him, she said. As Merit and her mother were unpacking what few things Merit had brought for her new room, Jenny asked, "What did you and Fergus do all that time when you were waiting in the hallway for us?"

"I don't know," Merit said. "We played, I guess."

Taped onto the pink plastic front door of her dollhouse was a thumbprint-size color photograph of *Dallas*-era Patrick Duffy. Merit had, twentyish-years ago, torn the picture out of a magazine. As she recalled it, Patrick Duffy was meant to play the part of the dead patriarch of her doll household. She had also—bizarrely, she thought now—cut out a white construction-paper frame for the picture and adorned the frame with ballpointed hearts. Even when she was a kid, Merit had already started to worry that she was a very strange person.

Caroline still hadn't said anything about her bedroom.

Merit took them into the bathroom.

"A *wood* tub?" Caroline asked.

Merit answered that while, yes, the outside of the tub was indeed wood, the interior of the tub was just normal tub material, although it did look like wood, too.

"Actually," Merit said, "wooden tubs were padded with cloth in medieval times."

She could tell that Wyatt thought she sounded like Fergus just then. Made sense, really, since Fergus had been the one who'd told her that.

On the abdomen of Caroline's toga was a red handprint. Wyatt, his own hands stuffed cozily within his Chadwick head as if it were a muff, squinted through the peephole in the bathroom door. Merit's right hand, she noticed now, had some nail polish on it, too.

The vanity did contain, as Merit had hoped, a Cutex bottle. She had no way of knowing if the bottle had been there for two decades or not (the label design did look somewhat dated), although, thinking about it, the nail-polish remover inside probably would have evaporated in that amount of time.

Tiny dark hairs coated the sink. A man had shaved there today.

Not only was the red nail polish on Caroline's hands, forearms, and both elbows; some of it had seeped through the sheet onto her shorts and thighs. Merit soaked a tissue with yellow nail-polish remover. The liquid, cold and substanceless, stank. She asked Caroline to hold her hands out.

Wyatt, having seen what he wanted to see through the peephole, was now looking at himself in the beveled mirror, futzing with the Chadwick head.

"*Jesus Christ,*" Wyatt said, "I can't see *anything* in this room."

The nail-polish remover was turning Caroline's hands a cracked, witchy pink.

Wyatt tried to fit the Chadwick head on over his glasses. *Not* going to work, Merit could already tell.

"Did you wear glasses when you worked at Cedar Point?" Merit asked.

"I've worn glasses since I was four years old, Merit."

As he tried to maneuver into the head, he knocked his glasses off; they fell onto the ceramic-tile floor.

"You'll still wear it, won't you? Just when we make our entrance?" Merit asked. She picked up his glasses. Both of them appearing there without costumes would offend Fergus and Lowell too much, she knew.

Wyatt said he wouldn't be able to see in the head. "Or, more importantly," he said, "drink."

"It'll only be for a few minutes," Merit said. "I'll hold your hand."

Caroline looked momentarily pained, but it could just have been the deathly odor of nail-polish remover.

"And your hand, too, Caroline," Merit said.

Descending the main staircase, they came upon a painting, which looked as if it were a billboard someone had defaced. The painting was *Richard III*, and Polaroids were tacked up over it.

"What is *that*?" Wyatt asked.

Merit said she had not a clue.

This particular painting had always frightened Merit. The dead and bloody white horse on the ground might have had a little something to do with it. Jenny had told her they were unable to sell this one because it was a direct rip-off of Francis Hayman's painting of David Garrick as Richard III. Merit had still never seen the original painting, or even a reproduction of it, nor had she ever read or watched *Richard III,* so she didn't know what scene Lowell was meant to be enacting. In Jenny's painting, one spiderish, withered Lowell arm was semiobscured by a red cape; in the other arm was a sword. Merit had never been certain if he was supposed to have killed his horse or if someone else had done it.

The portrait of Fergus (as Hamlet—blonder than the real Fergus, and much more menacing) next to it remained intact. Jenny had told her they couldn't sell Fergus's picture because nobody wanted a painting by Lowell Haven whose subject wasn't Lowell Haven. Jenny had always been embarrassed by that painting. She didn't know how to paint anyone other than Lowell, she once said.

Merit got a better look: The photos were all of Lowell, posing outside in a suit of armor (face and arms armorless) and a cape. He was wearing some kind of prosthetic nose. They were pictures Fergus had taken.

Merit tried to peel a picture off. It wouldn't budge.

Wyatt asked her if she thought her mother was responsible for this.

Merit said no way.

"Maybe they're protecting it from potential vandals," Wyatt said. "What? You know how people can be at parties." He removed his glasses, folded them, and tucked them into his shirt pocket. He took a deep, audible breath, as if preparing to do a cannonball into a pool, closed his eyes, and pushed his own head into Chadwick's. Wyatt always closed his eyes whenever he put his sweaters on, too.

The *Richard* picture was now worth—what, exactly? Ten thousand dollars? A hundred thousand? Merit didn't know. Did it really matter?

The defaced-picture thing wasn't doing much to alleviate Merit's party anxiety. She took Wyatt's hand and then Caroline's and led them toward the great hall.

Wyatt was blind in the mask, so they couldn't really get very far into the hall; instead, they hovered at one of the entrances. Above this particular entranceway was, Merit knew without looking up, a stag's head with alarmingly huge antlers. She leaned against the wall, Wyatt and Caroline flanking her.

Wyatt towered like a Harlem Globetrotter over everyone else in the room. The Chadwick head sort of had this dead basementy smell to it, and it looked moist and grayish now that they were out in better light. Chadwick's pupils were little screens. The right one had come detached and was curled up a bit at the bottom.

Being this close to the head of a famous character really did do something to kill the make-believe, didn't it?

The harpist was now playing a song Merit had heard before, many times. It was "The Ash Grove."

For several years after Lowell presented the sheet music of "The Ash Grove" to her, Merit thought he had composed the song for her. It was so beautiful. She played it every day on the cheap upright piano Jenny had bought for her (the piano was not a grand piano like Fergus's), and she heard it in her head every night before she fell asleep. The song became an obsession. As a child, she already possessed a poetic inclination, and the song made her long for her own youth. "The Ash Grove" actually made her long for her childhood, when she was still a child. Only a true artist could awaken such feelings in a very young person. Merit shouldn't have been programmed yet to understand longing, but she was. She did. When Lowell presented "The Ash Grove" to her, she already knew he wasn't the painter. But she still wanted to believe he was an artist, somehow.

In her sixth-grade chorus class, her teacher distributed a packet of sheet music of songs for their upcoming spring concert. The packet consisted of the following: "The Drinking Gourd," "I Don't Know What's Wrong with These Kids Today," ("from the Broadway Smash *Bye Bye Birdie*," the title page said), "Careless Whisper," and "The Ash Grove." The author listed on Merit's sixth-grade chorus-class version of "The Ash Grove"? "Traditional."

Merit had slipped the sheet music into her folder (although you were supposed to leave sheet music in class) and taken it home with her. For the next few months, she sat on the floor in her room after school, holding the two versions of the song side by side. Music, lyrics: identical. It sickened Merit that she continued to study Lowell's handwritten copy. She knew she'd find no answers in it. There were no answers to find, just as there were no answers to find about him in Jenny's pictures. Merit had never talked to anyone about Lowell's lie until she met Wyatt. He'd sung "The Ash Grove" as a Boy Scout, he said.

It was not lost on Merit that her last name became Ash.

Merit steadied herself against the cold wall. She'd read it in Jenny's journals: She really had called Lowell "Daddy."

30

After all the man-hours of thought given to the topic of "How Will Jenny Respond?" I was surprised by how much her reaction startled me.

There was something dangerous behind that black sheet. I knew it.

"Oh," I said, gallantly making eye contact with each member of my attention-rapt cluster (yet clearly addressing Jenny), "I just couldn't move comfortably in front of those paintings anymore. Those *absolute frauds.*"

Jenny once created things, too, but then, like most women, stopped. She never had any respect for her own talent.

"Could you say that again?" Dormer asked, fingering a microcassette recorder. "Into *this?*"

Where did *that* come from? I don't know whether I asked this question aloud, or merely thought it.

I leaned into the recorder and repeated myself: "Lowell's paintings are *frauds.*"

I asked Ray-Ray to pretend temporarily that my Otto I reproduction scepter (which had quite a good likeness of the Holy Roman Empire's imperial insignia, and was therefore worth every penny) belonged to him, so I could get a firm two-handed grip on the recorder. Ray-Ray set his disturbing drink down and fondled my scepter orb disturbingly. Embedded in Ray-Ray's wig were a few pieces of what appeared to be confetti.

Clutching the microcassette recorder (sweaty already from Dormer), I bellowed into the microphone hole, "*Lowell* is a *fraud.*"

I half-savored how those words felt in my mouth.

Jenny's Pulcinella mask's brow was frozen in a permanent furrow, its eyeholes down-turned, cheerless, its bird nose aged, tragic. Standing there with the swathed painting (or possibly really big mirror) balanced on her shoelaces, pulling frantically at her red rope belt's cayenne pepper–shaped tail, she could have been anyone. But even the costume couldn't erase her.

"Fergus," Jenny said, my name screaming like a launched bottle rocket, "you don't know *what* you're talking about."

A knife turn in the chest—no, not in the chest, in the *gut,* where death makes its first appearance. Even after all this time, it was still the way it always had been: Jenny loved Lowell more than she loved me.

I needed Preston Lympany and Merit now. I *needed* them. But they weren't here, and they would never be.

Now, I used to think, I'm not such a bad man; if I can make my exit from life without having destroyed too many people, without having added much grief to the world, I'll have done okay.

But my ambitions, you see, have always been so wildly out of line with my talents.

I batted away the microcassette recorder (this was between *Jenny* and me). I'll always regret what I said next. I wanted to hurt her. So I thought of the worst thing I could say. I thought of the very worst thing I could say, and said it.

"What happened to you, Jenny? You used to be the dauphine, the heiress to the throne! Now look at you: a frown, a wrinkled lip, a sneer of cold command. You're a shattered visage! A lifeless thing! It really does break my heart to see you this way."

It wasn't confetti in Ray-Ray's hair, I could see now. The white dots were litter from a hole puncher. Unholes, as it were. Ray-Ray had been making holes in white paper before the party, while wearing his wig.

"It's *my* hand that mocks *you*, monster," Jenny said.

Oh, why hadn't I worn a mask tonight?

"This is Jenny Meatyard?" Dormer asked me, although Jenny was right there. Oh, yes, Jenny was undeniably there.

As I said before: He had done his research.

Dormer introduced himself, then went into toadying mode immediately. He said he'd love to chat with her, if possible, when she had a moment.

Jenny didn't even bother with a reply. She hoisted whatever was behind the sheet and said to me, "I'm getting Lowell."

Helplessly, hopelessly, I watched Jenny blast through the mounting crowd. Cruel, beautiful Jenny in her shapeless commedia dell'arte costume. It looked as if she'd actually *pushed* Ellis Beckerdean out of the way, although I couldn't be sure. Ellis's costume was a straitjacket, and in it, his balance was even worse than it usually was. He'd been in my gymnastics class a few years ago, where he'd fallen, rather famously, off of a low balance beam and chipped several teeth. Had I been feeling differently right then, I would have tried to remember to get a good look at his new front teeth.

"I'm gonna talk to her," Dormer said.

But he wasn't supposed to leave me high and dry, too, was he? Not Dormer, my shadow, my shade, who needed me more than he needed anyone there.

I dug into my tight little right front pocket and unceremoniously unbounded a hundred. He took it, pocketed it, thanked me, and rewound the tape in his microcassette recorder. Mouse sounds for two seconds, then play.

". . . is a fraud," said someone whose voice sounded much less captivating than mine.

"Just checking to make sure it works," Dormer said. "They're such cheap asses."

I didn't care to contemplate who the cheap-assed "they" he was referring to were. Jenny was gone, having vanished into the maw of the great hall. They would hate me, Jenny and Lowell. Oh yes, they would. And now they would hate me together.

Jenny and Lowell, Jenny and Lowell: Jewell.

Dormer had his ear against the microcassette recorder, listening, listening. The recorder probably felt hot against his face.

I asked him if I really sounded like that.

"Oh, that's you, man," Dormer said. "You always think, Who's that prick when you hear yourself, but it's *you*." And then, despite all that had happened between us, he trudged off after Jenny. Away went my blanket; away went my shadow.

Ray-Ray returned my scepter to me. I'd anticipated more of a struggle.

"I need to find Lowell, too," he said.

Now I was losing *Ray-Ray*?

I did a quick search of the great hall for someone else to talk to. Penny Murphy from the bank was there with a trash-can lid on her head and wearing a sandwich board whose block letters said WHITE TRASH. It would have been funnier if she'd written merely WHITE, I thought—the TRASH part was self-evident. There was the mime, and the fire-eater, and there were other people, but I didn't want to talk to them. And anyway, mimes and fire-eaters don't talk.

"I have to give Lowell a handkerchief," Ray-Ray announced.

"*Okay*," I said.

I asked him to explain himself. I wanted to engage him. I wanted him to stay. Well, he said, before battle, a maiden gives her lover her handkerchief. I said I was aware of this tradition, but was unable to understand what it had to do with the little celebration we'd planned for tonight.

He stared mutely at the mime. The mime was trapped either in a cage or a box.

A hole-punched confetti bit had landed snowflakelike on Ray-Ray's sizable right brow.

"Ray-Ray," I said, "I have to ask. Why did you punch holes in a piece of paper earlier today?"

"Not paper. The *handkerchief*," he said, as if this were just so excruciatingly obvious. He was clearly running out of patience with me. One would have thought he would have been more impressed with my sleuthing, but then again, I'd always gotten the feeling he hated me. He was still watching the mime. "So Lowell can put it in his *notebook*."

We're all always thinking about posterity. All of us, the Ray-Rays of the world included.

At dinner on Ray-Ray's final night here last year (that afternoon, I'd done what Lowell'd told me to do, making sure Ray-Ray knew he was no longer welcome), he'd silently wept, hunchbacked at the table in my dining room. With his tears, he'd traced the same word (or words, depending on your point of view) onto the tableclothless oak. I'd refilled his iced-tea glass several times, hovering over him with my pitcher for several seconds longer than was customary. He hadn't seemed to mind, though. During refill number five, I'd deciphered what he was writing:

"RAY-RAY."

"Ray-Ray," I said, handing him a hundred, "don't do anything stupid tonight."

"Why are you giving me this?" he asked, and considered the bill.

"As a token of my esteem," I said. "Naturally."

"No thanks, Fergus," he said, passing the Franklin back. "I won't even take money from my dad."

I realized just then how young Ray-Ray was. I'd never thought about him as being any particular age before. Do tree photographers, of which Ray-Ray was one, really make any money? Marin County, unlike Summit County, isn't a bargain.

And then Ray-Ray, in his fight-promoter wig, was gone, too. Again, I was left alone.

"You there!" I said to the mime, shaking the hundred at him.

The mime gestured exaggeratedly to his solar plexus with those obscenely expressive mime hands. "*Moi?*" he mouthed.

"I want to give you a big, big tip before I forget."

The mime clapped giddily, precisely, and made three scrupulous little leaps over to me. His leaps couldn't be felt on the floor.

"You've been doing such a fabulous job tonight," I said. I was now unsure whether this pint-size blanched-face mime was a man or a woman.

Teasingly, I dangled the bill in front of the mime. The mime's hands were on his/her hips, his/her ballet-slippered foot tapping like a cartoon rabbit who had somewhere big to be. I gave it up, the money, and the mime brought it to its red lips, kissing it with more exquisite tenderness and longing than I could perhaps recall ever having seen.

As I was reaching into the same pocket (front right) for another bill for the mime, I felt a fond little shoulder tap.

Drisana-Nari was wearing the same pink track suit. Still no shoes. Her blue eyes were immensely open, as if propped up with toothpicks, and bloodshot. Had she been crying?

"Okay, stare at me," she said. She peered disconcertingly, candidly into my eyes. "This is the art thing I'm doing tonight."

I looked at the mime and the mime looked at me. We shared some kind of subtle nonverbal communication. He/she shrugged theatrically, like an old Borscht Belt comic or a child actor, and blew me a kiss.

That airborne kiss had weight. I know because I felt it.

"Are you trying to put me under?" I asked.

In such a situation, you would have asked the same question.

"Staring contest," Drisana-Nari said.

I didn't understand this girl at all.

I looked around for some help, but there was none to be found. Anna Gainsworth-Dougherty was wearing a padded sumo wrestler's suit. R. J. Sultan was in red dress, white wig, pearls: Barbara Bush.

"Fergus!" growled a voice that was, in its silver-tongued menace, unmistakably Lowell's. "What the bloody *fuck* have you done to our paintings?"

He was, my heart, hand in hand with Jenny. He was. She was hand in hand with him. She was.

Jenny was now maskless, her mask on top of her head, her dark hair poking up through the eyeholes. Absent was the black-sheeted whatever-it-was. Lowell was wearing a latex mask of his own face. Tonight, Lowell was himself.

"I don't even know quite where to begin with you, you bastard son of a mongrel bitch," Lowell said. I couldn't see his face, or watch his lips move, but the tone was understood. *That's* how good an actor Lowell is.

The rose, my rose, was on the floor. It had, at some point, fallen.

"You *think* you can destroy us that easily?" Lowell asked.

"You've got Merit over there crying. Do you know that?" Jenny asked. She jabbed at my chest with her sharp finger. It hurt. I wrapped my cape tighter around myself, as tightly as I could with one hand (scepter, thermos).

Merit was here? Merit was *crying*?

"But I *love* Merit," I said. I tamped gently down on the rose head, feeling it, experimenting with its weight and texture. I wanted to crush it. It felt ugly, and more like actually killing something than you'd think. "I would never . . . I would never . . . do anything . . . I mean, *Merit?*"

I was surrounded now by hangers-on: Dormer, Ray-Ray. Drisana-Nari seemed, in my peripheral vision, to have been sucking her thumb, although that could have been my high-strung mental state at work. Paying these three off wasn't an option, not now. I felt for my money, just to make sure my pocket hadn't been picked. I should have stashed my inhaler in a pocket instead.

"Anyway," I gasped, "Andrei. Did. It."

They were watching me, and that made it worse. Dormer was trying to get the microcassette recorder underneath my nose, as if this were Zaire and I were Ali and about to say something significant. I was trying to breathe, and couldn't. I was making sounds. With the orb of my scepter, I dashingly scraped the dead rose matter from the sole of my shoe.

"*Andrei?*" Lowell asked, his maskface inert. As far as I could see, there were no holes in either the nose area or the mouth area. Lowell has always been respiratorily blessed. His black eyes, his real eyes, flared. The ire there, was it real? It was.

There was Jenny. A gut jab reminded me again what I'd said.

"*Andrei?*" Lowell snorted through the mask. "Why you pathetic little coward."

"Excuse me for a moment," I stammered, and turned toward the entrance to the great hall. Tears, my tears, tears that I had myself made, were clouding my eyes. I set down my thermos at my feet and, with my hand, made a hygiene shield over my nose/mouth area. Very soon, a sneeze would occur. It was going to be an important one, although no one else knew that yet. Not only had I not thought to bring my inhaler; my pockets contained no Kleenex. (I've never owned a cape with pockets.) My garters were digging into my thighs (I was, like Henry VIII, wearing two), and my only talent was bringing harm to the people I loved. I wiped my tears, and my nose, and spread that nasty pink-fingered hand out over my heart. Breathing, I've found, is sometimes easier that way.

Although I wasn't looking at them, everyone—including Lowell, including Jenny—in my otherwise-antagonistic assemblage (and even some people in some other, more easygoing surrounding cabals) said, in unison, "Bless you."

"Thank you," I said. But I still wasn't looking at them. A firm but fair hand was on my back now. I didn't know to whom the hand was attached. Jenny and Lowell have the same touch.

On my beautiful floor were my podiatrist's discarded fiesta-hued calamari toothpicks. Lowell, Jenny, and everyone else in my group were murmuring among themselves. I tried not to listen, although I did hear Jenny say, "He doesn't *create;* he only *destroys.*" As I bent over to do a little toothpick pickup, I kept watch on the entranceway for Preston Lympany. The unknown hand wasn't on me anymore, because I was now kneeling on the floor.

Making her trembling way through the entrance was a girl, whose pale, freckled face I recognized but couldn't place. She was costumed as a punk rocker, her hair platinumed and moussed into three reptilian spears. If she'd known me better, which she never would, she'd have hated me, too. Her T-shirt was one of those mass-produced MADE IN HEAVEN ones that used to really set Lowell off. ("They're not even aware of the origin of that phrase," Lowell used to say. "They don't even know whom they're trying to be.") The punk-for-a-night girl seemed to have come alone. She spotted me there on the floor and gave me what appeared to be a kind of patriotic salute, although I might have been imagining that.

She was headed toward me. Rather than standing up hostlike to shake her hand, or even possibly embrace her, I found myself sinking even lower into the floor. I made sure my back was facing my anti-Fergus contingent (this, as I learned from the way in which Jackie O. once dealt with me, is the high-class way to snub). MADE IN HEAVEN was advancing toward me, and Lowell's velvet-slippered feet were now directly in front of me. I knew, from the way his feet were so severely positioned, that looking up at him wasn't going to be a good idea.

I waved at the girl, a signal to her, I hoped, that her approach was not only permitted but welcomed.

Jenny's feet, in low-heeled sandals, were now planted next to the velvet slippers. Jenny's painted toenails and Lowell's slippers were an identical red. Were they holding hands again?

"Get *up*, Fergus," Lowell's voice said. You can't tell, when studying someone's feet, whether or not that person is actually speaking. I collected all the toothpicks I was able to reach without moving.

A new pair of shoes had been added to my small shoe theater: blue Air Jordans. Not the footwear choice of any punk rockers I'd ever known, but my punk days were indeed decades behind me.

"Hello, dear," I said to her jitterbugging athletic shoes. Everything you need to know about someone, you can learn by their shoes—how they move in them.

"Lovely *shirt*," Lowell's voice, oozing with disdain, said.

"Lowell!" Jenny admonished. I may or may not have heard her giving his arm a smack. I lined the pretty toothpicks up in a row on the floor. They went: aquamarine, fuchsia, lime green, orange, aquamarine, fuchsia, lime green.

"Hi Mr. Goodwyn!" the girl exclaimed. She flopped herself down next to me, the flexible bugger. There was her face. I knew I'd very recently seen it. I searched the foot-busy floor for another orange toothpick. Symmetry is key, always has been.

Jenny's voice, overhead: "We were never going to sell those anyway." She transferred her weight now to one foot and held the other foot behind her, like a cat with a twisted ankle.

"But *Merit*," Lowell said.

The girl asked me, her mouth moving, "How are the calamari? I talked to Lance today, and he said he had to get them flown in from this guy in *New York*."

The caterer. Well, of course.

"I'll be," I said. "New York? Of all places." Given that I had no available pocket space, and no available hands, I knew I'd be unable to collect the toothpicks. Lowell's impatient right foot went *rat-a-tat-tat* on my floor.

"Fergus?" Lowell asked. "Is that *thermos* down there *yours*?"

Both of Jenny's feet were solidly on the floor now. They were holding hands—I could feel it—Jenny and Lowell.

"*Girl*," I said, addressing the caterer but paying breathless attention to the person I'd just seen come through the entranceway, "do me a favor and clean up all the toothpicks off the floor. If someone slips, I'll get sued."

"I'll finish *you* off later, Fergus," Lowell's voice said. "You're *not* going to destroy us." He sounded muffled, far away, as if speaking through plastic (which he was).

"But—" the girl said. Lowell's and Jenny's feet went away, away, away, out of my sight. "I'm not—"

"Here," I said, burrowing into my pocket and wheedling out a hundred. I handed it to her and stood up. She hadn't expected to make *any* money tonight, as I recalled.

"Preston!" I called across the great hall, and concentrated on my breathing.

"Fergus!" he cried.

I gathered up my scepter and my thermos and ran toward him. I didn't even glance back at the place, or the people, I'd been delivered from. The rose material on the sole of my shoe made the already-hazardous buffed floor even slicker. I slipped once, but only in a very minor way. In preparation for a really big one-armed hug, I transferred my scepter to my thermos hand.

Preston Lympany had gotten a haircut, Caesar-style, and dyed his brown beautiful youthful hair partially silver.

We hugged. His touch felt real. His denim shirt was wet from the rain.

"Do you like my costume? Trevor did my hair yesterday, before he went to Columbus."

Lowell and Jenny (her mask back on now) buzzed by me, going through the entranceway and then into the foyer, which contained Lowell's *King Arthur.* They were trailed by Dormer (microcassette recorder aloft) and Ray-Ray (wig askew and waving a hole-punched handkerchief). Drisana-Nari was not present. Not one member of the gruesome foursome said hello to me as they passed.

"I like the way Caesar operated," I said. "Big fan. Better to run a manageable little Iberian village than be second banana in unruly Rome, I've always thought."

I unscrewed my thermos lid and downed some of my lukewarm Kahlua and skim. The thermos hadn't done such a great job of keeping my cocktail cold.

"I'm not Julius *Caesar!*" Preston Lympany said, nudging me with his edible exposed elbow. "I'm George Clooney! Remember what you said? 'Salt-and-pepper'?"

In the foyer, Lowell and Jenny were talking, although it wasn't really much of a conversation.

LOWELL: "Oh my *God*."
JENNY: "I told you it was glue."
LOWELL: "*Oh* my fucking God."
DORMER: "So who do you think did this?"
LOWELL: "You're a bit *slow,* aren't you?"
DORMER: "Hey, I'm a naïve little boy. Can you just say it into the tape recorder?"
JENNY: "*What* magazine is this?"

"Fergus?" Preston Lympany asked. "Hel*lo?* Anybody home? Knock, knock?"

"Yes. I'm sorry, Preston. I'm just . . . I've just . . . I don't know what's wrong with me, to tell you the truth."

"But aren't you happy to see me? Trevor decided to go to his parents' fiftieth this weekend instead!"

Animal sounds were coming from the foyer. Whose noises were they? I didn't know.

"That was probably the right thing for Trevor to do," I said. My nose was running again. I did a George W. Bush and wiped with my hand. There was no alternative.

"It was between that, or your party, or the hair convention. I think he made the right choice, too. Plus, I really wanted to see you alone."

Another snot dollop had reclaimed its place on the tip on my nose. Somehow, rather suddenly, I'd become one of these cat fur–covered, correct-change, drippy-nosed old men one invariably winds up behind in the checkout line.

"Would you perhaps like to go upstairs with me for a moment, Preston?" I asked. "I'm afraid I need to make a bit of a Kleenex run."

The animal sounds in the foyer were coming from Lowell.

We sneaked through the kitchen and up the back stairs. (Mrs. Valdez said she wanted a word with me about the meal, but I told her that right then wasn't really the best time.) It felt like the old days, fleeing my own party. I'd done this before.

Had I been Lowell, I would have invited Preston Lympany upstairs for only one reason. But my intentions, in life as in art, had always been much purer than Lowell's. It would have been unseemly to lead him any deeper into that lightless hallway. At the end of it was the room Lowell and I had once shared. The bedroom closest to the back stairs was Merit's. The door to Merit's room was already open. All I had to do was turn on the light.

"*What* is this *room?*" Preston Lympany asked.

I'd been around Andrei long enough to know he didn't seem to suffer from any kind of sinus condition. I did, however, recall I'd emptied a box of Kleenex into his/Merit's bathroom's alabaster Kleenex holder last week (just in case he needed it).

"The dollhouse!" he said. "Whose is that?"

"That's Merit's," I said. "You'll meet her."

If, I forgot to add, she hasn't left yet.

"My stepsister had that exact dollhouse. Blast from the past! Who's Merit?"

"She's my daughter," I said.

"Your *what?*"

As I always do when I'm in her room, I made a beeline for the mortise-tendon oak toy box at the foot of her bed. Merit isn't even aware I still have her toys. "It's hard to know someone, isn't it?" I asked. "I mean, really *know* someone."

"Maybe," Preston Lympany said, "but there are so many different people. You never told me you had a *daughter.*"

I slid my thermos and scepter underneath the very high bed. I opened the oak chest again. I do this often, but never when anyone else is in the room.

The dolls were positioned differently from the way they'd been the last time I'd gone through the box.

"What's this house?"

Andrei had gone through Merit's toy box?

"I had it built in the seventies. Youthful indiscretion. You know how it is. Now it's more of an albatross than anything."

One of Merit's erased-faced dolls—the one whose blond doll hair we once lopped off (I'd been making a point to her about the oppressiveness of magazine notions regarding feminine beauty)—seemed to be missing. Madly, I ransacked the box.

"No, I mean this house over here. This toy house. Did you have it made of your mansion?"

Preston Lympany was holding, by its angled wings, a miniature model of what appeared to be my house.

"Is this another toy of your *'daughter's'*?" Preston Lympany asked. "You're kidding me about that, aren't you?"

"Oh Preston," I said, rushing toward him, toward my house (was it made of Styrofoam?), "one must never lie."

I snatched the little house from him. I felt it (not, thankfully, Styrofoam, but, rather, a low-cost lightweight plastic). I examined it. They'd only given it three chimneys, rather than the accurate twelve, and they'd missed several of the windows in the tower section of the house (they hadn't even *tried* for any kind of stained-glass look), and the roof in no way resembled slate. But it was, unmistakably, my house.

"On Ne Peut Pas Vivre Seul holds more of a public fascination than we sometimes think, Preston!" I said.

"On the back it says *'Hecho en México.'* "

"A *worldwide* public fascination!" I said. "Although, were I a betting man, I'd say it's probably an American company."

"Yeah," Preston Lympany said. *"Probably."*

The tower's crenellation felt good to the touch (although, truth be told, a bit dusty). The people who'd made this phony On Ne Peut Pas Vivre Seul had actually gotten the crenellation's limestone border right, having outlined the tower with a thin border of brown paint!

"There has to be some kind of copyright-infringement issue here, don't you think, Preston?"

"I don't know. I think you should just be more flattered than anything."

On the tower's middle tooth was a splotch of red something. It appeared to be nail polish, or very new blood.

"It is flattering, isn't it?" I said. "It *is.*"

"Yeah, it is!"

The splotch was sticky. Nail polish, not blood.

"Preston," I said, "do you really think I'm important?"

Upon the red rug on which Merit had danced barefoot when she was a little girl, I placed the house. Houseless, defenseless, I stood before Preston Lympany. Preston Lympany stood before me.

His nostrils had shrunk in size . . . or else I'd just gotten used to them. He'd recently—an hour ago, perhaps—shaved. Underneath his right nostril was a blister of blood.

"You're *so* important, Fergus," he said.

His brown eyes fluttered.

"Really?" I asked. "I mean, it's just a house."

He reached for me, my face. I closed my eyes and allowed myself to feel his hand.

I was unsure whether the tingle I felt was imaginary; or perhaps my nose was, in fact, running.

I liked Preston Lympany too much to chance it, you see. I couldn't risk it with him; I couldn't risk *anything*. The Kleenex box in Merit's bathroom would have meant leaving him. So out of my right front pocket I removed a hundred-dollar bill. I patted my nose with it.

My makeshift Kleenex hadn't done much to deter him, however. The money smelled old. Both of Preston Lympany's hands were cradling my face. It was more difficult to look at him now than it had been. Preston Lympany's own house was a rental unit, I knew. I was afraid the house talk was making him uncomfortable.

"Did you," I asked, changing the subject at once, "see my photographs downstairs? Of Lowell?"

"Those were so good," he said softly, moving in closer to me. "He looks so young in those."

"No, he doesn't," I said. "He looks the same."

"No," Preston Lympany said. "He looks older now."

"But," I said, "if *he* looks older, how must *I* look?"

I flattened the bill out underneath my nose. There was something ugly-smelling about that money now.

"Tell me," Preston Lympany said, his hand in my hair now, the other still on my cheek, "is Lowell as much a victim of his own self-interest as Trevor says he is?"

"Oh Preston," I said, the familiar tightness in my throat, the heat in my face, returning, "you understand me better than anyone." No one— other than Lowell, of course, and Jenny and Merit—had ever been able to make me cry. Preston Lympany, I feared, had that ability.

I wanted to give him something, wanted to make him happy, in the only way I knew how.

"Here," I said, pushing the hundred-dollar bill at him.

"What is this, Fergus?" he asked.

"I just want to give this to you," I said. I was trying to get the money into his hands. He wouldn't take it.

"I don't want your money, Fergus," he said. He backed up into the little model of my house, stumbled over it. The collision knocked the house belly-up. It was roomless, wall-less, hollow inside, as if made to swim through.

"Is this not enough?" I asked. "There's much more where that came from."

I twisted my cape around and dove my hand into my back pocket. I'd never been given many gifts myself, and I suspected Preston Lympany hadn't, either. When I'd paid a visit to his rented house last week he talked about what it was like, having no money, how when he was younger, being poor seemed like a game. ("Okay, the contest this week is," he said then, "how to spend only forty dollars.") No longer was it a game, he said.

I was holding, I estimated, three thousand dollars.

"You're *paying* me?" he asked.

"It's not a payment," I said. "It's a *gift*."

"I can't believe you're paying me," he said. Then again: "I can't believe you're fucking *paying* me."

He went toward the door.

"But Preston," I said, running for him as I had before. This time, *I* knocked over my miniature house. It went upright again.

"You think you can *pay me off*? You must think I'm so fucking *small*."

"But Preston," I said hopelessly, grasping the back of his denim shirt. "You can't go! You'll miss the blimp!"

The last thing I heard Preston Lympany say before he walked out of Merit's bedroom, away from me forever: "You didn't even tell me you *had* a daughter."

In the air was a scent I hadn't inhaled since Merit lived with me, all those years ago. Acetone. Was nail-polish remover still made with it? I guessed it probably was. Human beings: always looking for another way to kill themselves.

I sat on my floor, Merit's floor, with my house in my lap. And into the lethal air I said, to no one really, I was sorry.

31

8 April 1985

I'm crying all the time when I'm sober and alone, but when I'm with other people and drunk, I'm vociferous and mean. Which is worse? Yet, I'm not quite as far gone as Lowell, who's developed a perverse fear of, among other things, leaving the house and being around other people. We're going mad. We've gone mad. Maybe Fergus has made us this way. The studio is our prison. If there were windows, would it all be different? Even when he showed me the blueprints of the studio a couple of years ago, I begged Fergus to put some windows in, but he said windows in this part of the house would spoil the "line" outside. Oh, I still remember the tone in his voice when he said, "As an *artist* yourself, I'm *sure* you understand *all* about lines." He thought he was flattering me! Or was he trying to be condescending? I've lost all ability to decipher human intentionality. I've become someone I don't recognize.

But this morning, temporarily, there was a sudden burst of hope. Lowell and I were in the studio, and I was finally working again. We had three good hours in there, and I thought, If I can work like this every day, I'll be able to finish *Self-Portrait Emphasizing My Feminine Features* in a week! Lowell appeared to be both busy and serene—two things he hasn't been for a very long time—organizing our slides at the desk. He would hold a slide up to the chandelier, write something on the slide's white frame, then place it in one of the many slide stacks he'd made. We could have kept going like that for hours had Fergus not pounded on the door and told us he'd made a mussel gratin for lunch (already getting cold!), and that he and Merit were ready to take the pictures for our next project. Lowell said he was getting rather hungry, come to think of it, and it might be good for him to eat some solid food. He left the studio. I went over to the desk and looked at the slides. The first stack I went through followed no order. There was a slide from the *Cohiba* project, followed by one of a sketch from *Procter and Gamble*, and one of a photograph I'd taken of Lowell in his Wife of Bath robe. Every stack was like that: random, systemless. And what had he drawn on the upper right side of each slide? A five-pointed star.

I alone know Lowell's pathology. He says Merit and Fergus must never know how "very weak" he really is. His performances for them are both frightening and fascinating to watch. Yesterday, when he told Merit his mother sang at the opening ceremony of the Panama Canal, he was so convincing, I almost believed him myself.

For an hour, I tried to sketch my own face, but I hated what I did. I cannot draw myself. I cannot draw anything except Lowell. Is this what a nervous breakdown feels like? I forced myself to go downstairs and let Fergus take his agonizing pictures. I hadn't seen Fergus yet today, or

Merit, and I shuddered at what I saw. They were wearing matching wide-wale fuchsia corduroys and apple green button-down shirts.

Fergus seated all three of us on a bench outside. Luckily, the ordeal only took about forty minutes, and twenty of those were spent with Fergus jabbering self-justifications: "Ooopsie! I think I got my thumb in that one" and "Ooopsie! This thing has the most *atrocious* focus." He also spent a few minutes applying styling products to Lowell's hair, and to Merit's.

Merit was between us, Lowell and me, and looked bored. At one point, Fergus scuttled buglike underneath the great hall's lavender-colored awning, put his ear to his camera, and shook it, as if he were listening to the rattle of a toy inside a plastic egg.

Lowell was trying to have a conversation with Merit, something it's been impossible for him to do with her, or anybody else, lately.

"How is math class treating you these days, Merit?"

Lowell's black eyes had a dim, faraway look. Could Merit sense his disengagement?

"It's good, I guess," Merit said. "We're doing this thing called 'magic squares.' I think it's neat to see how you can get the same number."

"I didn't do magic squares until I was much older than you are now," Lowell said slowly. His accent was slighter. Did Merit notice that, as well? "And how is your music class?" he asked.

"The teacher says I take too long to learn things," Merit said.

"Good," Lowell said distractedly. He slid a few inches down the bench, away from Merit, into a shadow. "Always listen to what your teachers say."

Lowell's eyes have grown lackluster only recently. Is it the guilts that have invaded his heart? Does he suffer as much as I think he does, or more?

At noon, Fergus called it quits. ("Taking pictures is such hard *work*," he said when he closed up shop.) Lowell went to the gaming room, which is where he goes now when he wants to drink. Fergus waddled off somewhere, but I didn't pay attention to where. I made myself some lunch (unexpectedly, Fergus never complained about how I'd skipped his *moules*), and Merit asked if she could have some, too. So I carried our lunches (peanut butter and jelly, potato chips, and an apple for Merit; Manchego cheese, a spot of foie gras, Spanish olives, and a plastic cup of a maddening pinot noir for me . . . but then again, everything seems to drive me mad these days) outside. Merit said she wanted to watch the emus. I'm going to get frayed and desperate again if I let myself think about the last time Merit and I did something together, alone.

"Can I feed some potato chips to the birds?" Merit asked.

"Sure," I said. There were six black emus behind the fence. "Don't see why not. Those guys eat anything."

"They're *girls,*" Merit said.

How could she tell?

A few days ago, Lowell asked me if I thought the deception was taking a toll on his face. Without waiting for an answer, he asked if he was "a classically tragic figure," and whether I thought he'd ever in his life made a "meaningful connection" with anyone. Did it even occur to him how such a question would hurt me? To be acknowledged as nothing: a pain worse than childbirth. I ran away from him, ran outside, as far as I could get without actually leaving. I took along some food for the emus. I fed them a paper bowl of black coffee, a tube of Necco wafers, and some pickles. They ate the Necco wrapper *and* the cardboard coffee bowl; when I reached over the fence for the empty pickle jar, I was sure my hand was going to be the next to go. (So why *did* I reach my hand over the fence? Why *was* I so careless?) Lowell would certainly have a tough time managing his artistic career if I were suddenly Mrs. Hook Hand. Or would it be the best thing for him, the best thing for everybody, if I just *stopped* and put the bullshit completely behind us? I could get a clean start; I could use my name. I would still paint Lowell, only the signature would be different; nothing would change! The rage and powerlessness I feel about our success! Lowell would say I'm being an absolute self-dramatizer again. He would also remind me that I'd have no career without him.

Merit ate a potato chip, then hurtled over to the fence and dumped the rest of the bag into the pen. The fence is about two feet high, although the emus are themselves about six feet tall. They clustered immediately around the dusty chips. I told Merit it seemed as if the emus really loved her.

"Uncle Fergus said he loves me," Merit said. "He counted to a hundred and said he loved me a hundred times. He said he wishes he could grow down as I grow up. That way, we'll be the same age someday, and then we can be together forever. This one's name is Julie."

My temperature shot up by about thirty degrees. I reminded her again how I didn't like her calling Fergus "Uncle." She stared at me, chillingly. Merit, in that one cold stare, summed me right up. I have to get us out of here. I must get us out of here. When Merit asked if she could feed the emus, my thoughts were of sickness, fever, paranoia. I suppose I said something about how Manchego cheese comes from La Mancha, Spain, and mentioned Don Quixote, because Merit asked me, "Why does Daddy say it like this, 'Don Quicksoat'?" She boinged up and down in the air like a piston. "Quicksoat, quicksoat, *quicksoat!*" she singsonged. She pogoed back over to me. "Daddy says 'Quicksoat' because he cannot stand who he is," I said. Her fuchsia corduroys swelled on her; they were so big that the cuffs were rolled, the waist pinned. But I hadn't rolled them for her, nor had I done the pinning. Who had? Fergus had. Neglectful, negligent mother. Should Merit be taken from me? Will she?

Merit bit into her apple, turned it around in her hand, examined it. She took five bouncy little steps to the fence (her ponytail bobbing in its daisy clip, her hair within the clip a richer brown than it used to be) and held out the apple flat in her hand, as if she were a paying visitor at a petting zoo. She told me the emu's name was Anita. Anita ate Merit's apple in one gulp, without chewing.

The apple seemed to take a long time to work its way down Anita's gullet; the apple lump in her neck reminded me of the time when Fergus wrecked his knee during tennis practice, so long ago, before we lived in this daze.

"Is that normal for the apple to make a bump like that?" Merit asked.

"I *think* so," I said.

"Okay," Merit said, taking me at my word for once. I clutched her hand. While the bird wasn't displaying any outward signs of distress, the situation, from where we stood, didn't look all that good. Do emus express their feelings? Do humans, or is everyone just pretending?

Merit asked why Anita wasn't swallowing the apple, and I said I didn't know. The apple really did appear to be lodged in the animal's throat. It wasn't blinking its red eyes.

"Why isn't she swallowing it?" Merit wailed.

"Let's go get a pair of gloves," I said.

"Can *Daddy* get it out of Anita?"

What an absolute failure I must be—*am*—as a mother. Failure I *am*. My child wouldn't even dare to think of me as a plausible solution. How has this happened? Everything I was, and wanted to be, has been pillaged, demolished.

"Yes," I said. "Let's go get Daddy."

There is so much wrong with me.

Lowell was alone in the gaming room, playing chess. His opponent: himself. The chess pieces: on one side, shot glasses of claret; on the other side, glasses of muscat. Whenever he moved a piece, he took a drink. On the floor next to him were two open wine bottles.

"I killed Anita, Daddy!" Merit wailed. "I *killed* her."

"What's all this now, darling?" asked Lowell from the couch, then drank a shot glass of red wine. He refilled and drank again. He had, sometime after our useless photo shoot, changed into the scarlet taffeta jacket Fergus had bought for him. "Remind me who this Anita character is again?"

I explained what had happened, and Lowell replenished his glass with red wine. I wasn't sure he was even listening. I've been dreaming about him again, every night. In my dreams, he revisits me. In my dreams, he is something I've already lost.

"Why don't you go fetch your uncle, Merit? He'll give the old girl a good thump on her back and the apple will come blasting right out of her beak like a cannonball. Just make sure you're out of firing range. *FERGUS!*"

Lowell clapped three times. Fergus has somehow become the solution to Lowell's problems, when, in fact, Fergus is the problem itself. From within the bowels of the grotesque house, an echoing Fergus voice shouted, "I'll be right there!"

Merit's bottom lip quivered and she softly asked Lowell if he was going to go outside, too. He said he was so tired today, and that he'd already been outside once, but maybe later. He stroked his arm as if the jacket were a luxurious pet.

Then Fergus, in his besocked gnome feet, skidded into the gaming room. The camera was still around his neck. "Oooh, you're playing my favorite game, Lowly Worm. I love to sit and watch him do this one. I'm always rooting for the red wine. Beats me why!"

I explained the problem with Anita.

"Oh my goodness!" Fergus said. "Which one is Anita?"

"She has little white spots down around her tummy and a blue neck and light brown on her face in the shape of an S," Merit said.

"Oh! Harry Bailey Two! No time for gloves. The last time this happened, I had to stand on a chair and go in and yank it out with my own two hands. It was just like sex! Did I tell you about this, when Harry Bailey Two ate a golf ball?"

"Goiters frighten me," Lowell said. He moved a muscat glass and swallowed the wine down in one gulp. "The more distance I can get from a goiter, the better it is for everyone. This is one of the reasons I rarely visit Chicago. That and bratwurst."

He sounded like the old Lowell for a moment. He was drunk, or getting close.

Although Merit is almost as tall as Fergus is, he picked her up and carried her toward the door.

Bitterly, Lowell said, "Merit, darling, don't you *love* your new mommy?"

Merit hugged Fergus's florid neck and said, "Mommy!"

She giggled. Fergus giggled.

I lunged at Fergus. I shouted at him to put Merit down. As he ran down the hallway with my daughter in his arms, I screamed, "How fucking long has it been since you've been *sane*, Fergus?"

And then they were gone, and Lowell and I were alone again, as always. Lowell sunk deeper into the couch and closed his eyes. He was backlit by blue, the only lonely color. I was crying. In his real voice, he asked,

"What have we become, Me?"

The madness that has assaulted us.

32

"I can't see in this head," Wyatt said.

Merit told him he'd be allowed to remove it very soon, but not yet. "Besides," she said, "you're not missing much."

She was unable to locate Lowell, Jenny, or Fergus, or anyone else she knew in this crowd. Why was it no matter where you were, no matter what the situation—even if it was your *own* party (which this wasn't)—the crowd always felt hostile? The entranceway under which the three of them were gathered was constructed of some sort of cold gray stone. Merit was still leaning against the wall. Her wedding was the last time her parents had seen one another. Jenny and Lowell had behaved themselves at the wedding, but Lowell didn't show up afterward at the reception. An hour and a half through the two-hour reception, right after the bartender tapped Merit on the shoulder and said they'd run out of chardonnay, Merit knew she finally had to concede that her father wasn't coming. Before dinner started, Merit hid for twenty minutes in the bathroom at the country club and wept. Jenny said nothing about Lowell's absence at dinner. Two days later, Jenny called Merit three times at the Ritz in Maui, although she didn't mention Lowell then, either. The third call, Jenny reminded Merit to bring her back a bag of Kona coffee, ground for a Melita filter.

"I don't like it in here," Wyatt said. "It makes me feel too vulnerable."

"Don't worry," Merit said. "I'll protect you."

Fergus had cleared all the furniture from the great hall, including that awful white bearskin rug by the fireplace. Merit had probably spent *years* of her youth on the floor in here, trying to figure out where the bear's genitals were (or had once been). There was, Merit recalled, a little fur protrusion that stuck out midway down the rug's left side. When Merit was very little, she was of the belief that this protrusion was (or had been) the bear's penis. Later, she decided (based on no evidence) the bear had been a girl anyway.

Over the entrance hung a stag's head. Caroline gazed up at it with great interest. Fergus had once told Merit that this particular stag's head had the biggest antler spread on record. Merit thought then, as she thought now, that this was a weird thing for somebody to be proud of.

"Did he kill that?" Caroline asked.

Merit said she could guarantee he hadn't killed any animal before, not with his own hands. He did eat animals, though. Borderline contemptible behavior, if you asked Merit. If you're going to eat an animal, Merit thought, you had better be able to kill it yourself.

It occurred to her she hadn't actually known about whom Caroline was speaking. Fergus, Lowell; Lowell, Fergus: It didn't really matter much, because her answer would have been the same.

Merit was pretty sure Caroline had never been to an adult party before. Last week, when Merit had called Shelley and asked her if it was cool if Caroline stayed with them this weekend, Merit had explained her father's boyfriend was throwing a big party and she hoped to be able to take Caroline to it. The silence that met Merit on the other end of the line made her think she'd maybe given Shelley a little too much information. Also, Shelley already knew who Merit's father was.

If they were ever able to thread themselves over to the bar through these people, Merit would order Caroline a nice big Shirley Temple, heavy on the grenadine.

"So does Lowell look purdy tonight?" Wyatt asked.

Merit said she hadn't seen Lowell yet, so she couldn't say.

"You still have my glasses, right?"

Merit said she did. She felt to make sure they were still in her front pocket (they were).

Three yards or so in front of them a heavyset blondish man in a frog costume was chowing down on a little plate of something. One right after another, he plunked these small brown fried-looking things into his mouth. After he'd cleaned his plate, he sucked on the last fried-thing's toothpick. Merit didn't feel this was very polite at all. His costume wasn't a good likeness of a frog, either, now that Merit was getting a better look at it. The green sweatsuit was, Merit supposed, an inevitable component of the hastily compiled frog costume, but it was the frog eyes on top of the man's high-foreheaded blond head that really bothered her. It looked as if he'd taken somebody's (his *daughter's?*) fuzzy Eastertime rabbit-ear headband, dyed it green, and glued a googly plastic eye on each of the ears.

Merit was very close to making a comment about the overall lameness of the frog guy's costume, but then she remembered how any kind of frog-related issue wouldn't be the way to go with Wyatt tonight. He couldn't really see anything anyway, and so he wouldn't be able to join in on the laughs.

On Thursday night, when Wyatt finally noticed the frog tank on top of his dresser (Merit was stepping into her flannel nightgown; it was cold in Wyatt and Merit's house, even in August), he said, "I'm going to walk out of here now, without saying anything. After I've regained my composure, we'll talk about what you've done." He came to bed about forty minutes later. After two days, they still hadn't talked about the new addition to the household.

She had, in the last two days, started to worry about Wyatt. He seemed vaguely off. She was afraid he suspected.

"How do we get that lady with the tray of food to come over here?" Caroline asked.

Who smelled like nail-polish remover? Was it Merit or Caroline? Merit said they seemed to be just slightly out of the food path but that she'd still be glad to summon a waitress, or waiter, if she saw one.

"That lady over there has food," Caroline said.

The pointy-haired woman at whom Caroline gestured looked a hell of a lot like Claudia from Merit's office. Had Mrs. Valdez really said Claudia was here tonight? Claudia, or the Claudia look-alike, was wearing a man's tuxedo, although without the jacket.

Wyatt was breathing Darth Vaderishly through the Chadwick head.

"Are you okay?" Merit asked.

"I'm great!" Wyatt said. "I've decided parties are actually even tolerable this way. Anything's tolerable if you can't see. Maybe I'll just stop wearing my glasses entirely, except at work. It's hot in here, though."

Merit had no doubt now that the woman serving a platter of toothpicked food to a killer clown and a Pilgrim was indeed Claudia. Claudia was, Merit knew, very entrepreneurial and enterprising, after all.

"I think maybe we should go back to the main staircase," Merit said.

Caroline asked Merit why she wanted to do that.

"I've decided I need to go back and look at those pictures glued up on that painting," Merit said.

"Why, *Merit,*" Wyatt said, "I've never seen you take such an interest in your parents' artwork before."

"Can I go over and get some food while you're doing that?" asked Caroline.

"Yeah," Wyatt said. "Maybe we should go out there and, as they say, mingle. Am I allowed to take this off now?"

Wyatt's real eyes blinked rapidly behind the little Chadwick eye screens. How blind *was* he without his glasses? Merit waved her hand in front of him (a kind of high-five maneuver). He didn't say anything, nor did he move, nor did he make any signs of recognition.

Sure, Merit said. Take it off.

He definitely didn't know, or suspect.

As he pulled the thing over his head, Wyatt's eyes were closed. Merit caught a little whiff of their basement, which she found, at that particular moment, a very reassuring smell. Claudia, carrying her platter, was moving closer toward them, although Merit had no reason to believe she'd seen her. She would be brave. She would not run away from Claudia.

Merit unfolded Wyatt's glasses and slid them onto his face. They were slightly misaligned, and Merit was annoyed by that, so she took them off, readjusted, and slid them back on again. He opened his eyes and blinked. His hair was matted down on the right side. Merit tried to fix that, too.

There was no way he knew.

Across the great hall, Merit saw the chorus director from her church and the chorus director's husband. She was spacing on their names. They were dressed as weird Bavarian yodeler people.

"Hi, Claudia!" Merit said boldly as they drew near her. Merit felt Claudia could have been a little more aggressive at passing the hors d'oeuvres plate around. Fried calamari, Merit's most dreaded appetizer.

"Hey," Claudia said. "What's up?" Not that Merit knew her very well, but she felt Claudia had this very cool way of cutting to the heart of the matter. Merit liked that. No sorority-pledge-week "Oh-my-God-you-look-*amazing*-did-you-get-a-*haircut*?" pleasantries for Claudia.

Caroline helped herself to an ovoid calamari piece.

"My dad really knows how to throw a party!" Merit said.

She was hunching herself to Claudia's height, she realized. (As if Claudia cared how tall she was!) And although Claudia actually hadn't asked Merit why she was here, or even seemed surprised (or, frankly, in-terested) to see her, Merit said, a little too eagerly perhaps, "This is my dad's house!"

Caroline was looking around for somewhere to spit her semichewed calamari. Merit burrowed into her bag, feeling for a Kleenex.

"Good to know," Claudia said.

Wyatt gave Claudia his name and displayed his hand for her to shake. Claudia, who was clearly unable to take Wyatt's hand, merely grimaced. Merit remembered again how rude she could be about party introductions. She introduced Caroline and Claudia.

Caroline and Claudia nodded at each other. Caroline was good at this party stuff already. You couldn't even tell she had calamari chipmunked in her cheek. Merit passed Caroline a Kleenex of debatable age and status.

An elderly gentleman in an old-timey red-striped bathing suit gin-gerly approached Claudia's platter. "May I?" he asked.

"Get on in there," Claudia said.

Claudia's lips were the same color as her face. Actually, maybe it was the other way around: Her face was the same color as her lips. *Lip pink:* That was a good name for the color of her face.

Caroline turned her back to the group and, Merit knew, spit into the Kleenex.

"Thank you kindly," the gentleman said. He selected a piece of fried calamari ("This looks like a good one," he said of a particularly rotund specimen) and chewed.

"Is this"—Merit didn't know how to say it—"another *job* of yours?"

"Ummm . . . *yes,*" Claudia said.

"Delicious," said the older gentleman. "Thank you. Would you like my toothpick?"

"You can just put it on the tray here. Off to the side," Claudia said.

The gentleman placed his toothpick on the tray, gave Claudia a tip of his straw hat and a little wave of his cane. He strolled off into the crowd.

"Claudia and I *work* together," Merit said, although they didn't really. "And her *husband* works with me, too," she added.

"Ohhhh," Wyatt said.

Merit couldn't remember if she'd ever told Wyatt about how Claudia from her high school cleaned her office.

"Used to," Claudia said. "We lost the job yesterday."

Merit felt boneless and watery again, just the way she'd felt in the car before she blacked out. Claudia paused, focusing horribly on Merit. Claudia knew. She *knew.* Merit cleared her throat and asked her to explain "used to."

Claudia said the building owner had accused them of stealing someone's credit card yesterday morning. "I've never seen Paul so pissed," she said. "He said he's going to have someone's head on a platter."

Paul was Claudia's husband, the tiny guy with the floor buffer.

Merit studied the plate Claudia was carrying. It would definitely be too small for Randy's head . . . although it did seem to be the perfect size for Merit's.

"Oh my God," Merit said (or thought she said; she wasn't paying attention). "That's *terrible.*"

Caroline said she was very sorry. Wyatt, who was crunching on a fried squid nubbin, said nothing.

"You think we're not going to sue?" Claudia asked.

Wyatt said, "Well, you definitely should."

"Well, we're *suing,*" Claudia said, and gave the three of them a last chance at the calamari. Wyatt took one, although Claudia didn't stick around long enough for him to return his used toothpick. She may or may not have said "See you" before she split.

"She seemed nice. Although it's strange you didn't indicate you knew her before we came over here," Wyatt said. "Hey, would you mind putting this in your bag?"

Wyatt displayed, and then handed off a little wad of trash that contained his appetizer napkin, his orange toothpick, and Caroline's calamaried Kleenex, which, for some reason, he'd been holding. The napkin and the Kleenex were discarded into the abyss of her bag, but she kept the orange toothpick. She jabbed it into the palm of her hand. She wanted that pain. She deserved that pain.

Claudia had vanished. Short people probably hated crowds even more than Merit did. The toothpick probably wasn't sharp enough to draw blood anyway, but Merit was definitely trying.

"I hate," Merit, the big blurter, said, "*my job.*" Although that wasn't really what she meant. That, Merit knew, didn't even hint at the problem.

Wyatt said she and her friend over there had a lot to commiserate about, in that case.

Some life-defeated former *Ohio Is* ad salesman once told Merit the ceiling in their office was made of asbestos. Merit, for some reason, thought of this now. "Have you noticed how everybody's coughing all the time?" the salesman had asked her. Yes, she'd replied, she had noticed. She certainly had.

She didn't know how much longer she could last without crying.

Caroline was rubbing at the nail polish handprint on her toga. The way Wyatt's hair was messed up made him look like some kind of doddering grandpa. Merit brushed his hair back again. He smelled like sleep, closed windows, their bedroom. And Caroline: Had she even really wanted to come to this party? Her delicate nostril wings flared in a stifled yawn.

They were Merit's family. *They* were. Not the other three, wherever they were.

Merit hadn't had time to do laundry for almost two weeks, which meant she was wearing the same white shirt from a couple of days ago. Her shirt reeked of patchouli (high note) and Randy's skin (low note).

If Wyatt loved her so much, couldn't he tell how close she was to crying?

"Thank *God* you're here. Hello, Caroline. And . . . *Wyatt.*" It was Jenny.

Days before Merit and Wyatt got married, Jenny had told Merit it was good, actually, that Wyatt wasn't her match. "*I* married my match," Jenny said, "and look what happened to me."

Jenny was pink-faced and sweating, having clearly only recently been demasked. She was dressed as some kind of Italian clown. She held a big black-sheeted canvas.

"Have you seen what he's done?" Jenny asked.

Merit was crying now, and she let everyone see. She would not, she decided, hide.

Jenny ordered Wyatt to hold "my painting." Merit found the "my" significant. Jenny embraced her. Another blast of patchouli. Jenny certainly wasn't a patchouli wearer, but patchouli, even aged two days, would dominate any aroma competition.

Jenny hugged Merit and told her not to cry, which, of course, made Merit cry harder. Jenny said *this,* finally, was the last bit of evidence they needed to have him *committed.*

"I tried," Merit said (seeing now how her emotional state could work to her advantage), "I tried to get the pictures off." She couldn't bear to look at Wyatt and Caroline. She drew a tiny bit of blood with the tooth-pick, and she was pleased by that. She wiped the blood off on the back of Jenny's white tunic thing.

"Could I get you to say that on the record?" It was a man's voice, but it didn't belong to Wyatt.

"*Why* are you FOLLOWING ME?" Jenny asked.

Merit attempted to blot up her mascaraed tears with Jenny's shirt. Although she knew she was in no way presentable, she showed her face to him. He was a large square man with a low-slung jaw. He was costumed tonight as a surgeon. She wasn't really clear if he was actually a reporter, or if that was a joke. He rudely thrust his tape recorder in front of her mouth. He had a weird hand tattoo.

"Are you Lowell Haven's daughter?" he asked.

Merit sniffled and said everyone is someone's daughter.

Very helpful. Thanks, Merit.

"Caroline and I are going to go look for the bar," Wyatt said. He always got very nervous whenever anybody started talking about Lowell. His Chadwick head was nestled, uncomfortably, it appeared, underneath his arm.

360

"It's over there, in front of the window," the guy with the tape recorder said. "Full bar!"

"Out*stand*ing," Wyatt said. "Can I give this to you, honey?"

Wyatt made an audible almost-groan as he hoisted (one-arm) the mystery painting over to Merit. It would have made more sense for him to give it back to Jenny. The sheet was wet and the canvas might still have had that subtle, lingering almondy paint odor, although she could just have been imagining it.

A *new* painting?

"You're *leaving*?" Merit asked.

Rarely did Wyatt and Caroline devastate Merit. Rarely did they try. It didn't matter whether they were trying or not, for Merit was devastated now.

"We'll get you a drink," Wyatt said.

Merit didn't understand why she did what she did next. She would always regret it. She seized Caroline by her toga and whispered, so no one else could hear: "Do you hate me?"

The panic and pain and longing with which Merit asked this question must have repelled Caroline. (Merit was, it seemed, good at repelling people.) Caroline backed away. It was true, what Jenny had written in her journal: You could never tell someone everything. Caroline wrapped her toga tightly around her body. Wyatt went over to Caroline and slung his arm over her shoulder. Caroline gave Merit an uncomfortable little wave as she turned to go. The two of them walked away.

Merit wanted them back with her, her little family.

After four years, Jenny decided it was time for her to take Merit away from Fergus's house. Jenny sat on Merit's canopied bed, the bed Fergus had had made for her, and held Merit's hand and made her look at a picture of their new house. Merit, it still shamed her to admit, had cried horribly when she saw the picture. "It looks like a barn for poor people," she said, sobbing.

"That," Jenny said, smacking her hand on the red bedspread, "is exactly why we're moving! What a poisonous attitude!"

But that was not the real reason for the move. Jenny told Merit once that her head would have exploded if they'd stayed there one more day. She didn't want Merit to grow up around such "warped and perverse disillusionment," she said.

Up until five years ago, Jenny still went over to Fergus's house at least weekly. Up until five years ago, Jenny still painted Lowell, and Fergus was still taking his sham pictures. Merit had been, as she'd always been, the only one without anything to do. But when Merit helped Jenny make the decision to stop painting Lowell, the outcome wasn't the one Merit had intended: Jenny stopped painting entirely.

Merit made this happen with the help of an "interventionist" (cost: fifteen hundred dollars). The interventionist wasn't technically a "professional." The interventionist was Merit's former Women's Studies professor.

In the months after Merit graduated from college, she and her Women's Studies professor (with whom Merit had become close after she dropped the classroom bomb about Jenny second semester junior year) had sent each other E-mails more or less daily. Her Women's Studies professor's E-mails typically began something like this: "Hey, Merit! I wish you were still here so we could get together and commiserate. I'm drowning again." They typically ended something like this: "Your mother will never be fully human so long as she continues to allow herself to be exploited."

Lowell and Fergus were in Italy the week of the intervention, the invited guests of the old duke or whatever who'd bought a bunch of paintings years before (for which Lowell wrote Jenny a huge check for thirty thousand dollars, although Jenny contended the sale was for much more; Lowell never gave her a cent from the later Saatchi sale). Merit decided to take action the night Jenny, while preparing dinner, accidentally happened to set on fire a book about or by (Merit wasn't sure which) Willem de Kooning. (It was the first and last time Merit would ever, she hoped, use a dry-chemical fire extinguisher.)

After the fire, while Merit was mopping the kitchen floor, Jenny said, "You know what, Merit? I've never even been to Italy."

A banal statement, yes, but one of the saddest things Merit had ever heard. Later that night, Merit made a phone call in her bedroom.

"It's time," she said. "Let's put the Jenny Liberation plan in motion."

"Finally!" her Woman's Studies professor exclaimed, and said she could be there the next day . . . although it was a four-hour drive and although she'd be missing her Tuesday/Thursday classes. She also said the going rate for intervention was four thousand dollars but that she'd cut Merit a break.

The next night, Merit and Wyatt (they were the only intervention participants; it wasn't a big intervention as far as interventions go) met the Women's Studies professor at the hotel (a converted grain silo) downtown. The professor handed each of them a questionnaire and explained how the intervention the next day was going to work. The hotel-room TV was on at a low volume. *Nova,* Merit recalled, a show about sharks.

Back at Wyatt's house (which was not yet equipped with any motion-activated lights), sitting at the table in the eating area, they studied their papers. The questions had to do with the ways in which Jenny had hurt them, and herself. Before he'd even brought yellow mechanical pencil to paper, Wyatt said he didn't really feel as if he had enough data to answer the questions accurately. But he said he'd answer them if Merit thought it would help. She said it would, so he did.

Merit could no longer really remember all that much about the paper's specific questions, but she did remember the essay (which Wyatt had opted out of). In it, she wrote that her mother either had to start taking credit for her work, or she, Merit, her daughter, her only child, would never speak to her again. Jenny would become, Merit wrote, "historical" to her.

When Merit let Wyatt and the Women's Studies professor into Jenny's house the next morning at 7:45 (Wyatt picked the professor up at her hotel downtown), Jenny, in her white robe, was in the kitchen, removing a coffee filter from a green-and-red Melita box. The kitchen still smelled like fire and smoke. The professor introduced herself (her name was Margie) and explained the reason for her visit.

"Get out of my house," Jenny said.

Merit held a shoe-box "time capsule" Merit's grandmother had made after Jenny graduated from high school. When Merit's grandmother had died a few years earlier, and Merit and Jenny were cleaning the house and getting it ready to sell, Jenny found the box in the attic. Jenny said she hadn't thought about it for twenty years.

Jenny didn't cry when her own mother died, not that Merit saw, but she did cry that day when she opened the box. She took it down to her childhood bedroom and opened it there. Merit was with her.

Wyatt said maybe *he* should make the coffee and Jenny, Merit, and Margie could go and sit down in the front room.

Jenny glared at the box.

"*That,*" Jenny said, "is not *yours.*"

Although Merit usually didn't drink coffee, she knew she needed a cup now. Wyatt measured out teaspoons of ground coffee from the orange

Café du Monde can. Margie blinked in a weird way, which made Merit think Margie was having a problem with her contacts.

The kitchen was getting smaller, smaller.

Merit opened the box and pulled out an old sketch of Jenny's, drawn in gold crayon. Jenny had done self-portraits at one time. She was beautiful in this picture, and looked much older than she really was, although she was even younger than Merit was now. A crown of stars haloed her head.

Jenny lunged at Merit. She snatched the drawing from her and ran out of the kitchen. Everyone, including Wyatt, ran after her.

Merit thought Jenny was going to lock herself in her studio/bedroom, but she was wrong. Jenny had collapsed on the living room couch. She was lying facedown, sobbing. The drawing was, presumably, underneath her, for protection or destruction, or both.

Wyatt looked as uncomfortable as the hat tree. His hands were in his pockets and he seemed to be swaying slightly, back and forth, back and forth. Behind his glasses, his eyes went from Lowell picture to Lowell picture on the wall. He seemed a little scared of the pictures, as if he were expecting them to do something to him. But they couldn't do anything; they never did anything, other than hang there and watch you.

Wyatt must have really loved her to be there with her, Merit knew now.

Margie sat down at the piano bench, although she wasn't there to play piano.

"I want you to look at that picture," Margie said. "I want you to look at it and tell me who that little girl is. Tell me what happened to her."

Jenny arose in slow motion, like Frankenstein, like Rip Van Winkle, like something that had either been dead or extremely asleep. Her white robe and white slippers added to the overall narcotized vibe.

When she was fully upright, she considered the drawing again. Then, in one swift motion, she crumpled it up and threw it at the wall, at a full-scale picture of Lowell. In the painting, Lowell was naked in front of a blimp whose side said *The Spirit of Akron*. Merit remembered the day Fergus had taken those pictures. They'd left her alone on the grass that day, in the shadow of a blimp.

"I've destroyed my life," Jenny wailed. "I've destroyed my life, and yours. And his."

A button from Margie's long blue skirt (which had a row of buckling buttons snaking down the middle) spontaneously popped off and hit the floor. It made a sound as it landed underneath the piano, resting by the forte pedal. Jenny stopped making noise. For a few seconds, they all stared at the button. Everybody seemed grateful, Merit felt, to have something else to momentarily look at.

Margie covered the three inches of her newly exposed thigh with Merit's and Wyatt's questionnaires.

Merit tried to steel herself for what she had to say. It came out sooner, and meaner, than she'd planned, as everything important always does:

"It's me or it's him," Merit said.

Merit had never had her mother's attention. Even in Jenny's journals, Merit was nothing more than a postscript. And this was during Merit's sacred *childhood,* when she should have been her mother's *life.* (When Merit was a kid, all her friends were their mothers' lives.)

Jenny was still staring at the button, but she was crying again, harder now. Wyatt went over to her with a handkerchief.

"But who would I be?" Jenny asked. When she used to crawl into Merit's bed at night, she'd been this tortured, this pink and liquidy, too. But that had been a long time ago.

Jenny patted her eyes with Wyatt's handkerchief and stared at Merit. Her eyes looked as if they'd sting your finger if you touched them.

Again, Jenny asked, sotto voce this time, "Who will I *be,* then, Merit?"

For the rest of Merit's life, she would always hate herself for her response:

"I have no idea."

Merit brushed the blood-tipped toothpick onto the floor. Tonight, Jenny had no drink in hand. Not yet. The reporter guy edged his tape recorder closer to Merit, although she wasn't exactly saying anything. Even if she did have anything to say, why would anyone want to tape it? He was looking at her in such a way that she couldn't tell whether he wanted information from her or sex. Maybe they were the same thing.

And he *was* sexy, sort of. *Yeah,* there was definitely a sexy un-Ohio something about him. His eyes weren't as blue as Randy's.

"Stay here," Jenny said. "And *don't* look behind the sheet."

Then Jenny whispered, "I can't do it to him, not now. Not tonight. And *don't* let anyone see it."

(Actually, to be fair, the mothers who appeared to have no lives of their own, and no inner resources, nauseated Merit, even when she was a child.)

Merit had never seen Lowell hide his face before. He had arrived now in the great hall with an entourage of one. He was wearing a translucent plastic mask, through which you could kind of make out his real face, but only kind of. His hair was even more poofy and black than usual; Merit had never before wondered if he dyed it. The weird spiny guy to his side was wearing a crooked Al Sharpton wig. He was fanning Lowell with a white handkerchief.

Merit was now thinking of the one and only time Lowell ever picked her up at school. Eighth grade. Lowell had stood at the end of the eighth-grade hall, silhouetted and backlit in front of a windowed door, waiting. Waiting for *her.* He'd never waited for her before. As she was gathering her books and things from her locker, she overheard some kid (Bobby Petikind) a few lockers down say, "Hey, check out the Mr. I'm Steven Tyler freak show. What, is it Halloween?"

Merit was rarely alone with him in those days, and she still recalled how insubstantial and nobodyish she'd felt on the ride back to On Ne Peut Pas Vivre Seul, where she was staying for the night. That was her fault, though; Lowell was as charming as could be. "Tell me *everything,* darling," he said. She shrugged and looked out the Jaguar window and said she didn't have much to tell because she was boring. Then he'd asked her some questions—about school, boys, music class, whatever. While listening to herself give some horrible, boring answer, she'd felt that she was probably the most uninteresting person in the world. Or at least certainly the most uninteresting person *he'd* ever met. Even his lies had style. Merit's lies didn't have any style at all.

Merit looked up at her mother now. She wasn't feeling so hot again.

"*What?*" Jenny asked. "You're concerned about the painting? I'll explain later."

Merit wasn't actually concerned about the painting at all, but it was just like Jenny, and Lowell (oh, and Fergus), just to assume she was thinking about them all the time.

Jenny kissed Merit's cheek, pulled her mask down over her face (like a medieval soldier lowering his helmet for the big battle), and laced through the crowd, heading toward Lowell and his follower. Merit couldn't look.

"Hey," the reporter said, "I'll catch up with *you* later." He smiled in this weird way, then tucked his tape recorder into his doctor pants. His pants were baggy, and he could probably feel the tape recorder on his cock. "You look like you could use a drink."

"Oh," Merit said. Wyatt was supposed to be getting her a drink. "Gee." She often got flustered when in a situation that required the ordering of an alcoholic beverage. "I don't know. White wine?"

"You got it. Name's Brad, by the way."

"Hi there, Brad. If going to the bar isn't a problem, I mean. Or water, if that's easier. You know what: Don't worry about it. I'm fine."

"Ho, you're not getting off that easy. One white wine coming right up."

Merit couldn't tell if she was being hit on or if he was using some kind of time-tested journalistic technique. It probably didn't matter what his intentions were anyway. She tried to imagine what it would be like to have sex with him, but she was unable to get much of a picture.

This is how her other slippages had begun: She would meet the guy, imagine having sex with him, and then, before she knew it: the slip. She herself had initiated the affair (if it could really be called that) with the orange-handed boy; she herself had decided they would become bath buddies. A bath seemed, she'd thought, like a low-stress activity for two strangers to do. She had ended their bath relationship when he began sitting on top of her, facing her, and trying very subtly (he seemed to think) to stab his dick into her. As if she wouldn't notice.

She couldn't find Wyatt and Caroline. There seemed to be a lot of tall people here tonight . . . or were they just wearing tall costumes?

Lowell and Jenny were now involved in some kind of intense, heavy-looking conversation. Jenny's mask was off again; Lowell's was still on. It was weird to watch. His face was as inexpressive as a mannequin's, but he was gesticulating like a madman. Jenny might or might not have been crying. Had Lowell seen Merit? If he had, her presence left him indifferent. Was she going to cry again?

Merit understood something she'd never understood before. Every room in this fucking house contained a box of Kleenex because everybody here was *crying* all the time. It was a house of misery, a ghost house, a death house, sick with life-sucking torpor. When she read "The Fall of the House of Usher" in seventh grade, she imagined it taking place here.

An iciness, a sinking, a sickening of the heart. Merit nowhere in anyone's dreams.

And where were Wyatt and Caroline? She still couldn't see them anywhere. She shouldn't have brought them; why had she brought them? They hadn't wanted to go, and neither had she.

Fuck it. You know what? She had to get out of there.

Merit, quavering, as always, between anxiety and lust, told this Brad guy she was going outside for a smoke. When she said it, she moved too close to him.

"Right behind you," he said. "Not really my scene, either. It's just, you know, the *job*."

He gestured toward his crotch, although he probably meant to indicate the tape recorder. He asked if he should meet her out by the front door after he took care of a small business matter.

"Back door," Merit said.

"You got it," said the really quite surprisingly attractive Brad guy.

Because she'd lost her umbrella somewhere back at the house, she was holding the sheet-covered canvas over her head. She was going to the car. She needed a cigarette. And a serving of white wine the size of Lake Erie.

Her cigarettes were not, in fact, in her bag. (She'd practically dumped the insides of her purse out on the floor in the great hall while looking for them. Annoyingly, a mime—like, a *mime?*—had squatted down next to her then, mimicking her sad little cigarette search. Had she really looked *that* desperate?)

Merit found her car. The damage she'd done to it wasn't even that bad. She opened the trunk and placed the canvas there, gladly obeying her mother's no-peeking decree; she didn't really want to know what was behind that sheet anyway.

Her cigarette pack was in the front seat. Had she sat on it? Crushed: Yes, thanks very much, she had. She pocketed her crushed cigarettes and returned to the back terrace.

On the other side of the paned kitchen window, people were spooning together plates of meat-looking food. The guy in the John Deere shirt and hair net seemed to be wearing latex gloves. As Merit was watching, a woman, also in a hair net, came up in back of the guy and, as far as Merit could tell, appeared to goose him. They were facing away from her, so she couldn't tell what the woman looked like.

The kitchen door banged open. Cold air and meat smells. There was

Merit's new acquaintance, Brad. He was, as they called it in college, "double-fisting" it. (Merit personally always thought the term noxious.) A white wine, as requested, in one hand and a very large glass of what was either bourbon or scotch (she still wasn't clear on the difference between them and didn't care) in the other.

Brad kicked the door shut with his big heavy workman's boots. Merit liked the way he did that. She also liked his boots.

"Hey!" Merit called. She thought he probably hadn't seen the step below. "Careful there!"

"Hey, there you are! I felt like some double agent, sneaking in through the kitchen. Fergus gave me very strict instructions about where I was allowed to go here and where I couldn't. He was like, 'I daresay the kitchen is most indubitably off-limits to the likes of you.' "

"Did he really? That's horrible."

Fergus had never set such rules for Merit when she lived here.

"Nah," Brad said. "I'm just shitting you. He seems like a good-enough guy. I *guess.*"

He offered Merit her much-anticipated glass of wine. He didn't have braces. She had to remember not to suck her wine down too quickly; she would try to make it last for at least ten minutes.

Brad just stood there and watched her drink. It seemed like something he shouldn't have been allowed to do, not yet.

He asked, "How's the wine?"

She said, "It's good! Cold. *Good!*"

"Secret party trick: You get the white wine really fucking cold and your guests won't be able to tell how cheap it is."

"Oh," Merit said. "Wow." She'd never thought of that before. This Brad guy really seemed to know his stuff, she could already tell.

She took a last drag (oooh, she was being such a rebel tonight) off her cigarette, dropped the stub into a puddle, and pushed it around with her clog.

There was so much wrong with her.

"So," Brad said, "you come here often?"

He took a sip of his extremely big iceless beverage. The tattoo on his hand seemed to be a logo of some sort, a hieroglyph she didn't know anything about.

"Well," Merit said, "I lived . . . My father . . . I mean, I *lived* . . ."

"I'm just joking with you. I know all about *you.*"

He set his cocktail on the ground, dug into his pocket, and took out his tape recorder and a pack of cigarettes. He placed the tape recorder and cigarette pack side by side on the window ledge. Inside, the people in hair nets (two more women were there now) were lining up plates piled with grotesque amounts of food on trays.

Everybody seemed to know things about Merit lately.

"Big pocket," Merit said.

He reached for his cigarettes.

"Damn straight," he said.

The sound of rain on the awning made her feel, for some reason, a little more comfortable with him, a little more taken care of, than she probably otherwise would have felt.

He reached into the same pocket again and came out with a matchbook. He lit, he inhaled. Pretty smooth, the way he flicked the spent match out onto the terrace.

"So," Brad said, "no mask for you tonight, Merit Haven Ash?"

She hadn't even told him her first name. About three-quarters of her wine had already been knocked back. She didn't think it was a very good wine, although it was true she didn't know much about wine.

"Oh," Merit said, "I'm not creative that way."

"Well, you *know*," Brad said, stretching around for his tape recorder, "in medieval times, people wore masks as an excuse to commit adultery."

Merit swallowed the last of her terrible wine. Did she have the adulterer's telltale clammy sheen?

She asked if the mask thing was true.

"True story," he said. "You don't mind, do you, if I tape this?"

Merit said she wasn't very good at talking into tape recorders (although she couldn't really remember ever having talked into one before).

"Your mom told me you were an 'unimpeachable source.' Her words exactly."

"Damn," Merit said, "I thought *I* was the only person you were interviewing."

He was lying about Jenny. Merit's wet white shirt had gone see-through. Great day to forget to wear a brassiere, Merit. Well done. Bra-fucking-*vo*.

He depressed the red record button and the black play button simultaneously. Merit couldn't help but wonder if there was some more advanced recording technology out there. Had to be, she felt.

"OK, so. Beatles or Stones?" He laid the tape recorder on his manly lap. He exhaled smoke through his nose.

He seemed to be more interested in examining his drink than in examining her. This brought some temporary relief to Merit, whose arms were now crossed over her chest.

"Ummmmm," she said. "Pardon me?"

"I start all my interviews that way: 'Beatles or Stones?' Breaks the ice."

She had heard of reporters implementing such tactics before. She wished she had some tricks up her sleeve, too. But Merit, she had no tricks.

"*Beatles*," Merit said, as if this would forever be the final word on the subject.

She was mentally preparing herself for how she would answer what she assumed would be the next question. (George.)

"Are you cold?" Brad asked.

Merit thought about it for a second. She said she wasn't. She wondered if it would be rude to ask Brad to get her another glass of wine.

"The way you're holding yourself, you look cold."

"No," Merit said. "Just . . . hugging myself."

She wondered if that look he gave her meant he'd be willing to hug her, if it came to that. Merit decided she liked this Brad guy, although he was a liar. She had to remember not to take her arms down anytime soon.

She had an extra shirt in the trunk of her car, she remembered.

"I'm more of a Stones guy myself. I always worry about the guys who answer 'The Beatles.' If you know what I'm saying."

Merit said she understood where he was coming from.

" 'Lowell Haven' in there said he chose the Beatles."

"He *did*?" Merit asked. She found it sad that she'd never known this about Lowell, if it were true.

"Nah," Brad said. "I'm kidding around. I didn't really get to have a conversation with him at all. There were all these stupid little fuckers mincing around all the time."

Brad was sort of interesting in the same way Randy was interesting, but he wasn't interesting in the way Wyatt was interesting. No one was interesting like Wyatt. So why, then, was she dealing her husband such cruelty? Did she love him as much as she should? She thought she did. She knew she did. But why didn't *he* love *her* enough to know she was having an affair? And was she still having an affair, or was it in the past tense already? Was Randy already historical? She wanted to run inside and grab somebody's mask and put it on and scream at Wyatt about how oblivious and blind and dense he was, and had been. She always loved people more than they loved her. It was, she knew, one of the many ways in which she was doomed.

She was thinking about asking Brad if she could have some of his whiskey, but then she'd have to take at least one arm down from her chest area.

"So you seemed pretty upset in there. Must be hard on you, seeing your estranged father, being around all his, you know, *lies* again."

But Brad couldn't have known. She was scared. She wanted that liquor in the glass on the wet bricks between his boots.

"Would it be possible," she asked, "for me to share a little bit of your drink?"

"Merit Haven Ash," he said, "it would be an honor to share my beverage with you."

He gave her his glass. She unpeeled one arm from her shirt. Again, he watched her drink. She was fully aware she was probably flashing him one of her breasts.

"What magazine is this again?" Merit asked. She'd very quickly consumed half the glass.

He told her the name of the magazine, then discussed at some length his magazine's circulation and high-caliber demographic. She thought about telling him she worked for a magazine, too, but it was too embarrassing. He'd probably laugh at her for thinking her shitty little regional publication could even be considered, in the outer-Ohio world, a magazine.

"You'd be surprised how *good* it feels," he said.

Merit wondered aloud, "How good *what* feels?"

"Seeing yourself in a national magazine. Telling the truth so a million people can read it."

She removed her other arm from her chest. She sat back. She wasn't totally sure what she was doing. Actually, that was a lie: She knew exactly what she was doing.

"Shit," Brad said, looking away from her, glancing out to where the pond with the dauphin was—but he didn't know that, couldn't have known that, because it was August and the daylight had departed hours ago.

"You want my shirt?" he asked.

Merit said she had another shirt in the trunk of her car, but thanks.

"Hey, you never know when you might need an extra shirt." He reclaimed his cocktail glass from the wet ground. He seemed not to have been aware Merit had polished his cocktail off. He kind of sniffed his glass a little bit, which seemed strange.

She hadn't really planned for this little trip, not now, but she told him she was going to the car.

"Mind if I come with?" Brad asked, leaning into his tape recorder. Merit knew the tape recorder had been on all this time, but she hadn't until now noticed the red light, and how steady it was.

As they squished through the grass on the way back to the car, Brad talked about how important "Lowell Haven's" work was to him. He wasn't very specific about why, but he did say he hated almost all contemporary art, and that the art world was a joke, and that "Lowell Haven" was the only artist he liked. He made dread-inducing air quotes whenever he said Lowell's name.

"The first time I saw his stuff, when I was in J school, I went, This is great! *This,* I can relate to. No squiggles and lines and broken plates and bullshit. It seemed like nobody was painting faces at that time. I mean, who wants to look at anything else, really?"

As documented in Jenny's journal—and Merit definitely did remember thinking this way—Merit had had the same opinions about faces when she was a little kid. The rain had slowed to a spritz. Fergus told her once that whenever the leaves showed you their backs, look out for a storm. Merit still remembered how he'd made it sound as if the leaves made their own choices about things.

"He's like a vain woman. You know what I'm saying? There are no ideas in his paintings; there's only his face. His face is the only thing. You know, like a woman. Women only have themselves as a subject. No offense."

She hadn't noticed before how gangrenously moist her feet felt within her clogs.

"Faces," Merit said, "are important." She did a quick calculation and figured out Brad was roughly Wyatt's age.

"And then with all the rumors going on about 'Lowell Haven's' paintership . . ."

There'd been rumors? There'd been no rumors. Merit, the see-through-shirted faux naïf, asked, "*What?*" She sounded, she truly hoped, deeply shocked.

She delved into her bag for her key, which, as it was a key chain–less spare, wasn't immediately locatable.

"You know, your mother was the one who wanted to do this story all along. Didn't she tell you that?"

"*Really?*" she asked. That came out as more of a squeak than she'd wanted. Was he lying? He was lying.

She imagined how she'd sound when Brad, in his hotel room up in Cleveland, or in his Park Avenue apartment, or in his Fifth Avenue office, played this tape back. He'd play it for his wife, or possibly for his coworkers, those pipe-smoking, leather-arm-patched wits who would gather around Brad's massive burled-wood desk, listening to Merit's voice and pointing to the tape recorder and laughing reverberatingly.

She felt the key in her bag. The cobbles ground underneath her clogs. She wished she were a little drunker than she was.

"For every letter I've ever sent to 'Lowell Haven,' I sent your mother two."

Air quotes were also sometimes called "scare quotes," Merit remembered. Now she understood why. The Jaguar appeared more black than green tonight.

"So *this*," Merit said, "is my car."

"Jag-u-wire?" Brad said. "Well, well, well."

The car looked much less impressive than it often did in parking lots, sandwiched as it was between two menacing SUVs.

"Five years I've been trying to get this story. *Five years.* This story should be in kindergarten now."

Some seedpods from the tree above had fallen onto the trunk. Five years ago? Merit and Wyatt had gotten married. Jenny had stopped painting. She twisted Wyatt's cold spare key into the lock. One of the seedpods slid off the trunk as it popped up, whirling down, down, and finally adhering to Merit's left clog.

"Have you ever talked to anybody about this? I mean, it must be hard, keeping it to yourself all the time."

Atop all the other junk in the trunk was Jenny's black-sheeted canvas.

"Repression causes cancer, you know, Merit Haven Ash."

"Does it?" Merit asked. She plucked the seedpod from her clog. When she was little, she and Fergus used to pull open seedpods and stick them on their noses.

He was still having a hard time looking at her, she felt. He rubbed his index finger on the hole area of his tape recorder, as if dusting it. Yes, her shirt was totally stuck to her boobs. But what could she do about it?

"Hey, I thought you people ate early in the red states. During the network news, you know: pull a little TV tray up to the La-Z-Boy."

She hated it when people said mean things about the place she was from. Brad crept closer to the trunk.

"I'm just fooling around. I'm from Wilberforce. But now I'm a new Park Slope home owner, if you can believe it."

Merit didn't know what Wilberforce was, although it sounded kind of familiar. She nodded politely. The trunk was an embarrassing mess. To either side of the black-sheet-obscured picture, the following items were visible: ice scraper, three-gallon water bottle, one steel-toed boot, one very wet-looking formerly lavender-colored (now a soggy plum) leg warmer, and two protein bars.

"Protein bars?" Brad asked.

"Yeah," Merit said. Water droplets spotted the silver wrappers. "They're cranberry. My husband likes cranberry."

The cranberry bars were also probably about four years old, but Merit neglected to mention this.

"Aren't you hungry?" Brad asked. "It's late."

"Yeah," Merit said. "I didn't eat any of that stuff back there."

"Do you mind if I have one?" he asked, eyeing the protein bars. "You did drink all my J&B. Quid pro quo."

"Get on in there," Merit said.

"So, I saw your husband inside." His thumb was over the tape recorder's red light. "With the head."

Was Brad talking about Chadwick's head or Wyatt's head? Her glasses were spotted with rain and her shirt was now officially too wet to remain on her body.

"Does he know?" Brad asked. "The 'husband'?"

The tip of his thumb glowed radioactively. You could see the ghost of the bone within, a dark tree against an orangy sky.

"He knows," she said, although she was lying. She didn't know what Wyatt knew. "Believe me: He *knows*."

She'd never met a man like Wyatt before, someone who just *knew* things . . . but then again, she'd never met a man like Randy, either, or Dougie or Andrew (those were the names of her other two slippages). Or Brad. She'd never met a man like Brad before. That was the problem. One of them.

She wondered now, as she had lately, if sexual or emotional promiscuity, or whatever it was, was hereditary. A drop of rain fell onto her shoulder. The rain wasn't hereditary. She liked that about rain. She was growing stronger.

He slid the tape recorder into his front pocket. The tiny red light pulsed through his green pants, closer to his prick than he probably knew.

"Not to change the subject," Brad said, reaching into the trunk for the topmost rain-stippled protein bar, "but I can see right through your shirt." As Wyatt had feared, the trunk hadn't closed properly.

Merit said she knew about her shirt.

The air was expectant. It buzzed; it hummed.

He pocketed the cranberry energy bar without examining the nutritional information, then plunged back into the trunk.

"Everything is wet in here," he said. "Do you know everything is wet? Is your trunk fucked-up? I'm looking for your shirt."

"Thank you," Merit said. "Is it?"

The rain was stopping; was Brad making it stop?

"This picture underneath the sheet here is totally soaked. What does it look like, your shirt?"

Merit told him it was an itchy red plaid wool thingy.

"You know, your mother told me your father defaced her painting in the doorway in a 'final effort to destroy her' she said. Those were her exact words."

Merit coughed. She couldn't help it. She gazed back at the house, letting her focus grow slack. If anyone had been looking at her (which no one was), she would have appeared dead-eyed. She coughed again.

"We've got to get you out of that shirt," he said.

"Asbestos," she said.

"Somebody told me tires are made with asbestos. I get a cough sometimes when I come back here, so maybe the guy that I heard it from was right."

Against the mist, the crimson house assumed a gruesome silhouette.

They were all in there, the good ones and the bad ones; her little family. She hoped Wyatt and Caroline weren't mad at her right now. Were they at the table yet? Had they noticed the empty chair? She wished she hadn't asked Caroline if she hated her. She hoped Claudia would stay away from Wyatt. She hoped Wyatt would stay away from Fergus. She hoped Fergus would stay away from Jenny. And Caroline. She hoped Lowell would stay away from everybody.

"I'm looking, but I can't find the shirt you're talking about. Why don't we just use *this*?"

He said maybe she could use it as a shawl or something. She looked away as he peeled the sheet off the painting.

This was freedom, wasn't it? To look away when she wanted to?

"Whoa," he said. "I've never seen *this* 'Lowell Haven' before."

She was in the dying rain with somebody who knew everything about her. Everybody knew everything about Merit, it seemed. They took one look at her and they *knew*. Merit was an open book. Merit had no mystery, not like her parents. Mystery was a thing to be embraced; had she ever embraced it, or anything, before?

"So how do you know all these things about me?" Merit asked.

Was she shivering, or was it the ground?

"Because," he said, still gazing into the trunk, "you're a very open girl." The light shone up on Brad's long face, making him look like something from Halloween.

She was now able to imagine having sex with him. What else was there to do but let go? What else was there to do but let herself feel it all?

She looked both ways, and she jumped. It was very dark and there wasn't a hand to help her. The puddle was invigorating. Wyatt had told her once that she was the most thrillingly alive person he'd ever met. Merit had never forgotten this. When she remembered it, as she did now, it kept her strong.

"Tell me, Merit Haven Ash," Brad said. "Tell me everything I *don't* know."

Feel it all, but let go.

Tragedies happen, Merit thought, when people get too close. That was her family's tragedy, one of them. She would not allow it to be hers.

Let go, but feel it all.

She was brave. She glanced over into the lit, dripping trunk. She'd never before seen it, this "Lowell Haven" painting. She wished she hadn't seen it now. In it, Lowell, dressed as an eighteenth-century fop, was thrown up into the air on a blanket. The blanket was held by four Jennies, each wearing her costume from tonight, but none with a mask. In the painting, the Jennies looked wicked and sadistic, each lit with a cruel vitality. Lowell was limp, aloft—inhuman, or pretending to be.

Merit was struck by an alternate vision of her life, one in which she wasn't born to sustain a lie, one in which she wasn't *nothing*. Her mother was right: If you tell someone everything, you will be hated. They will hate you. Merit knew this now, but she would be brave. How many guilts should be allowed to invade one person's heart? Secrets: her family evil.

She held open her black sheet. When he came to her, she wrapped it around him, too.

She was going to tell him *everything.*

"Holy Christ," Brad said, gazing skyward, his eyes open against Merit's face and the soft muttering wind, the tape recorder against her thigh the only warmth, "what is *that?*"

33

Like Preston Lympany, Jenny hadn't taken it well, either, when I tried to give her some money once.

Even after she'd removed Merit from me, she occasionally came back to the house. She still loved Lowell. And Lowell still loved her. (I, naturally, preferred not to concede this at the time.) Now, however, I'm ancient. These days, I'm ancient, *and* I'm aware. It was *me* she wanted to get away from, of course. The truth ceases to be frightening when you decide, finally, to tell it.

A few days after they left, Lowell tremblingly showed me a photograph of the house Jenny and Merit had moved to. The house looked like the last place you go before you die. I hated to see Merit in such an awful milieu. I was prepared to tell Jenny so. But I needed an opportunity to give her my opinion.

The next month, Jenny called Lowell to say she was planning a return. "But only, only, *only,*" she said, according to Lowell, during their phone conversation, "for an afternoon visit." Lowell and I were delighted. We were over the moon. I wanted her return to be special. I spent the whole of that Saturday morning whipping up a pitcher of sweet iced tea and a little snack of baked aubergine with Italian parsley and melted Gouda. (Also, I arranged on a plate a party pack of Pepperidge Farm cookies—shorthand for *class,* I thought in those days; the memory of it now embarrasses me, quite blisteringly so.)

After our brief, and really very nice, repast, Jenny followed Lowell into his studio, where, in my memory, they remained for several hours. It doesn't take a tremendous imaginative leap to get a picture of what transpired there . . . although I do want you to know I didn't hear any suspicious procreational sounds as I was lying down, my ear to that thick and shadowy door. It was the first time I'd ever lain on the floor and listened without Merit by my side.

I couldn't bring myself to ask Jenny why she hadn't brought Merit that Saturday.

When Lowell and Jenny finally surfaced, I was waiting in the library, patient as a poodle. Nuzzling on my lap were the picture of Jenny's house and a check for twenty thousand dollars, made out to Jennifer M. Meatyard, signed by me, Fergus Brainard Goodwyn.

"Hallo, my dear Fergie," Lowell said upon spying me on the tufted leather couch. The pine-needle scent of turpentine. "What the devil are you up to there?"

"Oh," I said, "I just missed you two so much. But I know I'm not allowed to bother you. Not when you're in the *studio.*"

"Fergus," Jenny said, "your nose is running."

It had been only about a month since I'd seen her, but I felt then as I'd felt downstairs in the breakfast room during our refreshment several hours before. I was ravenous for her face. It was as if I were gazing after a lifetime at some lost lover with whom it had always been impossible and hopeless and, above all else, absurd, and whom I must forever hate for leaving me.

(Keep in mind that it only had been a month.)

"Trying to ween myself off Kleenex," I said.

Damned if I would let either of them see the little runny-nose droplet that had plopped onto the Polaroid of the unsightly new Meatyard homestead. I tried to brush it away. A discolored slug streak was the consequence.

"Oh, for God's sake," Lowell said, rushing toward me as he did in the old days, when I was something to be cared for. He extended a handkerchief. I'll always remember that handkerchief's unnatural smoothness and its synthetically sugary smell.

I thought it wise to turn away from them as I did my business. Jenny and Lowell were whispering, plotting against me. But I'd grown used to that.

"This photograph," I said, talking, like Miles Davis, with my posterior facing them, "is of abysmally low quality."

"A real estate agent took it, Fergus," Jenny said.

I'd forgotten, in the month since she'd left, how utterly dismissive she was about everything, how she disappointed me again and again. And idiot me: returning again and again, only to be disappointed again.

What I didn't tell her was that for the last month, every night, when the terrors were at their worst, I'd cried silently in bed, the pillows muffling my sobs because I couldn't trouble Lowell, not when he'd been troubled so much already. Jenny never knew that every afternoon I'd sat on Merit's floor and thrown Lincoln Logs at the dollhouse she'd abandoned.

My novelty Ziggy check smoldered in my lap.

I flapped the check at Jenny.

Before I'd even gotten a chance to explain that it was just a little gift to help them get back on their feet, she started screaming at me about how she'd never come back to the house again if she were going to be condescended to in such a manner (this remark was directed at Lowell), and how *one* of us had never even *been* in a darkroom before (this remark was directed at me).

I should have known already, even then. Even in those days, Lowell did not come to my rescue.

There wasn't much else to do in Merit's room after Preston Lympany left me, other than pull myself over once again to her toy chest. The last time I'd looked in it, there had been six dolls. Now: only three. Because the dolls had no faces, they were recognizable only by their hairdos. (And, yes, the lesbian doll with the caterer downstairs's haircut had indeed been one of the missing.) The doll with the French-braided blond hair was Jessica, the one with the kinky blond hair (we took a crimper to her hair once, all those years ago; I'll never forget the smell) was Nicolita, and the one with the knotted, unstyled hair was Constanza. Merit had named them. I clenched the dolls (Hello there, my old friends; how does it feel to once again endure such a grip?) and crawled back with them to my new small house, my cape dragging along behind. Me: a curious King Kong with spectacularly hairless fists.

When Jenny left me, do you know that she didn't even let Merit take any of her toys to their new house? *I'd* given them to her, you see. Such is my contagion.

"*Fergus,*" a female voice said.

The claws of my mind protracted.

The voice was Jenny's.

I turned. She was wearing the mask again. Everyone's eyes shine with a livid wrath behind a mask. (It is difficult, for this reason, to make an accurate evaluation of someone's character on Halloween.) But I already knew Jenny—oh yes, I did—so I could see how sincere her rage was.

Hadn't this been what I'd wanted?

"I *knew* I'd find you here."

I squeezed the dolls together and gave the little house, the one into which Preston Lympany and I had both collided, an apprehensive stroke or two.

"In *Merit's room,*" Jenny said. There were, to Jenny, a thousand injustices contained within that innocuous observation.

I readjusted two of the three dolls into sitting position, their arms extending catatonically in front of them, as if falling. It was the position of an infant startling in sleep. It is said that our infant-era startling reflex is evidence of prelife memory, when all we are is abject matter, falling through space.

I seated the two dolls on Merit's rug.

When I imagine myself falling, I never presume to fantasize I'll be caught.

"*Fergus,*" Jenny said with lacerating control, "Lowell and I have been trying to untangle your motivation." Her incensed eyes landed on Constanza, stayed there. Constanza was Merit's favorite doll. "But because we're not insa—"

Her words came to a halt.

I turned Constanza toward me and rotated her head, which had no face. *No,* Constanza's faceless head squeaked. *No, no, no.* Then, with a mocking horror-show slowness, I turned Merit's doll to Jenny. I twisted her head, her Ophelia hair swaying like seaweed underwater. I looked Jenny in the eye, as if we were both animals but I was the bigger one and this was the moment before I had to kill her, and made Constanza say, No. *No, no, no.*

In Constanza's voice I said, "Constanza says no one loves you. Constanza says Lowell loves me more than he loves you, and I'm Merit's real mommy and I'm the true artist."

I have no memory of Jenny's face when she tore her mask off, because I didn't see her face. I tumbled away when she dove at me, you see, and Constanza hurt me when I rolled on top of her, as if she were something that had been put there to hurt me, and Jenny grabbed madly at my cape and screamed words to me I'm not really sure were hers, words I'll never know if she actually said:

"*I'm* the artist. *I* painted the pictures for Lowell. Do you see, you *creature?* How could you not have known? How could you not have seen? Didn't you ever think it was me? How could you not have thought it was *me?*"

Jenny was still screaming and crying, but by that point, I'd rolled underneath the bed, and onto my scepter, and covered my ears with my hands.

"No," I said.

"No," Constanza said.

It was the first time Jenny had ever needed me to confirm her existence.

The three dolls—the two startled ones and unkind Constanza—were unable to fit inside the mini On Ne Peut Pas Vivre Seul because it was made for much squatter dolls. They couldn't sit on the roof because it was slanted. If they'd been rather more correct, anatomically speaking, I could have impaled Jessica, Nicolita, and Constanza on their own private chimneys. But that wasn't a possibility, either, not with these prim eighties-era Barbies. These days, though, who knew what the doll industry was up to?

When the trumpets heralded the start of dinner, I was still on the floor in Merit's room, crying.

As far as parties go, it was safe to say this one hadn't been much of a success yet.

I took the circuitous non–grand staircase route to the dining room, electing not to view the damage I'd done to *Richard III*. The music room was empty of all life except for the suits of armor and the harpist. The harpist was still plinking away. See? Happy moments were still possible. If a party's a disaster when Carolan's on the jukebox, the host has only himself to blame.

Dawdling uneasily in the rotunda between the music room and the great hall, I found a surprise. *Two* surprises, actually. The Automaton and Merit's stepdaughter. Why was I surprised? They hadn't been invited.

Lowell and I have always agreed that Merit could have done much better in her choice of a groom. Lowell didn't want to go to Merit's wedding because, he told me, he disliked Wyatt. Lowell had just abandoned painting, and he was full of hate for everyone and everything, except Merit. But guess who convinced him his paternal duty required his attendance at the wedding of his only child? And they *did* look glorious, Lowell and Merit, walking down that no-frills UU church aisle. (Merit, who never inherited her familial interest in fashion, let me choose her wedding gown, although I knew she was merely humoring me. She'd decided she couldn't tolerate my existence by that point.)

The Automaton gawked at my model house. The girl, Caroline, gawked at my dolls.

"They're for Merit," I said. "Hello." Although I was otherwise faultlessly gracious, a handshake was impossible for me. The Automaton had his hands full, too. He was holding the head of a sporting-event mascot. I couldn't say for sure, but I thought I'd once heard that the University of Akron's mascot was a squirrel. He was also clutching a beer.

The girl was Caligula. That much, I knew.

But where was Merit? I needed Merit.

"She was sad a few minutes ago," Caroline said. "We think maybe she went to the bathroom. We left her to go get something to drink. She was sad."

Merit, I knew, by my nausea and heartache, was being told by her parents to stay away from me. Finally. Forever. Mentally, I was crumpled upon the floor of her room again, rocking away with grief.

I'd brought the dolls with me to show Merit.

"Do you . . . like the music?" I asked. The dolls, the dolls would make her happy. My Merit. "Carolan was blind, you know. Smallpox." That reminded me of something. "You really should get vaccinated, Caroline. Have you thought about doing so? *I'd* be concerned if I were you."

Wyatt took a swig from his pilsner glass, swallowed, said, "I don't really think Akron is a big biological-terror target."

There was a musty je ne sais quoi about him. He seemed about my age. Poor Merit.

I would get Merit away from Jenny and Lowell and I would show her what I'd kept. It was so silly, really, I'd never told her.

From the rotunda, I assessed the state of the guests in the great hall. They hadn't done much of a job at filing into the dining room, but that had always been the way. In the past, it had taken at least three trumpet heralds and one stern directive from Lowell to get the mob moving.

I suggested to Wyatt and Caroline we set an example and sit down to dinner. I reassured them that Merit was already at the table, waiting for us, her little family. But I didn't believe it.

We were in motion. In an effort to ignore everything unpleasant, I held the dolls and the house straight in front of me and watched them, as if they were a new cutting-edge kind of cake.

"Are you sure that's not Merit's house?" Caroline asked.

There's a possibility Wyatt might have pinched Caroline lightly and shushed her with a "*cut it*" motion across his throat. I'm not able to confirm this, however. My eyes were on the prize.

"No," I said. "We bought Merit's Dream House at Children's Palace in 1983. Hers is much larger. This is Andrei's. Remind me to introduce you to him."

Concentrating on the house like that, the guests swilling formlessly around me, had put me in a distinctly underwater frame of mind. The house was bringing out something seasick within me. The tight squeeze into the dining room was doing little to alleviate this unwell feeling.

I tried very hard not to look at the injuries I'd inflicted on the *Canterbury Tales* cycle, which was painted by Lowell Haven. What I saw instead was that one of Caroline's side braids had come fully detached. The self-consciousness with which she tried to reattach it was Merit, pure Merit. Merit rarely visited much when she was a teenager, although she might say I rarely visited her, either. Caroline loved Merit. I saw that tonight for the first time. And despite the fact that Wyatt kept bumping into me with his large mildewy squirrel head, I found myself liking him more, too.

The only good news of the evening so far: Preston Lympany's sudden departure did mean one extra seat at the table for one of my surprise guests. Merit stopped sitting in my lap when she was eight.

"I'll have to do a bit of rearranging," I said, "but I'd love it if you sat next to me tonight."

The chairs to either side of my seat at the head of the table were empty. Merit wasn't yet there. The dragon ice sculpture centerpiece had been a mistake. How stupid it looked, a long red candle burning in its mouth. Within the party-favor bags on each seat was (in addition to a ka-zoo, a miniature tricorn hat, a baby blankie blue blimp eraser, and other items) a pad of paper on which the guests were asked to name the dragon. If I'd had the hand-strength, I would have shaken those paper pads out of each bag and ripped them into confetti.

"Love to," Wyatt said, but he wasn't looking at me. He was hunting around the dining room for Merit. His search possessed a twinge of des-peration. I liked him for the first time.

Wyatt helped me pull my chair out. I arranged Merit's dolls and An-drei's house atop the bread trencher in front of me.

"Would you mind," I asked, regarding the chocolate place card to my left, which read, in florid gold script, PRESTON LYMPANY, "sitting to ei-ther side of me?"

Caroline got herself situated in Merit's chair, Wyatt in Preston Lympany's. When seated, each examined the contents of his/her party-favor bag.

"Excuse the reach," I said.

Wyatt scooted his chair as close to the table as the squirrel head in his lap would let him, although this was unnecessary. I yoinked the choco-late place card away from his plate, broke it in two, and popped the PRESTON LY segment (it wasn't a tremendously symmetrical break) into my mouth.

Caroline, who was watching me very intently, picked up her MERIT HAVEN place card, broke it, and ate it, too. That hurt me. I was hurt. Wy-att had no place card to eat, as I hadn't given myself one. Medieval cui-sine being what it is, though, he wouldn't have to wait very long for his sugar fix.

The thought of a clovey restuffed peacock in full feather and a Lom-bard pie had just set the well-known gag reflex back in motion. I gripped the edge of the table and breathed.

We were the first ones seated at the table. Ellis Beckerdean, a lit cig-

385

arette poised between his clenched teeth, teetered into the dining room. He was being led by a tanned and ankle-braceleted lady friend, uncostumed, also smoking. I couldn't remember where I'd seated them. I didn't know how many more toxins I could take tonight.

Wyatt seemed charmed by the blimp eraser. He mouthed something about it to Caroline. She dug around in her little drawstring party bag.

Ellis Beckerdean and his lady friend were visibly hammered. They swayingly stopped at each place setting on the Wife of Bath side of the table, searching for the chocolate place cards with their names on them. With every place card Ellis and friend rejected, they were getting closer and closer to me. I could already smell them.

Caroline passed her blimp eraser across the table to Wyatt.

I was trying very hard to ignore the covered pictures, the *Canterbury Tales* cycle that Lowell had painted.

"Fergus!"

It was Drisana-Nari, still in the track suit. Had she again been crying? (Had she ever been crying?) She said she wanted to tell me something. She was very petite and thus didn't have far to bend to get to my ear.

"Lowell just pulled me over and told me to get out of here by tomorrow."

"Oh," I said. Her situation sounded familiar. "My."

"I was like, "Fine; I'll just leave *now*, then. I don't really like parties anyway." So I wanted to tell you bye. And . . . thanks for everything. But mostly thanks for telling me about Lowell. It's been hard to be around him since you told me the truth."

The two smokers, Ellis Beckerdean and his friend, were disastrously close to me now. I was gasping. My hand was on my heart. Inadequate organ.

"Don't be so upset!" she cried. Her curly hair swooshed across my cheek. "The thing is, he was in this delirious mood when he told me just now. He couldn't stop laughing."

I'd never known this girl at all, this vagabond, and now she was leaving. I'd never known her, so she'd never been real to me. Was she ticklish? What town did she call home? Who were her people and what did she dream at night?

"Too bad about your staring contest," I said. "It sounded like a fun game. And I wish we could have gotten to know each other a little better."

"That's okay. There are different levels of knowing somebody. Anyways, I got an E-mail from my boyfriend, Karl, yesterday. He sounded depressed and said he missed me and wanted me to come back to Pittsburgh. He's never said he missed me before."

Ellis Beckerdean was shuffling toward Caroline. He stopped. He tilted forward. His friend plucked the cigarette from his mouth and stubbed it out in the bread trencher before them. The friend said, "This is where you're at. I must be on the other side." It had never before occurred to me a bread trencher could be mistaken for an ashtray.

"Karl sounds like a catch," I said. "Congratulations to you."

"Lowell just kept laughing and saying this was just what they needed to bring them back together."

"Together?" I asked.

"Remember how I told you I think it's good to tell people everything everybody says about them?"

"Oh yes," I said. How my throat clenched. "I remember."

"Well, Lowell told me nothing you could do to them mattered. 'My wife and I are united tonight,' he said. 'Against *him*.' I knew he was talking about you. I thought you should know."

My throat in flames. My thwanging, thwanging lungs.

"Hey, Fergus," Ellis Beckerdean said as his friend started to work at untying his straitjacket. "Sandy wants to know why in the heck there aren't any forks on the table."

Before even seeing them, I could feel them. The atmosphere was suddenly altered. Lowell and Jenny. Masked, holding hands.

I think I heard myself muttering a word or two about how forks didn't come into fashion until the seventeenth century. At the opposite head of the two-headed table, where a Manhattan with two cherries awaited him, Lowell sat. Then Jenny sat. Where did she sit? Here's the exquisite torture: on his lap.

"Well, I guess y'all're gonna be eating with your fingers, then!" Sandy said.

Lowell and Jenny, in their masks, embraced. They were entwined, as if they were one body. One body with one revolting brain.

I contorted myself in my chair, furiously searching the room for someone to help me. Drisana-Nari was gone. Had that conversation even counted as good-bye?

Ellis Beckerdean was otherwise engaged: he wriggled out of his straitjacket, lobbed it at Sandy. He lit a cigarette.

I would have even momentarily taken the sycophantic company of a certain hackish magazine journalist. But Dormer wasn't there, either.

Even *Ray-Ray* would have been an acceptable companion.

Covering each of Lowell's *Canterbury Tales* pictures were my photographs of him. I allowed myself to bask in what I'd done. I was weak and I was stupid. All I could do was sit back, relax, and prepare for my persecution.

Sandy got into position across the table from Ellis Beckerdean and lit a cigarette, too. Caroline's elbows were on the table, her braided head between her hands. Wyatt tooted on the kazoo, but it made no noise, as if in a nightmare. He stared woefully at the dining room door. He didn't know what I knew: Merit was not coming back, not to me. When people leave me, they leave forever. I suspect it's not this way for everyone else.

Lowell dipped into his Manhattan and fed Jenny a cherry, through her mouth hole. Jenny rubbed Lowell's hair with her gloved hand and delicately unpinioned herself from him. She faced me now. I couldn't tell if she was still chewing. She tapped Lowell on his quilted shoulder: an order of some kind, unknown to me, unknowable. Then he faced in my direction, too.

And he laughed.

He held Jenny closer, squeezing her like a schoolboy. He rested his head on her shoulder. The two-headed beast named Jewell.

And she laughed, too.

Their faces were mannequin-soulless. With a long cocked index finger, Lowell pointed at me. Their laughter was becoming strident. I understood, with a growing sickness, why they were laughing.

I inhaled, but there was nothing good left to breathe. Smoke and dust and only that.

I tried to speak, but I couldn't. Lowell: beckoning me. Lowell: laughing.

Without asking, I seized Wyatt's little blimp, as well as my tiny fake house and Merit's dolls, and I ran as fast as my legs and my lungs would allow. I didn't dare look behind me when my chair clattered to the floor. I couldn't help it, though: As I ran, I did look back at Lowell and Jenny. Neither turned to look at me.

Lowell's latex mask was, like a football, crosshatched up the back with shoelace-heavy brown thread.

Their demented laughter, distorted through plastic.

I was running through the kitchen. Mrs. Valdez jostled me. I had no breath with which to tell her not to. She said she couldn't "get him out of there." She was talking about Ray-Ray, who was blocking up the assembly-line plate-preparer path. He was stooped piteously over the sink, splashing his face with water, but what did I care? I thrashed around, trying to get unmoored from Mrs. Valdez. Apparently, I was making sounds, because Ray-Ray, with great effort, unbent himself, swooped around, and glowered insanely at me. His wig was dripping. He patted his hole-punched handkerchief to his cheek.

"I didn't know he had a *wife*," Ray-Ray said dazedly.

It had stopped raining. Lying on my back within my hole-plagued tent, the perforations looked like stars, whole constellations whose names I didn't know. I breathed. I'd set the blimp eraser, the replica of my house, and Merit's dolls on my chest, balanced there, just the way you do with an infant. I never knew Merit when she was a baby, you know. I never had that with her. Neither Lowell nor Jenny had ever told me whether Merit ever thought she was falling at night when she was a baby.

With a horrible finality, I understood I would never find Merit again to show her what was hers. Wyatt and Caroline would find her again, but I never would. I had wanted to tell her two things tonight: that I loved her and that I was sorry. Who ever wants to be told anything else?

I love you. I'm sorry.

She'd never heard either of those things from me.

Lowell had left me five years ago and hadn't come back. When Lowell retired, he took *my* art, and *me,* with him, too. I begged him not to quit. I told him, "But you owe it to your talent, to those of us who have none. . . ." But I'd done the one thing I wasn't allowed to do: I'd stayed around too long. I was now obsolete. Do you know how that feels? To be told you've exhausted your worth?

But how could I blame him for turning away? Lowell has a child and he has his art. What more is there? What more could he need?

Then, with much less joy than I had anticipated for this moment, I heard above me the blimp's slow, lifeless drone.

I rubbed my eyes and wiped my wet fingers with what money I had left. My teeth chattering the way they do before disaster or destruction, I unzipped the tent flap and crawled out into the mud, listening to the whir and the wind.

It happened with a chilling slowness. The blimp, which was, I could already tell, floating lower than it should have been, briefly blinked the message I'd paid for:

LEAVE ON NE PURT VIVRE SUEL LOWELL HAVEN.

Whatever pains come to inflict me the remainder of my life, I can at least take some comfort from the knowledge no one else saw the words on the blimp before it crashed into my house.

Before it went down, I closed one eye and mimicked its flight path with my blimp eraser. The real blimp's nose was tipped suspiciously downward. It pitched and swayed. The sickly sluggishness with which it floated into the chimney above the dining room made the impact look deliberate, although it wasn't deliberate, it couldn't have been.

The deflating blimp coiled itself around the chimney, an embrace from some abominable lover.

Then it erupted into a fiery sphere, a flame world.

As I was running, running back to my house, running back to them, my only thoughts were of rescue. Rescue, release, freedom. I would save them; I would save them all. They needed me. My little family.

The nearing fire: so beautiful to watch. That particular sinuous red: Lowell's signature color.

Let it go.

Let go of it *all*.

I pitched the blimp eraser down like a dart. It stuck muzzle-down in the muck.

One night years ago, I had awakened from a nightmare. I was crying. I remembered only the end of the dream: There had been a fire, and all of us—Lowell, Merit, Jenny, and I—were in it. I told Lowell about my terrible dream. He got me a Kleenex from the box on the nightstand. He held me. Then he cried, too. Jenny and Merit had moved out the previous year, and this wasn't the first time I'd seen him cry. I remember how dark it was in our room that night.

"Why are you crying, Lowell?" I asked. "Are you afraid, too?"

"No," Lowell said, "I'm not afraid. You've just never told me your dreams."